THE SHROPSHIRE LADS

Graham Holbrook

GET Publishing

Special thanks to the following people who generously read earlier manuscripts of this book; your suggestions were invaluable: Nick Butcher, Margaret Cotton, Deborah Plunkett, Peter Kennedy, Katie Holbrook, Ro Brookes, Amy Jacobs, Ali Thomas, Emma & Alistair, Martin Monk, Peter Moulton, Juliet Still, Jake Leighton-Pope, Peter Hankin, Sara Hankin, Peter Duckers, Graham Bence, Eric Bence, John at Pengwern Books, Sue Robertson, Nigel Stewart, Debbie Elliot, Alexis Castagna, David Holbrook, Caroline James, Rob Thomas, Jo Allen, Alex Heydel, Dr John Ferries, Carole Masheter, Connie and Reggie Monk, Catherine Levy, Graham Coreless.

To Katie Merrifield: thanks for the encouragement

Cover illustration by Christopher Evans

Published by GET Publishing, 57 Queens Road, Bridgnorth, Shropshire WV15 5DG
info@getpublishing.co.uk

ISBN 978-0-9556464-6-1

Printed in the United Kingdom by Hobbs the Printers Limited, Brunel Road, Totton, Hampshire SO40 3WX

Dedicated to my late father, Ken, who was in the last draft of newly trained soldiers about to leave for France just as the Armistice was signed in 1918.

'The street sounds to the soldiers' tread,
And out we troop to see:
A single redcoat turns his head,
He turns and looks at me.

My man, from sky to skies so far,
We never crossed before;
Such leagues apart the world's ends are,
We're like to meet no more;

What thoughts at heart have you and I?
We cannot stop to tell;
But dead or living, drunk or dry,
Soldier, I wish you well.'

From *'A Shropshire Lad'*, by A. E. Houseman.

Author's note

Many of the characters and all of the settings in 'The Shropshire Lads' are genuine. George V visited Shrewsbury just before war was declared; Bernardo Verro fought the Mafia in southern Italy; Mansfield Cumming, Vernon Kell, Captain 'Hex' Hesketh-Pritchard and his sidekick Colonel Langford Lloyd are all important figures in histories of WWI. Room 40 played an enormously influential role, intercepting the famous Zimmerman telegram that finally brought the US into the war. PMS2, a department set up within the British Secret Services to discredit pacifists and socialists, was embarrassed in the High Court for persuading a group of students to send harmless 'poison' to the Prime Minister. Anti-war marches were organised by various left-wing groups in the hope of provoking the authorities into violence. The articles from the Shrewsbury Chronicle and the Catalonian Excelsior are taken from the relevant copies.

I have tried to represent the recruiting, training and fighting experiences as accurately as possible by following the many histories of the Great War. Dates, places and key events such as burying the dead at the Somme are faithfully taken from the detailed accounts of members of the 6th Battalion, KSLI.

There are some staggering accounts of the Great War, many of them listed at the end of this book. If you are an historian and have found inaccuracies in my account, I apologise. It wasn't for the want of trying to get it right. For the non-historian, any war anecdotes in the book that you find incredulous, please accept them as true. Some recruiting officers really did ask enlisters to hop on one leg and shout, 'Who goes there?' and little French boys did deliver newspapers to the trenches.

The Free 'n Easy is based on what I imagine the Corbet Arms at Uffington, just outside Shrewsbury, might have been like, ninety years ago. Randle Pugh is inspired by the anonymous author of

'I walked by night,' a wonderful description of his life as The King of the Norfolk Poachers.

I am indebted to Major H E Hesketh-Pritchard, whose first hand account of 'Sniping in France' is a case study in how to write a technical book whilst being aware that the reader wants to understand how the sniper's art was applied in real life and death situations in WWI.

Graham Holbrook, Shrewsbury, 2008

The craters at Carnoy, France, August 1916.

The mud-splattered lorry made its way wearily along the rutted road to the quarry, exploding puddle water onto the trunks of the plane trees. The head of the only occupant in the back banged softly and repeatedly against the wooden frame. Jim Downing, sensitive, sincere and shell-shocked, smiled. He was looking forward to his execution.

The vehicle slowed briefly before it moved off again, the driver struggling to find a gear. They turned a corner and stopped, the engine fell silent and a door opened and closed.

Light flooded into the rear of the lorry and Jim Downing held his hand up to his eyes and squinted but didn't recognise either of the two men who stepped up.

'You ready, Private?' asked the soldier.

'Let me, please,' said the other man. 'Private, is there anything from the Bible that you want me to read to you, before…..?'

Jim looked up at the regimental chaplain and shook his head. 'No, thank you, Father. My interests are more secular. I believe in the prophecies of another book.'

'And which book is that?'

'That's all you get, Private,' interrupted the soldier. 'Here, put this on.' Jim took the canvas blindfold, pulled it over his eyes and tied a knot at the back of his head, noticing the smell of horses and damp hay as he did so.

The soldier held Jim's elbow and Jim stood and turned towards the light that he could make out through the cloth. For the first time in his life he wondered how the network of material was woven. He had been surrounded by canvas for two years. Canvas tents, canvas puttees, canvas camouflage, canvas bags for dirt, body parts and food, and it had never occurred to him, until now, that someone had had to make it.

The two men helped the disgraced twenty-year-old towards

1

the back of the lorry and down the two steps of the wooden block that had been placed there.

'God bless you, my boy,' whispered the churchman. This was his fifth execution and the sight of young men walking towards the stake brought Christian images to his mind and a lump to his throat. Jim said nothing, but walked on steadily, guided by the firm grip on his arm.

'Stop now, Jim. Just a few moments and you'll be free,' said the soldier. Jim felt his shoulders being turned until the post rubbed against his back. His hands were tied and footsteps moved away. Only now did his heart beat faster. What if something went wrong?

'Squad! Ready... take aim...'

Jim recognised the voice and turned his head towards it.

'Fire!' The discharge from the twelve .303 Lee Enfield rifles reverberated around the quarry. Clouds of rooks were well into the sky before the echoes subsided.

The condemned man's legs gave way and his head slumped forward.

Sergeant Hamish Rutherford, best friend to Jim Downing and a few others, saw the red liquid drip from his victim's mouth and barked out the orders for his men to retire. He followed them out of the quarry. At the gate he stopped, looked back at Jim's profile and saw him smile.

Book one

1

July, 1914. Shrewsbury School.

David Wilson rubbed the last of the chalk from the blackboard and cleaned his hands on the seat of his trousers, as he had done for the best part of fifty years. He leant on his desk with one hand to take some of the weight off his old legs.

'Well boys, that's it. Your last lesson at Shrewsbury school.' Smiles above high collars and cravats greeted him across the room. 'Most of you are going up to Oxford and Cambridge. Some of you are even reading classics and that makes me proud. It's a wonderful grounding for life. The more you learn about The Heroes and how they met their challenges, the better you will be able to deal with this fast-changing world. Milton, will you stay behind for a few moments please? The rest of you, 'Intus si recte ne labora.''

The boys moved quickly but civilly to the door and soon the corridor was full of excited conversation and the sound of feet descending the stairs of the old building. Only the master and the boy remained in the classroom. The latter's complexion was pale, as if he hadn't been outside for months, which in Neville Milton's case was true.

The master closed the door and returned to his desk. He stood and looked out over the park with the rooftops and spires of Shrewsbury behind it. The idle brassy waters of the river Severn drifted by a hundred feet below the window.

'Over the years, many great men have walked out of this room and gone on to achieve much in life, in politics, the church, the arts, even business. You, Milton, are such a man.' He turned to face his protégé. The bespectacled, unremarkable face gazed down at his still-open book.

'I....I don't feel...'

'Men with your intelligence often take a while to find their feet out there, Neville. Brasher, more confident types will race past

4

you up the steps to success and riches. The fact that you come from a less privileged background than your peers has not given you their confidence, but it will come. You see, you have an important role to play in this world but we don't know what that role is. I have rarely, if ever, encountered a brain quite like yours and believe me, I have taught and worked with some of the most gifted intellects. But I am worried about what is happening out there.' He continued staring through the window for a while. 'The ancient Greeks thought that all the great tragic figures in their mythology had something profoundly in common. They called it hubris, an overweening pride, a reckless arrogance. You will remember the motto written up over the temple of Apollo at Delphi, the most sacred spot in the Greek world, 'nothing in excess.' I fear that we have broken that rule, Neville. Great Britain, Germany, France, Russia, Austria-Hungary; we have all become too proud, too arrogant, and the inevitable consequence of hubris is nemesis. We are heading for a violent shock as the state of balance and order is restored.'

'Are you referring to what happened in Sarajevo, sir?'

'Germany mostly, Neville. Their Kaiser Wilhelm reminds me of Icarus and we know what happened to him. But he is not alone. There are many leaders who share the same flaw. The Greeks had a word for this also: 'hamartia.' It means 'missing the mark,' a fatal flaw that stops some people reaching full maturity, which ultimately leads to tragedy. Macbeth, Hamlet, Don Quixote, Samson even; they all had it. The word appears in the New Testament where it is translated as 'sin', or 'trespass'. I fear that we will see much trespassing before the year is out.'

The master looked at Neville, saw his concern and walked over to his desk. *Silly old bugger*, he thought, *letting my geriatric melancholy dictate the mood.* 'Come, come, my boy. Don't look so glum. Change provides opportunities also. You are speaking at the end of term debate tonight, I hear.' Milton rose and his master guided him to the door.

'Yes, sir.'

'And what is the subject?'

"Social classes are inevitable in a free society,' sir.'

David Wilson laughed. 'I shall be sad to miss that one. And who is taking the opposite view?'

'A gentleman from Naples, I believe. He is touring the country explaining the communist cause.'

'Hmm. Be careful Neville. It is difficult to argue with an ideology.'

'Thank you, sir, for everything.' He extended his hand and they shook.

'Good luck, my boy, good luck.' He watched Neville walk along the corridor and down the stairs, and went back to his desk to gather his cloak, for the last time.

*

'Thank you, lords, ladies, gentlemen and not least the boys for inviting me to talk here today. My name is Bernardo Verro and I am a communist.' The man spoke perfect English with a soft Italian accent. The image of the Grand Tour foreigner was underlined by the cream linen suit over the chocolate open-necked shirt. 'I shall tell you why I think that class is wrong, why it is evil, how it leads to suspicion, then hatred and eventually to war and death. I shall speak from my heart about my own life, my own country.

'Southern Italy is at war. The outside world beyond Italy does not know about this war because it does not think that it affects them. The sides do not fight battles in the open, but in living rooms, in bars, in courtrooms and behind the doors of police cells.

'In 1860, Garibaldi did the Italian nation a great disservice by uniting the mainland with the cesspit of the Mediterranean, Sicily. In doing so he gave the pirates and brigands of that island an opportunity to export their way of life: intimidation and murder. When I moved to Corleone in Sicily, the malnutrition, infant mortality and working conditions of the peasant class were truly disgusting. Farm girls were being raped for fun. All of this was policy, created by the greedy landowners who were scared of the power of the people. They wanted their pounds of flesh and the local thugs enforced this policy. In Sicily these criminals call themselves 'Cosa Nostra', or 'our thing'. In Naples they are the 'Camorra', in Puglia they are the 'Sacra Corona Unita', and so on.

'Many years ago in Sicily I helped create a 'Fasci', or a group of peasants who wanted to change things…..'

Five minutes later, Verro looked up from his notes and realised that his audience's attention was drifting. He improvised.

'Now, this is not a debate about Italy, nor crime, but about division, about the allocation and use of resources. In Italy I am a marked man. Here I feel safe. You are lucky. The culture of your country is a good culture. The culture of the gentleman. But you risk losing it, by not sharing more equitably what you have.'

Verro looked around the hall. Four hundred boys in stiff, dark uniforms and high white collars looked up at him as he stood holding onto the lectern that sat on the stage. Gaslight chandeliers glowed even though it was still light outside. Huge wooden boards boasting the names of scholars and captains that had honoured the school throughout its auspicious past, hung on the walls.

'There is a Chinese proverb that says fish rot from the head. Much of Europe's ruling elite is like rotting fish. They have been there too long, lying in their baskets providing no nourishment to the people. The people are hungry; they are bored with their repetitive, dangerous jobs and their poverty. They look at those who own the factories and the land, and they see the big houses, the health, and they compare these to their own lives. Every year the differences grow more obvious and every year there are more people to notice those differences. Industrialisation has made the rich richer and the poor poorer.

'Be careful. There is a war coming. But not a war between peoples. It will be between the elites who will fight for the resources that can make them even richer. They risk ignoring the zeitgeist, the passion of the common people to use this moment to change things for the better, to dismantle the old system, the class system, and create their own society. Classless….shared resources….everyone working for the common good.

'I read in the Times newspaper this week that half the land in Great Britain is owned by just four thousand people. This leaves the rest to be shared between thirty million. That cannot be right. Yes, you are a free society, but then so was ancient Rome, relatively speaking. Be careful. Thank you.'

Verro walked across the stage and took his seat at the table with the headmaster and Neville Milton. The polite applause drifted away and Neville, almost reluctantly, stood up and walked to the lectern.

'Grazzi, signor Verro. I would like to start by saying that we cannot, must not, fight collective human nature. We can steer it, guide it, but history proves that if you require groups to behave in a way that human nature finds difficult, it will find a way round that requirement.' He held onto the lectern as if it were a rock in a tempest. 'It is natural to want to better your life and of those you love. In doing so we often benefit those that we don't even know. If that process generates classes then so be it. Factories provide jobs and wages. This is why people leave the fields to work in them. The idea of a classless society sounds impossible to me. The Emperor of this society wears no clothes.'

'Here, here,' shouted someone from the back of the hall.

Neville wiped the sweat from his brow with his hankerchief and held onto it. The feel of the familiar cloth in his hand comforted him.

'I also worry about a society where resources, money, jobs are available to all, as demanded by Mr. Marx and his friends. Wouldn't this make people lazy, less inventive? What we need is competitive individualism combined with equality of opportunity. Certainly, we are not a perfectly fair society. I know of none that is. The more classes you have the more differences you get and I argue that this degree of difference improves the universal lot. As an example, an aristocracy that inherits money may make us jealous, but a class that doesn't have to rely on votes for its income is more able to make decisions that are better for the long term good of all; more able than a career politician who cannot afford to put realism before voter sentimentality.' The audience applauded.

'I know that this is a controversial point, but I believe that the class most hated by the common man, the aristocrats, are an essential and beneficial part of our lives. Rulers need to have contact with the rulers of the past, to learn the lessons of the previous hundred years. In this country we do this by letting a group of lucky people grow up amongst those who are used to leading, who learnt how to lead from their forbears, often in the house that their great-great-grandfather built. An 'elite emeritus,' if you will. These aristocrats dare to defy both the arrogance of intellectuals from above and the emotions of the masses from below; dare to resist the entrepreneurial imperative; dare to raise the level of public conversation. We are here tonight because we love debate and we are able to debate. Long live variety and choice! Thank you.'

Cheers and applause exploded from the audience as Neville returned to his seat. The headmaster slapped him on the back, and said, 'Great speech, Milton, great speech. I agree with your sentiments entirely.'

Neville felt elated. It was over. He hated public speaking almost as much as he hated football. But as a scholar, it was expected of him. The school demanded it. You didn't get to public office, that finest advert of the quality of your education, without being able to get your point across to the masses. But he didn't feel justified. His speech was based on the only politics he knew, and he was intelligent enough to know that this wasn't a good enough platform from which to convince. If he hadn't persuaded himself, how could he expect others to be?

The headmaster rose and the applause stopped almost

immediately. 'Thank you, Signor Verro and Master Milton, for two excellent arguments about a subject that is often deemed too difficult to discuss. As you know this school prides itself on facing up to its challenges. Now I invite questions from the floor.

Immediately a hand went up. 'Yes?' asked the head. A tall, thin boy of seventeen stood up. He wore a brown jumper with holes at the sleeves and stained black trousers.

'I would like to ask the second speaker if he has ever been to the slums of Manchester or Birmingham?' asked Jim Downing.

Chair legs squeaked on the polished floor and an awkward silence descended on the hall.

Neville stood up. 'No. No, I am afraid I haven't, but....'

'Well, you bloody well should have, mate. How can you stand there and talk about what the man in the street needs when you haven't seen the squalor that he lives in?'

Someone to Jim's right shouted, 'Hey, I know you. You're the idiot who tried to shoot the king with a strawberry!' Jeers ran around the room. Some boys behind Jim stood up and pushed him.

'Karl Marx was right,' shouted Jim. 'I quote: 'The modern bourgeois society that has sprouted from the ruins of feudal society has not done away with class antagonisms. It has but established new classes, new conditions of oppression, new forms of struggle in place of the old ones."

'Throw him out!' someone cried. A few of the bigger boys surrounded him and pulled him towards the aisle.

But Jim hadn't finished reciting. 'Our epoch, the epoch of the bourgeoisie,' he screamed over the boos and whistles as he was forced to the back of the hall, 'possesses this distinct feature: it has simplified class antagonisms. Society as a whole is splitting into two great hostile camps, into two great classes facing each other. Bourgeoisie and Proletariat.' The sound of Jim's voice dissipated as he was carried out of the hall and into the bowels of the school buildings. The mocking crowd turned back to the headmaster. He tried to make a joke.

'One of your disciples, Signor?' he asked Verro.

'One day, perhaps, headmaster. One day,' the Italian replied, smiling.

*

The four distinguished officers, serving and retired, sat around the polished table watching the Secretary to the First Sea Lord close the door behind the departing tea-lady. Cigar-smoke and the smell of leather filled the room.

'Thank you for getting here so swiftly, gentlemen. I am afraid I have grave news for you,' said the immaculately dressed gentleman at the head of the table.

The hooked-nose officer, facing him at the other end, stopped stirring his tea and gently placed the silver spoon onto the white china saucer.

'Tomorrow morning we will declare war on Germany,' said the First Sea Lord.

The faces in front of him showed no emotion.

'As you know, we have been preparing for such an eventuality for some time. The Cabinet cannot envisage any circumstances under which Germany will withdraw her troops from Belgium. The Prime Minister has asked us to make the necessary preparations.'

The Secretary, who had taken a seat at a small table under the painting of Admiral Rodney, paused, pencil at the ready.

'I have called this meeting because I would like to tell the Cabinet what our Secret Services are doing to ensure that these islands remain safely in British hands. Admiral, would you go first, please.' The First Sea Lord gazed over the top of his glasses and smiled at his Director of Naval Intelligence, Henry 'Dummy' Oliver.

'Yes, sir. Tomorrow, the Telconia will start cutting through the German overseas telegraph cables. This will leave them having to use wireless or foreign cables, which as you know we have access to. We are already intercepting transmissions with help from Marconi and the Post Office, but unfortunately we are having difficulty deciphering the codes. The codebooks stolen in Germany by our friends in the Secret Service Bureau turned out to be fake. If you could find your way to give us more cryptographers, sir, I am confident that we will be able to understand what the Germans are up to.'

'I don't want to know what they are up to, Henry.' The First Sea Lord removed his glasses and fixed his eyes upon his employee. 'I want to know their intentions.'

He turned to the man opposite. 'Commander, what do you have?'

Mansfield Cumming, Head of The Foreign Section of The Secret Service Bureau, stuck out his prominent chin. He was known in Whitehall as 'The Eagle' for good reason. The clearest, cruellest green eyes sat in his bird-of-prey profile. 'We have agents in Berlin, Rotterdam, Brussels, Paris, St. Petersburg, all over Europe, sir. They have come up with nothing. The Germans have kept their plans very secret. Even the French Deuxieme Bureau has drawn a blank. Their military people think the main attack will be through the Ardennes but that may be wishful thinking because that is what they have planned for. Our contacts in the German shipyards report a massive increase in steel stocks, and the Zeppelin factories are working twenty-four hours a day. Other than that, we are blind. We could do with many more people, sir.'

'Thank you. Over to you, Captain.'

Captain Vernon Kell, the son of an exiled Polish countess and a British officer who had distinguished himself in the Zulu wars, was the perfect head of the Secret Service Bureau. He was fluent in seven languages, including Russian and Mandarin by the time he was thirty and had first hand experience of both espionage and counter-espionage before he came to the Admiralty's attention. His organisational and diplomatic skills had been honed during his time as the captain of the Queen Mary before ill health had grounded him. With a staff of three officers, a barrister and seven clerks, Kell was about to pull off one of the greatest intelligence coups of the twentieth century. He was a worthy successor to the great counter-intelligence exponents of the Elizabethan era.

'We have a list of all the German spies operating in Britain at this time, together with their addresses, contacts and objectives. After this meeting, I will send pre-arranged coded telegrams to Special Branch offices in those areas and they will arrest and detain them. There are twenty-two of them, sir.'

'And how do you know that you haven't missed someone, Captain?'

'Because we caught another five last year and persuaded three of them to work for us as double agents. Their lives depend on our success.'

'Excellent. Well done, Captain.'

'Thank you, sir. However, if Lord Kitchener is right about this being a long war, I believe that the main risk to national security within these isles will come not from Germany or her allies, at least not directly.'

Kell looked around the room. Now he had their attention. 'We already have problems with the miners in Wales and Lancashire and with the Fenians and the Protestants in Ulster. If the war should last, say, two years and we suffer heavy casualties, we can expect a shift in public opinion towards pacifism. This will play into the hands of the Germans, the anarchists and, God forbid, the communists.

'You fear the communists, Captain?'

'May I be frank, sir?'

'Please do. I've made a career out of it.'

'Socialism is the greatest political movement of our time, but no European country has met the socialist need and Great Britain is no exception. There is a groundswell of energy held back behind what the popular mind regards as a dam of conservatism and class interest. The slums in our major cities are a national disgrace. The communists have tapped into this and I worry about their ability to gain wide support across national borders. We have absorbed thousands of Russian immigrants over the last few years. Some of them will bring extreme political views with them. This war could be the storm that overfills the reservoir. We all know what happens to dams that are too short.'

'I see,' replied the Lord. 'Well, I suppose we have to hope that the war is shorter than you fear. Please keep me informed about tomorrow's counter-espionage operation, Captain. That is all, gentlemen. The British Expeditionary Force sails to France in two days. We don't want the enemy to know this until it's too late. I will ask the Cabinet for more intelligence resources tomorrow. Good luck and God speed.'

The men gathered up their papers and filed out of the veneered room. The First Sea Lord, Winston Churchill, sat back in his chair, looked at the row of portraits around him and sucked on his cigar. This would be his fourth war but the first that he would fight from behind a desk.

*

'Thank you for guiding us here, Ken. It must be difficult to run a pub and get up at this Godforsaken time,' said the Inspector in the full-length coat.

'I haven't been to bed yet, Will. And it's no trouble. I miss not being involved in this type of work, the intrigue,' replied Ken Downing.

'There's plenty of that surrounding this little jaunt. The boys have found out that Special Branch and the Service were put on standby all over the country yesterday.'

The two men watched the silhouettes move slowly through the fields of wheat. They formed a circle of a few hundred yards in diameter around a cottage that sat in a small garden. The sun was just coming up and a mist sat on the upper slopes of the Wrekin hill to their left. Up the lane behind them were ten plain-clothes policemen including two that were mounted and two more with lurchers at their sides.

'You know what this means, don't you, Will?'

The Inspector leant back on his shooting stick and crossed

his arms. 'It's been coming for a while. Might as well get it over and done with while we have a good reason. There are going to be a lot of unhappy women, though.'

He looked at Ken, his jaw firmly set. 'Why did you leave the Service, Ken?'

'I got fed up with kowtowing to the toffs. It's all very well working undercover but doing it as a butler does nothing for the ego. I got bored. We never found anybody remotely seditious. Why would you want to change things when you've got a big house and pots of money?'

'Many of them have tried in the past.'

'Not on my watch, Will.' He smiled at his old friend. Memories of his early days in the Service were what had kept him in for so long. The work in London had been exhilarating. He had mixed with rising stars fresh from the top universities and the military. This was how he came to know Cumming and Kell. But their careers had continued upwards where his had gone into a siding somewhere on a Yorkshire country estate. He had been forgotten and grew stale and bored.

He wasn't bored now, though. He was fascinated. Had the Secret Services been watching potential spies all over the country for months, years even, waiting for the right moment to arrest them? Vernon Kell was an institution in the Service. This operation had his paw prints all over it.

A thud reverberated around the small valley and men ran from all sides towards the cottage. Pheasants and partridges flew noisily into the mist from the woods and fields of wheat. A minute later two shapes were pressed up against the sidewall, arms and legs spread, frisked and cuffed. The policemen marched the man and the woman up the lane to where Ken and Will stood.

'Checked their mouths?' barked Will.

'Yes sir.'

'Good. Off to the Tower with them, then.' The party continued up the lane towards the police vehicles.

'They'll hang, you know. Not a good time to be arrested for

spying,' said Ken.

'Casualties of war, I fear,' replied the Inspector.

'This bodes some strange eruption to our state.'

'Hamlet. Act one, scene one?'

Ken laughed and nodded and followed the party towards the vehicles.

*

Hamish Rutherford and Jim Downing arrived at Shrewsbury Town Hall at seven in the morning and stood behind a couple of hundred other men in the square outside. This was the third time that they had tried to enlist. They had waited for hours on the previous two days before the soldiers had told them to come back the following day.

Hamish Rutherford was under no obligation to help with the threshing of the harvested crops, having made peace with his father at the weekend about enlisting. Jim was not needed at the Free 'n Easy until the evening and even then the weekdays were slow. He had not made up with his father since their fight. They were civil to each other, particularly in front of customers and staff, but something had gone. They were no longer friends. He hadn't told his father about enlisting. *Stuff him*, he thought. At least he wouldn't have to listen to any more quotes from Shakespeare.

The recruiting officer, other ranks, police and doctors arrived at nine. Someone shouted 'Where have you been? Don't you know there's a war on?'

Even with the help of the policemen, it took them a few minutes to get to the front door. 'If you don't move aside, you'll never get in the bloody army,' the officer shouted over the crowd.

Eventually the doors were unlocked and the suits and hats squeezed ever tighter, slowly shouldering their way to the front. As the morning wore on more enlisters arrived, mostly on foot, some by horse-bus and some by motorcars from the estates where they worked. One was driven by a woman who drew whistling from the queuing men. A group behind the two friends tried to outdo each other with stories that they had heard about what went on behind the walls of the hall.

'A friend of mine got in even though he's as blind as a bat. He read the small letters on the card on the wall when he walked in so when they took his glasses away he started at the bottom and they were so impressed he didn't have to read the rest which is just as well as his memory isn't that good either.'

'My mate got in even though he's got a glass eye,' another said. 'The doctor told him he only needed one eye to shoot with.'

'You're joshing Fred.'

'No, I ain't,' insisted Fred, 'And one of his mates read great with one eye. So when the doctor told him to cover that eye and read with the other he just dropped his hand and put the other hand over the same eye.'

'A fifteen year old got in by wearing his dad's bowler,' offered another. Jim and Hamish glanced at one another. They were both tall, tanned and fit with no physical problems and they had agreed to lie that they were nineteen.

An hour or so later the two friends were inside the hall. They looked around at the recruiting posters and military regalia in frames above the red tiles that made the room feel like a giant toilet. Even at this early hour the place reeked of body odour. Uniformed soldiers and white-coated doctors barked orders that echoed around the hall and men queued in the four corners before disappearing one by one through doorways.

'You. Yes you. Over there!' The corporal pointed first at Jim and then the queue that he was to stand behind. 'You, over there.' Hamish did as instructed and stood on the opposite side of the hall. He shrugged at Jim. Jim Downing, recently rejected by the girl he loved, shrugged back. He just wanted to get away from Shrewsbury and going off to fight seemed a good way of doing just that. God knows, he was taking a beating anyway.

When it was Jim's turn, he walked through the doorway into

a well-lit room whose walls had turned various shades of brown from years of smoking by its normal occupants. A bath of dirty water sat in the corner and at the far end stood a man whom Jim assumed to be a doctor. He asked questions of a pigeon-chested man wearing only a towel who stood on a weighing and measuring machine. A soldier came out of an adjoining room. 'Clothes off, bath, towel, dry. Then come over here.'

Jim looked at the water. 'Any soap?' he asked hopefully.

'No. Just do as you are asked.'

'I'd be cleaner without the bath.'

The corporal took one long step towards Jim and looked him up and down.

'You got lice?'

'No.'

'Then get your clothes off, get into that towel, skip the bath, stand over there. Understood?'

'Yes.'

'Next,' the corporal shouted over Jim's shoulder.

He stripped and wrapped the white towel around his waist, gathered his clothes and walked over to the weighing machine. The doctor dismissed the previous applicant and turned to Jim. He too looked him up and down.

'Put your clothes on that chair. Hands out in front. What do you do in civvy street?' he asked as he walked around Jim, appreciating the muscular frame.

'I'm a farmer,' he lied.

'We need to keep the farms going. Soldiers can't fight without food.'

'My father runs the farm.'

'Age?'

'Nineteen.'

'Open your mouth. Good. Now close. Any problems? Eyesight, hernia, ears, lameness?'

'No.'

'Open and close your fists five times. Alright. Sign this attestation form. You get a shilling a day. Please report to Copthorne Barracks no later than Sunday. Bring a change of clothes and a blanket.'

'Don't you supply those?'

'Of course we don't. This is Britain's first mass army, which is quite something when you think of the wars we've been in. We've had to start from scratch. You'll get a uniform and maybe even a gun in due course,' replied the doctor.

And with that he told Jim to read out the oath of allegiance and to get dressed. He dismissed him and having earned himself another two shillings, he went back to his paperwork.

Hamish was waiting for Jim outside in the sun. 'Bloody hell, I thought mine was quick!' exclaimed Jim.

'All they did was ask me to hop on one leg and ask 'Who goes there?' replied Hamish. Jim hugged him and they ran down the street to the nearest pub singing, 'We're in the army, we're in the army!'

And on that Sunday they did join the army, newspaper parcels under their arms. It was the 16th August, 1914, the same day as the Austrian, Adolf Hitler joined *his* new army.

*

The blond athlete closed the small stained glass window and the noise from the children in the village streets below the Swiss castle died as the lead met the old stone.

'Thank you. Now perhaps I can think.' Bernardo Verro sat on one side of the long table massaging his temples. He was dressed in his trademark linen suit and dark shirt 'We have never had such a security breach. You seriously caught two of the agents telling people from….outside, about the organization?'

'Yes sir, but they were dealt with, as were the people that they told.'

'How can you be sure that no-one else was told?'

'They were, how do I put this, interrogated separately and their stories checked.'

'Good, good. And the next of kin?'

'All dealt with.'

'Put to sleep?'

'One of the agents had a wife and no other family. She had a heart attack. The other man's family died in a house fire. The local police are treating it as an accident.'

'Well done, Gabriel. Nothing disappoints me more than betrayal. We gave these men their lives back. They were doomed without our intervention. They knew our approach to security.'

'Quite, sir.'

'What are you going to do about replacing the two traitors? This section has a vital role to play in the movement's objectives. We cannot afford any more mishaps like this. Everything would be lost if the section cannot perform it's duties.'

'As you know, sir,' replied Gabriel, 'We operate a very tight ship. Quality above quantity. At any time we only work with between ten and twenty agents. Some are sleepers and there are those who provide logistical support. Only a few will be turned into soldiers. The key is finding the right type of individuals. They need to have the proper political outlook and have a skill that we can use. This takes time, sir.'

'Gabriel, it is vitally important that we take advantage of the developments happening in Europe right now. The madness of war provides both opportunities to recruit and risks to our long-term objectives. I do not want our descendents to blame us for losing our way. Do you understand me?'

'Perfectly.'

'Good. Thank you for your update, Gabriel. I meet Ulyanov next week to discuss strategy. He doesn't need to know about this.'

Verro stood up, gathered his black cloak around him, unlocked the ancient gothic door and disappeared into the gloom of the castle corridor.

2

Jim and Hamish sat on the grass under the large oak tree. From there they could see the hundreds of men milling aimlessly around the parade ground, occasionally disappearing into the buildings that surrounded it on three sides. Others meandered across the field in pairs or groups. Jim finished the picnic that he had bought in town and leant back against the tree.

'Not very well organised is it, Jim?'

'I've never seen bogs like it, not even on a Sunday morning at the pub.'

'You seen any officers?'

'Just the two at the gate and I saw another trying to tell a group of chaps to clear something from somewhere. They told him where to go. A few minutes later, three corporals beat the living daylights out of 'em.'

'How do you tell who's an officer and who's not?' asked Hamish.

'The proper officers have bands on their sleeves, the other ones have stripes. The more stripes, the more important. And I think the officers wear hats.'

The conversation dwindled and they fell asleep. They woke to the sound of bugles and whistles. Uniforms ran around the parade ground, shouting and whistling at the men trying to get them into some sort of order. The friends jogged over, leaving the contents of their parcels under the tree. They went to the back of what now partially resembled an oblong of men about thirty deep by forty wide.

'ten-shun,' barked a voice at the front. Some of the men immediately took the position, others did so less confidently. Most looked at each other's feet and eventually nearly everybody had their feet together.

'Stop talking!' barked the same voice. 'Commanding Officer present.'

The hubbub died immediately. The sound of hobnails on a stepladder pierced the silence, and a face, then a body appeared above the front rank, just right of centre.

'Men of the King's Shropshire Light Infantry, I am Major Phillips and I am your commanding officer. You have done a brave and courageous thing. Aucto Splendore Resurgo. I arise again with increasing glory. This is our motto, gentlemen. You have the privilege of belonging to one of the king's great regiments, the KSLI.' A few heads dropped, they had heard it before, some more than once.

He consulted his notes. 'This regiment and its forebears have been the backbone of the British Army for nearly two hundred years. The Caribbean, the Peninsula, Egypt, Sudan, China, South Africa. You name the war, we were there. In a couple of week's time the Hun will come face to face with our First Battalion and will get a good hiding. I don't expect that you will get to France in time for the fighting but my orders are to process you through to Brigade as and when they can take you.' Hamish looked around and saw the unmistakable profile of Randle Pugh to the left. He nudged Jim and nodded in Randle's direction.

'Some of you have been here for a few days or more. You will be glad to know that a new fifth battalion, about a thousand men, will depart for Aldershot on or about the 28th of this month and a sixth battalion will be made up from the rest, to leave a few days after that. In the meantime you will have to put up with the overcrowding as best you can. We have just received two score tents and my N.C.O.'s will show you how to put them up.

'A final few words about cleanliness, food, and parade. Given the fact that there are about fifteen hundred of you and this depot is built for two hundred and fifty, I do not expect you all to shit and shave every day.' A ripple of laughter from the ranks. 'However, I will personally whip anybody caught crapping in the grounds. Dysentery is a killer, gentlemen. Crap in town, crap in the river if you have to. Just don't crap on my grounds. Second, you will have noticed that there is not enough food to go round. I am afraid that you will have to make do with what we have. Between parades and organised events you can go into town and find your own. We hope to be able to set up a field kitchen later in the week.

'Last of all, parade. Parade is where we drill. We drill to learn to obey orders as a group. As a group we fight more effectively. The next parade is here, tomorrow, at seven a.m. There are rules regarding drill. You will pick them up as you go along. The first one is do not be late. My N.C.O.'s enforce the rules and the two captains and the lieutenant here support the N.C.O.'s. I support the officers. I can order your destruction for disobedience or for deserting. This is the ultimate sanction, that I have used before. Welcome to the army.'

The major stepped down the ladder, saluted the sergeant major and left.

'Dis...missed,' the sergeant barked.

Jim and Hamish made their way through the mass of soldiers-to-be to where Randle Pugh was talking with one of the N.C.O.'s and another man, while he filled his pipe.

'Ah, the village idiots. What kept you?'

'Keeping the country running, Randle,' replied Hamish.

'Hamish and Jim, this is Sergeant Small and this is Rhys English.' They shook hands.

'Where do we sleep?' Hamish asked the sergeant.

'Anywhere you can, Private. But if you find a good space look after it. Same with any food or utensils. They'll steal the milk from your tea, this lot.'

'Our parcels Hamish!' Jim ran off, followed by Hamish to the tree, just beyond the end of the line of mizzen huts. As they neared it they could see that everything was gone, except for the empty newspapers which gently rolled away in the afternoon breeze.

'Our blankets too,' spat Jim. He felt his pockets. At least his book and his fags were safe.

*

That night Jim and Hamish slept, blanket-less on the floor of one of the huts with forty-odd other men. The beer that they had drunk at the Bricklayers pub anaesthetised them from the cold and hunger but both slept badly. The sergeant major shouted at them at 6.30. Jim woke to the smell of urine and vomit. He went to get some fresh air and Hamish went back to sleep.

'ten-shun,' shouted the sergeant major to the massed ranks just as Hamish stumbled out of the hut tucking his shirt in, a match in the side of his mouth.

'Name?' asked the sergeant without turning his body.

'Rutherford.'

'Rutherford, what?'

'Rutherford, Sergeant.'

'One week jankers, carrot-top. Get in line. And take that damn match out of your mouth.'

Hamish ran and stood on the end of a rank towards the back.

'Men present and hopefully correct, sir.' The sergeant enjoyed the joke with the captain.

The officer flicked his cane against his black leather riding boots and walked slowly up and down the front ranks.

'My name is Captain Bartlett and I am your parade officer today,' spoke the tall, thin officer without mounting the stairs that had been put there. He was an ugly man with pitted skin, small mole-like eyes and the nose of a lower-order bird of prey. His voice had a west country lilt, almost mellifluous in its sarcastic charm. Those standing at the back of the block of men could not understand every word but they recognised the sound of a man who was used to being hated. It wasn't arrogance exactly. It had that accentuated high-pitched clippiness uttered by those who enjoyed the only type of attention that they were going to receive. Dislike.

'Today we are going.......'

A door to one of the huts swung open and the handle hit the wooden walls with a noise not dissimilar to that of a muffled bass drum in a concert hall. The boom echoed around the parade ground. All eyes moved from the captain to the apparition in the doorway. Rhys English blinked in the sunlight. He was less than five-and-a-half feet tall and broad across the chest. He patted down his blue and cream striped jacket, straightened his tie and moved the boater so that it rested marginally to the right of his head. He walked slowly from the doorway towards a point to the near side of the group, without so much as a glance at the officers and N.C.O.'s at the front.

'Holy mother of God. What is *that*?' asked the captain of the sergeant major.

'You! Stop. Come 'ere.' The sergeant major pointed at his blemish-free brown boots. Rhys obliged at a saunter. 'Take that stupid bloody hat off. Now!' Rhys obliged again. 'Name?'

'English, Sergeant Major. Rhys English,' he replied in his Welsh accent.

'You're having me on.'

'No, Sergeant Major.'

'But you're Welsh.'

'What? I heard the army changed you, but that's ridiculous.'

'One week's jankers for being late. Another for being an idiot and another for being Welsh. That's three weeks of bog cleaning. Do you understand?'

'Yes, Sergeant.'

'Now get in line.'

The captain continued. 'As I was saying, today we will split into companies. These may not be the companies that you will be in when you get to France. However we can't parade two whole battalions at the same time.'

He counted the number of men on the front rank and then put his arm up the line between two of them. 'Everyone to my left move one pace to the left.' The men shuffled. 'Your other left, you idiots!'

Once he had made a gap between the two groups, he marched

past fifteen men at the front of the larger group, tapping each of them on their heads with his cane as he did so. He then made a break down the middle of this group. He took a few steps backwards and addressed the whole parade. 'You, on the left are now A Company under Captain McLeish. You, in the middle, B Company under Captain Atherton. You on the right, C Company under Captain Fox, who has joined us today. Lieutenant Laughley will show him the ropes as Fox has been out of the army for a number of years. Do not be easy on them, Fox.'

'Don't worry. I won't,' Clive replied cheerfully.

'Good. Carry on, Sergeant Major.'

'When I say, 'dismissed', A Company to follow me, B Company to follow Sergeant Willis, C Company to Sergeant Small.'

'Dis....missed.'

*

C Company followed the captain, lieutenant and sergeant across the parade ground and around the edge of the grass field. Jim, Hamish, Randle and Rhys found themselves in the same company, having joined the parade at the last minute. The sergeant held his hand up and told them to form up in lines, ten deep.

'The captain would like to say a few words. Attention!'
Clive Fox stood on a bench just outside the fading boundary line of the cricket pitch.

'Men, my name is Clive Fox. Captain Clive Fox. I have been out of the army for a few years as you can see from my shape.' He patted his stomach. 'I cannot do much about the food or accommodation problems, I am afraid. What I can do is do something about our fitness. My time in India and South Africa taught me many things, particularly the importance of personal fitness and rifle care. Rifles are in short supply at the moment so we will have to make do with something else.'

'ooooh,' sung someone. Clive struggled to keep a straight face.

'You won't like me saying it but I intend this company to be the fittest group of volunteers that Aldershot has seen this summer. I will be feeling the pain with you. The fitter we are when we get to Brigade the better it will be when the nasty stuff starts. Now, I need some volunteers of my own. You are three hundred men. I have one lieutenant and a sergeant. I need another lieutenant and three lance corporals. Is anyone from public or grammar school?'

A hand went up. 'Good man. Name?'

'Milton, sir. Neville Milton.' He had a nervous, almost feminine voice. Jim's jaw dropped. This war was conspiring against him.

'Mr. Milton, would you come out here, please.'

All eyes were on Neville as he wound his way slowly to the front, apologising to anyone that he brushed past. He was slight and his hair that had not seen soap for weeks.

'You wear glasses,' stated Clive.

'Yes sir, but only for reading.'

'Then why have you got them on now?'

Neville hurriedly removed them. 'Sorry sir, I was reading when reveille sounded.'

'Alright Mr. Milton, I am going to recommend that you become Lieutenant Milton.' Jim wanted to be sick. 'Sergeant, please record that when we get back to barracks. Now, I need three lance corporals. You, big man. What's your name?'

'Randle Pugh, sir.'

'Mr. Pugh, would you do me the honour of being an NCO?'

'Delighted to, sir.' Randle stepped out to the front.

'And would you please nominate two others to join you.'

'Hamish and Rhys. Out here,' barked Randle.

Clive smiled at the sound of Randle giving orders already. At least this was going well, which was more than could be said for the damnable embarrassment of Captain Bartlett still being in the regiment. Surely someone should have shot him by now.

*

Over the next few days C Company went about getting fitter and learning the drills with Clive and his N.C.O.'s leading the marches. Clive let Sergeant Small and the lance corporals cajole those who couldn't make it in any way they liked, including Second-Lieutenant Milton and himself.

A life-time of poor nutrition and housing coupled with appalling working conditions meant that many men collapsed during training and no amount of persuasion from fellow soldiers or superiors could get them to move. Eventually the effects of fresh air and regular meals and exercise would prove their worth but in the first weeks of training, under-developed bodies were cruelly tested.

It became obvious during these runs that Rhys English was an exceptional athlete. His stamina was never tested and the speed at which he ran up and down the group of sweating, swearing men astonished everybody. At the end of the first week Hamish foolishly challenged Rhys to a five-circuit race. By the end of the third lap Hamish was half a lap behind and the men had drifted off, bored with watching a one-horse race. Only Randle, Neville and Clive remained to see the humiliation. Rhys slowed towards the end, not wanting to rub his new friend's nose in it.

'Well done, Lance Corporal. That was some run. They obviously kept you fit down the mine,' Clive volunteered after the runners had shaken hands.

Rhys tried to hide the disappointment he felt at the quip.

'No disrespect, sir, but the mines are too low to walk in, let alone run. And the dust doesn't help none neither.'

'Ah. So how do you keep fit?'

'Ask Randle, sir.' Rhys, put his hands on his knees and studied the grass in front of him while he got his wind back.

'He boxes, sir. Lost the South Wales flyweight championship just before he joined up. It was rigged apparently.' He winked at Clive.

'Very interesting. Lance Corporal, the Regiment has a

reputation for producing fine boxers. You would do yourself no harm at all by putting yourself forward for that, once we get to Aldershot.'

'No thanks, sir. I've hung up my gloves. Fed up with the cheating. That's why I joined the army.'

'You'll see plenty of cheating in the army, Lance Corporal, that's what makes it work. However, the fights that I am talking about aren't done on points. You either throw in the towel, get knocked out, or win.' Rhys looked up, a twinkle in his eye.

'Mind you,' Clive continued, 'there are only three weight divisions and you are probably too light to take on some of the thugs who get involved. Never mind. It was just a thought.' Clive walked off to join the rest of the company.

*

The new friends shared the same tent along with fourteen other men. The group decided that daytime cards were friendlies, no money or goods being allowed to change hands. Evening games were different, where large sums were won and lost. Rhys, who seemed to have a limitless supply of packs of cards, played banker with the huge Randle as his enforcer. If someone ran out of money they would exchange items like cigarettes, tobacco, soap, razors, even blankets for money. Randle was the valuer and his judgment was final.

The winnings were mostly shared out between Jim and Rhys, both expert card players until Neville developed a habit of winning the big hands. At the end of a particularly tense evening session only Rhys, Jim, Hamish and Neville were left in. Randle watched, having again lost his daily allowance for the day.

'Are you God-fearing, sir?' asked Hamish, as the cards were dealt.

'Only when I'm losing,' Neville replied.

'Which isn't often,' said Jim. 'Can't imagine why that is, sir.

Given that you only learnt to play cards from us.'

The players picked up their cards and pretended to concentrate. They all knew what had happened at the school debate and exchanged nudges and sly looks at the awkwardness between the two protagonists.

'I'm a quick learner, Private.' Neville looked at Jim over the top of his glasses. 'By the way, how does army life compare to the slums of Manchester or Birmingham?'

The group took fleeting glances at Jim. 'I don't know, sir. I never went. I'm in for a ha'penny. What about you, Hamish?'

'Me? Er.....me too. And raise you to a penny.' Nothing more was said about it, but as is the nature of many friendships, the one that developed between Jim and Neville benefited from a common difficulty, overcome.

Rhys suddenly stood up. 'I say old man, you're not counting the cards are you?' He stared accusingly at Neville.

'What does that mean?' asked Neville, genuinely having no idea what Rhys was talking about.

'It means, sir, that you can predict which cards are in which hands just by remembering how they go back in the pack after each hand.'

'That's impossible,' said Hamish.

'Actually, I can predict which cards you can't have. I find that more effective,' said Neville quietly, almost apologetically.

Everyone stared at Neville. 'Am I not allowed to do that?'

'No, you are not. If you get caught counting the cards in serious card schools they throw you out on your ear, after they've taken all your money off you,' replied Rhys tersely.

'Sorry. I didn't know.'

'From now on, we shuffle after every hand. Alright, gentlemen?'

They were still staring at Neville, some open-mouthed.

Jim leaned forward, and looked round the table. He whispered, 'Don't tell anyone about this. Sir, your secret is safe with us. You didn't know so you can keep the money. Gents, this is our path to riches. The lieutenant has a unique gift. Whenever we play against other companies, we don't shuffle the cards until asked. Alright? Sir, will you agree to share your winnings with us when we play in other schools?'

'Yes. If you reciprocate.'

'If you what?' asked Hamish.

'It's agreed then,' said Jim and they all shook hands.

*

Matters took a turn for the worse in the second week. Major Phillips called the officers and N.C.O.'s to the officers' mess for news on the war. Drinks were served on arrival and the men milled around introducing one another and exchanging stories of the last couple of weeks.

'At ease, gentlemen,' said the C.O. as he walked onto the stage and stood at the side of the lectern. 'I have just had some news from the front. As you know, the Germans have been pouring through Belgium and Luxemburg and attacked the northeast frontier of France. You may also be aware that our boys gave a good account of themselves at Mons forcing the Hun back. However, because the French had to retreat, this exposed our flank, so we were forced to follow suit.'

He coughed and looked down at his notes. 'Over the past two days the Second Corps has been fighting for its life near Le Cateau against the German First Army. The outcome is by no means clear, gentlemen, but I can tell you that there have been many casualties on both sides. It appears that the Germans have learnt their lesson from Mons and are not approaching our dug-in positions. Instead they are picking off our men at a distance, using guns fitted with telescopic sights. Dastardly way to wage war but then this is what we have come to expect from the Hun.'

'I thought we learnt that lesson in South Africa,' whispered Clive to Neville at the back of the room.

A free-for-all debate developed amongst the men around him. The major tapped the side of the lectern with his knuckles.

'I have some more bad news, I am afraid. We are getting news of a major battle around Tannenburg in East Prussia. It appears that the Russians have been surrounded and are in the process of being destroyed. A whole army is being wiped out.'

The men looked up at their leader, stunned.

'I do not need to tell you that war is a bloody business. Some of you here today and many of the men outside that window will not make it home to their families. Your job is to train them well, train them hard and to take the battle to the enemy. The 5th Battalion leaves for Aldershot tomorrow at 1500 hours. That's A and B Companies. You will be split into further companies when you arrive. The officers go with the men this time. Captain Fox, please carry on your excellent work with C Company. We will use it as a model for the others as they arrive. You'll take your men to Aldershot on 10th September with the two other companies that I need your help creating. This will make up the 6th Battalion.'

'Thank you, sir.' Clive tried not to show his feelings but inwardly he was glowing. The implications of what the major said were obvious. He just hoped no one blew it for him over the next week.

He returned to his company just as it finished its morning run.

Neville called the men to attention in a voice noticeably more authoritative than a week before. He had been scared rigid when he was first made an officer, particularly when he realised the number of men that he was meant to command. But he was part of a very large machine that had been forged in the furnace of war over many centuries and it had been designed not to fail. Each cog was important in its own right but was also supported by cogs either side, underneath and above. His softly-softly approach and deft use of his N.C.O.'s had earned the respect of the men. He was starting to feel fitter and stronger than he had been since prep school and it showed in his confident demeanour and he could see the men starting to leave the worries of civvy street behind them as well.

The soldiers-to-be lined up quickly. 'Men, you have done well. The C.O. has remarked on your development to date,' said Clive looking along the front row. 'Before you get carried away, let me tell you that in tomorrow's papers you will read some unhappy news about the war. I do not think that this will be a short war. Far from it. There will be some terrible times that you will have to deal with.

'The rest of the battalion leaves for Brigade tomorrow. We leave in two weeks. That means helping me and the new recruits as they arrive. We shall be asking for more volunteers to become N.C.O.'s. Private English?'

'Here, sir.'

'You are off jankers from Sunday. Well done for taking your punishment without complaint.'

'Thank you sir. Can I just say one thing, sir?'

'Go ahead.'

'My grandfather was English and I hear the sergeant major's grandparents were German so I reckon we're even. Oh, and he never had a mother. Sir.'

The company dissolved into laughter.

The captain spoke up. 'After lunch, to celebrate the private's admission that he is one of us after all, we will have a sports competition. First cricket, then rugby, then football. Second-Lieutenant Milton, I assume you know the rules?'

'Yes sir.'

'Then over lunch, work out a way of getting as many meaningful matches completed by 1900 hours. I want a winning team and a 'Sportsman of the day,' to join the C.O. and me down the pub for a beer tonight.'

*

That afternoon was the finest day of many of the men's

lives, combining those virtues that humanity thrives on: competition, laughter, exercise and learning. Referees, experienced or otherwise, were appointed and each platoon played the others at the three sports, points being awarded for wins and draws. Over the evening meal, the conversations were of who had done what to whom; Randle's uselessness in goal but brilliance in the scrum, Rhys' tries, Neville's wickets, Clive's unfair refereeing.

And then Captain Bartlett arrived with the sergeant major. They marched through the row of tents to where Clive was sitting on a log eating with some of his men. Those queuing for the last of the food turned to watch the approaching men.

The sergeant major took up a position with his back to Randle, as if this were part of the plan.

'Captain Fox, I hear that you have withdrawn the punishment that I gave English on the 17th August.'

'Actually, the S.M. gave it. And yes, I have withdrawn it.' Clive did not stand up but continued looking up at Bartlett, occasionally spooning food into his mouth.

'On what grounds may I ask?' Bartlett was tapping his cane against his boot.

'I am allowed to rescind any order given by a more junior officer or NCO.'

'You have obviously been away too long, Fox. Regulations state that orders given whilst on parade are those of the parade officer. That was me.'

'Oh, come off it, Nicholas, you are leaving soon. What difference does it make?'

Bartlett flushed with fury. He tapped his cane faster and hunched his shoulders like a falling falcon going in for the kill. 'Because you have undermined my authority and as you know that is the worst crime in the major's book.'

At that moment, Randle whispered something in the sergeant major's ear. It took about five seconds, long enough for the blood to drain out of the man's face. Randle returned to his seat.

Clive looked up at Captain Bartlett. 'Have you told him?'

'Not yet. He is at Division Headquarters. But I will. Unless of course you wish to rescind the rescission.' The sentence was delivered slowly, with his top lip curled into a sneer revealing a row of beautiful white teeth.

Clive knew that all his good work with these men was about to go up in smoke. He could either take the blast from the major with its myriad of implications or loose the respect of his men. It was an easy choice to make. He stood up.

'Alright, you jumped up....'

He was stopped short by the sergeant major. 'Captain Bartlett sir, I'm afraid that there has been a misunderstanding. I have just remembered that regulations state that no order is an order, if it is illegal.'

'Illegal? What are you talking about, man?'

'Well, sir.' He cleared his throat. It was the first time any of them had seen the sergeant major stuck for words. 'Well sir, I gave English three weeks jankers, the third week was for.....being Welsh, sir.' He seemed genuinely surprised at his own immaturity.

'And, Sergeant Major.'

'That was wrong, sir.'

'Say it,' whispered Randle behind him.

'It was unpatriotic, sir.'

Captain Bartlett stared at him. His cane hit his boot with added violence and his face turned a dark red. He looked as if he would explode with rage.

He turned to Clive. He spat the words into his face. 'They should never have let you back in Fox. You cheated on your wife, and worst of all, on a superior officer. Your time will come, you'll see.' Bartlett turned and marched back the way that he had come, swiftly followed by the sergeant major.

Clive's gaze followed the two men out of the camp and then at the many faces that were staring back at him. 'I would thank you never to repeat any of what just happened. Now get back to what you were doing.' He looked over to Randle. 'Lance Corporal, please follow me.'

Clive and Randle walked out of the small camp. 'And what exactly did you say to the sergeant major?' asked Clive.

'I told him that I knew he and another sergeant at the enlisting hall in town were running a black-market operation with bogus enlisters and our kit sir. I told him that if he didn't say it was an unpatriotic order, I'd tell you about it.'

Clive looked up at Randle and tried to look serious. 'And how did you come by this information, Lance Corporal Pugh?'

'We know the same people, sir.'

*

In their last week at Shrewsbury, live ammunition arrived for the men to use. Companies were taken off to the butts for a day at a time by their officers and those few sergeants who had experienced shooting in anger. Most of the men had never fired a rifle, let alone a powerful one like the Lee-Metford or the Lee-Enfield. Both fired a .303-inch calibre bullet capable of penetrating eighteen inches of oak at two hundred yards.

Clive asked his officers to attend as many of the battalion's shooting sessions as possible to ensure consistency of tuition within his company and to identify potential sharpshooters. The men were asked to lie down in the prone position and five rifles were allocated to each fifteen-man group. The men took turns to fire five rounds each, at targets set in front of a large mound of earth a hundred yards away.

Captain Bartlett stood behind the prostrate men, looking through a telescope that sat on a tripod. He commented caustically on the quality of shooting as holes appeared at varying distances from the bullseyes on the large targets in the distance. Some missed completely. He laughed at Hamish's first shot, then at his second, but stayed quiet after the third, fourth and fifth.

'You've got wonky eyes, boy. Try shooting at the target to the left next time and you might hit your own. Nice grouping though,' said Bartlett sarcastically.

Hamish handed the gun to Jim. Jim replaced the magazine and asked Bartlett where Hamish's grouping was. 'Eighteen inches at three o'clock, if that means anything to you, Private,' came the reply.

Jim smiled at Hamish as he put the gun under his chin and took aim. He fired. Bartlett said nothing, nor after the second, third, fourth or fifth shot. Jim lay the gun down and turned to Bartlett who had taken a step back from the telescope. He looked at the target in the distance, then at Jim. He walked back to the telescope, had another look and said, 'Four inch grouping around the bull.' His voice was softer this time.

The other officers and N.C.O.'s who had been to many of these sessions over the past few days, looked at Bartlett. They rushed to the telescope, pushing each other away to get a better look.

'That is the finest shooting I have ever seen. By anyone. What's your name, Private?' asked Bartlett.

'Downing, sir. Jim Downing.'

'Where did you learn to shoot like that, Private Downing?'

'My dad taught me from the age of four, sir.'

'I didn't ask you who taught you. I asked you *where* do you shoot.'

'Mainly by the river, sir. Sometimes in the hills, with Hamish here.'

'What, old Cross-Eyes? He just missed every bloody German bearing down on him.'

'The rifle's shooting to the right,' replied Jim.

'Rubbish. I zeroed the sights on all the rifles this morning.'

'Then the rifling's worn out since you zeroed it, or the front sight has been knocked,' suggested Hamish, still smarting from the insult.

Bartlett moved towards the two friends and lay down between

them. He changed the magazine with one from his bandolier, assumed the firing position and let off five shots.

'Eight-inch grouping, eighteen inches to the right of the bull. Just like Lance Corporal Cross-Eyes next to you, but his grouping was better.' It was Neville peering through the same telescope. 'I think you owe Mr. Rutherford an apology, sir.'

Bartlett got to his feet. 'I beg your pardon, Lieutenant.' His eyes bored into Neville's.

'I was only saying...'

'I know what you were saying, Lieutenant. You were asking me to apologise to a junior officer, in front of these men.'

'Then do so, Captain.' It was Major Phillips speaking from the side of the row of white wooden huts. 'You did, after all, incorrectly accuse him of being a poor shot.'

Every muscle in the dried-up husk of undeveloped masculinity that was Captain Nicholas Bartlett tightened to breaking point. He stared at the major, then at Neville, then at Hamish. 'I...I....I can't, sir.'

'Very well, Captain. In that case you had better come with me.' The major turned and disappeared from sight. Bartlett followed him back to his office.

'Take a seat, Captain Bartlett.' Both men sat down on opposite sides of the desk. The room was sparse and cold despite the summer heat outside. Bartlett shook. 'Captain, I have got some bad news for you. You are not going to France.'

'But, sir....'

The major held his hand up. 'Captain, you are not cut out for leadership. Your men fear you but for the wrong reason. You are a bully. A manipulative coward who has come up the ranks by currying favour and threatening the unaware. This is the end of road. I am transferring you to non-combative duties. Frankly, men in battle deserve to be better led.'

Bartlett's face was white. He had never been spoken to like this before. How would he cope with the shame? 'May I ask for the transfer to be done discreetly, sir?'

'Of course. You never know, a while behind a desk might change you, but I don't hold out much hope. Now, please start gathering your personal affects. Better this be done swiftly.'

Bartlett stood, saluted and left, and as he packed he made a promise to himself. He wasn't finished with Clive Fox and his men. Not by a long way.

*

C Company marched behind a brass band through the town to the station, together with the new A, B, and D Companies. The recently promoted Major Fox and first-Lieutenant Milton proudly led the men over the Welsh Bridge and along the riverbank. The local papers had announced that the new 6th Battalion, King's Shropshire Light Infantry would be passing out that day and it seemed that the whole town was there to see them off. The men marched the mile to the station in suits and hats, followed by their belongings on the carriages at the rear. Some of the men's families were standing on the pavement waving their flags with the rest.

Clive Fox waved to his wife and two daughters at the bottom of Mardol, and Jim's and Hamish's fathers stood by the riverbank and doffed their caps to their marching sons.

As the men approached the station, Randle caught sight of a familiar face up on the ramparts of the lower wall surrounding the castle. His mother waved. He nodded and then disappeared into the station entrance. Neither of them had felt as proud as at that moment. Neither of them knew whether they would see each other again.

3

Loos, France. Ten months later.

Otto Spielmann removed his green and blue Jaeger regimental hat and placed it on the ledge at the bottom of the trench, Saxon cockade to the front. It was a superstitious gesture he knew, of no practical use except that his fellow soldiers might remember that he was out hunting and would not over-react when he started shooting.

He crawled through the hole at the base of the trench and out into no-man's-land, stopping briefly in the cover of a large piece of corrugated iron and looked along the front wall of his trench. Rubbish was everywhere. Rats scurried from tin to tin and back again, making the quiet rustling noises familiar to their human neighbours all along the trench line that stretched for miles in front and behind him. He looked up into the blackness. A few stars twinkled, but the moon had gone down an hour ago. He could see forty yards ahead. No danger of being seen by the enemy.

Spielmann checked the position of the Gewehr Mauser 98 rifle with the Zeiss telescopic sights that was strapped to his back over the canvas painted sniper suit, and moved off into the long grass. He moved fast and low, confident of his route, knowing that no German sniper had been killed or wounded in this sector since the two armies had dug in. That was eight months ago. Otto enjoyed easy pickings against the British battalions that defended the trenches further down the small valley. This was his hunting ground. Twenty-eight kills later, he was the top marksman in his brigade.

A new unit had taken over the British trenches. He had seen them through his five-times magnifying sights scurrying up the communication trenches just before dawn. It had been just too dark to get off a successful shot. He could wait.

He was a member of the elite Jaeger Regiment attached to a Saxon battalion. The Jaegers, or 'hunters,' had been employed as scouts in the successful Prussian Armies of the Seven Years War more that a century and a half before. Recruited from the mountainous and forested areas of Germany, they had excelled at providing long-range intelligence of enemy formations and at rapid fire and movement. They were the inspiration for Wellington's much-vaunted 95th Rifles of the Peninsula and Waterloo campaigns. Some of these tough soldiers specialised in scouting and observation, some at operating behind enemy lines and some at sniping, though each was highly trained in all three disciplines. Otto was a sniper, his dark facial hair distinguishing him as such from his fellow soldiers.

He had been taught to shoot and hunt by his father, who in turn had been taught by Otto's grandfather. You didn't grow up in the Rominter forests without learning how to kill boar and deer. The men would enter the forests before dawn and wait, rifle at the ready. They stood in the waist-high bracken, brain getting used to the sounds and sights of the forest as it awoke. As the night disappeared and the canopy let in the early rays of sun, tiny movements would be picked up by their heightened senses. A twitching ear, a scurry, a snapped twig underfoot. It was the same at dusk, when the animals felt safer in the gloom and were hunting for their supper.

Spielmann reached the partially destroyed wall in less than five minutes, unclipped his gun belt and carefully brought the gun and its sight around his right shoulder so that it was underneath his chest and between the forearms that supported him on the hard, cracked earth. He removed the sandbag ragging from around the sights and gently pulled the right edges of the two loose bricks in the fifth and sixth rows of the wall a couple of inches towards him. He peered through the gap to where he knew the clean-lined British trenches to be. Sirius was low in the sky. It was 5.50 a.m. In half an hour, the sun would rise behind him.

*

41

Two hundred yards down the gentle slope, Corporal Hamish Rutherford chewed on his last match. He spat the wet pulp into the gap between the neat rows of sandbags and the earth below and took yet another look through the periscope. He moved it to the left and right. Nothing. He looked at his watch. Ten minutes until stand-to relieved him from this mind-numbing task. He had volunteered to do the first night sentry in the trench because he wanted to show his section that he wouldn't fall sleep. He was exhausted and bored witless and was looking forward to the cup of tea that one of his men would bring him after stand down.

It was nearly a year since they had left Shrewsbury for months and months of training in the fields of southern England. The facilities had been pathetic and the weather awful until at last, by the spring of 1915 the British Army had got to grips with training a million men from scratch. The battalion had left Cowshot in July, a fit, well-trained corps of soldiers eager to get to the fight.

The first two weeks in Flanders had been full of night marches over cobbles in full gear, inspections by generals, training in bombing and machine-gun work and using the new gas masks in rooms filled with tear gas. The 60th Infantry Brigade had camped and billeted around Argues and together they had marched to Borre and then onwards through bland border villages with unpronounceable names. On the 10th September, the battalion was posted to front-line trenches in the Le Trou area where the West Yorkshires showed them the ropes. Every company spent a day in the trenches on their own and then six more days being relieved daily by other companies in the battalion.

The only fatality during their time in this quiet sector was a sergeant who was blown up by a German mortar, fired in response to the battalion's own naïve mortar test firing. The Germans hadn't taken kindly to the shattering of the 'live and let live' arrangement that they had shared with the previous brigade. Four privates were injured in other incidents, two accidentally. New drafts of men arrived weekly. Their training had taken less than half the time of the September 1914 draft, much to the latter's disgust. The battalion had been relieved by the 6th Ox & Bucks on the 24th and spent a night in billets before marching here to Loos with the rest of the 20th Division. Their orders were to defend the left bank of the Grenay to La Bassee canal.

Hamish could remember everything from Major Fox's speech before they came into the line. Fox had stood in the middle of a clearing surrounded by the four platoons that made up A Company under his command. It was a fine, warm day and the men sweated in the sunshine. Hamish recalled what the major said about mercy, that it did not exist in this primordial world, as it was misunderstood for fear. Such misunderstanding was made for death. 'Kill or be killed, that is the law.' The death sentence would be meted out for desertion, mutiny, leaving the trenches without permission, cowardice or sleeping while on duty. Only the latter worried Hamish.

Most of all, he remembered the feeling of excitement of going into battle for the first time. This was what he had trained for, for nearly a year. No more soft sectors, no more handholding. He and Jim had chatted excitedly for hours about going over the top, as they marched between the lines of trees that bordered the miles of dusty roads. When they had fallen out and grabbed some much needed rest, Jim played bars of notes on the harmonica that he had found by the side of the road and Hamish had read poems out loud from the book, 'A Shropshire Lad,' sent to him by his father. It provided solace and melancholy in equal measure. He was embarrassed about his reading, but no one had laughed.

'Stand-to,' whispered Sergeant Small as he ducked into doorways, kicking men from their slumbers. He knocked on the homemade door in the rear wall of the trench and opened it without waiting for a response. 'Stand to, sir,' he called into the dug-out.

'Thank you, Sergeant,' came Neville's sleepy response. Men rose stiffly from their foxholes. Someone farted. Another giggled. A rifle fell and clattered on the duckboards.

'The next man to make a sound, any sound, is on a charge.'

Hamish's twelve men looked at him through the semi-darkness. They were still getting used to this man's ways. One minute friendly, the next an aggressive disciplinarian. Young, too.

They readied themselves, facing the front, holding their rifles in the vertical position along the section of trench between the two firebreaks, about thirty yards apart. 'Bayonets,' whispered Hamish. The men removed the eighteen-inch blades from their webbing and clicked them into place below the muzzles of their rifles.

The dawn chorus drifted across the valley from the woods beyond.

They all moved to the front of the trench and up onto the fire step. Hamish checked to make sure that all heads were below the top of the parapet. 'Keep those heads down, lads. Fritz is probably out there now waiting for one of you to take a peep over the top. Jones, get that cap off now!'

Neville stumbled into the trench from his dugout. His tunic buttons were not done up at the top. Hamish noticed the pale beard growing on his officer's chin. It reminded him of the bad old days in the filthy, sodden tents near Aldershot where they washed and shaved only when ordered.

'All men present, sir'.

'Carry on, Sergeant.'

The clumsy thud of a man and rifle falling onto boards came from the section to their left. The noise of the shot came afterwards, echoing down the valley. 'Oh God. Stretcher-bearers! Get the fucking stretcher-bearers!' screamed Jim. Hamish ran to the fire-break and stared at the dying man shaking on the boards, face down, blood pouring from what remained of the back of his head.

Hamish looked up at the parapet. In the half-light, he could clearly see the gap in the neat line of sandbags where one had been blown open. Dirt continued to pour into the trench, mixing with the blood and brains on the boards. The men stared at the jerking body.

'His knees, his knees, they just….loosened. Rhys! Rhys! Don't die. Please God. Don't die,' cried Jim, as he cradled the Welshman's head. Men stood and stared. One vomited down the front of his uniform.

Hamish ran at the men on the fire step. 'Get down! Get down! Get off the bloody step!' He yanked and pulled at as many as he could, weaving over and under them as they fell like ninepins. He turned back to his own section and rounded the corner just as a sandbag exploded over the head of Private Ellis, covering his head and shoulders with dirt. Everyone dived for cover, some crouching on the boards, others curled in the foetal position in the shadow of the front wall, hands over heads.

Hamish bent down and rested his hands on his knees, panting for breath. He heard Neville shouting as he ran further up the line pulling at the men's bandoliers as he went. Hamish stared at his men, then at Ellis. 'You alright?'

'Yes, Corporal. Are we safe down here, sir?'

'From bullets, yes.' He looked up at the wounded sandbag. 'You got lucky, Ellis. Your lack of inches saved your life. He must have seen a hat or something and guessed that we were all lined up behind the parapet.' Hamish kept staring at the bags, getting his breath back. 'They're too level. You could see a mouse running over that lot.'

'In this light, Corporal?' asked another private.

'With the right telescopic sight, yes, you could. Half light, sun behind you, five to ten times magnification. But to shoot that mouse, that's fine shooting.'

'Are we going to get the bastard?' asked Ellis weakly.

Hamish looked again at the emptying sandbag and then at the hole made by the bullet in the rear wall of the trench.

'We might Ellis, we just might. Keep your heads down and no-one touch that bag or that bullet-hole. I'm going to talk to the sergeant.'

*

The black Labrador steered his master home from the paper shop as retired Captain Clive Fox cast his eyes over the jobs pages in the *Shrewsbury Chronicle*. The dog lead dangled from Clive's left forearm and he managed a polite 'Morning' to those he passed, glancing briefly up from his newspaper.

Today was Chronicle day. Once a week he was able to catch up on local and national events whilst dreaming of doing other people's jobs. He didn't mind being a surveyor. It was what many ex-officers did. The exams were relatively easy, the pay wasn't bad and you got out of the office some. But he had done the same job in the same building with the same people for three years and now he was getting itchy feet.

Maybe it was his military past. The army regularly posted you to all parts of the Empire and it was anything but an office life. He had done eleven years and had some great memories. Many of those that he had signed up with in 1900 hadn't been so lucky. He had seen incredible and terrible things during his travels. The creativity and disrespect for life of the Chinese, the heat and poverty of India, and the majesty of southern Africa. But his mind was restless again.

Job done, Boris took a drink and fell into his basket by the back door of the semi-detached Victorian house in Bellevue, one of Shrewsbury's better areas.

Clive's two daughters, Belinda and Catherine tried to jump on his lap as soon as he sat down.

'Morning, my lovelies. Could Daddy have a few moments peace reading his paper?' His eldest sighed and ran back with her sister to the kitchen where their mother was making breakfast.

'Tea coming up.'

'Wonderful,' he replied, already absorbed in what he was reading. The first few pages were full of local news and adverts despite the fact that Great Britain had declared war on Germany only three days before. There was a notice from North Western & Great Western Railways explaining that all excursion and reduced fare tickets were cancelled until further notice and that train services throughout the country may be discontinued as circumstances arose. In the next column there was an advert for the Cunard

Line declaring that its ships *The Aquitania*, *The Mauritania* and *The Lusitania* were the fastest mail and passenger services in the World. Local horse sales, Punch & Judy shows, children's parties and flower shows filled the first page. Inside he found articles about cricket matches, horticultural shows, an eisteddfod, a cancelled bicycle carnival and an apology for the reduced size of the paper, which was due to 'disorganisation of local businesses caused by the war'.

Towards the back, Clive found what he was looking for. Articles entitled 'United in danger', 'What Germany has done,' and 'The men to whom we look,' brought Clive up to date with the situation facing the country and started the irreversible emotional response in him that affected so many.

Agnes stood behind him reading the same reports as she placed Clive's cup of tea on the little table. Her eyes couldn't move from the title 'Vacancies for ex-soldiers.'

'You've seen it, haven't you?' asked Clive.

'Hmm'mm'. She glanced at the bookcase beside her. It was full of books on military history and she shuddered. She thought of putting her hands on her husband's shoulders, but realising that the hands of fate were already there she crossed her arms instead.

The room was silent for a while. 'They're panic buying in town, it says here. The KSLI were mobbed in the streets on the way to the station. Brass bands and everything. They even erected another platform to get all the hardware on,' volunteered Clive, wanting to say anything to break the mood.

'Hmm'mm`.

He turned in his seat and looked up at his wife. She passed him his cup and saucer.

'They are billeting the Cheshires and the Welsh Field Artillery here. Shrewsbury will be swarming. They are looking for homes to put soldiers into. We could take one,' suggested Clive.

'He'll get drunk'.

'I could join him,' replied Clive. His wife turned away and walked back to the kitchen.

'Bugger,' whispered Clive. He read on. The mayor was asking farmers and marketeers to keep prices down and for employers to keep positions open for enlisting soldiers when they returned.

'Do you know Agnes, there was nothing in this paper last week about the war. There was only a cartoon of the lady looking out to sea with the title, 'What of the dawn?' I remember it distinctly. The paper was full of the situation in Ireland and the gun-running, and news of Shackleton's dogs arriving with his ship. 'The Endurance,' I think it was called. Now everything and everybody is gearing up for this war. They are even looking for people to help with the harvest because so many of the farm workers are signing up. They'll never cope. 'A good time for war to come' it says here, as it's harvest time. Will they never learn?'

There was no answer from the kitchen. Clive folded the paper and placed it on the piano stool as he stood up. He noticed the large advert on the back page. 'Your country needs you. If you are able-bodied, unmarried and between eighteen and thirty years old, answer the call. Join the army today.'

'Well that's two reasons why I can't,' he said, rubbing his hands as he went in search of his wife.

*

The bells of St.Chad's church rang above the rondola and echoed down the narrow streets and alleys of the town and out into the fields beyond. It was the Sunday after that momentous Tuesday when Great Britain had entered the first global war. The armies of Europe were marching to catastrophe and the people were marching to church. Dutifully, obediently, for a good cause. 'My country right or wrong,' had been polarised to 'My country is one hundred percent right and the Germans are one hundred percent wrong'. It wasn't a case of xenophobia or power. At least to the ordinary man in the street it wasn't. German troops had been on neutral Luxembourg and Belgium's soil for nearly a week and the stories of atrocities were starting to trickle through, invented or otherwise. The Germans had had a bloody nose coming to them for years. It was democracy

48

versus militarism, fair play against the playground bully, the gentleman against the gun. Great Britain had guaranteed Belgian independence and would stand by that. It was that simple.

British women, like flocks of geese feeling the cold winds of change, prepared their feathers.

Clive and Agnes walked along the Town Walls from Bellevue, as they did most Sundays. This time the girls had stayed at home with the nanny. Agnes knew that this service would be difficult for Clive because St. Chad's was his old regiment's home church. Still, Clive was too old now and had a family so he could sate his conscience knowing that he would be joining up if he could. They passed the Boer War memorial above the park with its pith-helmeted soldier standing over the names of local lads who had fallen. Clive had known many of them, but did not give it a look. He had read them many times before.

They crossed the road, passed through the lines of parked carriages and tied horses and made their way into the cool church between the huge Doric pillars, stopping to wipe the mud from their shoes on the metal scraper. Two semi-circular staircases swept their way up to the first floor. The walls were covered with memorials to those of the KSLI who had given their lives in previous campaigns. Egypt, South Africa, Hong Kong, the Indian Mutiny, Sudan, Afghanistan, and further back to Salamanca, Vittoria, and St. Lucia. Agnes glanced at the last dedication before she entered the rondola. 'The fittest place where a man can die is where he dies for Man.'

The couple walked hand in hand down the middle of the nave and took their usual places half way along the row of pews to the left. The late morning sun poured through the stained glass windows turning the stone floors and aged dark wood into a pallet of reds, blues and purples. Clive's eyes followed the rising dust and saw that the upper story, similar to the dress circle in a theatre, was full of people. Some stood against the wall at the back, not able to find a seat. The whole edifice creaked under the weight and Clive for a moment wondered if it had ever had so many people bearing down on it. He felt oddly uncomfortable as if he were on a stage where the audience could see into his soul. He knelt and prayed.

A man in a black suit closed the large wooden doors at the back and nodded to the organist. The first chords of the hymn thundered through the round hall and five hundred worshippers stood and sang.

Agnes' heart sank. She looked at the other four hymn numbers hanging below the top of the brass and copper pulpit known locally as the 'coal scuttle,' found them in her book and whispered something to her husband. He smiled and sang even louder.

*

'Heels together, point toes. Hop and skip and hop and skip. Stop. Put umbrellas down, and up, hand out to see if it's raining. Lift skirts, walk around the umbrella on your toes and hop and skip back to your original position. Good. Well done children.' Clive's youngest daughter Catherine beamed at her father who stood at the back of the dance hall, arms folded.

'Look at me. Not anyone else,' demanded the octogenarian ballet teacher. She proceeded to torture her charges, placing a toy crown loosely on each of their heads which had to remain there while the girls practiced points and pliets.

Clive smiled. This is no different to the army, he thought. It was ballet, not drill and it was indoors not out in the freezing rain, or worse in the summer heat, but the basic elements were the same. Practice, threats, humiliation until the weakest got it right.

He had already made a decision about the army. If he was too old, he was too old. But he knew that it would be a matter of time before they needed more officers to help train the huge numbers of volunteers coming forward. Then the age limit would move upwards rapidly. At 32, he guessed he was a couple of weeks away from being expected to join up. He couldn't wait. It would be an opportunity to make amends.

He looked at his watch. He would tell Agnes after this evening's concert.

*

He took a slug from the bottle of whisky that sat on the shelf next to the mirror. He had seen injuries of all types before, but not for more than a decade. He tried hard to keep the bile in his throat when the Medical Officer showed him the damage to the back of Rhys English's head as he lay on the bloodied stretcher in the small dug-out in the communication trench.

The bullet had been found in the wall of the trench behind where English had been standing, a bull's-eye in a target of mud, brains and skull fragments. Clive had turned the cleaned bullet over in his hand. It was 7.92mm calibre, probably fired from a 98 Mauser. The design was sixteen years old but it was still considered one of the finest rifles ever made. Clive recognised the shape and size from the war in South Africa and he knew it was possible for this bullet to go though a sandbag at two hundred yards just as his army's SMLE .303 could go through two. Why hadn't the captain of the company that they had just relieved warned him of the danger? Clive had inspected the front parapet for loose bags when he arrived. All were filled and there were no gaps and no splits. If the Germans were firing through bags this could only mean that his men were being predictable and that the parapet was not up to the job of protecting them.

He went over to the table that stood next to the thick beam in the middle of the room. He picked up Rhys's identity discs and ran the red and green string around his index and middle fingers like a priest working rosary beads. The light from the candle reflected off the discs as Clive turned them over in his hand. Name, regiment, religion and number, that was all. He picked up the letter from the small table.

'Dear Mrs. English, your son......' Clive had found details of Rhys's next of kin in the dead man's pay book. He wondered if he had brothers or sisters, or God forbid was an only child. This was one of the tragedies of war, thought Clive. The sons that die are men. The parents are too old to make another one. If that was your only child, that was it. No more family. He looked at the photograph of his wife and two daughters sitting on the earthen shelf. It was dog-eared from too much handling and was spotted with damp from the wet winter months camped in the Sussex fields.

He was shocked at a thought that suddenly came to him. If he died, his wife and children would be grief-stricken, particularly his youngest. But they would survive. Life would carry on. His wife may remarry and his daughters would grow up and have husbands. For a parent to loose a child, particularly an only child, was beyond the point at which Clive wanted to imagine.

There were two firm knocks at the door. The huge stooping shape of Randle Pugh filled the doorway. He took off his cap.

'May we come in, sir?'

'Certainly, Sergeant. Who have you brought?'

'Corporal Rutherford and Private Downing, sir. We've been talking 'bout the sniper.'

'Oh, yes?' Clive looked up from the photograph and placed Rhys's discs on the table. 'Take a seat gentlemen. I'm sorry about English. You were good friends, weren't you.'

Jim's face was gaunt. Rhys and he had indeed been close. Both shared the same type of intelligence and quick wit. The Welshman had enhanced all of their lives, making the pitiful conditions and training at Aldershot bearable. He was always funny, even after weeks of rain, cold, lice and mind-numbing route marches. They had been in it together, even the motorbike trip to Marlow, where they had seen his charm with the ladies on display, but the journey had ended in tragedy for two of their number when a motorbike had come off the road. And what a fighter. Rhys' friends had got rich on the bets that Rhys had told them to make on his beating of John 'The Head' Roston in the boxing tournament. Third round he said it would be, and third round it was.

Clive lit another cigarette. Randle took this as permission to smoke his pipe and Jim took the packet of cigarettes from his uniform jacket pocket.

'You know Rutherford and Downing 'ere are good shots, sir,'

said Randle as he filled his pipe bowl with tobacco.

'I do. Thanks to you, apparently.'

'Well, sir,' he said, inhaling the pungent smoke. 'I give 'em the basics and then the private's father and their own competitiveness did the rest.'

'You taught them more than the basics, Sergeant. If there's a man in the British Army who understands stalking, scouting and shooting better than you, I'd like to meet him,' replied Clive.

'You obviously haven't met the Lovat scouts, sir,' said Randle.

'No, but I know of their reputation.'

'As I were saying, sir, these two can shoot. We think there's a way of getting back at the sniper.'

'Go on.'

'We've lined up the two holes that the bullets made in the trench wall wi' the bags that they went through using two pieces of wood, then made right-angles wi' the wood and the periscopes. We think we can see where the sniper fired from. It's a wall 'bout one hundred and fifty yards out on our left flank. No sign of 'im now though.'

Clive laid his cigarette in the shrapnel ashtray, sat back and crossed his arms. 'That was clever. Whose idea was that?'

'Corporal Rutherford, sir', replied Randle.

'You did well this morning, Rutherford. Probably saved a life or two.'

Hamish nodded his thanks to the major. He was thinking about the contents of the dugout and what they said about his commanding officer. The trumpet standing on its end on the earth floor, the ivory shaving brush by the white bucket below the mirror, the card cartoons on the wall, the pile of cigarette butts brushed under the table where the half-empty bottle of whisky now stood.

'So what are we going to do about Fritz?' asked Clive.

Hamish replied first. 'We need two good rifles with telescopic sights, sir. Not the SMLE, which for some reason has a telescopic sight fitting on the side of the gun. A Mauser would be fine and the more powerful the better. And the sights must be zeroed. If they are one hundredth of an inch out the bullet will miss by eighteen inches over two hundred yards. And we need some barb-less wire, some wood about two feet square and an inch thick, a piece of metal the same size as the wood, both with holes in the middle, a removable metal cover for the hole, and a piece of piping, about twelve inches long and four inches wide.'

'And paint. Green, yellow and brown. Some hessian and two telescopes of ten to twenty times magnification,' added Randle.

'Not quite the place I would recommend for a spot of painting,' joked Clive.

'It's for the sand bags, sir. If you look at the German trenches, there is no consistency of colour and there is rubbish all over their parapet. There are no clean lines. That's deliberate.'

'I've just had an idea,' interrupted Jim, looking around at the seated audience. 'When I was a kid we used to make things out of wet newspaper and glue. We could make some look like a Tommy's head. If we put it on a stick and somehow fixed that to a marker on the front of the trench, when Fritz fired at the head we could work out where the shot came from by fixing a periscope to point back down the line of the bullet.'

'How would you know that?' asked Hamish.

'You push a stick through the entry and exit wounds, and sit the scope under it. The top's a right angle. You wouldn't need the sandbags then,' replied Jim.

They all looked at Jim, taking in what he had said. Randle nodded in approval.

'Have any of you read Sun Tzu's 'The Art of War?' asked Clive. He walked over to the small shelf next to the gas blanket and pulled out one of the three books. 'This, gentlemen, is the finest book ever written on war. It's two thousand years old and the lessons in here are as true today as they were then, maybe more so.' He stared straight ahead as if trying for focus on a long-distant memory.

'All war is based on deception. Feign incapacity and inactivity, use baits and lures and be patient. He who is prudent and waits for an enemy who is not, will be victorious. Know the enemy and know yourself. Use the terrain and the natural forces around you. The wind, moon, sun, they are all important. Use secret agents to be your eyes and ears. Keep your best troops on the flanks. Finally, never let your enemy bring you to his chosen field of battle. Gentlemen, so far I think that the British Army has broken just about every one of those rules. From now on, we set about reversing that situation. I want no-mans-land to be ours. I want Jerry to be shit-scared of going anywhere near it. That is the key to winning this war.'

Clive went over to the table, dragged on the last of his cigarette and stubbed it out in the shrapnel ashtray. 'Sergeant, Corporal, Private, let's get some men together and fetch the stuff you want from the stores. I hope the QMS is in a good mood. Then we'll set about turning this into a fighting trench instead of some general's idea of a pretty one.'

As they entered the trench from the dugout, a French boy passed shouting 'Daily Mail, Daily Mail'. Clive grabbed three newspapers and handed them to Jim. 'There you go, Private, we'll call them Hans, Wolfgang and Claus.'

*

That afternoon, A Company prepared for the days ahead. Clive insisted that as much as possible of the work was done without the Germans knowing. He did not want to invite a dreaded minnenwerfer while his men were in the open.

They dug the trenches a foot deeper and made dugouts and shelters with better protection from mortar and artillery attack. They filled sandbags in their hundreds and splash-painted them with different colours and once it was dark they placed them over the old parapet, together with all the rubbish, tin sheeting, rags and trench detritus that the men could get hold of. The parapet top was roughed up and sniper-holes called loopholes were dug in and below the parapet by fixing the newly acquired wood and metal boards to sandbags so that the Germans couldn't detect them. Piping was placed into the loopholes to give the user more protection and to allow the guns to rest inside the parapet.

While Neville supervised this work, Clive co-ordinated the next day's plans in his dugout with Randle, Hamish and Jim. Randle tested his camouflage ideas using a mixture of empty sandbags, mud, grass, hessian and paint. Jim made his three heads by wrapping papier-mâché around large balls of clay dug from the bottom of the trench. He then stuck a pole up inside one of the necks and attached this to a brace which would later be fixed to the front wall of the trench. He found some rubber tubing in the sickbay that had been dug into the side of the communication trench and put this through the neck and into the mouth of the paper head. The room's occupants watched in amazement as he placed a lit cigarette into the tubing. He put a cloth hat on the head, stuck the pole into the floor of the dugout and put out the candles by flicking the wicks. He returned to his tube and a soft glow filled the room as Jim gently sucked on the end of it.

'That is incredible,' said a shocked Clive. 'Sun Tzu would have approved of that.'

'And to think that a year ago you thought that this war was someone else's, Jim,' laughed Hamish.

'Still do. I just want to remain alive until the workers of the world unite,' he replied without a trace of humour.

＊

Otto Spielmann crawled to his usual spot behind the broken wall feeling pleased with himself. Another four kills yesterday and a couple of possibles through the top line of sandbags on the parapet to his right. A few more today and he would have the most in the division. He looked at his watch. Twenty minutes until dawn.

Otto loved this job. It required a high level of skill and courage and he knew it was important to the war effort. It was because of men like him that his beloved country ruled no-man's-land. Nothing moved out here without he and his friends knowing about it. Even at night, they felt confident that patrols would return without casualties.

He could not understand the British. It was as if they did not expect to be here for long. Their trenches were obviously not deep enough and they offered very little in the way of invention. Why was the greatest empire in the world not using its reknowned powers of invention to work out solutions to defeat people like Otto? He had an inkling that vanity and arrogance had something to do with it. The fact that British officers made such good targets in their riding britches was but one obvious example.

He gently pulled the two bricks apart. They made the grinding noise that only brick sliding against brick can make. A fist came flying through the gap smacking Otto between the eyes and he lost consciousness.

Randle carried the inert body over his shoulder with Hamish covering his front and Sergeant Small his back. Not a word was said as they jogged down the slope and through the gap in the wire that they had cut on the way up. They lay in shell-holes when verey lights went up, and as they passed Rhys' old machine-gun team in their nest, Hamish gave the password and ran on.

The three of them fell into the front trench to find that the whole company had been waiting in case things had gone wrong. Those closest to the returning NCOs sheathed their bayonets and helped Randle offload his booty. The unconscious, bearded German lay face up at the bottom of the trench.

'Is he alive?' asked Neville.

'I bloody hope so, sir,' replied the panting Randle, wiping sweat off his brow to reveal the skin above his burnt cork-blackened face.

'And this is his gun. A Mauser .287 with Zeiss telescopic sights,' said a proud Hamish. Hands reached towards the prized weapon. 'Hands off! We've protected the sight fitting. Let's keep it that way.'

'Alright everybody, let's get on with the plan,' ordered Neville. 'Sergeant Small, please take the prisoner to my dugout and keep Rhys English's friends away from him. Tie him to a chair and gag him. It's not exactly regulations but it's better than shooting him like other units do. Sergeant Pugh, Corporal Rutherford, take that gun with you, get togged up, bring the telescope and go out to the left flank. Make sure you take the correct ammo and remember the map, paper and pen. Private Downing, the major is waiting for you down below. You two are going to the other flank. Remember that .350 has a kick like a mule. Happy hunting, men. Private Morris, fix 'Wolfgang' to the brace.'

4

Jim Downing stood behind the bar of his father's pub, the Free 'n Easy, checking the glasses for smudges and chips. He was grateful for the solitude as he wanted time to collect his thoughts before the onslaught that usually started at six o'clock. He let his eyes wander around the bar area, absently taking in the photos and paraphernalia on the dark wooden walls.

This was going to be one of the most humiliating evenings of his life. He had stayed away from the pub since the evening of the catapult incident, until now. His father had been furious. Jim reacted badly to the criticism and accused his father of being in league with 'the bourgeoisie and parasites who run this fucking country,' and that had got him a cuff. The fist came when he told his father that he had rolled over like a dog when he worked as a butler in Jim's early years.

Jim peered under the snob-screen towards the door. He would get a serious amount of stick tonight after his name and story appeared on the front page of the Shrewsbury Chronicle under the headline, 'Local youth charged with cruel prank on King.'

He had come round in the back of a police lorry, eyes watering from the smelling salts. He didn't have a clue which of the coppers around him had hit him. Hamish visited the next day and said that the two men who laid him out cold were not in police uniform. There remained a tenderness where he had been punched, but remarkably, no bruise.

The Free 'n Easy was an institution across the county. His father, Ken had bought it fifteen years previously, supposedly with the wages and tips that he had carefully squirreled away during a career as a butler serving in some of the country's most prestigious houses, but rumours persisted that Ken had another source of income.

'We supply the beer, you supply the songs,' ran the posters in the windows and over the years the pub had become the most popular venue for disorganised singing and dancing for miles around. If you couldn't walk to it you rode a bike or a horse, or you rowed or sailed the river Severn that

passed the rear of the pub. The lucky drove one of the few motorcars that were starting to appear in the area.

The weekdays' trade was made up of locals, passing botanists, anglers, darts players and the bowls teams that used the green at the back overlooking the river. Ken was pleased with the variety of types that he served. It kept the place alive, he said. He didn't fancy the chances of some of the working men-only pubs in town as modernisation reduced the need for traditional crafts and industries.

'Ready to face the music?' asked his father as he unbolted the double doors at the front of the pub.

'No,' Jim replied.

He reached up with both hands and took a half-dozen beer glasses off the shelf and poured some stout into each glass. When the last was half full he drank it in one and started to pour again.

*

The girl with red hair studied the silhouette of the young man for some time. He leant on the fence that formed the boundary of the pub grounds as it met the steep bank to the river. To her right the bowls match was coming to an end. She took a long slug from her glass of bitter and walked up to the fence.

'Fine view,' she said.

He turned his head towards her and smiled. 'It just got better'. He saw her blush and he wished he hadn't been so sure of himself. Girls, nice girls at any rate, didn't like that in a man.

He stood straight and extended his right hand. 'My name's Jim. Jim Downing. My Dad owns...'

'I know. And you work behind the bar. Which is obviously a cover for your other work.' She shot him with her imaginary catapult and strawberry and giggled. 'Sorry, couldn't resist.'

Jim gave her the same world-weary look that he had given all the other jokers that evening. He had come out here to get away from the pissed-

up rabble inside. *Any more shootings and he thought he would go mad.* He turned to the west again and Jessie followed his gaze along the river some forty feet below where the boats continued to sail upstream even at this late hour. The sun was just setting behind the saddleback of the Breiddon hills over at Welshpool and the air was full of the fleeting shadows of swallows and bats. Jessie joined him at the fence.

'Would you like a drink?' asked Jessie after a few moments.
Jim was stunned. *A girl hadn't asked him if he wanted a drink for, well, probably ever.* He faced her now. The setting sun picked out the flecks of raspberry and poppy in her hair.

'Thank you. A pint of stout please.' She smiled, curtsied, finished her beer and made off along the gravel path to the back of the pub. Jim watched her go. She wore a black full-length skirt over her petticoats, and some kind of corset. He had been so taken with her hair that he hadn't realised that her arms were bare. He sensed that she was a little older than he was and that he had seen her somewhere before.

When Jessie returned, he was talking to the captain of the home bowling team.

'Patrick meet....sorry, I haven't even asked you your name,' he spluttered.

'Jessie Appleby,' she replied. She shook hands with Patrick as he removed his hat, and with a 'pleased to meet you, Miss,' went back to packing the bowls into the wooden boxes that sat on the bench.

She was wearing a pink shawl over her shoulders now, which accentuated the redness of her hair. 'How did you know my name?' Jim asked, not being able to think of anything else to say.

'My secret.' She supped at her beer, meeting his gaze over the glass.

It had not been easy for her tonight. *She had arrived with a party of other girls, who knew about her plans for the evening, as girlfriends do. It was they who had strong-armed her into being more obvious about her 'desires' for this young man. Now she was outside with the man she had fancied for at least a year, half-tipsy. He was brasher than she expected, but he seemed genuine and showed some humility. Her only close experience* of men was living with three older brothers and father which was enough to give her confidence in assessing the opposite sex's qualities, or lack of them.

He was not classically good-looking. His chin was too small and his eyes were too deeply sunk but he had a great smile, long legs and broad shoulders. This boy had awoken something in her and it had happened even before they had spoken.

A fiddle struck up from one of the bars and the sound of jumping feet and girls' screams soon filled the warm evening air.

'Shall we dance?' asked Jim, who had become tongue-tied and was glad of the diversion.

She hooked her arm into his and walked into the pub, giving a little skip as she did so.

The pub was full of people, smoke and noise. Union Jacks hung from picture rails. The couple made their way towards the fiddle player who was now in full flight, through the laughing crowd and into the swirling, kicking mass at the far end of the room.

Most of the men wore dark trousers and waistcoats with light-coloured shirts and the girls spun in kaleidoscopes of petticoated skirts. The floor swarmed with the old and the young. Caps and neckerchiefs were stuffed into pockets and the swirl of dancers oozed sweat, fun and sex.

Jim put his right hand around Jessie's waist and clasped her opposite hand with his left. 'Hold tight,' he shouted as he guided her around the floor, firmly, swiftly, expertly, sometimes taking the lead, sometimes letting her do the work. She loved every minute of it. The chaos, the letting go, the music, oh the music. They were both, literally, being swept off their feet by the joy of the evening and the energy that they had both felt when their eyes had first met.

They danced reels, jigs, hornpipes and polkas. More fiddlers were playing now and then the uilleann pipes started up followed by a harp and the accordion. The Irish farm workers who came to the county for the build-up to the harvest were there in droves. The music of the shoes drummed on the bare boards and grew louder and louder until at times the dancers couldn't hear the players and they danced by instinct. Sometimes the music stopped in the middle of a dance and the shoes kept the beat until as one the players struck up again.

Every hour or so the dancing stopped and gave way to singing. The Wild Rover, Danny Boy, the Black Velvet Band were shouted not sung. Ken Downing provided free Guinness to the band all evening. He didn't care who they were and how many of them there were. That was for them to sort out. All he knew was that he sold fifty guineas of beer, wine, and particularly whiskey every Friday and Saturday night. He was happy, his customers were happy. 'Long may it continue,' he thought.

Much later Ken called time at the bar several times and the punters slowly staggered their way to the front and back doors. He stood by the bowling green to make sure no one pissed on it and closed the gate in the fence above the river once the last couple had left. He watched the boats going up and down river for a while. The half-moon's light barely got through the clouds coming up from the south, but he could still see the flotilla of tiny boats moving slowly back whence it came. It astonished him that after so many years of running the pub no accidents had been reported. Lost boats certainly, but no deaths. He touched the wood of the fence and walked back into his pub.

Jim and Jessie stood in the hallway, arms around each other's backs, sweaty and smiling. They had just said goodbye to some of the musicians as they wobbled their way down the hill on their bikes, somehow holding on to their instruments.

'Jessie's friends have gone without her. Can she stay the night in one of the guest bedrooms?' asked Jim.

'Where do you live, Jessie?' he asked kindly.

'Pontesbury.'

Ken Downing put his hands in his pockets and looked down at the floor. The signs of alcohol abuse showed in his face.

'You must be gone by the time the cleaners arrive, which is seven o'clock. You understand why?'

'Yes sir.'

'Good. It has been a pleasure meeting you, Jessie. You two look good together. What a night, eh?' And with that he walked past them to his ground floor quarters.

Jim dropped his hand from around her waist, suddenly feeling awkward.

'This way.' He showed her to the first guest bedroom, asked her if she needed anything and retired to his room at the end of the corridor. He closed the curtains, undressed and fell into bed, exhausted. His whole body was alive to what had just happened to him. He knew absolutely that he had fallen in love for the first time. He turned on his side and closed his eyes.

He didn't hear the creaks at first. He was so used to the old house's night-time noises that he didn't appreciate the meaning of the steady light notes until he heard the hinges of his door squeak. He sat up in bed and watched Jessie close the door behind her. She was naked apart from the pink shawl. She faced him from the door, feeling the cold brass of the handle in the small of her back.

'I lied', she whispered, 'There is something I need.' She looked magnificent. Her shawl barely covered her breasts and Jim could see the nipples trying to poke through the cloth. Her tummy-button was surrounded by the firm muscle of youth and her legs made smooth long shadows on the wood behind her. She moved towards the bed and lay next to Jim. He leant over her, stroked her hair and neck and kissed her on the lips.

*

The rowing boat made its way upriver, cutting through the water, mirror-like in the midday sun. The flow of the cool river was slow against the bow and the rowing was easy. Promenaders, cyclists and horse riders on the banks casually glanced at the tall adolescent leaning in and out of the strokes. Cricketers ambled about the park and brass band music filled the air. The striped tent of a visiting circus stood near the old town walls. Swans drifted on the tiny currents and tired breezes.

He pointed the craft towards the bank, tied the boat's tether to an iron hoop and looked up to the steep hill on his left.

The chatter of voices found its way down to the riverbank and Jim walked swiftly up to the Boathouse pub garden, already full of people. He tried to arrive at the pub by noon most Sundays to reserve a place at the bar or in the summer a seat in the garden. Nothing was ever arranged; he found friends or he didn't. He carried a copy of 'Das Kapital' in his jacket pocket to keep his mind occupied if he were alone.

Today, he knew he would not need the book. Jessie would be joining him. He had eventually found her address and left a message on her doorstep under a brick. She phoned him the same evening from the house of a friend and they had agreed to meet here today.

As Jim walked along the bank, he heard a new sound from the garden, different from other Sundays. More earnest and serious, like people discussing implications rather than events. He had heard the same in the Free 'n Easy over the past couple of weeks. The papers were full of stories of people joining up and the queues at the enlisting halls and although he had seen them for himself, he had been strangely unmoved by the whole thing. It wasn't cynicism; he was too young for that. He just concluded that falling in love and thoughts of war were incompatible, and being a romantic he naturally favoured the former.

Jim opened the small gate in the picket fence just as the Shrewsbury School clock struck noon and made straight for the aproned waiter holding a tray of pint glasses above his head.

'I'll have two thanks,' he said as he took a pint of beer in each hand. 'I'll make up later.'

Jim chose a seat in the shade under the willow tree, facing away from the pub towards the river and the park. He propped his feet on the bottom rung of the railings that fenced the garden off from the steep bank and watched families playing in the park opposite. He tapped a cigarette out of the packet and lit it.

He loved the oldness of Shrewsbury, the Tudor buildings, the hills, the churches and the pubs. It wasn't every town that could claim as sons the chief architect of the British Empire, Clive of India, the founder of Civil Engineering, Thomas Telford and the author of the 'Origin of Species,' Charles Darwin.

'Hello. Are you expecting anyone?`

'Jessie!' Jim jumped up and hugged her. She was wearing her

Sunday best outfit. A grey cotton skirt with white lace petticoat peeping out from underneath, pink shirt done up to the neck and she carried a bleached white bonnet in her hand. Her red hair hung in wisps about her forehead and he felt its cool sensuality on the back of his hand as the hair fell down her back.

She took the seat opposite him.

'Great to see you, Jessie'. He noticed tiredness around her eyes. They were a little narrower that he knew, less alive and her face was passive. 'What is it?' he asked.

Jessie turned to look at the river through the gaps in the railings. The hand-pull ferry meandered dangerously across to the other bank, its occupants holding on to the sides as the standing pilot somehow kept hold of the rope above his head.

She leaned across the table, held his hands and looked into his eyes, which were now full of fear. 'I cannot see you again, Jim.' She held his hands tighter.

'Why?' he asked, his voice just managing not to break.

She looked down at the old wooden table. 'You know that I have three brothers?' Jim nodded. 'The eldest two, Jack and Simon are in the army. They are in France already. Robert enlisted last week.'

Jim stared back at her. 'Jesus. Are they allowed to do that? The army, I mean.'

'Oh yes. Thousands are joining up every day. The army doesn't care where they are from, so long as they can see and run straight.'

There was a long, painful pause. Jim waited for Jessie to explain further and then he realised that she couldn't.

'And you don't want another man in your life.......'

She nodded, tears falling down her cheeks.

'And what makes you think that I will join up as well? I think the whole thing is bloody stupid. It's not my fight. It's theirs'.' He pointed towards the Shrewsbury School buildings.

'You will, Jim. You're the type. As soon as you see your mates joining up you'll be there beside them. In any case this isn't about losing you to the army, or to God. This is about me not having enough room in my

heart for anyone else. Don't you see? I am scared. Really scared.' She was sobbing now and she lifted all of their hands to wipe away the tears from her face. Jim shivered at the touch of her smooth, wet face.

'No, I don't Jessie. I absolutely do not understand this. The other night was the best night of my life. I cannot accept that there won't be any others.'

'Jim, don't. Please try to understand that I am dying inside. I did not expect to fall in love with you and I did not expect to see my brothers being put in mortal danger. I could loose the three men who mean the most to me. My father is heartbroken about Robert. It's as if Rob is already dead.'

'It's good to know where I come in the pecking order of your life, Jessie.'

She covered her mouth, realising what she had just said.

'I'm sorry. I didn't mean that.' Jim released his hands from her grasp, sat back in his chair and looked around for inspiration as he surely needed it now. He instinctively reached out for one of his pint glasses and downed the contents, thumping the empty glass back onto the metal table.

'You could always come with me, Jessie,' he joked.

'What?'

'You could dress up as a man and learn football songs. No one would notice. You'll be one of the lads.'

Jessie sniffed and smiled. 'I think that these might give the game away.' She stuck out her ample chest.

'Two good points,' said Jim. They smiled at each other, the lines at the corners of their damp eyes creasing in mutual love and respect.

'Daft bugger,' she whispered.

'Must be.'

'May I have some of your beer, please?' she asked.

'No, you may not. First, you take away my virginity, then you break my heart and now you want to drink my beer. Mouths of babes come to mind.'

'That was your first time as well?'

'And the last by the look of things.'

'Oh, give over, Jim. You'll find another girl.'

'Yes, Jessie, I probably will. But I cannot see me meeting another Jessie Appleby. And there's the rub. I know that I want to spend the rest of my life with you and yet in meeting you my life will be forever poorer.'

'But you are only eighteen. You cannot know what or who is right for you.... for ever.'

Jim looked at Jessie and then down at the river. 'Did you know that swans mate for life?'

Jessie shook her head.

'There's another thing about swans that only boat people see. They're graceful on the surface but under the water they are paddling for England, or Wales or wherever they are from. That's going to be me from now on, Jessie. I'm going to pretend that I'll find another Jessie Appleby. But underneath, my heart and my brain are going to do everything to get back to the genuine article. Because we deserve each other and although I'm young and we only spent one night together, I know absolutely that what we have is more special that what many people accept is love. When this war is over, I will come back for you, and if you have found another Jim Downing in the meantime, then you'd be a fool.' He rose from his seat, poured half of his second pint into the empty glass and gave it to Jessie.

'To beer, the end of the war and the genuine article.'

Jessie stood. 'To beer, the end of the war and the genuine article,' Jessie replied.

They clinked glasses, downed their drinks and kissed lightly on the lips.

Jim backed away from her towards the gate, winked and nodded towards the waiter who was moving towards their table, looking for payment.

Jessie's jaw dropped. 'Men! They're all the same,' she shouted at Jim.

'Not true, Jessie, not true at all,' he said quietly as he turned and opened the gate. He didn't turn to wave but continued down the slope to the river and grinned the grin of a boy who suspected that he was, at last, becoming a man.

*

The expert hand rotated the lens of the telescopic sight until the trench further up the slope came into focus.

'Bloody hell, sir. I feel as though I could touch it.'

'See anything of interest, Jim?'

Jim moved his right hand an inch or two each way. The view flashed across the eyepiece and he had to slow the whole movement down until he could pick out recognisable objects. Sandbags, rags on the wire, small shadows in the early morning sunshine, seeds perched on the long grass between him and the enemy, goblets of sparking dew on rusting metal that littered no-mans-land. 'Oh yes, oh yes.'

Clive's heart was racing. He lay just behind Jim's left shoulder watching this prodigious talent shape up to do the job that Clive knew the boy was born to. He was easy with the gun, confident with his technique and abilities. Quiet, more intelligent than he came across at first and unobtrusive in a way that Clive remembered that he had been when he first joined the army. Strength of character was what was needed, with an understanding that the best way to beat the system was to go along with it, stay calm and win your own little victories. Despite Jim's sensitive nature, he had a calculated manner that was at once cynical, removed and controlled. The death of Jim's friend, Rhys had added a determined glare to his eyes and Clive hoped that this reflected an increased desire to survive. The alternative was that he was somehow mentally removing himself from his environment. That wasn't good.

Clive felt wonderful, his senses alive in every way. This was the way it was meant to be. Taking the fight to the enemy, turning the tables bit by bit. And if he failed, he failed. Better to die out here in the battlefield than being blown to bits cowering in some hole in the ground or having one's head blown off by someone you never saw and who would kill again tomorrow. Clive looked along the barrel of the Mauser .350 with the Ross telescopic sights mounted above it, as it rested in Jim's hold. A foot and a half long piece of card stuck out from the top of the front of the sights, another trick of

Sergeant Pugh's. He had seen the chamois hunters of the Pyrenees use them when shooting into the light.

Pugh was an enigma to Clive. Another one who was comfortable in his own skin. Supportive of all, particularly the less able, but intolerant of idleness and foolishness and above all those who thought they were grander than Pugh knew them to be. After the war, Clive wanted to get to know this bear of a man better. He had heard the stories of Pugh's dabbling in investments and of his poaching life and wondered why Pugh had volunteered for the fight. In fact, he asked himself that question of all his men and concluded that he was only asking because he knew what war was like. They didn't. Yet.

Clive pulled out the grey metal telescope from his inside pocket, put the fingers of one hand over the top of the front lens as he opened it and put the telescope to his eye.

'Now somewhere in the dark recesses of my mind I remember reading that British scouts accompanied snipers into the hills overlooking Sevastopol in 1855 and with telescopes such as these they were able to point their mates towards their targets. If I've got a telescope twice as powerful as Jerry's telescopic sights…. or those huge field glasses that I can see in front of me then we should be able to have some fun. See him?'

Jim looked at the direction of the telescope, moved his position to the left and peered through his scope.

'Two hundred yards. See him? Do you think he's looking for the chap we nabbed this morning?'

Jim didn't answer. He saw the young German officer holding the field glasses. He held his breath.

'Kill him, Jim.' Clive didn't know whether to look at the result of what Private Downing was about to do or at the boy himself, pulling the butt tight into his shoulder, knuckles going white as his front hand gripped the stock, breathing out, slowly releasing the air through his nose as he curled his forefinger round the trigger and gently pulled it back. Clive saw the front of the muzzle spit flame and lift slightly, followed by a wisp of smoke. He watched it rise slowly in the crisp morning air as the boom rolled up the valley. He looked through the telescope to where the field glasses had been and saw them tumbling down the front of the German parapet, trailing their leather strap until they came to rest on the earth at the bottom.

'Get down, get down,' hissed Clive. Both made themselves as low as possible, their eyes boring into the muddied knuckles of their hands. 'Cover all skin,' they had agreed the night before in case they ran into trouble. The camouflage of mud and grass must not be broken. German snipers would pick it up like a fingerprint on crystal.

After a few minutes, Clive whispered to Jim. 'The smoke from the gun. It'll give us away out here. The gun's too powerful. We can only use it from the trench. We'll lie low for the rest of the day. Understood?'

'I think I killed him, sir.'

'You did, Jim, you did. Well done.'

Jim said nothing. He felt sick.

*

Randle didn't need the telescope to see the smoke rising above the patch of marsh grass by the small stream that ran diagonally across the field. The tiny cloud was only about six inches across with a foot long tail that seemed to point downwards from whence it came. Randle could see the wisp clearly as it slowly dissipated in the morning sun.

'Hamish, get those periscopes. Now.'

Hamish squinted through the Zeiss sights, saw the two periscopes turning above the trench in front of him and fired.

'Missed.' He fired again. 'Got one.' He fired again. 'Got two. The gun shoots a couple of inches to the left at this range. Fritz must have had a different grip to me.'

71

Randle held his hand a foot or so above Hamish's new gun, ready to shake away any smoke from the muzzle. There was none.

'Now we wait.'

'Until what?'

'Until, my dear boy, I've finished my maps and notes of the German front line and what's behind it. Or it gets dark. Whichever happens soonest.'

'Dusk is fourteen hours away, Randle.'

Randle put his eye back to the telescope. 'Welcome to the world of sniping and scouting, Hamish. If you can't cope with fear, hunger, thirst and staying still for hours then this is not the job for you. Oh, and you can't shit for days either. Fear does that.'

As the years had gone by, Hamish began to realise that the more he thought he knew Randle, the less he knew *about* him. Did he really know these things or was he making them up?

Hamish stared out from the shadow of what was left of the beech tree. 'I'm sure I'll cope.'

'Good. Then keep an eye out for snipers. We'll change over every half hour.'

'Not sure about Jim and the major, though. Nothing to smoke for a whole day.' Hamish shook his head and grinned.

'There's a lot going on behind Jerry's lines,' said Randle. 'Wonder what they're up to?'

*

Back in the trench, Neville was speaking his first German since school. 'Would you like a cigarette, Otto?' he asked.

'No. I don't smoke.'

'Yes. I can see how that would be inconvenient if you are trying to conceal your whereabouts.'

'I am not a sniper. Please, you have to believe me. I was ordered to go to the wall by my officer this morning. The regular sniper was taken ill yesterday.'

'So, Otto. Let me see where we are.' Neville paced across the dug-out, hands in his trouser pockets. 'You have a beard and are wearing what can only be described as a camouflage suit. And of course, you had that wonderful gun, lethal at over a mile. Yet you say you are not a sniper. Perhaps you were rehearsing for a play, with you as the deadly caterpillar?'

'I was given them this morning.'

'And the beard? Is that borrowed Otto?' Neville pulled hard on a fist full of the German's whiskers. Otto moaned through clenched teeth but did not scream. 'And why were the bullets in the magazine facing backwards, Otto? We saw what happened to Rhys' head. We found the bullet. It had split in two at the back.'

Otto knew he was cornered. This was not the way it was meant to be. Had he got careless? Had he been lulled in to a false sense of security by the ineffectiveness of the British troops? How had they found him before he had fired a shot?

'There's a pebble sitting on the table in my dugout, Otto. An ordinary beach pebble. It belonged to the man you shot. His young sister gave it to him just before he joined up.'

Neville went back to his chair, facing his prisoner. Otto was sitting on the floor of the dugout, arms bound to the table that was lying on its side behind him. He seemed to read the German's mind.

'Otto, has it occurred to you that we knew you were there. How did we know that, Otto?' The German stared back blankly. 'Sergeant, please go and get Claus for me would you. And an empty sandbag,' asked Neville.

'Otto, do you know what the British Army does with captured snipers?' Neville saw the briefest look of fear cross Otto's face. 'We shoot them. We shouldn't, of course. You see, we British have our own code of conduct. Most of the time, we behave like perfect gentlemen. But when we think the other side isn't playing fair, we get nasty. Very nasty, Otto.

'Some of us think that German snipers are the worst of a

very bad bunch. We didn't want to fight you. We just got to the Empire before you did. But you wanted what we had. That was why you invaded Belgium and France. You wanted those channel ports. Calais, Ostend, Antwerp, Boulogne. Once you got your greedy hands on those jewels, you could rule the waves. Why do you think we helped create an independent Belgium? Oh, it would have taken many years to roll back the Empire but it would have happened as sure as eggs are eggs. A few years down the line one of your Kaisers would have said, 'Europe isn't enough. I want the British Empire.' But we don't want to be run by an army, Otto. Oliver Cromwell tried that. It doesn't work. You have to be able to debate issues Otto, and let the press and the people decide who's right. It's called democracy. We believe that the masses make better decisions than the few. Wouldn't you agree, Otto?'

Neville had worked himself up into something close to a temper. 'That's because the masses cannot, by definition, have a conflict of interest. Unlike the few.'

Sergeant Small returned with the clay and paper head called 'Claus' and gave it and its pole to Neville, together with the empty bag.

'Let me show you how we knew where you were hiding, Otto.' Neville unbuckled his leather holster and removed the Colt 45 pistol. Otto's eyes widened. Now he was afraid. He didn't want to die like this, not strapped to a table in a British trench.

Neville stuck the pole into the dug-out floor, slipped the bag over the head, walked back two paces, knelt down on one knee and aimed, holding the gun with both hands.

Otto couldn't take his eyes off the bag.

The explosion from the gun deafened them all. A soldier put his head around the gas blanket. 'Everything all right, sir?'

'Yes thank you, Corporal.' Neville put the smoking gun on the shelf, and walked over to the wall picking up his stick as he went. 'You see Otto, if I have a hole in the trench with your bullet in it and a bag with two bullet holes in it and a stick, I can line them up like this.' He moved the stick through the air from the hole in the wall until it reached the bag. He pushed it through the hole and the damaged head until it poked through the first bullet hole on the other side. 'You see where I'm pointing Otto. Somewhere close to where the gun was. And of course, if I have two angles as you gave us yesterday Otto, and a periscope, I can be pretty sure where you are. We just hoped that being a German, you would be a creature of habit and keep going back again and again.'

Otto looked up at the lieutenant. 'Clever,' he said.

'I agree, Otto. The man smoking the cigarette through the tube thought it was clever too, until you shot his 'head'. Made him feel quite queer. But let's get back to what we do with snipers.'

Neville removed the sandbag from the head. The back had been completely blown off and shredded newspaper and clay stuck out like a child's homemade sunflower. 'Up there Otto, are the men of 3 section who lost a good man yesterday morning, just after dawn. His head looked like that, except there were blood and brains. He leaves a grieving mother and younger sister.'

'What do you want of me? Why are you telling me this?'

'For two reasons.' Neville leant over the German and put his hands on the table ledge behind Otto's head. His eyes bored into Otto's. 'I wanted to show off my German. I don't like the language myself. I think it was Nietzsche who said that the problem with it is that whereas French and English had developed in courts and salons, German came out of universities and seminaries. It encourages your innate arrogance, Otto. I also want to know everything you have learnt about being a sniper and I want to know what we are doing wrong. It appears that most of the British Army has forgotten about this great art. We want you to help us relearn it.'

Otto smiled. His yellow teeth had been stained from years of chewing tobacco. Then he laughed the laugh of a man who knew these men were desperate. His glorious homeland had already won. All they had to do was wait for the Tommies to come after them and mow them down until someone shouted, 'Enough is enough!' and they went home. Germany held the French and Belgian coalfields and most of their industry. She would keep them.

That was a mistake.

Neville gave the pre-arranged signal and both he and Small bent down behind Otto and lifted him and the table and walked him to the doorway.

'Corporal, give us a hand would you?'

'What are you doing, where are you taking me? You are not allowed to do this!' shouted the German.

'You are not allowed to murder Belgian women and children either, Otto,' replied Neville. They walked him along the front trench still tied to the table. Neville took the corporal's hat and put it on Otto's head. 'Now, lift.'

Slowly, Otto began to realise his fate. He saw the earthen wall of the trench, then the bags, then the fields in front. And then he saw the German trenches two hundred yards away. 'You cannot do this. It is not allowed. Please. Please get me down!'

Neville put the table leg under his shoulder and a bullet hissed as it passed Otto's ear. 'We can wait Otto, you can't. No one will know you told us. You will go to a prisoner of war camp...'

'Alright, alright. I will tell you. Please get me down from here. Please, quickly!'

5

The two sniping and scouting teams and Neville sat in the shade of the support trench, eating their bully beef with their fingers, washed down with cups of tea. Although their sector was a lot more active than some others were, the soldiers of the 6th KSLI had yet to endure the all-out battles that would become the norm as the war wore on. Tea-time was a relatively civil affair with both sides ignoring the smoke of the supper fires, only sending over mortars and shells at night time or in response to the other's attacks.

Jim finished his fourth cup of tea and poured himself some more from the large pot, stirring in two spoons of sugar. He leant back against the trench wall and the cool of the earth spread across his naked back. Major Fox pulled two cigarettes from his silver box and passed one to Jim.

'Sir, I can honestly say that I could not have lasted all day out there. Not in that sun and under camouflage. I was being cooked alive, and those bloody flies!' said Jim.

Sweat was still beading on Clive's forehead. He cupped his hand automatically around the match and lit his cigarette. He took a deep chest-full of smoke, held it for a moment and let it pour through his nostrils.

'Well, Private, you are going to have to get used to it, or find a different job.'

'But sir….'

Clive held his hand up. 'But nothing. This is serious stuff. We are facing a very capable, canny and ruthless enemy. You heard what the lieutenant said after interrogating the sniper. Those chaps lie out there sometimes for days on end. They piss, shit, eat, drink in the same place if it's a good position. You are the best shot I have ever seen and you are only nineteen. With you and Corporal Rutherford here we could shoot the bastards to kingdom come. You need to prepare ahead, work out what you need and fit your attack to best suit what you are capable of. If Rutherford hadn't seen that sniper taking aim as we returned we wouldn't be having this conversation.'

Jim lowered his head, letting the cigarette drop to the floor. He rotated his foot over it. This wasn't fair. No man could have taken that heat for much longer. He knew that the major was struggling as well. They had run out of water by nine o'clock that morning and by four his tongue had swollen to the point that he couldn't frame a sentence. The pain had taken his mind off the fact that he had just killed his first man.

'Fine drawings, Sergeant,' said Neville, leafing through the half-dozen hand-sized pieces of paper. The level of detail was impressive as was the perspective. Neville could see undulations in the German trenches, woods, communication trenches, broken villages to the rear, even impressions of people working in the cornfields about a mile or two away. 'Very good. I'll take these up to HQ later this evening. I think Intelligence will be very interested.'

'There's alot of activity behind their lines, sir. Hundreds of 'em moving along the communication trenches, both ways,' said Randle.

'I see. I'll pass that on.'

'What happened to the sniper?' asked Hamish.

'We gave him a shave and packed him off to the rear. He gave us lots of information about his unit and still more about their methods,' replied Neville.

'Did he now?' Hamish looked at Neville and his thin smile told him all that he needed to know about how the sniper was encouraged to reveal the tricks of his trade.

'Apparently German snipers pick off the officers at every opportunity. They can recognise them by the cut of their riding britches and the stripes on their cuffs. If they are carrying a sword, they are dead men walking.'

'You're joking,' said Randle.

'No. I've already told HQ. They are getting changed as we speak.'

Clive interrupted the laughter. 'Right, gentlemen. In five days we should be relieved. In that time, I want observation posts built below the parapet. Keep Jerry's heads down. Shoot anything that moves. We'll keep the Mauser .350 here to take out any snipers that shoot from their own loopholes. I want to see if that gun will shoot through the metal plates that our German sniper said they had. Blind the enemy, gentlemen, that's the secret.'

Clive drove his clenched fist into the other palm and stood up using Jim's shoulder as a prop. Jim thought he felt a reassuring squeeze or it could have been Clive's exhausted body looking for more support than he wanted to let on.

'If Jerry is building up to something, I expect Division will want us to take a look so get some sleep. Also with intelligence like this, Sergeant,' he said as he scanned through the drawings, 'I expect they will want more information on the whole sector. Hopefully, we can spread the load with the other units. I'll suggest Battalion use the Royal Flying Corps. It's going to be a busy week, men. Expect some fireworks tonight once Jerry realises that one of his stars has gone missing.' And with that, he departed down the trench, dropping and stubbing out the cigarette as he went.

'His name was Otto by the way. He was an officer of the elite Jaeger regiment. That much he volunteered without too much persuasion,' said Neville to the men as he watched the major turn the corner of the trench.

Jim grinned at Hamish. 'A plane, Hamish. He's going to order a plane!' They shook hands and followed each other's gaze up into the darkening sky.

*

That night, the men made observation posts in the trench front wall as silently as they could. Word travelled between the company commanders and some in the battalion followed suit, eager to try out the new tactics and take the fight to the enemy. Given the list of ideas from Clive's experiences in Africa, Randle's years of poaching and Jim and Hamish's shooting in the hills and woods of Shropshire, it was difficult to work out what to do first. And that was before Neville went through his notes from Otto's debriefing. Clive promised himself that he would write it all down when the battalion was relieved.

By the following morning, the trenches containing the soldiers of the 6th KLSI were dotted with rudimentary 'rooms', some no more than a gap at the bottom of the parapet, with a small opening out onto no-man's-land. On the opposite side of the trench from Clive's dugout, he and the men had fashioned a fairly impressive hole of about six feet wide and three feet high, backed by a blanket. Only a battalion captain or an appointed sniper or observer was allowed in and never when the sun was behind the trench. Enemy snipers would see the flash of light in the front of the trench and know it was an observation post. Everything had been thought of, from wrapping the gun in dust-free sacking for camouflage, to pouring water on the earth near the muzzle to stop dust being blown up when the shooting started. Each observer was issued with two telescopes. Ten times magnification for when the sun was facing you, twenty times for the afternoon. Jim assured the captain that with a five times magnification sight fitted to his gun he could get a six-inch grouping at a hundred yards by moonlight. Clive's scepticism was to be proved wrong time and time again.

Just after seven a.m. Clive put his head around the blanket and spoke to the prostrate Hamish, on telescope, and Jim, on rifle. 'In a few minutes, I will be firing the .350 Mauser from a loophole a couple of hundred yards down the line to the right. It's got a big flash and lots of smoke; that should attract some attention from their snipers. You'll be on their flank so you may see them. That's when you earn your crust, gentlemen. Good luck.'

Jim's heart raced and he breathed deeper, trying to slow it down. He closed his eyes for a minute and then looked through the telescopic sights. 'See anything, Hamish?'

Hamish scanned the scene in front of them through the telescope. 'No movement. Nothing.'

The unmistakable crack of the high-calibre Mauser rang across the fields, then another, and another, followed by metallic thuds as the bullet sliced through the metal loop-hole covers in the German lines. Shouts and whistles drifted through the still, cool air. Hamish and Jim looked through their scopes. Nothing moved. The Mauser fired again, and then Hamish saw it. The smallest of movements amongst the long grass, about a hundred and fifty yards to their right and a hundred yards out from their lines. 'There!' whispered Hamish. He pointed with his finger. 'By the broken oak.' Jim peered through the sights. Everything in view was vertical. The grass, the tree, the cross hair. Except for a dark line, about two feet long sitting above the horizontal cross hair. It didn't move. Jim scanned the area behind it. Tree roots and tufts of grass. 'I see it.'

'There's another, Jim. Forty, fifty yards between him and us.'

Jim lowered his gun a millimetre or two. 'In the orchard?'

'Yes. See him?'

Jim saw nothing. Just apple trees, grass and shadows.

Then the Mauser fired again and he saw movement. He didn't know where it had come from, but his brain had definitely picked it up. He looked to the left of the orchard and used the sensitive cells at the side of his retina to look for movement amongst the fruit trees. 'Got it. Watch this.' Jim fired at the shape by the wall and saw the gun fall. In three seconds he had lifted, pulled and returned the bolt, gone back to the line by the tree, aimed two feet behind it and pulled the trigger. The black line dropped and the grass mound shifted as the body underneath it rolled from the force of the shot.

'Fuck me, Jim. You just got two!' shouted Hamish, forgetting to whisper.

Jim grinned back. He was beginning to enjoy this.

And so started the vicious battle between the snipers of the opposing battalions that would go on until the following January.

The Germans had a year of experience on the 6th KSLI, but day-by-day the gap closed. The Germans became more cautious and the British more inventive. Autumn offered new opportunities. Grasses died and leaves fell and the judicious use of telescopes rather than field glasses exposed many of the hiding places that had been used to such effect by the enemy. Other battalions in the 20th Division sent officers to learn the tricks of the trade and gradually the battle for no-man's-land turned. The Times newspaper even sent a reporter to listen to the men's stories and in November it ran a story about the Shropshire Lads, who had enlisted at the same time and who used their skills to 'give the Hun a taste of his own medicine.' Jim was held up as the deadly secret weapon who had won the Aldershot shooting prize and who had more 'scalps' than any other sniper in the British Army. The article was read with interest in the drawing rooms, offices and pubs of Great Britain, a rare uplifting piece in a sea of awful news. It also sealed Jim's fate if he were ever captured. And in a train carriage somewhere between London and Bristol, an Italian gentleman dressed in a cream suit and dark shirt, read the article and smiled.

*

When the company arrived back at billets after being relieved from the front line, it was late afternoon and pouring with rain. The Division was preparing to transfer to the Ypres salient, a bulge in the British lines around the strategically vital but destroyed city. This was a shock for those who had been on leave or who were part of the new drafts from England. Ypres was infamous as a killing ground, a place where whole companies had been wiped out, battalions decimated. The men had heard the stories from the soldiers who had been posted there. The dreadful effects of gas, the random death from artillery barrages, the slaughter from the machine-guns. It was called the 'meat-grinder' for good reason.

A thousand men and their equipment and horses were loaded onto the transport lorries and tractors and they moved off to the north under the darkening sky. The roads were pitted from shellfire and over-use and it was impossible to sleep for more than a few minutes at a time.

As they got nearer to their destination the sound of a furious artillery barrage reverberated on the sides of the lorries. Tired and worried men looked at each other in the gloom, trying to find expressions of concern on the faces of their comrades. The long convoy stopped. All ears were tuned to the cacophony raging outside. Explosions could be heard between the booms of the artillery. Horses bellowed in panic, enclosed in the darkness of their lorries. One of the soldiers ventured out of the back of the transport into the driving rain. Jim, Hamish, Randle and Neville and the rest of the men followed. They went round to the front of the lorry where the driver told them that the road ahead was closed. Nothing was able to get into the sector where the artillery battle was taking place.

The horizon to the left was lit up with the explosions of hundreds of British guns. The watching men were near enough to feel the concussion and the white and yellow lights flickered across their rain-soaked skin. To their right the communication trenches cut mile-long zigzag scars across the destroyed fields and hamlets to the men cowering in the front lines. Far in the distance to the east, the clouds glowed with the reflected light of the German long-distance howitzers' firing. In the middle of these two terrible displays, the men of both armies received the four-inch-wide projectiles of death and misery. A two hundred yard-wide carpet of destroyed fields, woods and humanity curved through the Flanders countryside for miles from where they stood.

A young military policeman approached. 'Welcome to hell,' he said. 'This show will go on for some time, gents. I would get back in the dry while you can. Get some rest. You're going to need it.'

'We're not really going into that, are we, Lieutenant?' Jim

asked Neville as they filed back into the lorry. Neville either didn't hear or decided not to answer.

At two a.m. someone banged on the side of the lorry and shouted through the metal. They swore as they awoke and staggered outside. It was still raining, but the guns were silent.

Officers shouted orders to their men and the battalion lined up beside the transport. Colonel Ogilvy, wrapped in a black cloak and wearing his flat-topped officer's cap, stepped into the field just below the road, accompanied by his batman who held an umbrella over him. The rain ran off it and into the mud in streams of bright water.

'Men of the KSLI,' he shouted through a tin loudspeaker, 'This is where our war gets serious, where we show that we are real soldiers. We will have to rely on our wits, our instincts, our training.' He looked at his men for inspiration. Over a thousand men faced him looking for leadership, a reason to go into that dreadful place. 'We expect to be relieved in about five days but much depends on how successful Division HQ is at finding replacements for you. I know that you will do your jobs. Thank you and good luck.'

He walked back to the line of transports and stepped up to the cabin of one of the lorries. His batman closed the door behind him, saluted and got in the back to await the other senior officers.

Jim was terrified. This was much worse than the trenches at Loos. He had never imagined violence on a scale of the savage industrial storm he had just witnessed.

Each company lined up behind supply lorries where the men were loaded up with wooden stakes, ammunition, water, sacking, telephone and barbed wire and tins of food. Jim followed Clive Fox and the rest of the company for a mile along the rough road through a destroyed, still burning village. They turned right into one of the communication trenches and stumbled through the darkness and mud for half-an-hour. Progress was slow. A steady flow of men from the Royal Army Medical Corps supported and carried the wounded from the front trenches past the relieving men of the 6th. The incomers leant against the walls of the trench as the pained and shocked faces made their way back to sanctuary. All were covered in mud and soot. Most wore bloodied bandages. Jim stared with the rest of the men, not able to avert their eyes from the grisly sights before them. Uniforms had been torn open either by shellfire or by the medical orderlies getting to the wounds. One man's eyeballs rested on his cheeks like poached eggs as he groaned on the stretcher. Others had lost limbs or parts of them. Faces were distorted by pain and bone damage. Some of the men were unsteady and lurched into the walls of the trench, screaming in pain as their limbs touched the sides.

Further up the trench the walls disappeared and the men of the 6th crawled over the sodden earth, keeping low to avoid snipers. The bloated carcasses of horses lay in the remains of a field to the left, oozing their stench through holes in their bellies made by the shrapnel. Wrecked war equipment lay everywhere, reflecting the pale moonlight.

It took two hours for the company to get to the first of the three front trenches. Soldiers sat in small holes made in the sides, smoking through shaking fingers. Others slept on what was left of the duckboards, their bodies partially immersed in stagnant water. The air was foul despite the breeze. The latrines had been blown to pieces and the smell of their contents mixed with the body odour, lime and another miasma that Jim did not yet recognize. It was the smell of death.

They dug with shovels, trying to repair the destroyed trenches. Others pushed against the encroaching mud and rock with their backs while stakes and broken pieces of wood were knocked into place.

The newly arrived company immediately set to helping them, stepping over bodies, alive and dead alike. Water was everywhere. It rose as they worked, flowing into the already drenched dugouts below. It swallowed boots, putties, equipment and rifles. Some of the men sank into deep holes in the mud and cried out in fear.

At seven o'clock the sun came up and a pathetic attempt at stand-to was organized. They shivered in the rain, bayonets resting on the remains of the parapet of the forward trench, exhausted and sodden to their bones. Satisfied that the Germans were not about to attack, stand-down was called and the work began again. German snipers kept watch over the destroyed defences, taking the lives of any man careless or stupefied enough to show his head. Visiting what was left of the latrines became a lottery as the snipers picked them off one by one. The men dug a new hole in the reserve trench that soon overflowed, the mess mixing into the rivers that ran between the mounds of earth that had once been a trench system.

Jim found a periscope and peered out onto the landscape in front of them. In all directions lay desolation. The colours that adorned the countryside before the war had mixed into browns, greys and black. The fields had disappeared as if a giant farmer had used his plough to remove all trace of human endeavour and then scattered his victims across the featureless landscape like he were sowing seeds. The remains of the Highland regiments that had been slaughtered in the last few weeks lay in the mud and hung from the broken wire as far as the eye could see, their blackened bodies sticking out from under their bonnets and the kilts that shook in the wind. Rifles stood erect in the ground where their owners had bayoneted the earth in their death-fall. Grey smoke wafted up from whatever was still burning at the bottom of shell-craters and rats scurried from body to body, unable to decide which to feast on first. Jim stepped down into the middle of the trench, took a swig from his canteen, spat it out and drank again, walking off in search of somewhere to sleep.

*

It was one of those summer afternoons when the toil in the fields was amply rewarded by the beauty of the balmy evening. The low sun cut sword-like shadows from the stooks of corn and the swifts enjoyed an easy feast of midges and mosquitoes. A boy stood atop a haystack holding a fork larger than himself.

The last field was harvested and the Reverend Phillip Joyce felt a mixture of pride and end-of-term melancholy while he watched the families amble through the orchards back to the large farmhouse. Dogs ran with the children as they danced and chased their way through the apple trees. A shoot ended in the distance.

'I hope you've brought the communion wine Vicar, we drank all the cider these last few weeks,' joked Brendan Rutherford.

'That explains the lateness of this year's harvest. And silly me thinking it was the weather.'

The old farmer laughed his usual barrel laugh, put his arm around the vicar and walked up the incline to catch up with his son.

'Hamish, please tell me you've kept some of the beer that the brewery delivered on Monday. I've just joked with the man in black here about the cider being spirited away but if you haven't any beer left we'll have a situation on our hands that'll make Belgium look like a children's tea-party.'

'Don't worry, Dad. I got Jim to order an extra couple of barrels and some claret. Not that that'll interest you much.'

'Bloody right. French crap. Can't stand the smell of it, or them. You wait, Hamish. If the Germans keep going the Frogs will be turned over quicker than one of your mother's puddings.'

Hamish sighed. 'Dad, I know you think about it a lot but can we not have any war discussion tonight. I just want to enjoy the end of the harvest, get drunk and sleep. Any mention of Germans or war will upset the ladies and probably a few of the blokes as well.'

Brendan Rutherford said nothing as they both walked under the brick arch into the walled garden where the women were laying the table in the sunshine and the men stood around in groups, non-smoking hands in pockets. Most were dressed in the farm labourer's uniform. Heavy boots, corduroy trousers, off-white flannel shirt, braces, dark waistcoat, neckerchief and flat cap. Some had removed the garters that gathered the bottom of their trousers to keep the grain out. They needed drinks and

Hamish walked towards the icehouse where he had hidden the alcohol. He looked up at the old farmhouse. The barn attached to its side looked past its best. The wisteria needed supporting and a few of the upstairs windows were missing their panes.

'Right everyone,' Brendan shouted as he tapped the barometer by the stable entrance. Faces turned towards his fat, ruddy face framed by the doorway. 'Anyone who mentions the war will be put up against that wall and either shot or made to eat some of Sarah's damson jam. I'd advise the former. It's a faster death.'

*

Sarah Rutherford led the small party of girls and mothers from the farmhouse, over the wooden bridge to the long table in the middle of the lawn. Fourteen people sat facing one another across the longest piece of polished oak that any of them had ever seen. It was decorated with late summer wild flowers and heaved with drinking vessels of all kinds. Flagons, jugs, and glasses for cordials, wines, port, whiskies and brandies. The cider and apple brandy, (or 'Bees' as Hamish's father called it after 'Brendan's Best Beverage') were homemade. The beer, as always, was Bass from the Burton Brewery and the empty wooden barrel lay half hidden under a bush, discarded in frustration by a couple of the men once it was emptied. The famous red triangle at the end of the barrel flickered defiantly in the candlelight.

A cheer went up from the table as the ladies approached, carrying an array of puddings. Custard and fudge cream slopped in large china jugs.

Hamish glowed with pride at the sight of his twin sister Sarah, statuesque and noble in the flowing blue dress that he had bought her for this harvest celebration. She held the plate straight out in front, trying her best to appear like a head waiter serving the dish of the day to a royal party. Hamish could see the lights on the table reflecting in the dark welsh eyes that she had inherited from their mother, as she approached his seat at the head of the table. Her thick eyebrows, high cheekbones and full lips gave her a Romany appearance that was sympathetic with the occasion. She tried and nearly managed to look solemn.

'Your pudding, sir.' She carefully placed the dish on the table in front of him.

Hamish grabbed her waist and tickled her as he pulled her onto his lap. The party cheered again, banging the table with spoons warmed by eager hands.

'You're my pudding Sarah'. She screamed and tried to escape his clutches but he held on. She beat him about the head with her wrists, embarrassed but not wanting to hurt him. Eventually he let go and she turned swiftly, arms crossed and walked back to the kitchen.

The other girls pushed between the seats nervously and placed their desserts on the table.

After the course was finished, the ladies retired to the farmhouse. A baby's crying could be heard through the open windows and scores of bats undulated blindly above the men's heads. The men waited until the girls were out of earshot for they all knew what was coming. This had been an almost melancholic harvest supper. The war had galvanized the whole country, much of it represented around the table that night. The farmer and his son, the local vicar, gamekeeper, wheelwright, shepherd, railway worker, several labourers and banker, not including the second job that many of them had out of necessity.

The cigars were handed around followed by the port and spirits. The gamekeeper broke the silence. 'His Lordship's selling the horses and some of his lorries to the army. Good prices n'all.'

'The price of everything will go up. I reckon we should all wait for a few months, Mr. Rutherford,' volunteered the labourer with a moustache that covered most of his face.

Brendan Rutherford, seated at the opposite end of the table to his son, breathed his cigar smoke in the man's direction. He was wearing the bowler hat with the pheasant feather stuck into its band that he was famous for in these parts.

'First of all, Alf, they're not yours to sell. Second, the government has capped the price of food products. Third, it's my bloody country that needs the stuff and I'm buggered if I'm going to take advantage of the predicament that we temporarily find ourselves in.'

'Might not be that temporary.' It was the banker. 'This will be a bad war. We've not seen anything like this before. The American Civil War should have taught us the effect of machine guns on massed rank of troops, and in South Africa the Boer taught us the importance of movement and sniping.'

'And?' asked the vicar.

'Well, unless one side wins before the bad weather arrives, both armies will dig in. We are talking about millions of men on both sides being bombed to bits by artillery. Those men have no choice but to retreat or to attack. Retreat is unthinkable. There is too much at stake. Attack will be suicide.'

'Oh, great. I didn't know you were in Lord Kitchener's propaganda corps, Paul,' snapped Rutherford senior.

Every man joined in the debate simultaneously. Everyone except Hamish. He whispered in the wheelwright's ear who stopped in mid-sentence and turned to face Hamish.

'Are you sure?'

'Quite.'

Brendan Rutherford caught the look on his son's face. The light from the candles suddenly seemed to throw a dark shadow across his countenance.

'What is it, Hamish?'

'Randle joined up today.'

They all stared at him, not wanting to believe their ears. The banker dropped his head.

'We are going out one last time tomorrow night. He joins the KSLI on Monday.'

'Does his mother know?' asked Hamish's father.

'She will by now'.

'But why?' asked Alf.

'If you have to ask that Alf, you will never understand.'

'What about you, Hamish?' asked his father.

90

'I don't want one of those white feathers that the ladies are handing out, Dad. So I guess the sooner a whole lot of us enlist the sooner we'll win, machine guns or not'. He glanced at the banker. 'I'm a crack shot remember.'

Brendan folded his hands on the table, looked down at them and nodded his head for a few moments. When he looked up he had tears in his eyes, but his voice was strong.

'Yes, you are certainly that, my boy. I just hope they use that talent wisely.' He stood up, walked around the table to where Hamish had also risen and hugged his son, ruffling his ginger hair. Two tall, broad men at a crossroads in their lives.

Someone at the table raised his glass. 'Gentlemen. To all our heroes. May God protect them and deliver them home safely.' They stood up, and lifted their glasses in the direction of the farmer and the most important thing in his life.

'Mother.' Brendan shouted in the general direction of the house. 'Bring the girls out. We are going to dance. Phillip, give me a hand with the phonograph will you? I have a new W.C. Hardy song I want you to hear. It's called 'Memphis Blues'. Ragtime music, I think they call it.'

*

Hamish and Randle leant against the wooden fence surrounding the ring, their hands holding cards detailing the order of play. Occasionally Randle flicked a finger or nodded his head. It was almost imperceptible but the movement was definitely there.

'Are you doing what I think you're doing, Randle?' Hamish asked the big man.

'Depends what you're thinking, Hamish.'

'That you're bidding for these animals.'

'Not if I can 'elp it.'

Hamish stared at his friend for a few moments. The auctioneer's drone continued in the background. Hamish had not been to an auction this year so his ear was not tuned. He could make out the occasional instruction to the ring hand to turn the cows or bullocks around and the birth months for each lot, but that was about it. The prices were indecipherable to him.

Randle cast his eye round the ring at the farmers gathered at its edge. To casual observers they were a field of ruddy faces, heads and bodies clothed in browns and greens, the steam from the animals comically reflecting the ring of cigarette and pipe smoke that ascended from the ranks of their past and future owners. To Randle, they were players in a great game, the rules of which only became apparent after years of practice and even then new rules could apply depending on the referee, who in this case was the man with the gavel. Randle had his own rule. Be a linesman whilst wearing a player's kit. It confused the hell out of everyone, except of course himself and the referee.

Between them they kept prices high for the local selling farmers and the big landowners who came in from outside hoping to make a killing by buying cheaply in the hills. If Randle's bid was not matched, the animal would just be recycled a few hours or days later. The auctioneer paid Randle a couple of bob from his increased commission. A few locals knew his doing and accepted it as part of country life which was hard enough anyway. The Randles of this world oiled the wheels and made life a little easier and a lot more interesting. So long as he didn't steal from their fields, which he never did, then everybody got on fine.

'I'll explain later' said Randle and winked at his young friend.

*

Both were lying on a ridge on the shoulder of Caer Caradoc, looking into the long valley below. It was nearly a full moon and they could see for miles in all directions.

'The first lesson of field craft is to keep a still tongue in y'r head, Hamish. Gamekeepers don't like people like me and they positively hate those who boast 'bout what they done. The second is to study the moon. It's best to hunt for animals that are born blind when the moon is on the wax. They travel further from their burrows than when it's waning. Then there's the weather. You don't want to get stuck miles from home in a fog as you *can't see the stars to show you home.'*

A few lights twinkled in Church Stretton and the soft glow of Shrewsbury's gas streetlights could be seen on the horizon to the north. Before them stood the mighty Long Mynd. The only noises were an iron gate straining on its hinges in the warm breeze and the bleating of sheep in the area known as the Wilderness on the hillock to the south.

'Get the wind on your face to stop the animals and birds smelling you. Pheasants look into the wind to keep their feathers down so if you want to catch'em work out where the wind is.'

'Understand the sounds of the hills at night,' continued the poacher. 'The flight of the wood pigeon and the bark of the gamekeeper's dog. Never, ever, steal from farmers. Get to know whose land you're on and who owns the game that you want to take. The shepherds will leave us alone so long as we follow that rule. And if that makes me look like Robin Hood, so be it. More than once they've warned me where the man-traps are.

'Back in Norfolk we used the 'green roads' made by pirates o'er the centuries to avoid contact with people. They weren't on any map. We just knew em.'

Hamish smiled at Randle's tendency to speak in an accent foreign to his ears whenever he recalled the time before he arrived in Shropshire a few years ago. Randle became known to the Rutherford family after he saved Hamish's horse which had become stuck in the marshes. He came to the farmhouse in the dead of night and asked for help, risking his freedom to save the horse. Brendan Rutherford had let Randle use his land for night passage ever since.

Hamish also knew that Randle had to leave his native Norfolk after a term in Norwich prison. The stigma was too much and he and his mother had moved to Shropshire after a brief time in Manchester. The locals called him 'Cockney' because they thought his broad Norfolk accent meant he was from London. He lived off the small amount of money he made from selling his own paintings and ink drawings while he got to know the lie of the land. No one knew exactly what had happened to Randle's father but there were rumours that he had been deported for sheep stealing and never came back. According to legend his mother kept a bottle of his urine on the mantelpiece to this day. 'Once it wastes I'll know he's dead,' she had said. The bottle and the urine had been with her for fourteen years but no one could vouch for having seen it.

'Did you ever get into trouble for pranks, Hamish?' asked Randle, keen not to monopolise the conversation.

'Not trouble exactly. Jim and I were known as the 'Village Idiots,' a while back. We did daft things but we never got caught. We once emptied a local copper's house by stuffing straw down his chimney and tying a rope to his front door. You should have seen him pulling his fat wife out of the window!' The men laughed out loud as Hamish remembered the copper trying to catch the two boys whilst his smoked-up eyes streamed with tears.

'Jim's going off the rails if you ask me. He used to be a good friend,' said Randle.

Hamish's face was sad. 'It's that political rubbish he's got into. He read that book by Marx and he changed. Almost overnight it was. He's gone all Jesus-like. Reckons he can change the world on his own. You heard what happened at the school?'

Randle laughed again. 'I wish we'd been there. We'd have sorted out the toffs. Still, beaten up twice in a week is some achievement.'

'Three times. His Dad had a go at him as well,' said Hamish.

'That man has a violent streak. He's another one with a dark side. The booze has got'im.'

'Jim's still a brilliant shot, though. He hasn't lost that. I reckon we might be quite useful in this war,' said Hamish.

Both men stared melancholically into the darkness for a while.

'The world is changing y' know,' said Randle. 'Not for the worse neither. Before the bike, most people never went ten mile from home, they married people they had known all their lives and took jobs in their area. Children used to work in the fields from morning to evening, many without shoes. A man wi' a whip would stand over them and they would get thr'pence a day. Now they can get ten miles by eight o'clock for a better job.'

'Sore arses though. Wouldn't be any good for horsework.'

Hamish got a cuff for his wit. 'Come on, let's go and catch some birds. Bring the net.'

'You ever had a girl, Randle?' asked Hamish as he caught up.

'Aye, many, my boy. Women like big men.' Realising that Hamish hadn't got the joke, he coughed and continued. 'The only girl I ever loved was Mary-Anne Goss. Great with birds she was. I found her a jay and a jackdaw and the three of them became inseparable. She would walk into town with them on her shoulders and when she went shopping they would wait for her on the roofs of the shops. But she couldn't stand cats.'

'What happened to her?'

'She was eaten by a lion.'

'What?' asked Hamish.

'Hunting she was, in Africa.' Randle was fighting to keep a straight face. 'Big bastard came at her. Ate her legs first, then her guts, and while she was still alive.'

Hamish looked out of the corner of his eyes and caught Randle's Adam's apple bobbing like a float on a nibbled line.

'You idiot,' he shouted, and raced at his retreating friend.

'Watch out. Behind you!' Randle pointed over Hamish's shoulder.

'What? Where?' He turned back towards the direction whence he came, feet wide apart, knees bent ready to receive whatever threat lay there. Feeling foolish again he turned back. Randle was gone.

'Yep. Should have seen that coming. Now who's the idiot?'

Hamish looked up at the stars and around the hills and valleys below. He knew where he was and he knew the way home, roughly. It would take him about four hours. He set off down the hill with the heavy net over his shoulder. At least he could salvage some pride by bringing that home.

After a couple of hours walking along the smaller tracks, he crossed a ford and as he reached the path into the woods on the other side, two figures stepped out from the trees. They wore the unmistakable attire of gamekeepers. Knee length boots, thick wool three-piece suits, white, high collar shirts and ties and leather straps over their shoulders. Two shotguns pointed at Hamish. Both men sported ludicrously luxurious moustaches.

'Where are you from, boy?' Hamish felt a trickle of cool sweat run *down his back.*

'I said, where are you from, boy?' The keeper stepped closer. Hamish, for reasons that he did not yet understand, was quite calm. He felt almost removed from the situation. His heart was beating no faster that it had for the past hour.

'Shrewsbury.'

'We're a bit off our territory now aren't we, boy?' He stepped a little closer to where Hamish stood, the water from the river spreading out from Hamish's boots. Hamish tightened his grip around the net that rested on his right shoulder. 'No game left in Shrewsbury? Can't say I'm surprised. The place stinks. Even the dogs are leaving. Too much shit. I reckon it's the people. Nowhere to wash except in the stinking brook that they call a river.'

Now, of all the things that Hamish liked about his home county, it was the river Severn for the simple reason that it was the best place to see kingfishers, otters and dragonflies.

'I think you must be mistaken, sir. The water has been clear since they stopped gamekeepers washing in it.'

The keeper hit Hamish hard in the stomach with the barrels of his gun and was about to kick him in the face when a booming voice cut through the gloom.

> *'When I was young*
> *Then boys were boys*
> *And went to bed at ten,*
> *and did not smoke*
> *Them stinking fags*
> *Nor ape the ways of men.'*

As he finished the last line Randle stopped, facing the gamekeeper who had stayed at the back. Randle put his hands on his hips and smiled. The keeper levelled his gun so that it pointed at Randle's not inconsequential stomach.

'And who the fuck might you be?' asked the keeper closest too him.

96

'Your worst nightmare,' replied Randle.

The river behind Hamish erupted and a plume of white water exploded skywards.

The two gamekeepers turned instinctively to look. Randle turned sideways and kicked the back of the keeper's knees with the underside of his great boot. The man let out a howl as he fell backwards. Randle gripped the gun with both hands and pushed against the man's chest with his other leg. The keeper screamed as some of his ribs gave way before the link at the end of the leather strap snapped.

Randle turned and dropped to one knee, gun at the ready. Between the ends of the barrels, he saw Hamish grip the other keeper's gun laterally with both hands, put his boot into the man's groin, fall into a backward roll and send the man somersaulting over his head into the river behind. Hamish grinned at the big man as he sat on the ground.

'You taught me that last year, Randle. Using a gun as a pivot.'

Randle was silent.

'And I guess the explosion was a piece of lime and rock in a bottle with a split cork?' Hamish suggested as the poacher stood over him

'Aye, boy.'

Randle dragged the concussed man out of the water. 'They'll live. Bring the net and the gun.' He walked to the river, picked up a brace of concussed bream that had floated to the surface and put them in his pocket. He set off at a trot in the direction that he had just come from.

When Hamish caught up, Randle stopped, gripped Hamish by the collar, put his eyes inches from Hamish's and said slowly, 'Three other lessons, Hamish. One, don't whistle when you don't want to be found. Two, never cheek someone with a gun. And three, if you ever use my name in front of gamekeepers again, I'll give yuh' a hiding that you'll remember for the rest of y'r life. Do y'hear?'

'Completely.' Hamish was shocked. He had never seen his friend angry, but he was in no position to argue.

'Good, shall we go and fight a real war, then?'

And with that, he took the shells out of the guns, put them in his pocket, threw the guns over the hedge into the gorse below and trotted off into the dawn.

6

Jim slept fitfully in a hole dug in the side of the communication trench and shouted in pain when someone who was laying the telephone wire stood on his leg. He was hungry and fed up with being cold and wet. He found Hamish in a smashed dugout trying to make a new roof.

'That won't protect you from much,' said Jim.

Hamish looked up at his friend. He wasn't in the mood for Jim or his wit.

'Hello, Private. Been sleeping?'

'I had my eyes closed. Not much of a sleep.' Jim watched his friend moving a heavy plank into place.

'Are you going to help me, Jim, or are you going to stay sulking up there like a girl with no-one to play with.'

Jim sighed and got between the planks and lifted.

'At least it'll keep the rain off,' said Hamish.

'Until tonight that is.'

'You've heard then?'

'Heard what?'

'That nightly shelling is compulsory in this sector. We've all been advised to write home before it gets dark.'

'No, I hadn't heard Hamish. I was just depressed about the bloody rain. Now you have made me suicidal.'

'You'll get shot if you kill yourself.'

Jim grimaced at the black humour. Nothing was going to get him out of his torpor and frankly he didn't want it to. His bad mood provided some kind of soporific anaesthetic against the awfulness of his surroundings.

'Have you eaten yet?' asked Jim.

'Since when?'

'Yesterday.'

'No, none of us have. We are waiting for the soup to arrive.'

'I've eaten my iron rations already,' said Jim.

'What? They're for emergencies only.'

'It was an emergency. I was hungry.'

'Well, don't come begging to me when the shelling starts and no food can get through,' replied Hamish.

'I won't. I'm going to eat the rats. Ypres rattus norvegicus. Boil in trench water using a few bones to make a stock. Interested?'

'Are you alright, Jim?' Hamish gave his friend a genuinely concerned look.

'Much better now, thanks Sergeant.' His stomach rumbled and they both laughed.

'You're a bloody idiot, Jim Downing,' said Hamish, 'but I love you. Now give me a hand with this cross-post.'

Jim did as Hamish asked. An hour later, the dugout roof was complete and both men shovelled earth on to the planks of wood.

'What happened to the bodies, Hamish?'

'A team of blokes arrived from the left flank and took them away on stretchers. The bits they put in sandbags between the legs of the bodies.'

'Christ, what a job.'

'It's a punishment. You can be strapped to a wheel for a day or bury bodies. You get used to it, one of them told me. The bodies that have been, well, bodies for more than a week, they chuck over the front. They get like overcooked chicken. Everything falls off the bone as soon as you lift them, so they let the rats have 'em. It all gets blown to bits anyway, once the shelling starts.'

'I've lost my appetite. I don't think I'll be having the soup.' said Jim covering his mouth. He dropped the remains of his cigarette into the pool at his feet and walked up a trench which had a wooden sign nailed to its side. 'Keep to trenches in daylight,' had been crudely written on it.

*

Major Fox and Lieutenant Milton finished their soup in the newly repaired dugout. They watched the candle flames make shadows on the corrugated metal roof. The water level had subsided a little, now that the rain had stopped and both men sat on chairs, their bare feet warming near the candle flames in front of them. They couldn't afford to let the water pickle their skin. Getting trench foot was a serious offence, and as they hadn't yet been issued with waders or whale fat, the only way to avoid it was to keep out of the water or to use the flame of a candle to dry their footwear. Their socks hung from string above.

They tried their best to write letters home, using pieces of wood as lap tables but the paper was damp and they gave up. Clive found another of his now famous bottles of whisky, opened it, took a slug and passed it to Neville. 'So, Lieutenant, when this war is over, what are you going to return to?'

Neville smacked his lips and took another swig. 'After university, I was going to do something in the church, sir. But now I think that I'm going to go into the arms trade.'

'That's quite an epiphany.'

'You could call it that. Certainly the devil would. But as you know sir, there have always been close ties between the church and war. Even the brass bells taken from the dissolved monasteries were turned into the cannons that sank the Armada. But I've been thinking....if I became very good at it, I could swamp the market with bullets and shells that were so unreliable and dangerous to the men with the guns that he would never dare fire them.'

Clive thought for a while. 'But then there would be no need for soldiers, Neville. We can't have that. What on earth would the generals do? Play croquet?'

Neville laughed. 'No, they'd.... did you feel that?'

Both men felt it. The ground lifted under their feet, almost imperceptibly but it had definitely happened. And then again. The candles flickered as if a draught had caught them. Clive was the first to react. He rushed to the dugout door, pulled back the gas blanket and ran along the trench in his bare feet. He blew into his whistle and shouted, 'Get down, take cover.' Neville followed him and as he got to the door, he heard the noise. It was as if God were tearing the silken sky down the middle. They saw the huge explosion a good two seconds before the concussion hit them, knocking them off their feet. And then another one. And another, getting closer.

They screamed at those that sat against the trench walls. 'Take cover, take cover.' Soldiers ran and dived in all directions. They doubled up into foetal positions, hands over cloth hats. The terrifying screech and flattening cacophony of the explosions triggered survival instincts in them all. Closer and closer. Half a mile, a quarter, two hundred yards....and then the huge shell landed just behind the forward trenches. The air left their lungs as the blast exploded over them, earth, rocks and wood showering the cowering men in the front trench. It seemed to take minutes to fall from the darkness.

Neville shouted at the men nearest him. 'This way! Follow me.' He ran to the next corner and up the communication trench to the reserve trench, twenty yards back. He was met by smoke and earth. The reserve trench had gone. It had disappeared into the fields above.

The explosions continued down the line of trenches.

Someone shouted, 'Digging party, here now!' It was Jim. He rushed past Neville and climbed up the huge pile of earth, dug his shovel into the top and began digging like a man possessed. Other men followed.

'Get off there, Downing,' shouted Neville. 'This is just the beginning.'

Jim kept on digging. 'Hamish was at the back here, sir. There will be men under here. We've got to get them out.' He spat the tears away from his mouth as he shouted.

It took them five minutes to get to the first body. Its arms were spread wide, mouth full of earth. They worked carefully to find the rest. Eighteen men had been buried alive by the one shell.

The diggers stood in the freshly dug trench, some bent over shovels, others smoked, their backs leaning against the walls, sobbing or praying as they did so. A few knelt over the bodies of friends or brothers. Jim hadn't found Hamish amongst the dead. And then they heard the next wave of shells.

*

Hamish and Randle pressed their bodies into the furthest recesses of the hole in the trench wall. Tree roots grabbed at their hair but the two men didn't feel them. The first shell had blown them off their feet and their hearing was temporarily impaired. Opposite them were three smaller soldiers huddled in a similar gap. The brave men who had been on the receiving end of the bombardments in this trench system over the previous months had dug and dug as far as the water table would allow and as the shelling continued, whatever natural drainage systems there had been were blown to bits. The soldiers who now used them had no idea whether the trench builders had survived nor did they care. They just wanted to get through to the morning.

The next wave of howitzer shells came in, exploding in the sector to the north as the previous shells had. And then they plunged into the company. Mashing, deafening, killing, maiming, destroying, maddening. There was no point Hamish or Randle leaving their little cave and trying to help their men. You were either under-cover or you weren't. Lucky or unlucky. Discipline and courage had no place here. In this hell only chance and physics ruled. If you were close to a shell when it exploded, you died. The only alternatives were terror, being buried under a ton of earth or being wounded. A 'blighty' one would get you out, hopefully for good. But with so much red-hot metal flying around there were equal chances of being killed, losing fingers, your face, your limbs or worst of all, your manhood. They had heard stories of that happening to some unfortunate fellows.

The men agreed that they would rather die. The smell of fresh piss and shit entered their nostrils but no-one cared.

Randle started to sing, 'Gunner, Gunner….' Hamish joined in and soon the soldiers cowering opposite did so to. Two hours later the shelling was over and the traumatized men slept where they were.

*

The next night was the same, and the next. Those who survived and rose into the dawn sunshine went about their business as if they were working at a factory. The men said little. What could you say to a friend who had survived the onslaught? 'Well done, but sorry about your brother?' There were jobs to be done. Shoring up the trenches, putting down duck-boards, drying your feet, eating cold breakfast, replenishing canteens, de-licing.

The bodies and the wounded were taken away by troops that appeared through the communication trenches. The shelling of the German lines had been particularly heavy that night and bits of field grey uniform dotted the otherwise British debris. Telephone lines were relaid, linking the front line with battalion and divisional HQ's. They wanted to know how many men needed to be replaced, but most of all they wanted to hear of any signs that the Germans were about to attack, en masse. Clive told them that it was impossible to tell as the wire had been blown to bits in places, so no gaps could be seen to have been cut by potential attackers. During the barrages no fool would be able to look over the parapet to see approaching Germans. It was just too dangerous.

Clive called Jim and Hamish to the remains of his dugout. It was no more than a gap in the trench wall, covered with wood. There were no serious defences left in the sector. The Germans could attack at any time and the division would be over-run, there was no doubt about that.

'Sergeant Rutherford and Private Downing, I am going to ask

you to do something that could save many lives, including your own. Division thinks that the enemy is about to launch an attack in this sector. The artillery fire that we have been taking is just softening us up. Some of our boys up the road have raided the German trenches and taken prisoners who told them that crack storm troops have just come into the line. Would you two be prepared to go into no-man's-land and keep a watch on the German lines while the shelling is going on?'

'How do we let you know if they are coming?' asked Jim.

'You'll be issued with flares.'

'And you'll see them while it's shelling?'

'I'll have men watching for them, behind the front parapet. As soon as we see your lights, we'll man those parapets, shells or no shells. I'll also warn the machine gunners that you are out there.'

'That might be useful,' said Hamish dryly. 'Won't they be watching anyway?'

'Don't fool yourself, Sergeant that the shells are for us. They've got the machine-gunners' names on them. We cocoon the machine gunners in places where they can't be hurt. We live or die depending on whether those machine guns are working.'

Jim and Hamish looked at each other. They were both exhausted and filthy. The whites and rims of their eyes were red and their cheeks hollow from terror and lack of sleep.

'Just get us good guns and lots of bombs, sir,' said Jim.

*

Just after dark Jim and Hamish crawled over what was left of the parapet, found a deep shell hole about a hundred yards from the British trenches and three hundred from the German lines, and waited in silence. Every twenty minutes or so they peered over the rim of the hole to look for movement in the east. Then they fell asleep.

The explosion of the first mortars woke them from their slumbers. They saw the burning fuses of the dreaded German mortars overhead as they followed the drums of high explosive and scrap metal towards their target. All along the British lines explosions of fire and noise erupted one after the other. 'Pop, pop, pop,' went the mortars just behind the German lines, followed by the hundreds of burning fuses fizzing their way towards the soldiers hiding under the soft earth.

'Minnenwerfer,' whispered Hamish. 'The attack will be tonight. The Germans wouldn't risk sending their men into no-man's-land when the long-range shells are coming in. Look at how accurate those bastards are. I think the major did us a favour sending us out here.'

'Oh yes?' replied Jim. 'Look at this lot, then.' Hamish turned to where Jim was looking. Thousands of men were emerging from the German trenches, wave after wave of steel-helmeted soldiers walking towards them with bayonets sticking out of the end of their rifles.

'Forget what I just said. Fire that flare, Jim.'
Jim didn't move. He stared at the hordes of Germans bearing down on them.

'Fire that bloody flare, I said.'

'Not yet. If we fire it now the Germans will know that they haven't surprised us and they'll take cover. We want them near our machine guns when the flare goes up.'

'Jim, if half the bloody German army dives for cover near our lines, we'll die with them. Either our own guns will get us or those bastards will.'

'I thought you were meant to be the hero, Hamish.'

'So that's what this is about. For fuck's sake, fire that fucking flare! Now, Private, or I'll fire it myself.' Hamish raised his big fist above Jim's face.

Jim looked at the approaching Germans, satisfied himself that they were close enough and fired the flare into the sky. The white trail drove into the darkness and burst into brilliant light above the battlefield. Many of the Germans momentarily stopped in their tracks and then someone blew a whistle. Thousands of soldiers broke into a run and charged towards the lines in front of them, screaming at the top of their voices. The mines stopped falling along the front.

A full ten seconds later, a machinegun opened up, tracer flying into the running troops. And then another joined in, followed by another. Troops fell as they ran, ten, twenty at a time, but still they came on. Jim and Hamish watched in astonishment as the waves kept running into the bullets, getting closer and closer to the trenches that they had been ordered to capture. Some of the men got caught in salvos of bullets, the force of the metal preventing them from falling forward. They flailed their way to the ground, limbs jerking in a dance of death.

But still they ran on. All along the front as far as Jim and Hamish could see, men of the German army started to reach the trenches to be met with a hail of .303 bullets fired from Lee Enfield rifles. As they staggered back, the machine guns stopped and British soldiers climbed over their parapets and ran into the enemy that they so despised. Bayonets flashed in the lights of the new flares that hung in the sky on their little parachutes. It was now savage hand-to-hand combat. Jim and Hamish fired over open sights at the retreating men from the cover of their hole, each covering the back of the other until there was no-one left to shoot.

The firing of the guns slowly gave way to another sound. Screams of agony and desperation drifted into the night sky. Jim and Hamish listened in resigned horror until just before dawn and then crawled their way back through the mud and the dead. They ignored the groans of the wounded. It was impossible in this light to see who was friend or foe. Once the sun came up it was harvest time for the snipers. You had to make your own way back; no one would come and get you. If you survived the day and could move, you took your chances once it got dark again. While the shelling continued every night this was the only way it could be.

They fell into their trench and went to see Major Fox, finding him having a shave in one of the other company commanding officer's dugouts.

'Morning lads,' said Clive, carefully removing the soap and whiskers with his cut-throat. 'My God, it's good to see you fellows. We thought you had left us for good. You've missed breakfast, by the way.' He wiped the last of the soap away with the towel and slapped it onto his shoulder. 'One of those bloody coal-boxes landed right between Lieutenant Milton and me. Didn't go off. Come and have a look.' He led them through a warren of collapsed earthworks to where two men were gingerly removing the back of a black metal object.

'Quite amazing. I think Lieutenant Milton and God must be familiar. Reckon I'll stay close to him next time there's a barrage.' Jim and Hamish didn't hear him. They watched wide-eyed as the kneeling men carefully placed the detonator on the mud at their feet.

Clive put his arms around both men. 'You've both been mentioned in dispatches. Well done, boys.' He shook their hands and walked away.

*

The poacher was pleased with himself. It was six o'clock on a fresh morning and Sir John Dawson's estate now had thirty pheasants less than a few hours before. The poacher had disabled the gamekeeper's gun that hung on the tree and the bitch on heat ('in use' he called it) distracted the guard dog. A pair of clippers saw to the wire of the run and the birds had come to the grain and sacks without any complaint. He wrung their necks, came into town with his load under hay on the cart behind and the stallholders paid him handsomely.

Randle Pugh's huge hands dangled off both ends of the bench and he chewed smugly on his pipe. He stared lazily down the hill of the Quarry park between the ranks of lime trees and watched the early morning rowers launch their skulls and fours into the river from the boathouse on the far side. The blue bandstand that he sat by every Saturday afternoon was away to his left.

He looked down at his mud-splattered boots, brown corduroy trousers and dirty grey shirt and imagined himself in a new set of clothes. Maybe a suit and new boots. 'Nah,' he said out loud. He was comfortable as he was. The poacher's uniform was simple. Look like everyone else and keep it dark. He had no need for posh clothes. Where would he wear them? Certainly not down the pub and if he wore them at home his mum would only laugh at him.

Randle Pugh, twenty-eight going on forty lived in an isolated two-room cottage with his mother on the outskirts of town. The smallholding was a cottage with one acre of poor land, half a dozen pigs, three hives, chickens, a cat to kill the vermin and Josh the sheepdog-greyhound cross that he used for work. A wonderful dog was Josh. The intelligence of an animal bred to work the land, with great speed and a gentle mouth. Randle and Josh were partners in crime as Randle saw it, though he still maintained that 'game was fair game,' as it was to be killed anyhow and the money would be used to line the pockets of the already rich who paid their workers less than a shilling a week.

No, today he would have breakfast by the market, have a few pints of light and dark and go home for a well-earned rest. He might even treat himself to a dance at the Free n` Easy that evening. He stood up, stretched in the sunshine and marched off towards the town centre.

*

There was a long queue at the bank. The Declaration of War had sent people into an irrational panic, fearing there would be a run on the banks. The fact was that Britain had by far the largest and most sophisticated banking system in the world and ordinary people didn't know that the country had access to more gold reserves than all the other combatants put together.

Randle knew all this. Business was his livelihood whether it was selling pheasants or trading shares. He just didn't care to show that he knew. His dress and accent were of one who lived off the land. He was brighter and more urbane than his peers and probably better read than most of the people in the queue but it was not in his social or financial interests to bring this to anyone's attention. His height was enough. He didn't want anyone, particularly the law paying him more attention than he already received. He ignored those in the queue who stared at him.

As he stepped inside the large, severe building he looked round at the brass spiral staircase, the portrait of King George, the safe, the weights and scales and the huge ledgers. The atmosphere was warm, stuffy almost. Randle smiled as he saw the coal fire glowing in the wall behind the counter. Bankers, he thought. Cold as fish.

'Yes sir. How can I help you?' asked a junior clerk still looking at his ledger.

Randle put his passbook on the counter followed by screwed up notes from different pockets in his coat and trousers. The clerk looked at the notes for a few seconds then slowly raised his eyes to the face of the man who put them there. This took longer than expected. At first he looked at Randle's neck, expecting to meet the customer's eyes, then up and up until he was staring at the most alarming sight that he had seen in weeks. He had to hold on to the counter to prevent himself from taking an involuntary step backwards. Randle didn't help the poor man by widening his eyes and curling his top lip into a sneer, showing off the two gold teeth at the corner of his mouth.

'You wish to pay this in, sir?' the clerk stuttered.

'Aye'.

'Very good. Well, what do we have here?' he asked no one in particular, focusing on anything other than that face. He unrolled the notes, dropping a few as he did so.

'Six, seven....'

'Hush y'r mouth, boy. Add it up in y'r head,' spat Randle. He took in the purple cravat, wing collars and long black jacket and wondered if they buried bankers in their work clothes. They all looked the same in life, probably in Hell too. Safety in numbers.

'Mr. Pugh. How good of you to drop in.' The manager arrived out of nowhere. 'I'll take over, Norman. Thank you.'

'Don't want no fuss, Paul,' said Randle quietly.

'Fully understood, sir.' The manager added the notes up again, wrote the amount into the pass book, adding the cumulative amount up in his head, checked it on the adding machine to his right, updated the book and handed it back to Randle.

Randle nodded to his friend and walked out of the bank. In the distance he heard a brass band. He looked up at the sun. It wasn't the time or the day for that matter, for the band to be playing in the park. Ladies and children ran past him. Horses were pulled up by their riders as people flocked like hungry sheep across roads and down the slope towards Smithfield, the main link between the railway station and anywhere else. Randle had time on his hands so he followed.

An astonishing sight greeted them at the bottom of Mardol. Buildings on both sides of the river were draped in flags, small triangular ones on bunting and enormous Union Jacks and St. George crosses fell from windows and guttering. The summer haze had lifted from the river and Randle could see the crowds stretching over the Welsh Bridge and up into the wool trading area of Frankwell. Trows, the local shallow-bottomed ketches that plied their trade through to Ironbridge and down to Bristol, were tied up on the far bank and their occupants stood on the decks to see what was happening. The breeze blew the sweet smell of river mud over everything.

The music grew louder and the crowd on the other side waved their flags even more furiously. Policemen held up the traffic at junctions to the road.

The commanding officer flicked his walking stick back and forward in time with the beat, followed by the band. As they crossed the bridge, the brass tops of the tubas glinted in the sun. Randle's heart started to race.

They turned into Smithfield Road and the full array of militaria was before him. He recognised the lapels of the colonel at the front, followed by the trombones, trumpets, bassoons, clarinets and drums, all carried by

110

red and black uniformed soldiers marching perfectly in time. Then came the officers and ranks of the 1st Battalion, King's Shropshire Light Infantry, a thousand and seven men stomping their way to the train station, rifles over their shoulders. Women dived out from the pavements to kiss the marching men. Some put flowers in their lapels then ran back dodging the officers on horses that guarded the procession. The older soldiers at the front of the long formation looked sternly ahead as if this were a common event to be got through as quickly as possible. The younger ones grinned and laughed. It was a beautiful summer day, they had a job, the ladies loved them and they were off to fight the Hun.

'God bless you,' the people shouted. 'Good luck.' 'Well done lads.' 'Stick it up the Hun,' one said.

Randle watched the rear of the column until it turned the corner. He was elated. He hadn't said a word nor waved a flag. But he had not felt so moved by anything since he found Josh guarding his bitch and newly-born puppies by the front door, a couple of years back.

He walked back up the hill and stopped at the chemist. Between Dr. Wansbrough's metallic nipple shields and Minderus Spirit for Hangovers, ('take every fifteen minutes with water until cured'), he found what he was looking for. Carbolic soap and lots of it. He was going to war.

*

Randle lifted the tin bath off its hook on the wall at the back of the cottage, blew out the dust and cobwebs and placed it on the path that ran between the herb garden and the pigsty. He went over to the large pot that hung over the fire and put his finger in the water.

'Good 'nough,' he said to no one in particular, wrapped his hand in the cloth at the side and lifted the pot from its stand. He poured the contents into the bath, stripped off and was about to lift a leg over the bath rim when he realised that his new soap was by his bed. His mother was at the range, boiling some clothes. He stooped under the ledge on which stood a bottle of yellow liquid and she caught sight of his bare backside as he went.

'Be careful. I saw a sparrow looking for worms earlier.'

'He'd have better luck with your broth, you old witch,' he replied. He found the soap in the guzunder beneath his bed and returned to the room that did as a kitchen, a scullery, a hallway and a sitting room. He kissed the top of his Mum's head, walked outside, stroked Josh on the way and got into the bath.

His mother followed him a few minutes later carrying a knife. She put her foot on the pedal of the grinding wheel and once it was rotating at a good speed she placed the knife on the stone. The noise was not one that Randle wanted to hear this morning, not after the beers that he had had the night before. He tried to get his head under the water but it was at least six inches too shallow so he straddled the far end of the bath with his long legs and managed to lower himself sufficiently so that the water lapped above his ears.

He lay there for a while, watching a pair of crows chasing away a kestrel and when he could no longer hear the infernal noise of knife on turning stone through the water and tin, he sat up, his long wet hair and beard glistening in the morning sunshine. His mother was close to him, kneeling in the herb garden. 'And who do we thank for persuading you to have a bath Randle?' asked his mother, expecting that it was a girl, or one of his mysterious City friends.

'The army said I 'ad to clean up and shave or they'd do it for me, which I don't fancy.'

The woman got up as fast as she could, which was painful to her. 'The army?'

'I joined up yesterday, Ma.' She was stunned and couldn't help showing it. Randle was thankful that the sun was behind her and he couldn't see her face.

'Randle. Randle. My boy. What have you done?' Her fists crushed the herbs in her hand.

He looked down at his enormous legs. 'I got to give something back, Ma. I bin taking for years. This is my chance to do something decent for once. T' have a real job.'

'To get killed more like.'

'Maybe.' He tried to find her eyes in the silhouette.

She recognised the challenge. The challenge to push it further or leave it alone. She knew from years of arguments like this with Randle and his father that it was better to leave some alone. This was one of those.

The moment passed. 'Now hand me that towel, woman.' He stood up and she wrapped the towel around him like she had when he was a boy. He put his arms around her shoulders. 'We'll be fine, Ma, just you see,' he said, chin resting on her crown. Josh lay in the sun on his side. He wagged his tail as his master looked at him.

'You better be. You better be,' she said, wiping the tears from her cheeks.

*

The hurdy-gurdy completed its cycle and started again.

'I'm fed up with that bloody music. Has anyone got a gun?' shouted one of the many men at the bar of the etape, one of the many houses in the partially-destroyed town which had been converted to entertain the allied troops when they were away from the front line.

'Shur'up, Barry. You're always moaning, you are. First it was the weather, then the mud, the officers, the food. Blah, blah, blah. Why don't you just desert and do us all a favour? I'll volunteer to join the firing squad. I'd gladly put you out of your misery,' said a soldier some distance from the target of his abuse.

As the rest of the section joined in the debate, Hamish whispered in Randle's ear. 'What are those men doing out there?'

Randle looked through the etape's small windows and smiled. 'That my boy, is the queue for the ladies.'

Hamish looked confused.

'Prostitutes. Ladies of the night. You know, you pay them for fuckin'.'

Hamish went red. 'But there are loads of them. I haven't seen any women in this village.'

'That's because they're all next door, earning pots of money.'

Hamish involuntarily felt in his pocket for his change, and then looked up at Randle, mortified that his friend had misunderstood his action.

Randle raised one of his eyebrows.

'No, no, Randle, I am not interested. I couldn't.'

Neville returned with three bottles of beer. 'Getting lively in here.' He looked at the blushing Hamish. 'You alright, Sergeant?'

'We were just discussing whether or not to join the queue outside,' said Randle before Hamish could answer.

Neville turned in his seat and looked out of the window. 'Ah, yes. A worthy distraction from the mundanities of trench life. Thought about doing it a few weeks back but didn't have the courage. I wouldn't know where to start, to be honest.'

'Try the back of the queue, sir,' quipped Randle.

'That's not what I meant.' Now it was Neville's turn to blush.

Hamish sat up in his chair, leaned over to Neville and asked, 'You mean that you've never done it before either, sir?'

Neville shook his head. 'Never really had the opportunity,' he whispered back.

The three men then looked at each other, then at their drinks. As one they downed them and walked to the door.

A cheer went up at the bar. 'We know where you're going,' came the chorus. Randle cuffed one of the men sitting by the door who dared to laugh.

They stood in line in the spring sunshine watching the men at the front disappear into the terraced house every few minutes and then back out again through a different door.

'Blimey you don't get long, do you?' said Hamish nervously.

'You won't need it if you've not done it for a while. You definitely won't need it if it's your first time,' smirked Randle, loving the moment. Some of the soldiers in front of them turned round, then faced the front and laughed when one of them said something.

Hamish was starting to regret leaving the etape. He needed another drink.

'Sir, this is a red light brothel. There's a blue light one up the street for officers,' Randle pointed out.

'No thanks, Sergeant. Quite happy to mix it with the men, so to speak,' replied Neville.

Those within earshot hooted with exited laughter. Here was an officer they could respect.

Hamish saw the children pointing at the queue from the end of the street and felt guilty. He thought of home and how wives, sisters, mothers would be queuing up for bread or tea. And then they were at the entrance to the little house. Randle pushed Hamish to the front.

A big military policemen, standing on the first step leaned over Hamish. 'Ten francs or eight shillings for ten minutes. Any trouble and we throw you out. Use the sink and powder after you've finished. Up you go.'

Hamish went up the bare wooded stairs with a heavy heart, got to the top and followed the buxom, middle aged woman to the door at the end of the corridor. The woman smiled, said 'Entree monsieur,' and left. Hamish peered into the darkness and walked towards the shape lying on the bed.

'Murnay.' The shape held out a hand, took the ten francs and stuffed it under the far side of the mattress. It sat up, undid Hamish's fly buttons and let his trousers drop. She pulled down his underpants and held his balls with one hand. With the other she dipped into a tin of borated Vaseline and rubbed this over his privates. Hamish's breathing got deeper.

The woman lay back down on the bed, lifted her skirt up to her neck and said, 'Ici, monsieur, ici.' Hamish did as he was told, followed his instincts, finished and collapsed.

The woman giggled, extricated herself from under her

customer's body and went to the sink in the corner. She washed herself, tapped Hamish on the back and pointed to the taps that were still running. He got up, shuffled to the corner with his trousers round his ankles, washed and started to do himself up.

She tapped him on the shoulder again and handed him the cup of disinfecting powder. He poured some of it into his pants, patted the front, said 'Au revoir', and departed. He walked past the squeaking beds on the right, down the stairs and went straight to the etape and waited.

Half an hour later, Randle and Neville walked in. They laughed and were looking very pleased with themselves.

'What kept you?' asked a depressed Hamish.

'Don't tell me you only went round once, Hamish,' asked Randle.

Hamish's mouth dropped and he put his head into his hands.

Randle patted Hamish's head. 'Don't worry, my boy. If you get VD, the M.O. will sort you out. And then he'll put you on a charge.'

'Officer present!' someone shouted. They all looked towards the door. There stood Clive, trumpet in hand. Everyone stood. This was no ordinary officer. This was Major Fox, the real McCoy. A warrior who cared.

'At ease, men. I haven't come to spoil your fun. Just to play this. Anyone play the piano?'

'I do, sir. But we don't have one here,' replied Neville.

'Oh, yes you do. You just need to ask the right person. Madame, please can we use your piano?'

The lady at the bar nodded, and Clive disappeared into a side room. 'Give me a hand, someone.' Several men jumped to help.

'Bloody hell, how long has that been there?' shouted Barry.

They pushed the upright into the middle of the room and men crowded around it. Someone passed Clive a drink that he downed in one and then blew gently into his trumpet. Neville took his position on a chair at the keyboard and played a few bars of improvised jazz. Clive joined in, tentatively at first but after a few more free drinks the duet was firmly established. The soldiers tapped their feet and sang a bawdy song, the musicians adapting to the harmony. An hour later they stopped for a rest. Someone shouted, 'Sir, we've just received a message. It's in German.' He held up a scrunched up piece of paper, opened it and pretended to read. 'I think it says, 'Please stop the trumpet and we'll go home! Signed Willy.'

7

Exactly eleven months after arriving in France, the battalion was posted to the Somme. They still hadn't received any Blighty leave. So many had died, many more injured. About a half of the original battalion was left, the rest made up of fresh drafts and transfers from other units.

They had left the Ypres salient a broken body of men. Those that had survived felt no guilt, just a sadness for those that hadn't made it, a cynicism about what the war was for. The locals' indifference as they marched from Frevent station hadn't helped one jot. The women didn't even look up from their lace-making.

Two men had been executed for cowardice, one of them a boy of seventeen who couldn't take the artillery barrages any more. He literally walked up the communication trench during an attack and refused to go back. So they shot him.

At least this break had given them a chance to catch up on letter-writing and opening parcels from home. A national endeavour to cheer up loved ones at war made the letters bland and false and the terrible experiences that the men had gone through gave an other-worldliness to what they read. Either the writers had no idea what was going on over here or they were lying about the English garden still being full of roses. The shocking sights that the wide-eyed men saw when they arrived at the trenches of the Somme told the soldiers that the letters must have been written before this, the worst of all disasters ever to befall the British Army.

They walked through the communication trenches of the old British lines in daylight, the front line being some way in front in the Serre sector. On both sides lay thousands of bodies like the high water mark of wreckage after a storm. Groups in their scores hung from the circles of barbed wire as if they were praying, their crumbling bodies turning blue-green in the intense heat. The flowers of Britain's youth had been hung out to dry. There wasn't a yard of ground as far at the eye could see in which a body didn't lay. In the gaps in the wire were heaps of men, like giant rugby scrums that had collapsed under the weight of numbers. Hundreds of stretchers supported by sack-faced men moved slowly and silently over the bodies. The soldiers of the 6th had grown used to the sights and smells of death but this was of a different league altogether. Whole battalions had been slaughtered on the first of July, and again and again over the following days until the generals realised that the attacks must be failing because there was no-one left to tell them otherwise. Huge swarms of bloated, black flies hung over the battlefield, diving at will to feast and drink on the dead.

Jim followed his platoon down into the cool bowels of the empty German defences and sat on the floor. Some vomited where they lay; others brushed the layers of flies off their uniforms and out of their hair; some just stared, tears falling down their dusty cheeks.

Jim tried to say something, anything. 'What.....what..... how.....?' but he knew in his calcifying heart that there would not be, could not be, an answer.

He looked around the room for that is what it was, a room; not a hole in the ground. He was surrounded by concrete and cables. On the floor in front of him were open boxes of machine-gun ammunition and stick grenades. Chairs were lying on their sides as if the previous inhabitants had left quickly to get up to the surface. As soon as the British barrage had stopped there would have been a race to the machine guns between the attackers struggling to get through the rows of undamaged wire and the men hiding in relative safety down here. The attackers had lost. At least for a week they had, until sheer weight of numbers had given the British a pyrrhic victory that the country would never recover from. Jim wondered if the Germans had just walked away one night, disgusted at the one-side battle.

They heard footsteps descending the many steps to the subterranean chamber. Someone pointed a rifle at the doorway. It was

Randle, ashen-faced from dust and shock. 'Don't get too comfortable down here. In an hour you'll be given stretchers, bags for identity-tags and sandbags for remains.' He left with eyes boring into his broad back.

A while later Randle returned with several men and the grisly equipment. As they handed it out, Randle took Jim to one side.

'Bartlett's back, Jim,' whispered Randle.

'What?'

'The major told me to warn you. Bartlett's commanding C Company. He's taken over from Captain Jones who copped it last month.'

'But...but...' stammered Jim.

'I know. Those of us who knew 'im are shocked too. But the army is worried sick about a mutiny after what happened here, so they're drafting in as many officers as they can get hold of. There's a lot of unrest at home too, so they say.'

'But he's an idiot, Randle. He'll start the mutiny, not stop it!'

'Just be careful, that's all. It was your shooting that did for him in the end, remember.'

'Aye, and it might be permanent this time!' hissed Jim.

'That's the talk that gets you shot, Private. Now get a grip and start collecting. Don't forget to tie a bag round your face.'

*

Jim looked out over the barren landscape and spooned the contents of the tin into his mouth, occasionally pulling on a cigarette that he had propped between tree roots that stuck out from the wall of the trench. It was quiet. The front was a mile away and the guns were silent.

'Not the healthiest way to eat, Private,' said a voice behind him.

Jim looked over his shoulder, saw Sergeant Small and grunted. He didn't bother to turn and carried on with his meal of beef and nicotine.

'Not a happy chappie are you?'

'No, Sergeant. But don't let it worry you. I don't reckon we're meant to enjoy this,' quipped Jim. He didn't take to the sergeant. He was too in control. Too precise.

'We can all find ways of coping, Jim.' It was the first time he had ever referred to him by his Christian name. 'We go a long way back, you and I.'

'Do we?'

'Yes. There aren't many of us left from the old battalion. We're survivors.

'So far.'

'My word, you are a doom-mongerer, Jim.'

Jim chucked his can into the mud in front of him and turned to face Small. 'I wasn't always like this you know.'

'I know.' Small's eyes fixed on Jim's, making the latter's neck itch. 'I remember your first day, Jim. You were funny, you and Rutherford and English. 'The Terrible Trio' we called you in the NCO's mess.'

'Really?' asked Jim. He was genuinely touched. 'Different times, different times.'

'Yes, they were.' They both paused.

'Do you think we'll ever get those days back, Sergeant?'

'Call me Gerald, for now. Life's too short to be formal all the time.'

Jim looked the sergeant up and down. His uniform was nearly spotless and his hair was freshly combed.

'I think you have to take your chances, Jim. No-one knows when this war will end. Could last for years.'

'What do you mean, 'Take your chances?''

'I just heard something, that's all.' The sergeant looked away.

'Heard what?'

'It's probably rumours. I just heard that good people could get out if they were prepared to let go of the past.'

'Blimey,' said Jim. 'That sounds a bit far-fetched.'

The sergeant laughed. 'Absolutely. But it's an interesting thought, eh? Leaving everything behind; starting from scratch; new identity.'

'You sound as though you've given this some thought, Gerald.' Jim couldn't help smiling, even if the sergeant knew he was taking the piss.

'Haven't you, Jim? Has nothing ever happened to you where you thought, 'Sod this for a game of soldiers,' so to speak, 'I'm off to discover the rest of my life'?'

Jim looked serious for a minute. 'Yes, of course, many times.'

'You'd be able to leave it all behind, family, friends, everything you grew up around?'

'Look at us, now.' Jim spread his arms and turned to the scene of desolation as far as the eyes could see. 'The only thing I have left is my mates and God knows how long they'll last.'

'Exactly.' Small patted Jim on the shoulder. 'Imagine the good you could do, knowing what you know.'

'What do you mean?'

'Well, Jim, it's no secret that you see this war as a class war. With your shooting skills, you could bump off a few of the idiots who started it.'

Jim went cold. He felt he was being trapped.

Gerald Small sensed it. 'Don't worry, Jim. I'm just larking about. Interesting chat, though. See you at stand-to.'

*

A week later they were in the forward trenches. The men woke and readied themselves for the stand-to. Some still had their eyes closed as they drifted into the line of soldiers underneath the parapet. It had been yet another bad night. Mortar bombs had exploded intermittently up and down the line and the exhaustion that they all felt wasn't enough to put away the fear that this could be their last night's sleep.

The last few days had been the most physically and emotionally draining of Jim's war. With the rest of the battalion, the company had buried bodies and bits of them and given bags of identity disks to the medical officers. These would be taken to Battalion so that telegrams could be sent to the relatives telling them that their sons or brothers had died a gallant death. Jim had given up counting how many men he had buried. The gallows humour that had helped them get through the worst of times somehow seemed inappropriate in these fields of wasted courage. Anyone who tried to make a joke was ignored. They were in the presence of the worst event of their lives. Nightmares were never this bad.

Jim's feelings about the war had moved from resignation at the start, through fear and disgust to an anger that he didn't know he was capable of. Trivial as it was, the return of Bartlett had irrevocably proved to him that the hundreds of thousands who had died in this war had died for nothing. If their leaders were capable of sending that idiot back to the men who had shown him up for what he was, they were capable of the gravest of errors. It wasn't war that was stupid. It was those that conducted it. And as they were the same class of people who pulled the strings in peacetime, he had all the evidence he needed that a revolution was the only way to stop the war. He hoped he lived to see it.

'Stand to,' said Hamish. The men clicked bayonets into place and gazed sleepily into the blood red dawn above them.

'See anything, Corporal?' asked Hamish of the man peering through the periscope.

'Nothing, Sergeant, just a mist. Weird colour though.'

Hamish pushed the man aside and took a look. 'Go and get the major, now!' he shouted at no-one in particular. Hamish turned the periscope from left to right, sweeping the battlefield. The mist was a mile wide and a hundred yards from them, drifting in the gentle morning breeze.

'Which way is the wind blowing?' he hissed to those near him. No answer.

'Fuck! Fuck! Fuck!' He rushed to the ladder and clambered up to the top, his upper body above the parapet. He felt the wind on his face.

'What the bloody hell are you doing, Sergeant?' It was Clive.

'The wind, sir. It's coming this way!'

'Have you gone mad? You'll get shot. Get down from there!'

'That's my point, sir. No one's going to shoot me. There's no one out there. Just that mist.'

Clive pulled Hamish down and rushed up the ladder himself. He looked up and down the line, raised his field glasses and twisted the focus mechanism so that he was staring straight into the cloud.

'Gas! It's gas.' He screamed in his men. 'Gas, gas, gas! Get those fucking masks on now!'

Panic set in everywhere. Rifles were dropped, men pushed each other away so that they had room to get their masks out of the pouches on their chests and strap them around their faces. The training was forgotten. It was too long ago and this was for real. Only a few did it in measured movements, getting those nearby to check the fitting around their cheeks.

They heard the screams from the company on their right, first. They were closer to the mist. And then the yellow-green cloud was on them, wispy fingers of death licking at their masks, looking for a way in. Men stared at each other, terror in their eyes. Someone coughed, then another. 'It's got in, it's got in!' one screamed. He clutched at his throat, tore off his mask and pushed his way past the soldiers towards the communication trench. He didn't make it. His legs gave way and he fell to the floor of the trench, clawing at his frothing mouth as his lungs and throat lining dissolved into the pineapple and pepper gas. His lips turned blue and the skin on his face took on a greenish black hue as he died the worst of all deaths. Soldiers forced the masks onto their faces with their hands and the terrified eyes disappeared behind misted windows. A few used the flappers to clear the gas out of the trench towards the reserve lines but this made breathing difficult so they stood where they were and waited for the wind to do the job for them.

It was hours before anyone felt safe enough to remove his mask even though the cloud has disappeared towards the rear within minutes of its arrival. Pockets of yellow mist hung at the bottom of the trenches which had to be cleared before Clive would allow anyone to remove their masks. They had all seen what happened to the unlucky ones. They swore and sweated in the heat as they moved the bodies to the rear, knowing that fate had again decided that their misery would go on. Hamish's actions had given most of them time to get their masks on. Other companies had been hit much worse. Dead and dying bodies lay in the communication trenches for a hundred yards, waiting for the relieving battalion and medical officers to process them. Clive's men stumbled past and over them on their way to the rear, too drained of humanity to care.

*

Clive Fox hung his helmet on the hook on the white-washed wall and stripped. He flung his clothes into the bath and got in with them, swearing as the cold water enveloped his body.

A young voice outside the door cried, 'Post for you, sir.'

'Thank you,' he answered. 'Please leave it outside.'

Clive felt disgusted. A year of unremitting violence, filth and fear hadn't eroded his sense of righteousness, the feeling that despite everything, this was a just war. Until now, until he had arrived at the Somme. Nothing justified this. This was insanity. He didn't hate the Germans for what they had done. We would have done the same, he thought. But the scale of the slaughter was beyond his understanding. Yes, take the battle to the enemy, but not like this. This was merciless leadership. They hadn't won the battle for no-man's-land before unleashing a hundred and twenty thousand unsuspecting men into the hot tearing metal.

He looked down at his hands as they rubbed the soap and water over his body. They seemed to have wills of their own. He didn't try to control them. They rubbed and rubbed, until the skin on his chest and thighs was raw. He threw the soap into the piles of clothes at the far end of the bath, and turning them over with his feet again and again he closed his eyes and fell asleep.

He woke up shivering. It was dark in the room except for the occasional flash of reflected light from explosions far away. He got out of the bath, dried himself with the towel, and rinsed and drained his clothes. As he got into his second uniform he remembered the post outside the door.

He took the only letter to the window and read in the poor light.

'Dearest Clive,

You haven't written in a while so I hope you are alright. Many women here have received the most shocking news. It is terrible for them and their families to be told like that, but I suppose with so many deaths it would be impossible to give such distressing information to everyone in a kinder way.

The girls are fine and are doing well at school despite your absence. They get upset when their friends lose their daddies.

I had a letter from a Captain Bartlett who told me that you had an affair with his wife when you were both in the army a few years ago. I don't want to believe it Clive, but I wish you were here to deny it. If it did happen, it seems strange for this man to choose now as the time to tell me.

Anyway, we all send our love, and hope you keep safe,
Yours,

Agnes.'

Clive leant on the windowsill and looked out of the window. He saw his reflection and felt guilt mixed with fury. The affair had lasted less than a month, Clive breaking it off when Bartlett's wife had got too fond of him. She told Bartlett that Clive was the reason that she was leaving him. The army had hushed it up, Clive and his family were posted away and he hadn't met Bartlett again until the embarrassing reunion in Shrewsbury barracks when Clive re-enlisted.

He looked down at his wedding ring. 'Bastard!' he spat.

*

The company left the horror of the Somme in late August, 1916 for the craters at Carnoy.

The front line was dominated by German trenches on the hillside above them, leaving the men exposed to sniper fire. Clive decided to improve their position by digging a sap, a lateral trench to the rise immediately in front of them and to start a new trench system from there. He asked for two sniper teams to cover the digging.

Hamish and Randle found a small shell-hole surrounded by long grass, giving an excellent view of the German lines slightly above their position. Behind these lines the ground dipped a little and then rose to the road that ran north-south about two miles to the rear. The small, shattered village of Fauouisser sat across it. Hamish and Randle watched through the telescope and telescopic sights as the Germans worked on what appeared to be a new railhead just outside the village.

'I wonder if our artillery knows about that railhead,' said Hamish.

'How would they?' asked Randle.

'Spies?'

'Maybe. But they would have a few problems getting the message through the German lines.'

'They use pigeons don't they?'

'I wouldn't want to be a pigeon around a million hungry armed men,' joked Randle.

'The major's right, you know. We are the only eyes the battalion has. If this set-up could be repeated throughout the army, we'd have a hell of an advantage,' suggested Hamish.

'That Otto chap wasn't making any notes of our positions was he?'

Hamish looked out over the fields. 'That's because his friends don't need to know. They don't want our positions. They want us to go after theirs.'

'Very observant, Dr. Watson.'

Hamish looked at Randle. 'Who?'

Randle sighed. 'Don't you read, boy? Dr Watson was Sherlock Holmes' sidekick, his friend, his partner in the pursuit of dastardly criminals.'

'Can I tell you something, Randle? I have trouble reading. It's not that I can't. It's just that I sometimes really struggle to read even short words. I get there by trying to read the whole sentence. I can work out what it probably means, doing that. The letters seem to float around.'

Randle thought for a while, looking through the scope. 'Best stick to what you're good at then. You love this job, don't you?'

'Yeah. For the first time in my life, it's what I say and what I do that matters to those around me, not what I can read or count. The farm work is all right but it's the same every year. This is different. I don't find it difficult to kill. In fact, I bloody enjoy it. Jim's all right with it, now. Good job really, seeing that he's done so much of it.'

'The major has great plans for 'im. I think he looks on Jim as a kind of son,' replied Randle.

'Talking of children, I got a letter from sister Sarah. You remember I told you about the girl that broke Jim's heart?' asked Hamish.

'I do.'

'She's had a baby girl. It's Jim's. It's a year old now.'

Randle turned his head to face his friend. 'Does he know?'

'No. Sarah asked me to keep it quiet. Jessie doesn't want Jim to know. She's trying to keep herself isolated from everything and everyone associated with the war. Her dad turned her out of the family home. He and his wife are alone now. All three sons are in the army. One of Sarah's friends has put Jessie up for now but food is getting scarce and they don't know how long they can support her. Dad's helping out of course but all his produce goes to feed the army. Even the horses have gone.'

'I see. Jim won't thank you for not telling him, Hamish.'

'But what would he do if he knew. He can't go home. She doesn't want him while he's a soldier. No good would come from telling him, Randle.'

'Alright. But would you mind if I sent a message to someone to look after her and the girl? Finance-wise I mean.'

Hamish was taken aback. 'Seriously?'

'Yup.'

Hamish nodded, and punched Randle softly in his side and went back to his scope.

*

Jim and Captain Bartlett watched the digging of the sap, fifty or so yards behind them and slightly to their left. Bartlett had asked Clive Fox if he could find out more about the tactics used by the snipers so that he could develop his own teams. Clive had willingly suggested that Bartlett spent some time in no-man's-land.

Eyes in the front trench trained on the ridge above where the enemy lay, looking for activity as the sap extended into no-man's-land, forty or fifty men digging and shoring up in its wake, throwing surplus soil onto the sides and topping it with sandbags. Machine gun posts on the flanks were manned and armed, waiting for the enemy to rush the new trench. German snipers tried the occasional shot but A Company had learnt its lesson and dug deep first and then long. Speed was vital as the diggers had to get as much frontage dug as possible by nightfall, increasing the chances of repelling an attack by firing from the new front trench.

Suddenly 'pop, pop, pop, pop,' sounds came from the direction of a thicket to the rear of the German trenches. Jim and Bartlett heard it clearly, the sound of four dreaded minnenwerfers. They watched the steel drums of high explosive and scrap metal sail into the sky just in front of them. They had seen the damage these things could do to a trench and didn't need to be told what they could do to a body in the open. Jim watched transfixed as the bombs reached the top of their parabola and started their descent.

'Jesus. The sap!' shouted Jim. Too late to warn the men he watched helplessly as they carried on their digging unaware of the danger until the explosions ripped up the ground amongst them. And then there was only the noise of falling earth followed by the screams. Jim had never heard noises like it. He lay frozen to the spot as the high-pitched wails reached and washed over him in waves. Again and again the shrieks of unimaginable torment and fear pressed into his ears until Jim could bare it no longer. 'We must help them. The poor bastards!' He tried to scramble out of the small shell-hole but was pulled back by Bartlett.

'Don't be such a bloody fool, Downing. You'll get shot to pieces. Don't leave me out here!'

'I don't care, sir, I've got to help them.' He scrambled to his feet again and this time Bartlett was too late. Jim hurtled through the small thorn bushes behind their position and sprinted through the long grass towards the smoking holes where the bombs had landed. He heard the rattle of a machine-gun to his right and the crack, crack of a sniper somewhere closer. And then a machine-gun opened up to his left followed by a similar sound from an unknown direction. The air was filled with noise. An explosion nearly blew him off his feet and he careered head first down a short slope, his legs not able to keep up with the energy in his body. Jim fell into the muddy pool at the bottom of the dip in the field. He got up, ran to the side of the hole and charged over the top.

Hamish, hiding in a shell-hole and guarding the flank of the sap, saw his best friend emerging from the bushes near where he knew Jim's position to be. He too, was aghast at what had happened to the men in the sap and watched those in the front trench run into the sap as soon as the smoke from the explosions starting to clear. He saw Jim and then the firing started. Hamish instinctively looked through his scope in the direction of the German machine gun and in three seconds had found the men sitting behind it. They must have been lying down when he made his earlier sweeps. He fired at the gun breach and disabled it immediately. He then turned the scope to where the British machine gun was firing, saw some soldiers feeding the Vickers with the belt of two hundred and fifty .303 bullets and tried to trace where they were shooting. He saw dirt fly off the top of the German trench at yard intervals and realised that they were trying to keep the German's heads down. Hamish looked at where Jim should still have been running but he was gone.

'No!' Hamish shouted. Jim burst out of the dip and sprinted, knees and fists pumping the air and jumped over the bags at the front of the sap. The firing stopped.

Four more 'pops' came from the same place as before. Hamish scanned the area where he thought the noise had come from. 'There,' said Randle. Hamish followed the line of the telescope and moved his gun and sights to the same place. At three hundred yards, he could see a team of ten or so Germans reloading the four minnenwerfers. A thick bush and the slope protected them from eyes in the British trenches. Not from where Hamish and Randle lay, though. Hamish fired five quick shots into the group and as it scattered he unfixed the spent magazine and pushed a new one into the breech from below. He watched the mortar explosions at the point where the sap met its mother trench, knowing that the men who had run to help those wounded by the first set of bombs had probably been caught in this one.

*

The scene that met Jim in the sap was one of carnage. The compression had forced the air from their bodies through the joints and the shrapnel had done the rest. Body parts were everywhere. Legs, hands, limbless torsos with exposed organs, shredded skin amongst the bones with smoking remnants of bloodied flesh hanging off. Jim saw small lumps of white-pink that he could see were brains and globules of smoking flesh. The smell of cordite, burnt flesh and blood caught in his throat.

Jim looked around this vision of hell and the whites of his eyes bulged in his blackened face. He heard the screams and moans as the cacophony above him lessened in intensity. A hand clasped his ankle and Jim looked down at the body whose uniform hung in tatters. He bent down and involuntarily tried to wipe the dirt from the man's face. The eyes stared past Jim and the voice whispered, 'Remember me, remember me.….,' and then he lay still.

Jim covered his head with his arms as the four mines exploded. He dug his face as far as he could into the soil, lying there motionless until the earth and stones stopped falling around him. He turned over, his eyes screwed up tight. Slowly he opened them.

His first impression was one of silence, and then of red. Blood red as far as his eyes could see. All the way down the sap were bodies and bits of bodies. As the smoke cleared he saw men lying in impossible positions, rifles, spades and earth all mixed together in a banquet for the devil. He stared and stared, not able to fully understand what had happened

He pushed himself up, brushed loose earth off his tunic and stepped over the mess as if he were floating a foot above it. He felt, smelt, and heard nothing. As he reached the entrance to the mother trench, he leant his shoulder against the wall of earth, wood and sandbags and looked down at his shaking, bloodied hands and felt his hearing slowly return. A lark sung above him.

He lifted his face to the clear blue sky and let the vomit cascade from his mouth.

*

The two biplanes flew over at noon, dropped a bomb each which blew up in the cornfields behind the German lines and then flew a circuit over the British trenches again. There was no waving from the soldiers below. Twenty-seven men from A Company had died and nineteen had been wounded. The remaining men and those who ran to help from other companies had taken two hours to get the bodies and wounded out of the trench system and back to the casualty stations in the rear. Body parts that could be collected in relative safety were put into sandbags and buried in shallow graves just behind the reserve trenches, below wooden crosses made from ammunition boxes. Soldiers who had had to pick up bits of friends sat on the floors of trenches and dugouts, silent in their grief.

The stretcher-bearers finished their work in the early afternoon just as the three scouts returned to the trench. Sergeant Small had delivered his report by the time Hamish and Randle found Jim with Neville and Clive in the dugout.

The smell of whisky met the two men as they stooped into the room. Clive had his feet on the table, crossed at the ankles. His leather belt, holster and revolver hung from a nail in the post behind his head and his uniform tunic was unbuttoned to the navel, revealing greying hair across his chest. As Hamish's eyes got used to the gloom, he could see Neville standing by the wall at the back. On the floor next to him sat Jim, propped up against the dark wood of Clive's cupboard. He quietly played chords on his harmonica. The air was full of smoke and the mud and stone floor was littered with cigarette butts.

Clive raised his nearly empty glass to the newcomers. 'Ah, the warriors return. What kept you? You're late for the party.'

Jim chuckled in the corner.

'We've had a right royal fuck-up here,' continued the major. 'Nearly fifty casualties. Did you know? Half my men. Blown to bits and pieces. We can't find some of the dead. Those minnenwerfers really, really are quite awfully ...' Hamish couldn't make out the last word as Clive completed the sentence speaking to the bottom of his glass. He poured himself some more whisky and offered the bottle to Jim, who accepted.

'I think you have had enough, Major,' said Neville.

'Enough? Enough? Do you know what they are about to do with me? No, of course you don't. I haven't told you, have I.' Clive got to his feet too quickly and had to hold on to the post and table for support. He walked over to the corner of the dug-out, unbuttoned his fly and pissed into the bloodied water that came half way up the inside of the white bucket.

'I'm to be sacked, gentlemen. Apparently, I should have told battalion HQ about the sap. Not sure what they would have done to help. Probably said, 'No,' or something equally inspiring. God, they are a stuffy lot up there. You can't scratch your arse without getting permission these days.'

He finished what he was doing, did himself up and slowly walked back to his seat. 'The C.O. will be here in a minute, with my dear friend, Captain Bartlett who is taking over the company. Positively Shakespearean, don't you think?'

He poured himself another drink and sat looking at his palms. 'I've got blood on my hands you see,' he said.

Hamish peered into the gloom at the faces in the room. They were a mixture of sympathy, shock and resignation.

'Jim, you alright?' Hamish asked.

Jim looked up at his friend and shook his head.

'He hasn't said a word since the explosions,' said Neville.

Hamish went over to where Jim sat, long legs stretching out into the middle of the room.

'Jim, Jim, you poor bastard.' He knelt down and opened his arms. Jim fell into them. They hugged and Jim sobbed into Hamish's chest, long, wrenching sobs. Hamish ran his hands through his friend's hair, 'We'll be all right, Jim. I'll look after you. Don't worry. We'll sort it out.'

He pushed Jim's shoulders back to look into his face. What he saw there he would remember for the rest of his life. Behind the tears, Jim's eyes were dead. The pupils were too small for the dark room, as if the irises were shielding their owner from the terrible world beyond. The candlelight reflected in them but there was no feeling from the other side. 'Jesus, what's happened to you, Jim? What happened out there?'

Jim mouthed some words but nothing came out. He was repeating the same phrase over and over again but there was no noise. No movement of arms or hands, just the muscles around the mouth pushing and pulling. Even Jim's tongue was still.

'Sir, what happened out there?' Hamish looked at Clive.

'May God prevent you from seeing it for yourself, Corporal. The private here saw it too soon. No man should see what he saw, not on his own.'

Light flooded in the dugout as the gas blanket was drawn back. Two shapes came down from the trench above.

Lieutenant-Colonel Ogilvy and Captain Bartlett stood at the bottom of the steps. They kept their caps on.

Clive Fox remained seated. 'I thought it was polite to knock or have we lost touch with civilisation already?'

Silence filled the room. The lieutenant colonel sighed. 'Major, you're in enough hot water as it is. Don't make this more difficult than it needs to be. Stand up and salute me now or I will have you court-martialled for insubordination as well as the dereliction of duty you showed today!'

Clive poured the remaining contents of his glass down his throat and gently placed the glass back on the table. He remained seated. 'Your move, Colonel.'

'You leave me no choice, Fox. You in the corner, stand up when an officer enters the room!' Jim got to his feet. The colonel reached for Clive's revolver belt hanging on the post and handed it to Bartlett. 'Get the red-caps in here would you please, Captain Bartlett.'

Bartlett couldn't suppress the smile. He looked down at Clive. Now this is very definitely check-mate, Fox, he thought. 'Certainly, sir,' he said and started to turn towards the door.

Clive's hand reached for the holster. In one swift movement, he opened the leather flap, took out the gun, pushed the safety catch to 'off', put the barrel into his mouth, and fired. The back of his head exploded, splattering those standing behind him with his blood and brains. His body slumped to the ground.

No one moved. It had all happened too quickly. All eyes fell on Clive's body as the smell of cordite filled the room.

Jim sank to the floor and closed his eyes, loving the darkness.

8

Hamish sat on the pile of hay that he had slept on, looking out of the barn's loft open window on to the farm and its yard below. He watched the chickens and a couple of goats wandering around in the morning sun, picking at nothing in particular in the parched earth. He scratched through the uniform material at the lice below his armpits. His rifle had been taken away from him while the investigation was underway and somehow the absence of weaponry made him feel safer. He was away from the front, away from danger and he had slept well, even managing to sleep again after the cockerel had woken the rest of the farm.

He had not spoken to anyone from the battalion since the incident as he had been kept in isolation, like all those who had been in the dugout that afternoon. He was not even been allowed to write home. The military policemen that Ogilvy had brought along in case of any problems were into the room within seconds of the shot.

Now as he looked over the sagging terracotta and moss-covered roofs of the French farm below, he wondered where this terrible mess would lead. His taste for the war had turned distinctly sour. He could take the filth, the fear and the lack of sleep. He had grown quickly used to the disgusting side of it, the deaths, the wounded, and the screams. But he hated the inter-personal feuds, the hatred between men of the same army.

He had spent the last couple of days looking back at what had happened in the dugout. The major being drunk. Jim's lifeless eyes. Neville's aloofness. He had been shocked at the major turning the gun on himself. But the thing that had really turned his stomach was listening to Bartlett's clipped, barked orders after Fox had shot himself. There was no doubting his efficiency but there was something about the steady, almost premeditated nature of Bartlett's delivery that made Hamish imagine that it had been rehearsed; as if Bartlett lay in bed at night creating situations in his mind where his political and sadistic ambitions came to fruition at the same time. Come-upances didn't come much better than this one. Bartlett's chief heretic humiliated before him, to the point where Fox felt that carrying on the fight was pointless.

Hamish's stomach rumbled and he got up from the straw bed. He climbed down the wooden ladder and went out into the sunlight. A girl ran across the farmyard shouting and laughing. Hamish smiled for the first time in days. As he approached the open farmhouse doorway, he heard the noise of a lorry struggling up the dirt path and he watched it bounce its way in and out of the potholes to the yard where he stood. Randle's face was behind the wheel, occasionally disappearing as the sun reflected off the windscreen.

Randle leant over to the passenger door and opened it as the lorry drew level with Hamish and stopped. 'Get in,' he said brusquely. Hamish stepped up into the lorry and closed the door.

'Have some o' this. You're going to need it.' Randle handed Hamish a flask. He opened it and smelt the contents. It was whisky.

'No thanks. I have seen the damage it can do.'

'Drink it.'

Randle stared out of the windscreen straight ahead. Hamish realised that the big man had not caught his eye since he came up the lane. He took a few swigs of the fiery liquid and replaced the stopper.

Randle continued to look ahead. He pulled on the safety brake and turned off the engine.

'Prepare yourself Hamish. Jim has been court-martialled.'

'For what?'

'Disobeying an order and leaving his post.'

'Leaving his post! When?'

'On the day of the mortars. Bartlett ordered him to stay in the foxhole rather than go t' the wounded. He risked not only himself, but also gave away his position. Bartlett has reported that had Jim stayed put he may 'ave got to the mortar battery before they fired the second salvo. Small's report was damning.'

'That's ridiculous. I could barely see them myself and I was better positioned.'

'I know. I told the court-martial that. Either way he disobeyed an order. The court-martial was a farce. The brigadier and captains on the bench wanted this affair dealt with as soon as possible. They made Jim a scapegoat.'

'Why would Small be so hard on Jim? I thought he liked him.'

There was silence in the cab. 'You know what this means don't you, Hamish?'

Hamish bent forward, put his head in his hands and nodded. Randle put his huge hand on Hamish's shoulder. 'That's not the worst of it, I am afraid.'

'What the hell could be worse that having your best friend shot, Randle?'

'It's regimental tradition that the immediate superior instructs the firing squad. That's you.'

'What?'

'It's at dawn tomorrow at the quarry at the end of this road. Just down there. I've named the squad. They didn't know Jim very well and in any case one o' them gets a blank so none knows if they killed him or not. The recoil is a bit different but not much. They'll meet you there. 0400 hours.'

'Christ, Randle you are talking as if Jim was history.'

Randle looked through the lorry window towards the woods. 'I know the army, Hamish. It sees discipline as everything and must never be compromised. If people get hurt in the cross-fire while discipline is enforced, so be it.'

'Can I see him?'

'No. No one from the battalion can see him. Only the military police that look after him. And the chaplain tomorrow morning.'

Hamish banged his head hard against the wooden dashboard. 'I cannot believe this. Are they really expecting me to shoot my best friend?'

'The court was serious stuff, Hamish. There was a brigadier on the bench. This has gone right to the top. If you're not there tomorrow Hamish, it'll be your turn next. And I am your immediate superior. Please don't put me through that.'

'We could all refuse to do it until the King has to shoot Lord fucking Kitchener,' shouted Hamish as he stepped down from the cab and slammed the door.

Randle gunned the engine, looked at Hamish and touched his own temple with his forefinger, as he drove off. Hamish ran across the yard back to the barn. He had lost his appetite.

*

'He's the bloody King of England, Hamish. They'll shoot us.' Jim Downing took another swig of his beer, drew heavily on his cigarette and shuffled the cards again.

'No, just you. That was the forfeit. You lost the game and we never back out, remember?'

'But I could get killed out there.'

'You were quite happy for me to take that risk, Jim. Anyway, no one's ever been shot for firing strawberries.'

Jim put his head in his hands and sighed. 'Oh well. In for a penny, in for a pound.' Hamish laughed and took the rabbits over to the bar and handed them to the landlord. A rabbit a pint was the deal. The trenches that ran alongside Offa's Dyke were rich hunting grounds that morning but the boys hadn't expected to catch this many. The free beer had exaggerated their courage and Jim was paying the penalty.

Hamish grabbed a handful of strawberries from the bowl on the bar and handed some to his friend, pocketing the rest.

Jim finished his pint of Bass and the two eighteen-year-olds walked out of the Yorkshire Arms into the afternoon sunshine, unsteady in the warm fresh air.

'Right, where is the old bugger?' asked Hamish.

'This way.' Jim set off towards the crowd lining the street at the corner of the square.

140

The older of the boys smiled as he watched his taller friend put his hands into his pockets and stride out over the bone-dry cobbles. He loved watching the drink-fuelled transformation from the chippy, self-aware aesthete to something a good deal more heroic. Fast moving, lanky and with trousers that exposed his sockless ankles, Jim looked like a university don in search of his bike.

Well-dressed people stood at open first and second storey windows on the far side of the street. Bunting and flags fell from balconies as far as the eye could see. The two young men tried to catch the eyes of the office ladies wearing their hats indoors, wanting to look their best for the visiting King George V.

Hamish put a match between his lips and returned the box to Jim as they joined the throng at the top of the street and looked down the hill in the direction that some people were pointing. Turning into the high street about four hundred yards down the slope was a single carriage, pulled at a slow, dignified pace by four greys, one ridden by a footman in gold and red livery and who sported a top hat. The four occupants of the carriage seated behind him were dressed in long-tailed morning suits and matching waistcoats. Children waved Union Jacks, and members of the St. John's Ambulance Brigade and Voluntary Aid Nurses stood to attention as they lined the route.

Hamish whispered in Jim's ear, 'You ready, Gavrillo?' in what he imagined to be an accent similar to the Serb who had assassinated Archduke Franz Ferdinand in Sarajevo a few days earlier.

'Normal rules apply, P.C. Plod.' Jim glanced at his watch. 'It's 1.24. If I don't make it, tell my comrades that I died a hero's death!' And with that, he crossed the road and disappeared into the crowd.

It was the first time that they had had a VIP target in their game and the adrenalin started to rush through Hamish's blood as soon as Jim was out of sight. Events in Sarajevo the previous week added to the sense of danger. He loved it.

Both friends knew the town, particularly the triangle of narrow and cobbled streets and alleys known as the 'shuts' that had not changed since the early middle ages. Six hundred year-old houses touched gables across the lanes, and the myriad of ancient shops and pubs seemed to be sinking into their foundations.

Hamish finished the count and walked across the road, turning left immediately. He walked quickly, hands in pockets and took the corner on the lean, hoping to cut his friend off. Before him at the end of the alley stood the church in the middle of the graveyard. He stopped at the edge of the square and peered around the corner of the tannery, leaning against the Colman's mustard advert as he did so. There were few people about, just two tall black suited gentlemen walking slowly around the area. A family hurried past him in the opposite direction.

He walked on, head down, feeling a little embarrassed that he was now a grown-up playing a child's game, fun as it was. He stopped again at the next corner, bent his knees and slowly put his head round the corner, peering between the wall and the black water pipe that stopped a few inches above the gutter. The passageway was empty. He could see the crowd at the end, lining both sides of the high street. The King would be passing any minute.

Hamish walked swiftly down the alley, pushed his way onto the street and looked over the heads and hats of the throng in the direction of the entourage. He saw the carriage, stationary by the statue of Clive of India as the king stepped down onto the street to meet the mayor and members of the town corporation. The band of the King's Shropshire Light Infantry struck up the national anthem as their patron started to inspect the first rank of the thousand and seven men of the 3rd Battalion standing to attention in the square.

'Bugger,' whispered Hamish. He had played this game so often that he knew his friend's modus operandi probably better than Jim did himself. He liked to step out of alleyways to shoot, maximising his means of escape. Hamish looked at his pocket watch. 1.30. He had four minutes. Jim must have seen the king's carriage stop, and decided to get closer.

That could only mean Grope Lane.

Hamish retraced his steps, walked very slowly under the floor of the storey above, focusing on the entrance to the lane where he was sure his friend was. He stopped just before the end of the wall, put his hand into his *jacket pocket and grabbed the catapult. He chose a large, hard strawberry from the selection in his other pocket, and slipped it into the leather pouch. Holding projectile and equipment in either hand, he crouched and peered around the corner.*

Sure enough, there was Jim looking up the street, standing in the shadows of the awning hanging from the luggage shop. Hamish took the dark side of the street and moved towards his quarry. He fancied his chances of a first-time hit. He kept moving, putting his heels down gently. A cat sauntered across the lane and into a hole in a shop wall.

Hamish was twenty feet away when he saw Jim raise his arm at the unseen target. The cheering from the street grew louder.

Hamish lifted the catapult and strawberry and pulled the pouch back until it was level with his ear.

A shadow moved swiftly across the end of the alley, pushed Jim's arm skywards with one hand and in the same fluid movement delivered a punch into his sternum, with the other. Jim dropped without a sound and a second silhouette fell on his prostrate body, pinning his arms onto the cobbles beneath. Hamish had seen it all and heard nothing.

He watched, not able nor wanting to move as the first man expertly moved his hands over the motionless body while the second put something into Jim's mouth followed by a couple of fingers.

'Nothing,' said one calmly to the other.

'Nor me', replied his colleague.

The men lifted Jim's limp body under his shoulders and hauled him up the alley away from the cheering crowds, his feet dragging on the cobbles. One of the men carried the two top hats. Hamish fell back into a shop doorway as they passed.

'You didn't see this, boy,' said one of the men. He peered into the darkness and continued on his way.

Hamish stood in the cool, dark entrance to the shop, not quite believing what he had just seen. The shop was empty. No one seemed to be minding the place. He stepped up into the street and looked up and down the alley. He saw only the crowd at the end, cheering the King and his fellow passengers as they passed by.

As his heart started to slow, he heard the pealing of the town's church bells for the first time.

*

Hamish didn't need the cockerel to wake him the next day. He hadn't been to bed, but stood for hours in the wood behind the barn, watching the flashes in the distance and listening to the rumble of the explosions, working out their distance in the same way that he used to when a child with lightning and thunder. His ears had become tuned to the sounds of the wood; the gentle sussination of the leaves above him, the creaking of the branches sliding across one another, an occasional owl followed by scurries in the undergrowth. It reminded him of countless adventures in the fields and woods at home, sometimes with Jim, sometimes Randle, occasionally all three of them together.

They had met on their first day in the playground of the elementary school in Shrewsbury when they were nine. Both loved football, and Hamish had played defender in front of Jim's goalkeeper. They had both been terrible then, and hadn't got much better since. Shooting had developed into their passion after Randle had taken them hunting in the hills one summer evening. Hamish had wondered at the pleasure he got from killing things, and Randle had told him that so long as he intended to eat it or sell it, it was all right to feel whatever he felt.

'Eating, drinking, trading and making babies are man's greatest needs and they're the most fun,' Randle had said.

And now they were here, ten years later, waiting for one of them to be shot by the other.

Hamish walked out from the barn where he had dressed. He felt his chin as he crossed the yard in the moonlight and thought that after the war he would try to grow a beard. Anything to make himself feel different from the way he felt now.

He walked up the path towards the quarry, looking to

acquaint himself with the place where he and others would kill his friend. He had reconciled himself overnight to the fact that his life would never be the same after today. But then his life had changed so many times in recent months that he didn't dwell too much on the philosophical side of this morning's events. He thought of Jessie and her daughter, neither of whom he had met. He thought of Jim's father. His only son, shot in disgrace. The Free n' Easy would fade away.

Hamish heard his own footsteps marching up the gravel path echoing on the walls of the small quarry. He saw the two buildings to his right, just by the entrance. The moonlight reflected off the slate quarry walls and as he approached, the iridescent quarry floor came into view, lit up like in one of the plays he had been forced to attend at school. Close to the slate wall, Hamish saw the stake, about seven foot high and four inches wide.

There was a dull light in one of the windows of the larger building and he walked over to the door. He turned the handle and stepped into the room. The light went out. 'What the hell are…?'

Hamish was pole-axed by the fist hitting his abdomen just below the sternum. His knees gave way and the air rushed out of his body. A hand went round his throat just before his face hit the concrete floor and then another arm pulled him round so that he sank slowly onto his back, fighting for breath. A small pistol was placed between his eyes.

'Name?'

'Rutherford. Sergeant Rutherford,' Hamish wheezed.

'Alone?'

'Yes.'

'Unit?'

'6th Battalion, KSLI. 'A' Company.'

'Reason for being here?'

'I am leading the firing squad.'

'Who are you shooting?'

'Jim. Jim Downing.'

There was a pause. 'Friend?'

'Yes. He is my best friend. Why? Who are you?'

'His saviour. And yours. If you do exactly as I say, Sergeant. If you don't, you both die…this morning.'

The blue light from the quarry reflected on the gunmetal and above it Hamish could make out the features on one side of the man's face. He had short, dark hair and pockmarked skin. His eyes were the darkest Hamish had ever seen. He looked almost, but not quite, African.

Hamish nodded.

'Good. You will go through with the execution. Your friend will not die, although he will appear to. Understood?'

Hamish nodded again.

'If you tell anyone of this meeting, you will die. So will one member of your close family. You may not know that they died an unnatural death. If you come looking for your friend, you and he will die. Understood? Good.

'Be aware, Sergeant Rutherford of whom you are dealing with. Be very, very confident that we will know of any deviation from the agreement that we are making today. Understood? Then lie there for one more minute. Let me finish what I am doing and I will be on my way. Do not worry about your friend. Everything has been prepared. He will be very useful to us, I think.'

The man stood up straight, turned around and walked to the shelf that ran along the far wall. Hamish heard four clicks that he recognised as something being pushed into their magazines. When he had finished the silhouette moved to the door.

'Remember Rutherford, if you love your family and your friend, you must forget this. He is with us now.'

He opened the door and closed it gently behind him.

*

Captain 'Hex' Hesketh-Pritchard was feeling decidedly ambiguous about life. On the one hand, he was happy that at last he had been able to set up the Sniping, Observation and Scouting school at Bethune under the patronage of Sir Charles Monroe, Commander of the British 3rd Army. The school was already paying huge dividends in the trenches. The officers and men who had attended the seventeen-day course were more than a match for their German or Austrian counterparts. Selection for the course was tough, testing shooting, athletic and intellectual prowess. In the sectors where the graduates had gone back into the front line, the battle for no-man's-land had started to turn, after two years of invaliant slaughter.

On the other hand the captain was fuming. He had not been paid for eight months and he had to take a demotion from major to obtain the role that he now carried out: spreading the message about the school and checking the accuracy of the telescopic sights and hunting rifles that had begun to trickle in increasing quantities into the divisions. He also carried out, on request, the occasional hunt for troublesome snipers. He regarded the sniping of men as the noblest form of hunting but he had been aghast at the standard of marksmanship displayed by supposedly the best shots in each battalion, most of it caused by poor setting up of the telescopic sights.

He was also bitterly disappointed with the lack of initiative taken by his fellow British officers in tackling the sniper menace. Didn't they understand that they would lose the war unless the German sniper was swept from the field? How could the allies attack when it didn't know where the enemy was hiding? The only initiative that he had seen had been taken by Canadian or Scottish officers with hunting experience like himself.

But the rest of the British Army seemed incapable of shrugging off the sense that there was a right way to fight and it didn't include hiding in bushes.

Hesketh-Pritchard and his companion, Colonel Langford Lloyd had been looking forward to this evening's visit to the headquarters of the 60th Infantry Brigade, billeted in a chateau, just west of Mauquissait. The two officers had heard much about the exploits of Major Clive Fox and his enterprising company and they were planning to discuss tactics and stories of derring-do with his team.

The Ford motorcar drew up to the front of the chateau where a subaltern stepped forward holding an umbrella and opened the car door. 'Sorry about the weather, sir. Please come this way.' He walked them up the stone steps into the cool interior, checked their papers and asked them to take a seat in the orangery that overlooked the lake and manicured gardens.

After a half-hour had passed, a young captain arrived and stood opposite them. 'I am awfully sorry, sir, but we were not expecting you. The brigadier telegrammed your office to cancel the visit.'

'May I ask why?' asked the colonel, with a voice full of gravitas.

'Apparently the person you came to see has died, sir.'

'Apparently or definitely, died. Captain?'

'Definitely, sir. He shot himself in front of his commanding officer.'

'And who is he?'

'Colonel Ogilvy.'

'Justin Ogilvy?'

'Yes, sir. Do you know him?'

'Indeed I do, Captain. Please would you go and find Brigadier Mostyn.'

'He's at dinner, sir.'

The colonel felt for the package in his inside jacket pocket.

'Perhaps you would read this.'

The captain opened the unsealed envelope and took out the headed piece of card. His eyes widened as he got to the bottom of the typed message and read the signature below.

'I will fetch him immediately, sir,' he blurted and walked off at pace taking the card with him.Brigadier Mostyn, accompanied by the newly promoted Major Bartlett arrived a few moments later.

'Langford. How are you, old boy?' The brigadier held his hand out and shook the colonel's, introducing Bartlett at the same time.

'Good, thank you John. This is Captain H Hesketh-Pritchard. You may have heard of him?'

'Indeed I have. How do you do, Captain.'

'Is there somewhere where we can talk privately, John?' asked the colonel.

Mostyn took them into a large room in which hung two huge chandeliers. They sat down at the table, the visitors on one side, the hosts on the other. Colonel Lloyd opened his notebook and put a pencil on the table next to it.

'John, as you can see from the card in front of you this is not a social visit. We are here because we are losing the war and the gentleman who signed that card believes that Captain Hesketh-Pritchard here can help us undo some of the criminal negligence that the British Army has so far been guilty of.'

'Steady on, Langford. That's a bit strong. We have all been through a tough time here. No one expected the Germans to be so well dug-in and armed and trained. They have had a huge advantage in numbers of machine guns, mortars, artillery.' Pointing to the card, he added, 'And in any event Langford, his Lordship is a bit off his territory isn't he?'

The colonel sat back in his chair. 'The Cabinet feels that the gentleman's first-hand experience of guerrilla warfare in Africa gives him impeccable credentials to look into this matter.' He stared down his superior officer. 'John, who orders the weapons? Who carries out the training? How many men have we lost in our own trenches to sniper fire? How many Germans have you shot in their trenches? How many of their snipers have you killed?'

There was silence from the other side of the table.

'There was a German sniper captured by Major Fox's team a

while back, I understand,' asked Hesketh-Pritchard.

'There was,' replied the brigadier.

'Do you have the interrogation notes? Apparently he gave us some interesting facts about the modus operandi of the Jaeger regiment.'

'We destroyed them. They contained information gained from a prisoner of war while under duress,' said Bartlett in a rather too superior manner.

'I see,' replied Hesketh-Pritchard barely able to contain his anger. 'And what do you call watching your best friend having his brains blown out by a sniper or drowning in his own body fluids while the chlorine in his throat burns his insides out? I would call that 'under duress'. Wouldn't you, Major?'

There was no answer.

'How many times have you been into no-man's-land, Major?' asked the colonel.

'Once.'

'Once. Major Fox and some of his men spent most of their days out there, apparently. They learnt a great deal. Why would he shoot himself?'

'When Colonel Ogilvy went to see him, Fox refused to stand up or salute him. Ogilvy took his gun away; Fox grabbed it and shot himself. He was drunk,' replied the brigadier.

'So are most of the experienced front-line officers that I meet. The ones that are left that is. But I still do not understand why he would shoot himself.'

'I don't know why.'

'And what of the private that you court-martialled?' asked the colonel.

'How did you know about the….'? Bartlett didn't get to finish his sentence.

'Don't be a bloody imbecile, Bartlett. Do you think that we would arrive here without scouting the territory first? That was precisely what Major Fox and his team were trying to do out there.

Preparing the ground.'

The silence could have been cut with a knife.

'I would like to speak to that private, Major,' demanded the Colonel.

'I am afraid that he was executed this morning for leaving his post.'

Colonel Lloyd put his pencil down. His demeanour was that of a man who was connected to the mysterious totality of life. He cared deeply about what had happened to these brave, enterprising young men. 'And who presided over the court-martial?'

'I did,' said the brigadier.

The colonel sat back in his chair again and looked up at the gilt cornicing in the ceiling above the chandelier. 'Let me try to sum up. The captain and I are here to meet one of the most enterprising officers in your division, who shot himself in front of that idiot, Justin Ogilvy. The private had left his post to help some wounded men. A private who won the Aldershot shooting prize, by the way. And this man was later executed on your orders, John.'

The brigadier stared at the wall behind the colonel. Major Bartlett looked down at his hands, not daring to take them off the polished table lest they reveal the sweat beneath.

Hesketh-Pritchard unbuttoned the pocket cover at his left breast and retrieved a tightly folded piece of plain white paper. He slowly unfolded it, laid it on the table and read the name.

'I need to meet with Sergeant Randle Pugh, tonight. He is just the man that I have been looking for.'

'I am afraid that won't be possible. He's in a raiding party.' Bartlett looked at his watch. 'They will be going over about now. Aerial photos have shown us that Jerry appears to be mining behind his front trenches. There's a lot of fresh earth that has been dumped in the area. We want to confirm it.'

'The same aerial photographs that Major Fox asked for?'

The brigadier nodded. He wanted this to end. Now was not soon enough.

'And would I be correct in assuming that everyone present at Major Fox's death is on that raiding party, with the exception of you, Major Bartlett and Colonel Ogilvy?' asked the colonel with a final, fatal slash of his rapier.

'Yes, sir,' replied Bartlett. The veins in his neck stuck out so much above his tight collar that they looked ready to burst. Hesketh-Pritchard didn't think their owner would mind if they did.

'Right then, gentlemen,' said the colonel as he pushed back on the Queen Anne chair and stood up. 'The major, the captain and I are going to Sergeant Pugh's trench right now and wait for his return. God help you both if he and his party don't make it back safely.'

*

Neville stood on the second rung of the ladder peering into the darkness of no-man's-land. He had given up on the periscope as it didn't pick up the subtler changes in form and shadow that he needed to identify movement, even using his peripheral vision. Small clouds of mist drifted from right to left, skimming across the bright puddles left by the heavy rain. It was a fullish moon and as it shed its light on the fields below, Neville imagined in his weary mind that the wasteland before him was a stage, the moon and stars lighting the set and his sixty men in an unscripted play.

The soft and regular crumps of noise and the flashes reflecting off the clouds further up the line added to the sense of unfolding drama. Clive had been right; all wars have the same elements: characters, conflicts and tragedies. Neville had stopped asking himself, *'When will humanity learn?'* because in the months that he had been in the front line he had learnt that it couldn't. Until the innocents were allowed to decide if their country went to war, there would always be war. And even then, Neville wondered if populations would shy away from it. The British public, given a choice would probably have voted for this, as he would have done.

Not now though. Not after what he had seen and touched in the sap. No one should go through that. And, if he were fighting to protect innocent eyes from seeing what he and many other men had seen, then hopefully innocence would be retained in his countrymen, who then in ignorance would vote for it to happen again, because a communal sense of injustice would always override a fear of the unknown. Quid pro quo.

He looked at his watch.11.15 p.m. It had been dark for two hours and there was no sign of action in front of him. An owl had flown slowly through the low cloud and bats had been hunting in the clean fresh air.

The trench was now full of men stepping quietly through the cloying chalky mud that seemed to be rising at their feet. Neville looked down from his eerie and saw Sergeants Pugh and Rutherford checking the equipment that their men were expected to take on the raid. Sixty-six pounds of it, the same weight as a mediaeval coat of armour. Rifle, two Mills grenades, two hundred and twenty rounds of ammunition wrapped around their torsos in bandoliers, wire cutters, field dressing, entrenching tool, two sandbags, rolled ground sheet, haversack, mess tins, towel, extra socks, message book and preserved food rations. Some also carried a weapon of choice. Entrenching tools with nails sticking out, coshes, knives, daggers, and knuckledusters. Six men from the machine-gun section carried two Lewis portable machine guns and replacement forty-seven round magazines between them. These fine weapons could fire five hundred and fifty rounds a minute and when fired from the flanks of a raiding party could wreak havoc on enemy positions, particularly if the party was withdrawing and being pursued. However, they were heavy and easily got clogged with mud. Neville smiled to himself as he remembered Rhys English's boast that he could strip, rebuild and fire the Lewis gun in twenty-seven seconds, blindfolded. Some wag had quipped that he hoped he removed the blindfold before firing.

Neville had sixty men for this raid, more than he'd been trained to lead. The tactics were his own.

The timing was bad. The moon was too full and the wet fields meant moving stealthily was going to be difficult to say the least. Orders were orders however and no matter what he thought of his new C.O, orders had to be carried out. He had seen what happened to those who didn't.

Clive's trumpet hung from a strap around Neville's neck. He blew softly into it, making no noise.

*

Hamish pointed the torch into the faces of every one of the twenty men under his command and asked if they were all right. Muted responses came back, not always supported by the expression on their faces. Hamish checked their equipment and their knowledge of the password and ensured every man's face and hands were covered with the grey mud. No skin must show. The Germans had started using searchlights that picked out skin, metal and movement as clearly as if it were day.

The occasional shell went overhead, the sound of tearing silk. Some of the men ducked, not yet battle-hardened.

Hamish kept getting flashbacks to the firing squad thirty-six hours before. The scared look on the faces of the men who formed the squad; the nondescript officer-in-attendance who watched proceedings unfold from the quarry shadows; the chaplain arriving and stepping up into the back of the military police lorry; the sight of the silent Jim with a blindfold tied around his head being led to the post by the M.P; the way that his own mind seemed to distance itself from proceedings as he had stood to the side of the squad and said, 'Ready. Take aim. Fire!' And then after some time he had pulled his eyes away from watching the smoke rise from the ends of the rifle barrels and turned his head to face Jim. He kept his feet where they were, facing the squad in case he had to look away quickly from his friend's dead body. Jim's knees had given way and his head and torso had fallen forward. The thick rope that tied his hands and waist stuck him to the post. He looked like last year's scarecrow.

Hamish had stared at Jim, looking for any sign of movement. A thin, long drip of red liquid had fallen from Jim's mouth. With the echoes of the gunshots still ringing in his ears, he could not bring himself to hope that he had not just killed his best friend.

Randle arrived from the communication trench with the rum ration and poured a generous quantity from a large metal urn into every man's cup.

'We can tell you aren't paying for that, Sergeant,' teased Hamish. Randle continued pouring his way up the trench softly singing, 'Come, come, Mr. Gunner,' to himself.

Sergeant Small pushed through the mass of men and equipment and found Hamish finishing his preparations. 'Evening, Rutherford. I'm coming with you.'

Hamish was stunned. 'But you haven't been briefed.'

'No matter. Change of plan. More hands the better, eh?'

'Fix bayonets,' came the whispered order from man to man.

Sixty 'clicks' sounded along the narrow trench.

'Up men, up!' Neville was walking quickly along the parapet urging his men up the ladders and into no-man's-land. 'You know the orders,' he whispered. 'Keep behind your NCO. Walk slowly. That's it, men. Steady. Keep low, bayonets front.' He walked a few paces forwards as his men emerged from what they called their 'lidless coffin.'

'Sergeant Pugh, you take your men to point A, Rutherford go to point B. Hello, Sergeant Small. You had better follow Rutherford for now.' He looked at his watch. 'It's 11.43….now. Check? Go in at 12.15 precisely. Seal off the flanks of the trench. Kill as many as you can, have a look around the back for signs of mining and get out. If you can get a prisoner or two so much the better. I'll prepare a surprise for them if they come after you. We'll be just on our side of the wire. If I think things are going wrong you'll hear this.' He held Clive Fox's trumpet up for the men to see. The brass glinted in the moonlight, incongruent amongst the greys and blues of the night. 'Happy hunting gentlemen.'

*

Hamish led his men at a stooping, slow run for about a hundred and fifty yards, stopping only when he thought the moonlight was too bright to run through. He avoided the tops of ditches or mounds in case the Germans saw his party in relief against the grey sky. He lay down at the foot of the barbed wire, checked that the men had done the same and removed the cutters from his trouser pocket. One of his men passed him the thick leather gloves. Hamish cut and folded as he went, followed by a soldier with the Lewis gun. When they got through the three lines of wire Hamish crawled to the left of the hole. The Lewis gunner went out to the right, keeping watch on the German trench over the sights of his gun. The third man returned Hamish's rifle and the rest crawled through the gap. The last man tied the whistle by its cord to the wire. He would stay at the gap and direct the withdrawing troops towards the hole. Twenty men waited for the order to rush the trench fifty yards in front.

Hamish could just make out the parapet but not well enough for him to worry that the Germans could see his own troop of men. It was going well. Stage one completed. He looked at his watch. 12.07. 'Damn,' he whispered to himself. Seven minutes to wait out here in the open, one minute to rush the trench. He looked to the right. He couldn't see the other party but hoped they had got through the wire. There was no wind. The only noise was the laboured breathing of his men.

Suddenly a flare fired from the German lines cut through the silence. It hissed as it climbed, taking forever to reach the top of its flight. The chemicals combined and the brilliant light started its slow descent to the earth below.

'Cover,' whispered Hamish urgently. He forced his face into the gap between his muddied hands. He could make out individual grains of soil and blades of grass in the white light.

'*Surely they can't fail to see us,*' he thought.

He lifted his head momentarily and looked to the right, seeing clearly the shapes of men in Randle's section lying along the base of the giant wire coils about two hundred yards away. He put his head down and waited for the inevitable shouts and whistles followed by the machine gun rattle from the German lines. Nothing.

They lay still as stone in the pitch-black silence.

Hamish looked at his watch in the moonlight. 'One minute. Pass it on,' he said to the man lying next to him. Slowly, quietly the men began to shift position keeping their eyes on the trench in front of them as they brought knees up to their stomachs. Hamish crawled through the tight crowd until he was at the front, still on his knees, looking ahead. He looked over his shoulders in both directions, nodding encouragement to his men. He looked down at his watch. Ten…five, four three, two, one. 'Now, men, now. Up, up, up!' He ran at the trench with the bayoneted rifle held in front of him, the eighteen-inch blade glinting in the moonlight. The group of twenty men spread as they ran and splashed their way through the puddles and up the German parapet.

They sensed the smells, low murmurs and soft lights familiar to them from their own trenches. A face looked up from the dark recesses of the nearest trench. Hamish fired at it and it disappeared into the blackness. Another and then another head appeared from holes next to the trench. One of his men fired from the top of the parapet and then another until it became a free-for-all. The bodies and faces of friend and foe alike lit up in the muzzle flashes. Momentarily it reduced in intensity and someone jumped into the trench, pulled open the gas blanket covering a large hole and threw in a Mills grenade. The explosion deafened Hamish and the blast knocked him off the top of the parapet.

'Jones, seal the flank with that Lewis gun. 'You others, follow me.' Hamish grabbed the bag of grenades from the man next to him and jumped into the trench. He rolled two up the communication trench towards the reserve trenches. Screams followed the explosions. He stumbled through the smoke firing blindly in front of him. His magazine emptied. 'Damn,' he shouted. He wished he'd brought the Lee Enfield with its ten-bullet magazine rather than the Mauser with the five. He tried to change the magazine but in his hurry he dropped the replacement. A white-vested German appeared from a side trench brandishing a bayoneted rifle. The German lunged at Hamish who sidestepped at the last moment. The blade went through Hamish's sleeve, cutting his bicep on the way. Hamish pushed his own into the man's belly, leveraging his rifle so that the blade sliced through the gut-sack and into a lung. The German collapsed at Hamish's feet, exhaling blood onto his puttees and boots.

Hamish picked up the magazine, wiped off the mud, slotted it into the underside of the gun and staggered on. He heard machine gun fire followed by the rattle of the Lewis gun. The machine gun fell silent. Red, white and orange distress flares went up to his right. The Germans were in trouble. All around him the air was thick with explosions and gunfire. Men screamed in fear and pain. Clouds of smoke and dust filled the air, reflecting the red and yellow of the explosions. Hamish ran on, shouting, 'This way men. Follow me,' until it grew dark again.

He stopped and turned, looking back at the fighting going on behind him. The flashes made the silhouettes look like dancers in a silent picture that he had seen in the Shrewsbury Music Hall just before he joined up. They moved left and right, arms wielding awful weapons, heads pathetically exposed behind empty hands. He saw Jones using the Lewis gun as a club and the huge shape of Randle kneeing a German between the legs before driving a knife into the back of his neck.

'The mines,' Hamish said out loud. He turned back towards the darkness of the German reserve trenches. Sergeant Small's frame barred the way. 'Sergeant. How did…'

'This way,' said Small. He darted down a side trench. Hamish followed, stepping in the water already disturbed by Small's feet.

'The entrance is in here.' Small dived down some steps into a lit room to the right. Hamish followed.

Small was waiting at the other end of the dugout, revolver pointing straight at Hamish's face.

'You really are an intrepid young man Rutherford, aren't you? Quite, quite intrepid,' said Small between breaths. 'However, I am afraid that you have to die, Rutherford. You know too much, as they say. A shame, really.'

Hamish noticed the two German soldiers laying side by side, a bullet hole in each forehead.

'We could have used you. We thought about it but decided that you were not of the right political outlook. Good shot but not angry enough.'

The explosion knocked Hamish off his feet and he fell across the stacked chairs to his right.

Neville stood at the top of the steps, smoke seeping from the barrel of his revolver. Sergeant Small's body lay in the middle of the room. Neville went over to the body, gun still cocked. He looked down into Small's eyes, saw the irises draining of colour and was satisfied.

Hamish lay on the floor of the dugout looking at Neville, then at Small's body. He tried to comprehend what had happened.

'Bloody, buggering hell, Neville. That was close.' He rubbed his throbbing earlobe.

'Still 'Lieutenant' to you, Sergeant. At least until the war is lost or won.'

They both stared at Small's body. A dark pool was spreading out from under his back.

'Occasionally, I give myself a pat on the back for my powers of deduction,' said Neville, removing his cloth hat. 'This is one of those moments.' Hamish's mind was whirling. The sound of gunfire and shouting drifted into the dug-out.

'When you told Randle and me this afternoon about your experience in the quarry, I started thinking. *You can't pull off something that clever overnight. But what a perfect way of getting someone out alive, without creating suspicion.* When Small asked to come along tonight in your section, I smelt a rat. Randle agreed. Hence my little ruse about staying by the wire.'

Randle stooped into the dugout. 'I think that we 'ad better be going, sir. German re-enforcements are coming up from the village. Hundreds of 'em.'

'Hold on,' said Hamish, getting to his feet. 'If I go back to our lines, Jim is lost forever. I can't tell anyone other than you two without endangering more lives. I told only you because I trust you both. The only other person I feel the same way about is Jim. He's my best mate. If there is somebody out there who is clever enough to get a condemned man out of this fucking mess, I want to know who it is and why they're doing it. Don't you?'

'So you are not going back to our lines?' asked Randle.

Hamish paused. '*I can't.* If I don't go back, if they think I'm dead, I can move about, I can try to find Jim.'

'If the Germans find you they'll shoot you as a spy. If the British find you they'll shoot you as a deserter, 'said Randle.

'Not if I can find Jim first.'

Randle looked at his friend, and then nodded. 'Back home they'll think you're dead as well, Hamish.'

Hamish didn't reply. He hadn't thought of that.

'You don't speak German do you?' asked Neville.

'No.'

'Right Hamish, get changed into one of those uniforms. I'll take the other.' He bent over one of the bodies and looked up at Hamish. Hamish's mouth was wide open. 'Quickly now.'

'For Christ's sake,' said Randle turning to guard the door. It was the first time Hamish had heard Randle blaspheme.

The two men got changed quickly. Neville gave Randle the trumpet.

'See you both after the war then,' said Randle.

'We'll meet before then, I'm sure,' replied Neville. 'Please tell them that you thought we were taken prisoner. I don't want my little sister to worry too much.'

Randle placed a hand on Hamish's head. 'Look after yourself, you young fool.'

'We'll make our way home, somehow. It'll give us time to think. There's no fly-fishing at this time of year to distract us. I'll give your regards to the girls that are missing you. That shouldn't take long,' Hamish replied, and winked.

'If I may give you some advice,' said Randle, 'ask Jim's father to help you. He is more than you think. And he may want to know that his son is still alive.' He bent down, picked up Hamish's rifle, turned and took the steps in one bound. He disappeared up the trench towards the front line to where the troops and a prisoner were waiting to leave.

Hamish went over to where Small lay and washed his hands in his blood. He smeared it on his face and uniform. 'Take us home, Neville.'

The two men walked out of the dugout. Neville threw in the last of his Mills bombs and walked Hamish towards the German reserve trenches, holding him as if he were wounded. The two bombs exploded with a 'crump' behind them as they rounded a corner and found themselves staring down the slope of the communication trench. They saw a long line of German troops nervously approaching. In the distance was the little French village of Fauquissart.

Half an hour later, they reached the end of the trench, crossed a field and climbed up onto the road that ran between Paris and Brussels. The wind blew in from the east.

In the distance Hamish fancied he could hear a trumpet playing 'I'll take the high road, and...'

Book two

9

Jim opened his eyes. The knot in his stomach told him that he was involved in something far, far greater than his imagination could comprehend. He focused on the cracks in the white wall six inches from his face as he recalled the events of the days before.

Jim accepted that he was an intelligent man. Enough people had told him so. He had been through enough in his life, particularly after his mother died, to give him that ability which only the traumatised understand: to be able to distance oneself whilst simultaneously getting involved in stressful situations. When Jim had used this survival technique in times past he worried that his character would fragment into subtly different personalities, some of which may not share the values that he hoped his spirit held dear. He didn't know that most thinking people shared the same fear.

Dark forces had been to work on Jim over the last few months. What happened in the sap would haunt him forever, he knew that. Jim felt far less emotion about what had happened in the dugout later the same day. Now, as he lay on the bed he could not reconcile his respect for Clive Fox and the relative ease with which he had come to terms with the major shooting himself. Clive knew he was finished, humiliated in front of his cherished band of brothers. The presence of Bartlett had made it unbearable for him.

Emotionally, Jim knew he had slipped a rung or two. He didn't care as much as he used to, about anything. About the war, about Fox, even Hamish. About home, about himself even. Something had happened in that sap that had left him less able to empathise with the world around him. He could now visualise the revolting scenes with a degree of dispassion, which both worried and impressed him. The nightmares were awful and he had woken many times each night since the explosions, drenched in sweat, his nails drawing blood through the skin of his palms. But his conscious brain knew that it had less conscience than before.

'Fine by me,' he thought. *'Revenge is a dish best served cold.'*

Immense as that day had been in its effect on Jim's psychological health, he could explain most of it. *'That's war,'* he thought. What had come afterwards, he could only describe as extraordinary.

The military policemen had taken him from the dug-out to a guardhouse about a mile behind the lines. The occasional shell had landed nearby and he had pulled himself up to the bars in his window and watched as men pulled horses and equipment to some kind of safety. And then he had been escorted to a large building on the other side of the square where the court-martial, in a couple of hours, had found him guilty of leaving his post against orders. He remembered the brigadier with the large greying moustache listening intently as Bartlett's and Small's statements were read out by a junior officer. Jim had been allowed a minute to explain his actions. He took twenty seconds.

'Sir, I was the nearest to the wounded men and I thought that I could help them in some way. They were screaming, some for their mothers, sir. The enemy attempted to seal off the sap at the trench end to prevent assistance of the wounded. I had to help them.'

Jim remembered the brigadier's answer. 'If we allowed soldiers to run around no-man's-land disobeying orders, then the war would soon be lost. We have to have discipline at all times. You gave away the whereabouts of your position to the enemy.'

Jim was led away as the brigadier and captains discussed the case. Two hours later a sergeant delivered the grim news to him. Jim remembered the calm way in which he had accepted his fate. Execution by firing squad. The sense of surrealism had degenerated into one closer to farce and by the time he sat down on the floor of his cell, alone, he felt like a child who has just been to a poor circus, one minute watching the ageing trapeze artists with an open mouth, the next yawning at the unfunny clowns.

When he had been moved to another makeshift jail somewhere in the woods behind the village, he knew that he had less than a day to live. The policemen had unceremoniously escorted him to a small, first floor cell, unlocked his handcuffs, made a couple of weak jokes about not seeing him again and left. He heard them exchanging small talk with the soldiers that he had seen on the way in.

He lay on the thin mattress with his hands behind his head and had fallen asleep. When he woke, he looked around the room to see that it had been rearranged. He didn't know how. It was just different to the one that he had fallen asleep in. There was a bucket in the corner and a small table and chair in the middle of the floor. The sky through the small window was the same colour as the walls of his cell, a light grey-brown.

He heard horses' hooves on the cobbles outside the window and voices and gentle laughter. A draught, followed by a door slamming preceded the sound of hobnail boots walking towards his door. A face appeared at the grille.

'Ahah. Awake at last, are we?' spoke the face, grinning widely. A bunch of keys rattled and a key turned in the lock. The bolt was drawn back and the door opened.

The stocky man stood in the doorway. His key hand was back in his pocket. In his other hand was a British Army pistol, pointing directly at Jim. He was about thirty years old, over six feet tall and he wore a British Army uniform.

Jim had sensed something was out of place. He couldn't work it out at first.

The man entered the cell, keeping his pistol pointed at Jim. He felt for the chair back and pulled it in front of him, the seat facing his knees. Slowly the man lowered himself onto the chair, leaning forward so that his gun arm rested on the chair back and his other hand spanned his left knee. The gun was pointing directly at Jim's heart.

'You may sit up, Jim. In ten minutes you will be brought some tea, bacon, sausage and egg. I understand that this is your favourite meal of the day.'

Jim had still not understood why this situation felt

instinctively off-beam. And then he saw it. The soldier, if he were a soldier, had removed all regimental and rank insignia from his uniform.

The man continued in a crisp English accent. Well-educated, with a hint of west country.

'In those ten minutes, I will explain to you why I am here. Please do not interrupt. Do not consider any attempt to overwhelm me. Not only am I very good at looking after myself but down that corridor is a mate of mine who will shoot me and you if I do not give him a code word the next time we meet. Do you understand, Jim?'

Jim nodded, still not quite believing that he had woken up. He gently pinched the skin at the side on his knee to make sure that he had.

'A while ago, you were identified as a very useful gentleman. You are a first class shot, you are brave and you have the correct political outlook. I expect that you can see the utter pointlessness of this war. Through good timing and a bit of luck we were able to make an opportunity out of a catastrophic situation for you.'

'Somewhere in the region of one and a half million men have already died on all sides, with another two million wounded, Jim. You look surprised. Accept it as the truth, give or take a few thousand.

'My job and that of the organisation that I belong to, is to identify men and women like yourself, who are too good to die, and who can help us do something to stop the slaughter and to prevent wars like this ever happening again.'

The man let the comment hang in the air. He looked at the floor of the cell, taking his eyes off Jim for the first time since he had stepped in. He pulled at the middle of his top lip with his thumb and forefinger, looking for the appropriate sentence to follow.

'Our organisation functions on all sides. British, German, French, Russian, Austrian, Italian. It is not nationalistic. The people who are lucky enough to pass through our hands come from all ranks and backgrounds. We would like to offer you your freedom, Jim and the opportunity to make a difference. Do you really think shooting a few middle ranking German officers from a hole in the ground is the best you can do, Jim?' Again he paused at a key stage in the speech.

'However, this freedom comes at a price. For all intents and purposes you will be dead. To your fellow soldiers, your friends, your family. Those who take part in your execution tomorrow will believe they have killed you. We will make sure that you survive. Your father will receive the customary telegram and letter.'

'After the firing squad has left, you will be taken by hospital lorry to a safe house, two hundred miles south of here. A few days later you will be taken to Switzerland where you will be given a new identity, training, money and projects to complete.

'In return, you will be expected to work for the organisation until such time as the organisation has no further use for you. This will not be full-time. Let's call it project work. It is the type of work that you will enjoy Jim, and you will be a force for good. Together we will ensure that the people who caused this war are never allowed to repeat the mistake. We will prevent those people who benefit from the prolonging of this war from doing so again.

'Jim, you will never be allowed to contact anyone that you currently know or have known. This rule is ruthlessly enforced.' He paused for the third and last time.

'If you decline this offer, my colleagues and I walk out of this building and you can pretend that this has all been a very strange dream. You will, of course, die tomorrow morning.

'Finally a word about your next of kin. If you decide to come over to us, Jim, you will join a group of men and women who believe passionately in what we do. We are not terrorists; quite the opposite in fact. We are trying to stop the terror. But the nature of their work requires the utmost secrecy. If you attempt to break this code of secrecy, you and your father will be killed. Your next of kin will also be killed should you leave behind any details about the organisation when you die. I make no apologies for this code. To our knowledge, no government or intelligence service has discovered our existence. We now have to find a way to stop this war killing millions more. Neither side has the political will to do so, so we will have to change the politics. This is where you come in, Jim. If the unrest in the armies gets out of control, or the people at home say 'Enough!' we think that revolution will happen in some countries. A revolution that will provide a wonderful opportunity for the masses to exert their power at last. National boundaries will be removed. Wars become history. The time of the elites is over, Jim. They have caused too much hardship. We need you to help us ensure that our opponents are removed. If you worry about the ethics of my proposal, then think of the torment that you have already seen at first hand. We want you to help us stop the slaughter once and for all by creating a new and better world.'

The sound of boots on concrete came up the corridor. Another uniformed soldier came into the cell with a cup of tea and a plate of sausage, bacon and egg. He passed behind the first man, put the cup and the plate on the table, then retreated from the room.

'I need your decision by 1800 hours.'

Jim looked at his watch.

'It is correct. I checked it while you were asleep.' The man smiled, and backed out of the cell. He turned the key in the lock and slid the bolt across the door.

'Have a nice breakfast.'

Jim sat there, staring at the locked door for a long time. Nothing in his life had prepared him for what had just taken place. He pinched himself again, only harder. He looked at his hands and saw the cuts from his nightmares. He knew he had no choice if he wanted to stay alive. That was the easy bit. What really concerned him was that the main reason he had for living at that moment was that he wanted to work for the man who had just left the room. His verbal delivery had been exact, steady, monotone and very, very persuasive. He had made Jim feel like an important part of their machinery, a friend almost.

Intellectually Jim was completely engaged. Emotionally, the man had got under his skin and Jim enjoyed the sensation. He wanted this stupid war to end just like everybody else did. Did he really care how it was done? Too many people were dying to worry about the legality of how it was stopped. He would gladly kill anyone who got in his way. If there was an organisation out there that needed his skills to prevent stupid people from creating mayhem in the world again, then this was where his future lay. He would commit to the cause, even give his life for it. If it increased the chances of survival for Hamish, Randle, Neville and the rest, then great.

Something deep inside his head rang alarm bells, alerting him to the shift taking place in his spiritual centre of gravity. He was able to rationalise that the terrible events in the sap and before had probably inured him to the old morality. He just didn't care any more. The war had to end. That was it. Nothing else mattered.

When the officer had returned at six that evening, Jim was exultant. He stood underneath the small window facing into his cell and smiled as he heard the footsteps come closer. He had given the man his decision and in return Jim was told how the 'execution' would work. It was important that he remained calm throughout. No histrionics, no ham acting, just the usual behaviour of a condemned man who had reconciled himself to meeting his maker.

He had no idea, even now, that beyond the blindfold his best friend had been watching his every move.

He roused himself from the past. It was the future that mattered.

He stood up, stretched and walked over to the unbarred window, rubbed a hole in the condensation with his sleeve, and gazed over the beautiful mountain scene in front of him. He caught a glimpse of his reflection and found that his dark hair was now spotted with grey.

'Welcome to Switzerland,' he said to himself. 'Welcome to a new life.'

He opened the right window frame, took a deep breath of the

crisp Swiss mountain air and held it in his lungs for a long time. He automatically slapped his trouser pockets, looking for his cigarettes. There were none and to his amazement he wasn't disappointed.

*

Jim opened the door to his room later that afternoon and strolled around the castle and into the church. There had been no attempt to stop him. He was free to move around as he pleased. There was no moat or battlements. Just a large house with castellation and tiny windows which was close to a town in the valley below and surrounded by snow-capped mountains. He crossed the courtyard from the castle's gothic archway and into the small church. To his right he saw the dull brass plaque that read:

'Cette église a été donner par l'évêque de Geneve a L'Order de St. Jean de Jerusalem en 1270.'

As he entered the church his eyes rose immediately to the heraldic ceiling. An array of boxes was divided into five spans by the beams of the nave. Each box contained an image. Some were heraldic shields, some were black eight-pointed crosses. There were mason's compasses, swans and burning oil lamps. The only Christian symbols that Jim could recognise were a chalice and four angels boxed around a sun in the centre of the display.

As he stared at the roof a quiet, calm voice came from behind him.

'Quite something, isn't it.'

Jim turned. The man's face was smiling, apologetic almost. His long light-brown hair was tied behind his head and his chin and upper lip sported a beard of a few days growth. He wore a loose-fitting white linen shirt and thick blue cotton trousers, braced-up over his shoulders. He was about six foot tall, just smaller than Jim.

'You must be Jim Downing. I am Gabriel Romano.' He extended his right hand.

Jim took it. 'Pleased to meet you.'

'And you, Jim. This church used to belong to the Knights of Malta, who you have probably never heard of. They are one of the many secret sects that maintain the power of the elites. A very reactionary and dangerous group. I like the irony of our using the church to destroy them.'

Gabriel put his arm around Jim's shoulders and moved him back to the church door. 'Over dinner tonight we will discuss our expectations of each other and how we will operate. Please feel free to go where you like. You are not a prisoner here!' Gabriel laughed at his own joke. 'By the way, we will be joined by a comrade from Italy. I believe you know each other.'

*

Bernardo Verro sat at the end of the long oak table and savoured the aroma of the glass of Chablis that he held under his nose. He held it to the candlelight and turned it gently in his finely-manicured fingers and smiled. He liked returning to the castle. He felt safe here. Switzerland was so civilized. He had to applaud the Swiss for taking on the role of Europe's neutral country, as they were uniquely well-placed to do so. Impossible to conquer because of the Alps and having no abundance of natural resources, none of their neighbours cast jealous eyes in their direction. But the really clever trick was to corner the market in secret money. The Swiss knew too much and could make life very difficult for anybody foolish enough to raise an army against them. It was the ideal place for his centre of operations. So long as they adopted the country's code of discretion, no-one asked any difficult questions. And they were very discrete.

He was in a buoyant mood tonight. He and Gabriel had come up trumps with the latest recruit, Jim Downing. He remembered him from the rowdy debate in Shrewsbury two years earlier and had been fascinated to read the article in the Times about his sniping prowess. The fact that one of the many sleepers was in his company made for a golden opportunity. They just had to wait until the conditions were right for Jim's removal. Verro considered the odds. About fifty sleepers in each army, one or two candidates needed a year. It felt right. So long as they were patient and only took the right person in the right way, the model worked. Quality over quantity every time.

'Sir, may I introduce Jim Downing,' said Gabriel from the doorway to the mediaeval hall.

Verro stood and walked eagerly to the two men. He extended his hand to Jim. 'We meet again, Mister Downing. In rather different circumstances, though.'

'Bloody hell!' said Jim before he could stop himself.

Verro laughed. 'Hello, Jim. I am Bernardo Verro. You remember me, then?'

Jim's mouth hung open. 'Of course. The debate. You're a communist!'

'Like you, I think.'

Jim paused and for a moment Verro thought he had blundered. 'Yes, yes. I *am* a communist. It's just that…that I have been through so much…I haven't really thought much about what I want, just what I don't want. That war is disgusting, it's an aberration, it's…it's evil!' Jim's eyes became moist as his words fell over themselves trying to get out first. His brain made a connection between the horror that he and his mates had been through and the person with a possible solution.

Verro grabbed him at both shoulders. 'Together Jim, we will put a stop to all this. This is our calling! There are millions of people out there who are waiting for someone to bring sanity back into the world, millions who believe in the power of the common man to change everything. You know this, we know this. We have to be brave enough, clever enough, ruthless enough to make it happen!' Jim raised his hands and gripped Verro's wrists. 'I can help, sir. I really can help!'

'Excellent. Then let's dine and we will discuss how we can use that help.'

They sat for dinner and were waited on by two men who wore the same type of clothes as Gabriel when Jim first met him. It seemed to be a uniform of sorts.

'There are not many of us who work in this part of the organisation, Jim,' said Gabriel. 'We keep it very tight. Tomorrow you will start your training and after it is finished, a few months from now, you will understand how effective very highly trained and motivated people can be. We carry out projects at the request of like-minded individuals across Europe. These projects are dangerous and require a lot of skill and daring. They are also essential to our objective of stopping the war through uprisings by the people, for the people.'

'So you want me to kill people, then?' said Jim as he sliced through his beef. He looked at Verro and Gabriel who sat at either end of the table.

'Yes. Is that going to be a problem for you, Jim?' asked Verro.

Jim smiled back. 'No, not at all. I've got quite good at it. And if it's for the greater good, so much the better.'

Verro and Gabriel exchanged glances. They had made the right choice.

'The war has now lasted for two years,' said Verro. 'As the slaughter continues we expect that some countries will implode. When that happens we need to be there to make sure that the revolutions succeed and the bourgeoisie doesn't take over and recycle everything in the way it has in the past. Each country has its revolutionaries but we only deal with those that we trust and those that are serious and organised. These people need to have learnt the lessons of past revolutions. Our enemies will be the bourgeoisie, the aristocracy and the army. If an army mutinies this is good for us because they become people, not soldiers. If an army does not mutiny then we have to find ways of dealing with that.'

'That was Engels' worry , sir,' said Jim.

'Exactly, Jim. Exactly. However, we are optimistic about the situation in his homeland. Some of our people are there now, in fact.'

'And what about my homeland, sir?'

Verro sat back in his chair and steepled his fingers. 'Great Britain has a liberal political climate but a criminal imbalance of asset ownership. More soldiers have died in this war than in all her wars for five hundred years, put together. It is only a matter of time.' He lifted his glass of wine and raised it to Jim. 'To the end of wars, everywhere.'

Jim and Gabriel stood and raised their glasses. 'To the end of wars.'

*

Jim rose at dawn. He had slept better than he had for weeks. He still had the nightmares but last night's had been less intense. The bright red, raw scars on his palms were dry and had started to heal at their outer edges. He gulped down the water in the glass, went to his door, opened it and saw the clothes on the floor of the corridor outside as he had been promised. A collarless white shirt, dark blue boiler suit and heavy boots. He shaved and got dressed quickly, descended the ancient stone staircase, crossed the sun-strewn courtyard and waited under the archway by the church.

At six precisely, a small door at the side of the archway opened and Gabriel beckoned him in. Jim closed the door behind him and followed Gabriel down a narrow spiral staircase that was poorly illuminated by the tiny leaded windows above.

At the bottom Jim found himself in a long underground room that had obviously been a crypt at some time in its history. The floor was made of the same flagstones as the walls. Huge candles burned in the two black iron chandeliers that hung on chains from hooks in the stone ceiling. Jim felt like he was entombed in rock.

'Welcome to the gymnasium,' said Gabriel. He stood in the centre of the room, hands by his side. He wore the same type of clothes as Jim. 'Good sleep?'

'Best all year.'

'Good. Today I am going to tell you about the training and the types of projects that you will be expected to perform and perform well in about six months' time. Experience has taught us that it takes about this long to build up the strength, speed, endurance, and automatic responses to every situation that you might find yourself in.'

Gabriel walked past Jim, drew back a curtain and pulled a large trolley into the middle of the room, on the bottom of which was a rolled-up rope mattress. On the top tray lay a grisly array of weapons, bottles and surgical instruments. He bent and picked up the mattress, resting it on his shoulders in one movement. Jim was impressed at the power in Gabriel's tight frame. The muscles in his forearms and neck were well defined and he moved with the confident grace of the seriously fit.

Gabriel rolled out the mattress so that it covered an area of about ten feet by ten.

'In 1410, an Italian by the name of Fiore dei Liberi wrote a book called 'Flos Duellatorum' or 'The Flower of Battle.' It is, even now, the greatest book on wrestling and the use of weapons ever written. Our organisation has tried to improve on its teaching over many years and failed. It is a perfect set of techniques. I will teach you how to fight with a knife but most of your time will be spent learning Liberi's seven rules of unarmed combat. These are strength, foot and arm speed, grabs, breaks, tyings, hits and wounds. You will need to build up your strength and stamina. It is a myth that excellent technique is enough to win fights. If you are up against someone who can fight well using these methods and who is stronger and fitter, you will lose. You must learn how to hit hard and fast. We will teach you good footwork, balance, reactions and agility.

'There are a number of points on the body that when pushed, pulled or twisted can manipulate the opponent and take him off balance or throw him. You will be taught these. Once you have grabbed your opponent you can then break his limbs in a number of ways. I will show you how to break fingers, wrists, elbows, shoulders, necks and spines and also how to use your legs to break knees, shins, ankles and feet.' Gabriel touched the relevant parts of his body as he said them. 'You will learn how to tie your opponent using only your body and how to escape from holds. You will learn how to use your fists, palms, forearms, elbows, head, knees and feet to strike your opponent. Eye-gouging techniques will be shown to you. Lastly I will illustrate which parts of your opponent are vulnerable to specific types of attack. These include the eyes, ears, nose, throat, collarbone, sternum, solar plexus, groin, knee, shin and spine.

'By the time you finish the training, Jim, very few people will be able to disable you without a firearm. If they have a firearm you will know how to maximise your chances of using this to your advantage.

'As far as operations are concerned, I will help you understand how to lead a clandestine life, to maintain personal security, to communicate in the field and to hold a cover story in the unlikely event that you are captured. You will also learn how to pick a lock and how to lose someone who is following you. I will teach you ways to withstand torture although you will be given some of this in a phial between your teeth.' He walked over to the trolley and held up a glass jar of clear liquid. 'It's saxitoxin. You must understand Jim that our security conditions apply even if you give anything underway under torture. It is for you to do all that you can to avoid being put in a situation where you feel that you must talk.'

'Apart from using your own body there are other ways of achieving your objectives. One drop of the saxitoxin in the target's food or drink will kill them instantly. It is also difficult to detect in the bloodstream if there is an autopsy. In this jar is methyl alcohol. It's tasteless. If you put a quarter pint into the target's beer they will die of alcoholic poisoning as they sleep. This is a Schelty needle and Braun ground glass twenty-millilitre syringe. Ram this into the heart through the breastbone or into the back of the head and the target will go into shock and die within thirty seconds. You don't need to fill it with anything. Air in the bloodstream is deadly. If you do it through the chest as you bump into him he may not even feel it. It gives you time to remove yourself from the vicinity and it also leaves no discernable wound. If the subject is sedated, you should insert the needle under the nail of the big toe. This leaves no wound. It is our most successful weapon, but it requires a lot of practice with this device here.' He held up a leather brace, similar to those worn by archers to protect the forearm from the bowstring. 'We obviously have nothing to teach you about rifle shooting....

'All right, Jim. We will start with some simple wrestling techniques. Before that, we stretch.'

As Jim walked towards the mat he felt he was crossing an imaginary line that separated the victims of the world's ills from those in control of their destinies.

10

The two bearded men rose silently at dawn and went about the tasks that they had perfected every morning on their journey back to England. The warm firestones were placed into the bottom of the packs that had been given to them by a Belgian farmer. Above these went the damp clothes that they had slept in, followed by the blankets and books. They both scratched at their skins in a vain attempt to remove the lice that had bred and rebred since they left the trenches, and naked, they went to the riverbank and dunked their heads in the cool, fresh water. The larger of them shook his head violently as he stood up, splashing the other with the water that had collected in his long, unkempt hair. The second man scooped his hands into the water and threw handfuls of the stuff at his friend who responded in kind.

And then they stopped and looked at each other.

'You look ridiculous,' said Hamish.

Neville laughed the laugh of the truly happy. 'My friend, I think we look like reunited shipwrecked sailors who thought we were alone on the island.'

They were a few hours' walk from their destination, the end of a journey that they would remember for the rest of their lives. Neville had talked his way through to the rear of the German formations where they had stolen civilian clothes, apples and bikes from a townhouse on the outskirts of a Flemish village. They found a canal that ran parallel to the coast and cycled along its towpath for sixty miles, stopping only to rest and to hide from German patrols. They had been shot at twice. Neville put their luck at not being hit down to their own erratic cycling.

The canal fed into the Ostend to Bruges waterway which they followed until they came to the harbour at Ostend. There, they found a Flemish trawler captain who was impressed at an Englishman being able to speak his native language and the offer of two bikes, and who agreed to take them to Boston on the Wash where he hoped to see a lady-friend and sell some fish.

From Boston they had again followed the rivers and canals, this time through Lincoln, Nottingham and down to Birmingham until they found the lower reaches of the Severn at Kidderminster. They had survived on the fish that Hamish caught using discarded tackle, and animals that could be caught in traps using the same wire. Hamish had never expected to use the survival lessons taught him by Randle while he was on the run.

They had been lucky to get a ride on a barge all the way from Lincoln to Birmingham with Alan Allen and his wife. No questions were asked about the men's backgrounds. They were expected to help with the loading and unloading of the cargo and for this they could sleep on deck and had food and drink bought for them at the numerous pubs that lay along their route. They celebrated a harvest festival of sorts as they idled past fields of recently cut corn. Their hosts took pride in belonging to canal families that stretched back to the early eighteenth century and claimed that they knew every inch of the British network. The barge was called 'The moon under water' for the very reason that Mr. Allen had himself been born three feet under water when the boat was fully laden and because their shire horse hated the moon and would jump into the canal to get at its reflection.

Now back in England they had spent the morning of the previous day lying up in the small wood that surrounded the main buildings at Hamish's farm. They decided well before they arrived back in Shropshire that it was in no one's interests to contact their families, who were meant to think that they were languishing in a POW camp, and that was the way it would stay. The families probably understood that this was healthier than the trenches anyway. But Hamish said that he knew where they could hide safely and steal some food. He looked forward to telling his father at the end of the war how the farm had kept them going in his hour of need

They arrived just before dawn and covered their position

with foliage and rubbish just as they had in no-man's-land. The Brecon Buff geese wandered around and over them.

They caught a whiff of burning coke which Hamish knew meant that a farrier would be shoeing horses. Piglets and chickens roamed around the farmyard, their hungry sounds becoming urgent as Sarah, Hamish's twin sister walked across from the house to the dairy carrying a wooden yoke below which hung two buckets of cream. Hamish whispered to Neville that the butter had to be made first thing in the morning when the air was cool and that at this time of year she would add a small amount of carrot juice to give it the yellow colour that would increase its chances of selling at market. The men listened to the churn being turned until at last the slap of the new block of butter could be heard against the witch-proof Rohan wood.

Children and adults who Hamish did not recognise ran from the pumping yard with buckets of water and poured the contents over the butter to remove the whey. Some of the little helpers walked over to where the farrier hammered horseshoes on the bick of the anvil, the noise echoing around the farm buildings. The big man wearing the leather apron and bowler hat led the horse to the stables in front of where his son lay in the undergrowth, telling the children that he had once knocked a horse clean out with his fists when it had turned on him. Hamish's eyes burned with pride for the father that he hadn't seen for two years.

Later that morning, when the farm hands had been at breakfast Hamish and Neville had stolen a piglet and cooked it on a makeshift spit down by the river.

They cleared the campsite of signs of their overnight stop and walked along the path above the riverbank towards the Free 'n Easy, five miles to the North. It was a clear, cool autumn morning, a time when England looks at its best. The midday sun reflected off the river to their right. Fields had been harvested and birds of prey kept watch over the corn stubble. The sound of cockerels pierced the balmy calm, and a light breeze eddied the river mists up onto the banks and into the fields and woods beyond.

Hamish could see the green weeds at the bottom of the river a few feet down, bending in the direction of the flow, a sign of further deterioration of the riverbed. Families of swans pushed off from the banks and bent their regal necks under the surface, searching for the fish that waited, deep in the shadows, for the flies to arrive in the sunshine. Hamish and Neville threw the cores of their apples into the currents, the swans investigated and swam away unimpressed, leaving them to the ducks and other lesser animals.

By mid-afternoon they reached the beach of sand and mud that sat opposite the river entrance to the garden of the Free 'n Easy, forty or so feet up on the other bank. A rope-and-boat ferry had been built linking the two sides of the river.

'That's new,' said Hamish.

'We've been away a long time,' replied Neville, ever-philosophical.

It had been two years since Hamish had last visited the pub. Hamish remembered it clearly; it was a couple of weeks before they joined the army. A lifetime ago. They were boys then. They thought they were men but they weren't, not by a long way. Hamish wondered where Jim was now and what he was doing, as he had done a hundred times since the 'execution.' He gave up now, not really trying. There was no point. He did not have a clue about what had happened to Jim. He didn't even know if Jim had gone willingly or was kidnapped by force. His face was so full of resigned misery when Hamish had held him in the dugout that he thought that Jim might even have preferred death to a new life.

Whatever had happened to his friend, he was going to do his damnest to find out, even if the result was as bleak for himself as it was for Jim.

He also had to admit to himself that he was intrigued at how anyone could get a condemned man out from under the noses of the British army. And more importantly, why?

*

181

Hamish and Neville clambered up the steep bone-dry path and stopped at the gate to the pub garden and bowling green. A few bowls glistened with dew.

'That's unlike Ken. He prided himself on putting everything away before he went to bed,' said a concerned Hamish. He opened the gate and they approached the large house. As they did so they saw a shadow move across the small window to the right of the pillared entrance. And then it was gone.

The men walked past the large number of wooden beer barrels and glass bottles that lay scattered across the path. Hamish knocked hard on the large blue door. There was no answer. He knocked again. Nothing. They walked around the building looking for signs of life through the dirty windows. Still nothing.

'I think we got here just in time.' Hamish went back to the rear garden again, found the black hook behind the half-barrel that now did as a plant pot and hooked the end into one of the brass rings that sat in the wooden covers to the beer cellars.

Neville watched. There was no point warning his friend. They had come this far together. They weren't going to give up now.

Hamish pulled the cover open, peered into the darkness below and walked down the steps as he had done many times before.

'A misspent youth,' he whispered up to Neville when he reached the bottom. 'Come on down.'

Hamish smelt it as soon as he lifted the cover. Un-kept beer. He looked around the large cellar, now bathed in sunlight. Upturned buckets and pewter jugs lay on the floor. Cobwebs hung from the rafters. Beer sloshed about the floor as Hamish and Neville found their way to the steps that led to the rear of the bar.

Hamish led the way up the steps and pushed gently on the trap door. It creaked as it opened and Hamish ascended into the dusty gloom above, followed by Neville.

'Stay exactly where you are and put your hands up,` said a voice in the darkness.

The men did as they were told.

An old man of medium build came out of the shadows holding a shotgun at his shoulder

'People like you make me sick, do you know that? While my boy lies in some Flanders grave, you parasites live off other's misfortunes. Prepare to die....'

'Jim's not dead, Ken,' said Hamish.

Silence filled the room. Hamish gritted his teeth, feeling his breath rushing over his top lip.

'Hamish?'

'It's me, Ken. I couldn't shout for you in case there was someone else. We are not meant to be here.'

'Who's your friend?' asked Ken Downing as he pointed the gun at Neville.

'Neville, sir. Neville Milton. I was Hamish's commanding officer in the army.'

'So?'

'He saved my life,' said Hamish. 'He also speaks seven languages and is great company when you are behind enemy lines. He taught me to read.' He couldn't think of anything else to say. It was the truth.

The silence enveloped them all. Dust drifted in the shafts of sunlight which crept between the curtains.

'What do you mean, my son is alive?' Ken asked, keeping the gun covering the two men.

'Were you told that he was court-martialled and shot?' asked Neville.

Again the pause. 'Yes, I received a telegram. Not a nice way to find out that your son is a coward.'

'He wasn't a coward, Ken,' said Hamish. 'He was court-martialled for disobeying orders. He tried to save some wounded men. The whole thing was a cover-up for Major Fox's suicide. Someone had to carry the can. It's a different world out there, Ken.'

'Clive Fox? He was involved in that?'

'We were all there in the dugout when it happened.'

'How do you know he is alive, Hamish?'

'Because I led the firing-squad.'

'You what?'

'Hold on, Ken. I arrived early at the place of execution because I couldn't sleep. Someone was changing the bullets and he jumped on me. He put a gun in my face and told me that if I wanted Jim to live, I had to go through with the shooting and stay stum. They sent someone into the trenches to kill me to make sure that I stayed silent. Fortunately, Neville got to him first.'

Hamish waited for Ken to speak. The dark silence descended again.

'The only people who know Jim is alive are us three, Randle and the people who took Jim. We escaped through the German trenches during a raid. Randle was going to tell the army that he thought we had been taken prisoner.'

Ken pushed the safety catch forward and placed the gun on one of the bar tables. 'That's certainly what your father thinks, Hamish. He was glad of that, given the amount of KSLI casualties.'

He came further out of the shadows into a thin ray of sunlight. Tears were running down his face. He looked what he was. A grief-stricken alcoholic.

'Jim is alive? Jim is alive?' He stumbled to Hamish, sobbing into his chest. Hamish put his arms around the old man. He reeked of alcohol.

'Ken, I'm sure that Jim survived the firing squad. I think that he was taken away by a group who want to use his shooting skills. Jim was an exceptional soldier. You must have read the Times article on him.

'But I think he is traumatised. He entered a trench full of dead and dying people who he knew, on his own. It took us hours to clear up the mess. He was also close to some explosions. The shock affects people in different ways. We've all been through so many horrors. When I saw him afterwards his mind had gone. Like he had run headlong into a mirror.'

'My poor, poor boy.'

Keys tinkled outside the front door. A woman's voice could be heard on the other side. 'I bet the old fool is still in bed nursing his hangover. Poor bleeder.'

'Stay down,' ordered Ken. He moved swiftly to the door just as the two ladies poked their heads in. 'Thank you, Mrs. Davies, Mrs. Evans, I won't be needing you today,' he said holding the door on the jam.

'But Mr. Downing, it's the big night of the week tonight. We'll need to clear up after last night.'

'We'll do it, ladies. I'll do it, I mean'

'Oh, it's like that, Mr. Downing, is it?' asked Mrs. Evans, giving him a knowing look.

'I'll pay you for your trouble next week, ladies. Goodbye.' He closed the door. 'Stay down boys,' he whispered. 'She'll be looking in through the windows.' He heard a giggle from behind the bar and grinned. It was his first smile in two months.

He blew his nose on a handkerchief. 'Well, I think that calls for a drink, boys. Don't you?'

Much to Hamish's relief, Ken poured them whisky rather than beer.

'To children,' said Ken raising his glass. 'They break your heart but by God, we love 'em.'

'There's something else I haven't told you, Ken,' said Hamish. 'Jim's got a daughter.'

Ken stopped in mid-slug. Hamish thought the content of Ken's mouth was going to be sprayed in their direction. Instead he swallowed the mouthful and poured himself another measure, topping up Hamish's and Neville's glass as well.

'I know. A mutual friend wrote to me. She's too proud to accept any help from me, though. I've had to be a little devious. She won't want for a roof over her head from now on.'

Hamish was stunned.

And then it all became clear. 'Randle,' he whispered. 'He

could have got the news about Jessie past the censors but not that about Jim's abduction. Ken, when we last saw Randle he said that we should come and give you the news about Jim and that you may be able to help us find him. Without evidence of Jim's innocence and abduction, Neville and I will probably be shot. Randle said that there is more to you than meets the eye.'

Ken paused and looked into his glass, swilling the last few drops around the bottom. 'Did he now? Bad lad. I could say the same about him, but then you have probably worked that out for yourselves. I think that we should find somewhere else to talk.'

They followed him out of the bar area and along a corridor. He stopped at the third door on the left, produced a key from his back pocket, turned it in the lock and opened the door. They followed Ken into the room. Expensive furnishings were draped across comfortable, sturdy sofas and chairs. There was a mahogany globe in a frame by the window and the walls were lined with books. Ken walked over to the grand piano and took a seat at the keyboard, placing his glass on the dusty surface. He showed with a sweep of his arm where the two men should sit.

'I have not played this since my wife died thirteen years ago. She was a wonderful player. Taught me how to play. Your news has removed the scales from my eyes, gentlemen. I am going to try to play Beethoven's Pathetique Sonata, that lively rondo after the solemnity of the second movement. Jill played it at our wedding.'

'It's one of my favourite pieces, also,' said Neville.

'I hope I do it justice, Mr. Milton. And when I have finished, you will both tell me everything, and I mean everything, that led up to my son's disappearance.' He played the first few bars and Neville closed his eyes and leant back into the luxurious sofa.

*

Ken Downing put the telephone back in its cradle and walked downstairs to where Hamish and Neville sat in his study. He unlocked the lid to his desk and pulled out a small drawer from the back, turned it over in his hand and slid the false bottom away from the rest of the drawer. He then took out two tightly folded pieces of paper and unfolded them on the lid of his desk. They were blank. He went over to his bookshelves and selected The Common Prayer Book and took it back to his desk, opened the back cover to expose the black lining and slid the open book over both pieces of paper from bottom to top. A form appeared on each sheet. He turned to the two men who had been following his every move.

'These, gentlemen, are forms declaring that you will be bound by the Official Secrets Act, should you sign them.' He uncapped the gold fountain pen that lay in a cubby-hole in his desk and offered it to the men. They got up, took the pen and signed the forms without reading them. They were too fascinated to worry about smallprint. Ken moved the semi-circular hand blotter over the signatures, folded the forms and put them in his jacket pocket.

'Hamish, Neville, you are now bound by the most onerous piece of legislation on the British statute book. If you breathe a word of what I am about to tell you without our authorisation, you will be arrested, tried and interned, perhaps for the rest of your lives. Do I make myself clear? Good.

Some years ago I worked for the Government. I am no longer on their payroll but I do keep in touch with those I used to work with. Most of my time was spent keeping an eye on various members of the British aristocracy, hence my profession as a butler. I never found much to alarm Whitehall and eventually I grew bored of it. However, whilst the threat to parliamentary democracy appeared thin within the boundaries of this island at the time, things move on.

'I have just spoken on the telephone with two senior people in the Intelligence community in London. They are Commander Cumming and Captain Kell. Their departments play important roles in the fight to prevent a return to the dark ages of ideological or military rule and they are very interested in how anyone can do what you say they have done with Jim. The implications for army security are awful.

'We will meet them both at Cumming's holiday retreat in the New Forest in three days time. Kell looks after threats residing in this country; Cumming is more interested in getting information about our enemies, though their interests often cross over. This is a good example of a threat lying in both their camps as they will explain when we meet them. Suffice to say that with all the strikes going on, Kell is very concerned about anything that has a smell of communism about it. The teachings of Marx and Engels are very persuasive, very powerful, as we know from Jim. A marksman working for the communists doesn't bear thinking about, particularly in the current environment with many countries at risk of civil war. So what makes me think that the story you have told me could be linked to the communists?'

He walked around the darkened room and stopped by the rows of books, casting his eyes over the titles. 'There is a principle of code-breaking that says that if you can't easily understand what is in front of you, work out what it can't be until the answer becomes clearer.' Hamish glanced at Neville, remembering the time that Neville admitted to card counting. For example, if a foreign country wanted to recruit someone with Jim's shooting ability they could find one in their own armed forces. What else makes Jim attractive to a secret organisation? Perhaps his political views. Certainly the fact that he can be made to 'die'. But a foreign power has no need to recruit people who don't exist, so to speak, as everyone in the intelligence community knows about the services that work for each country. It has to be an organisation that thinks no-one knows of its existence. The clincher for me is that it is inconceivable that the German's have infiltrated our armed forces to the extent that they can get people out to fight for them and neither do they need to. However, it is not beyond the bounds of possibility that there are some soldiers who have extreme political views, particularly after what they've gone through. But whoever this group is, they have made one mistake.' He looked at both of the men, enjoying his moment as chief detective.

'Sergeant Small,' said Neville.

'Exactly. He was the only person whose identity we have, who probably had a direct link to this group. I've suggested to Cumming and Kell that they start some digging. You will hide here until we leave for the south coast early next week. You can help me clear up. I haven't been myself recently, as I am sure you gentlemen can understand.

'And now I must have a shave. I'll run you a bath but don't go near a razor or the windows. We don't want you appearing in the Chronicle do we? 'Missing Salopians found in pub,' would not exactly add to our chances of making whoever this organisation is, believe that you are in a POW camp somewhere!'

*

Jessie Appleby wiped the tears from her eyes. 'Please, vicar. This means so much to me. Please don't do this to us.'

They sat on the front pew in the empty church.

'Jessie, I cannot allow Poppy to be christened in this church. You are not married and there is no father.'

Jessie burst into tears again. Poppy looked up at her mother and then at the brass candle holders. 'But he's dead, he's dead!' Jessie hissed. 'They bloody killed him.'

'My child, I feel so sorry for you. This war is a terrible thing. I have tried to comfort so many of my congregation but grief is not something one can treat. Only God and time can sooth the pain.'

Jessie was at the end of her tether. She had tolerated the ostracism and sly looks in the village; she had learnt to cope with the fear of losing her brothers, until she had read about Jim's execution in the Chronicle. The words hadn't sunk in at first and then she had dropped the newspaper and forced her face into the cushion, screaming, 'No! No!' Her eldest brother was convalescing in hospital after losing a leg and there was little news of the other brothers. But this was a complete shock. Not Jim. He was so young, so....so colourful.

'So that's it then, is it? Not content to take my brothers and father away from me, your God has now taken away my friend, Poppy's father, for good. And still he isn't content with the misery he has meted out. So he tells you to not allow me a christening for my child, our child.' She was no longer crying, she was angry, very angry and she said something that she never thought could possibly leave her lips. 'This is not the God I knew as a child. This is your God. Not mine. Vicar, you can stick your christening. I'm going to do my own.'

So she did. She went home and in the sink in the garden at the back of the house she poured water onto Poppy's forehead, kissed the tiny crucifix that hung from her own neck, placed it between Poppy's eyes and said a prayer.

She looked up at the sky. 'Sorry, Lord. Speak to your son if you don't understand this.'

*

The white-walled tyres of the Rolls-Royce Silver Ghost Oxford Open Tourer flashed past the trees in the moonlight, the immaculately engineered motor making easy work of the steady rise to the estate above. Cumming's chauffeur, goggles over his eyes, chatted with Ken about mutual acquaintances. Hamish and Neville sat in the back. They could smell the salty air above the Solent as the roofless car sped along the narrow dusty lanes.

Ken had given Hamish and Neville some of the colourful anecdotes that made up the legend of Commander Smith-Cumming, the first head of the foreign section of the Secret Service Bureau. Appointed by Winston Churchill as First Sea Lord, Cumming, or 'C' as he was referred to, had made a miraculous recovery from losing a leg in a car accident in France the year before, which claimed the life of the driver, Cumming's son Alistair. Cumming was trapped in the wreckage and used a penknife to hack away at his smashed leg so that he could get to his dying son. He was now to be seen speeding down the long corridors of Whitehall, his wooden leg supported on a child's scooter.

The London office was in his own London flat at the top of Number 2, Whitehall Court, reached by a private lift. Bernard Shaw and other celebrities lived on the lower floors but they didn't know that the headquarters of the Secret Service was above them. He owned numerous motorcars and yachts, and held pilots licences for both the French Aviators and Royal Aero Clubs. He was infamous for adopting various disguises whilst touring European countries even though his only language was English. His ambition, as he once told his secretary, was to write his memoirs, entitled, 'The Indiscretions of a Secret Service Chief'. They would be four hundred pages long and every page would be blank.

The car turned into the drive at the top of the hill and stopped at the gatehouse. A special branch policeman checked the chauffeur's papers and pointed his torch at the three men.
'Please go in gentlemen. 'C' is expecting you.'

The car stopped outside the Queen Anne house, the electric lights from the many chandeliers radiating across the driveway and gardens. A butler welcomed Ken, checked his papers again and took them all into the house. He took their orders for drinks and disappeared into one of the side rooms, closing the door behind him.

'One butler taking orders from another. I bet that's a first. Welcome to Burleston, gentlemen.' They all turned towards the cultured voice. A barrel-chested man of medium height stood in the doorway to the drawing room, dressed in a black, velvet dining suit and white shirt. He had a prominent, almost Punch-like chin below an engaging smile, hooked nose and piercing green eyes.
Ken introduced Hamish and Neville.

'The deserters!' shouted Cumming, smiling. 'I should have you both shot. Fortunately for you we can see how you both can be useful to us, in your different ways.' Cumming led them into the drawing room and introduced them to a large man with a twitch in a face so similar to Cumming's that they could have been brothers, and another, shorter man whose spectacles and serious demeanour made him look like an accountant.

'This is Captain Reginald Hall and Captain Vernon Kell,' said Cumming. The six men took their seats around the large room. 'I have been reading a lot about you two heroes,' said Cumming, sitting himself opposite Hamish and Neville. 'Quite an adventure you've both had. One of our contacts, a Colonel Langford Lloyd has been in France for a while now collecting evidence of the cover-up of Major Fox's suicide. He has given us some interesting views on the both of you following our recent enquiries. You know Captain Randle Pugh, I understand.'

'Captain!' said a staggered Hamish.

'Oh yes,' replied Cumming. 'After the raid in which you were supposedly captured, Captain Hesketh-Pritchard, from the Sniping, Observation and Scouting school was waiting for him. He has been invaluable in developing the training courses at the school. Many areas of no-man's-land are now under our control because of the great work that the school has performed. It doesn't have to comply with the regimented processes of the rest of the army. Hesketh-Pritchard, or 'The Headmaster' as we call him, thought Randle should be a captain so he became a captain. Remarkable man by all accounts. Anyway, the stories that he has told his colleagues about you two have filtered back to us. Not all of it's flattering regarding you Mr. Rutherford, but he does acknowledge your bravery.'

Hamish was speechless.

'Mr. Milton, I understand that you speak many languages.'

'Yes, sir.'

'And you can card count and do the Times crossword with ridiculous ease.'

'Well sir, I wouldn't….' Neville shifted uncomfortably in his seat.

'We'll give it a try shall we?' He took the newspaper from the side table and put the brass-rimmed monocle from his breast pocket up to his eye. 'Reggie, Vernon and I have been struggling with this one. 'A French emaciated ruler is selfish.' Ten letters.'

Neville smiled. 'Unthinking. Un-thin-king.'

'Not bad. Not bad at all,' said Cumming, filling in the last answer.

'There you are, Reggie. I knew we'd do it in the end.'

'Lieutenant, you gave up a place at Oxford to join the army in 1914, I understand?' asked Hall.

'That's right,' said Neville.

'   A patriotic act if ever there was one. I run a department that breaks German codes, mainly wireless transmissions,' said Hall, blinking regularly. 'We call it Room 40. According to your old classics teacher at Shrewsbury School and others who have crossed your path, you have an extraordinary brain. We want to use it. Would you be interested in joining us?'

Neville was stunned and it showed on his face. Only a week ago he was a tramp on the run. Now he was being offered a job right at the heart of Britain's Intelligence community. As he looked into Hall's intense blue eyes and cutwater chin he felt like a nut about to be attacked by a toucan. 'I've not done code breaking since I was mucking about at school sir.'

'Then would you mind mucking about to help us win the war?'

'I would be honoured to, sir. But the reason that I am here is to help Hamish find Jim Downing.'

'You have helped me just fine, sir. You must do this,' said Hamish.

'Good. Lieutenant, you will be working with your old friend Dillys Knox.' Hall stood up. 'Thank you Mansfield, for your hospitality. Neville, we will leave for London now. We will need to invent a story that explains how you got to London.'

'We're leaving now?' asked Neville.

'Now. I want you at your desk by 0900 hours tomorrow. There's a war to be won.'

*

Cummings rang a bell on the small table beside him. The butler appeared and took more orders for drinks. They handed him their empty glasses and waited until he left the room before any of them spoke.

Hamish looked across at Ken and saw that he had lost ten years in the few days since he had given him the news about Jim. He only hoped that Jim or fate did not let them down.

Cumming retrieved a beige folder from under his armchair. 'I can identify with your plight Ken. It is an awful thing to lose a son and if I can help you find yours, then I will. However we have to tread carefully. We have very little to go on and I don't want to field awkward questions from my boss about my allocating resources to helping an old friend find his son, when there is a war on.' He opened the file. 'Your Sergeant Small is an interesting fellow. Following a request from me, Colonel Langford Lloyd has kindly passed on this chap's background to me which we have followed up at this end. It appears Small was not his real name. He joined up with the KSLI in 1911 but Special Branch can find no record of his name in the town in which he is meant to have been born and brought up. Even the next-of-kin details on his enlisting form drew a blank. So we are obviously on to something.'

For the first time Kell entered the conversation. 'Hamish, have you been briefed on my role?'

'Yes, sir.'

'Good. I have been preoccupied by socialist subversion for some time. I have a bad feeling about all this. We had the uprising in Ireland last year, then the horrors of the Somme, and strikes in Glasgow and Manchester only last month. Munitions factories are being blown up, for God's sake. Some elements of the French army are refusing to fight and the Russians are in disarray. Socialist and pacifist organisations in this country are combining forces to bring down the government so if the communists start using clandestine military means to pursue their objectives we are in deep trouble. Hamish, Small is the only link we have to these people. Can you describe him to us?'

'He was about thirty-five years old, a little shorter than me, dark brown hair, moustache. Oh, and he was immaculately dressed. Even after bombardments he was better turned-out than everyone.'

'Anything else?' asked Kell as he wrote in his notebook. 'Scars, wedding ring, accent, anything at all.'

'He definitely didn't wear a ring, sir. Some of us reckoned he was a...a homosexual.'

'I see. Why would that be?'

'Well, sir, he was a good soldier and we respected him but he was just so well-mannered and polite that he didn't seem to be like us. He would spend ages looking after his fingernails. And he never visited the brothels, sir.' Hamish went red.

'Fingernails?' asked Ken Downing. 'Was he right or left handed?'

'He was both. He could shoot with both hands equally well.' Hamish noticed the briefest of mood changes pass across Ken's face and then it was gone.

Hamish asked, 'Is there any chance that Brigadier Mostyn, Colonel Ogilvy or Captain Bartlett are involved?'

Cumming looked up from the file. 'According to Colonel Lloyd, the last two were just makeweights who found Fox a threat, someone who rocked the boat and who was likely to expose their own incompetence. For disposing of the German sniper interrogation notes, Lloyd has had Bartlett returned to the desk job in England that he should never have been allowed to leave. Colonel Lloyd has known Mostyn for a number of years. He is a blabbermouth. Not the type of person likely to be useful to a group that wants to remain invisible. Ogilvy has been killed, by the way. A stray shell took out the battalion HQ bogs while he was paying a visit.'

'There is a God after all,' hissed Hamish through gritted teeth. 'But what about Jim? People at home think he was a coward.'

'Colonel Lloyd wants him to be posthumously pardoned. I have refused to pass on that request to the top brass on the grounds that, irrespective of the gross unfairness of it all, military discipline is everything. If soldiers get to think that their leaders are weak enough to admit making mistakes, we will have a mutiny. If you can't accept that, Hamish, then war has obviously taught you nothing.'

'So what do we do now?' asked Ken.

'We wait,' said Cumming. 'Jim is probably safe while he remains useful to these people, a hell of a lot safer than he was in his previous job. I ask for your patience. We'll expand our enquiries and I'll go through the files again to see if there is anything that we have missed.'

Cumming smiled at Hamish. 'Now what are we going to do with you, my boy? You can't hang around in Blighty waiting for some soldier on leave to recognise you.'

He sat back in his chair thinking. And then it came to him.

'Have you ever flown in a balloon?'

'A balloon? No sir. I've never flown in anything.'

'Marvellous. Marvellous. Tomorrow, I'll take you to meet Commander Pollock at the Naval Ballooning School at Hurlingham. We call him 'pink tights' because of an unfortunate incident a few years ago. He has a new invention that I know he's desperate to try out. We need to send you away for a while until we sort out what to do.'

'Where to, sir?'

'The Pyrenees, my boy. We've a safe house in a little village called Laroque des Alberes. You'll be just in time for the last of the Catalonian festivals.'

11

Hamish turned the key in the door of the modest-looking house and went inside. His baggage clattered as he dropped it to the mosaic floor and the noise echoed up the three-storey stairwell. He was exhausted after the two weeks flying from England and he needed to find a bed. *'No more sleeping outdoors, ever again,'* he promised himself.

He made a tour of the terraced house that was much bigger than it looked from the outside, in the traditional French style. Hamish counted the rooms. There were sixteen, plus a balcony shaded by enormous palm trees with views to the mountains beyond, a double coach-house and an empty cellar. If he could find food and drink he could live like a king. He checked for his wallet that contained the Francs that Cumming had given him, and he found it secured in his jacket pocket.

It was late afternoon. The house was dark. The shutters had not been opened for weeks. He found a bed, lay on it and recounted the eventful last few days.

The last words that Pollock said to him as they took off from west London were, 'The art of successful ballooning is uneventful flying.' It hadn't quite turned out that way. They had the English Channel, eight hundred miles of French countryside and the Massif Central to traverse, crosswinds that seemed intent on taking them over the trench system and a new system of steering that Pollock was trying out for the first time. To be fair to the commander he was a superb balloonist and it hadn't taken him long to get used to the effect of the weight of the heavy aero engine that the balloon had to lift. They landed daily at pre-designated stops to pick up helium for the balloon and aviation fuel for the engine whose propeller pushed them towards their destination.

They took off in the early mornings into the warming air

and landed in the evenings when thermal activity was at its lowest. Pollock used all his experience and skill to coincide this with the locations of the provisions. Hamish was amazed when Pollock showed him how winds gusted in different directions at differing altitudes. Now he understood how Pollock would return to England. 'It'll be quicker on the way back,' Pollock shouted, 'I can use the outer reaches of the Gulf Stream.'

They stopped west of Paris, trained into the city for a spot of entertainment and good food and returned with a crate of champagne to find the balloon basket taken over by a clutch of hens.

Pollock gave Hamish a history of ballooning and the new technology available to those that flew them. Hamish wept tears of laughter at the story of how the Germans believed rumours spread by British Intelligence that they had crossed pigeons and parrots to create a super-species capable of verbally delivering messages from spies behind German lines.

But Hamish would remember the beauty most of all. To take off in the early morning mists into the sunshine above and to look down on the French countryside, mountains and lakes, punctuated by the long shadows was a sight that he would never forget. Even the seasoned pilot seemed moved. Occasionally, he turned the engine off and they drifted silently, looking down at centuries of man's endeavours working in harmony with God's creation, with a terrible scar that ran from the Swiss border to the North Sea.

*

Rosa Jouie floated in the shadows of Collioure castle walls and wondered what it would be like to fly amongst the few clouds in the sky above her. She imagined herself to be an unborn child in a mother's fluid, the harbour walls holding her back from the world that she wanted to see. She listened to the sand shifting a few feet under her as the gentle waves lifted her body on their way to the beach. Her long raven hair drifted like seaweed in the current.

This was the highlight of her week, a swim in the warm Mediterranean Sea after the rigours of the days in the vineyards, and the trip to Collioure to collect supplies.

She had lived all of her nineteen years in the little village in the foothills of the mountains. Her loving parents, conservative Catholics, had worked hard all their lives and when Rosa was five years old they had bought a small vineyard below the church. Monsieur Jouie dug up many of the old vines and planted some of the newer, more disease-resistant varieties. These had aged and grew in yield and the reputation of the Jouie's vinification was now unmatched in the area as was the beauty of their daughter. Everything that they now did was for Rosa's future, their bodies beginning to falter after so long in the steep, gravely fields.

Rosa turned over and made for the shore. Even though she had bathed in the harbour many times before she was not immune to its beauty. The terracotta roofs shone below the cloudless blue sky, contrasting perfectly with the dark mountains behind and the green vineyards that clothed their lower slopes as they fell dramatically into the sea. She understood why the Parisian painters made their winter homes here.

But she wanted more. She had been surrounded by beauty all of her young life. But beauty without excitement, without…danger, was to her like eating farmed oysters. Less flavour, less intensity, less chance of finding a pearl amongst the grit.

She dried herself as best she could with the towel and pulled the black dress over her shoulders not bothering to remove her damp costume. The white lace at the top drew the eye to her neck and shoulders. Defined but still feminine, they gave hint of the body below.

Leaving the beach through the line of fishing boats she walked past the line of blue restaurant umbrellas that protected the diners below from the sun and occasional rain showers. Even in these autumn months it was still warm enough to eat al fresco. She stared ahead, not wanting to meet the admiring glances. She had learned years before that this was the safest and quickest way to go about her daily life. It was also the kindest for she had had to deflate many egos with gentle words of discouragement. She didn't really understand why she made it so difficult for them to get to know her, but in her rare moments of introspection, she worried that it might be because she did not want to fall in love with a Catalan. Fiercely loyal to their country and their culture just as she was, and passionate in everything that they did, it would take an earthquake of shattering proportions to get them to leave their homeland. Rosa had ambitions of her own. They did not include living here for the rest of her life.

She found her mother where she had left her, standing at the side of their horse that was tied to the railings just below the market. She kissed her and stepped up into the open carriage. Boxes filled the space behind her. Her mother kissed the cheeks of the two ladies that she had been talking to and reached up to Rosa who helped her to the seat beside her.

'Good swim?' she asked her daughter in Catalan.

'Yes, mama,' Rosa replied. She flicked the reigns and the horse slowly moved off up the gentle slope in the direction of Laroque des Alberes, two hours away.

*

Sunlight streamed into the room as Hamish awoke from twenty hours' sleep. He yawned and stretched out the stiffness in his muscles. Despite the ordeal of the balloon ride and the weeks on the run, he felt fit and light on his feet as he opened the shutters to the rooms that he thought he would use that day. Dust rose into the sunbeams as if the furniture itself were breathing the fresh air for the first time in weeks.

He stood on the huge orange veranda and took a deep breath

of the pine-scented air, listening to the sound of the garden in front of him. He tried to make out the insects that were making so much noise. Hamish could not imagine enough grasshoppers needed to make this high-pitched hubbub but he was sure that this was what had awakened him.

Hungry but happy he went downstairs, opened the front door onto the narrow street and went in search of food.

The months that he had spent in northern France had not prepared him for survival on his own in a Catalan village. He had picked up a few French words, enough to be able to buy a beer or a plate of sausage and chips but not much more. As he walked through the honeycomb of streets and alleys he realised that he was, for all intents and purposes, in a different country to the one in which he had fought. The red and yellow striped flags of Catalonia hung everywhere, in the bunting that zigzagged its way up at first-floor height between opposing rows of houses, above the Marie and the Church, even hanging below the bread and cheese for sale in what appeared to be open-sided living rooms. Bottles of local wine stood between huge vegetables and beige flagons of olive oil.

The clothes were different too. Whereas the French and Flemish of the North had worn simple, formal clothing, here the dresses and shirts were more embroidered, with lace seeming to border every edge. Even the waistcoats were tied together with leather lace.

Every girl over the age of twelve, it appeared to Hamish as he wandered, wore a long, gold chain around their necks, suspending a locket between their breasts. The men wore dark suits over white shirts and ties, topped with flat or peaked cloth caps, an image that Hamish thought looked faintly ridiculous as old men stopped for breathers as they staggered their way up the steep, shuttered streets in the bright sunshine.

Goats, horses and cattle roamed the streets, often unsupervised and occasionally Hamish had to step into the gutters to let them pass.

He bought an Excelsior newspaper at the tabac for ten centimes and sat at a table by a bar, shaded by palms. He ordered a red wine and pommes frites and looked at the paper. The front page was a large photograph of the Tsar and Tsarevich visiting the Russian Front, saluting a Russian officer who held a sword in a formal and threatening manner.

Hamish reflected on what had taken place over the past few months. *So much had happened to him. Was it fate? Or did these sorts of things normally happen to people who put themselves in harm's way and then did everything they could to survive. It happened to people in books. He had loved listening to his father reading how the heroes of Rider Haggard had faced exotic trials and tribulations again and again.*

Hamish allowed himself a brief moment of self-congratulation. 'I have survived,' he whispered as he sipped on the wine. A lizard appeared on his table and looked him in the eye. Hamish looked away and his complacency evaporated as he saw the lorries arrive.

*

The convoy of green transports came to a halt at the bottom of the hill, just below where Hamish sat, a red cross against a white background on their sides. Soldiers and nurses jumped down from the cabins, drew back the pins at the side of the rear barriers and placed wooden steps on the road. Slowly the men made their way into the sunshine, blinking where bandages did not cover their eyes.

'Les blessés,' said the waiter.

They both watched as more men stepped down to the ground, many on crutches, most holding onto their helpers. Many had an arm or leg missing, sometimes both. They wore coats even though the day was warm. A nurse brought a small wooden cart, only just bigger than a child's go-cart from one of the lorries and with the help of a doctor, gingerly lowered one of the men into it.

She gave the long handle to a man with one arm to pull, and moved on to attend to the rest.

When the lorries were emptied of their cargo, the sad party set off up one of the boulevards lined by the plane trees that Hamish had seen all over France. The tree bark reminded him of the camouflage suits that Randle had made. A cyclist rode past the pathetic line of men and shouted, 'Vive la France, viva Catalonia,' his fist raised high above his head. He got no reply.

*

The screech of the peacocks met Ken Downing as he opened the car door and stepped onto the gravel drive. He remembered the old house. How could he forget? It wasn't just the size of the place; it was the elegant dimensions and restrained use of Palladian principles that most appealed to the eye. A pet cemetery rested in the middle of the garden, surrounded by topiary tunnels and statues that overlooked the ha-ha. As Ken reached the bottom of the steps to the front door a voice said, 'Yes, may I help you?'

Ken saw the butler blocking his way to the door. 'Yes, you may. I have come to see Sir Alfred.'

'He doesn't have visitors in the morning. He does his papers. You should have phoned or written to make an appointment.'

'I see,' said Ken. 'In that case, please will you tell Sir Alfred that I am staying at the Bull in the village. I have information about Gerald that may interest him.' Ken turned and went down the steps.

The butler's jaw dropped. 'I say, you can't expect....what did you say your name was?'

'I didn't,' replied Ken. He walked to his car and slowly drove back up the long drive. It wasn't long before he saw the large car in his rear-view mirror, as expected. He slowed to let the car pass and it stopped no more than ten feet in front. The driver got out and strode earnestly towards Ken's car, holding a walking stick in his fist. He peered into Ken's open window.

'What do you want? Who are you?' And then his expression changed. He looked unsure of himself. 'I know you.'

'Get in the other side,' ordered Ken. Slowly, the old man obeyed.

'What do you want?' asked a distinctly less aggressive Sir Alfred, once he had taken his seat.

'Sir Alfred, I wish neither you nor your family any harm. But I have reason to believe that Gerald Sutcliffe knew about my son's disappearance.' Ken looked straight ahead. He could imagine the conflicting and extreme emotions going through the old boy's head; he didn't want to embarrass him any more than was necessary. The threat of it was far more frightening than the experience of it and he *did* want to frighten him.

'What do you mean, 'knew?' Where is he? Is he alright?'

'No, sir, he is dead. Died on a raid on the German trenches.'

'Dead? God, no! The poor man.' Sir Alfred's eyes welled up.

Ken waited until the man composed himself. 'When was the last time you saw him?'

'I haven't seen him since…who are you?'

'I visited your house many times in a professional capacity some years ago. I now work for Her Majesty's Government.'

'The Government? What the hell was Gerald up to?' asked Sir Alfred.

Ken turned to Sir Alfred. He needed to see his eyes. There was genuine sadness mixed with a yearning there. 'We need you to find that out for us, sir.'

'Me? How am I supposed to find out anything about Gerald?'

'Do you know where he went after your disagreement?'

'How do know about that?' asked Sir Alfred.

'Sir, it was my business to know as much as possible about as many people as possible, in my area of interest. Which was people like you…..and Gerald.'

The old man's eyes bored into Ken's. He could see that Ken meant what he said. 'And if I don't?'

'Then we will let it be known in the village that you had an unsavoury relationship with your previous gamekeeper.'

'Who would believe you?'

Ken withdrew a bundle of letters from his inside jacket pocket. 'As many as we want to believe it, sir.'

Sir Alfred was stunned. 'You…you cad! Those are mine!' He grabbed for the letters. Ken caught the man's thumb with his free hand. He twisted and pulled in one movement until it dislocated. Sir Alfred screamed and Ken let go.

'Be under no misunderstanding, sir, that this is a deadly serious matter. If you whisper a word of this investigation to anyone, we spread the news and release a couple of these letters.' He took out a piece of paper from his jacket pocket and gave it to Sir Alfred. 'I expect a call on this number by the end of November. Use your wits, you must have heard where he went after he left you.' He leant over and opened the passenger door. The man got out nursing his thumb and kicked the door shut. Ken gunned the engine and drove past the stationary car towards the gates to the estate. He smiled. *'Thus the whirligig of time brings in his revenges'* he thought. He had wanted to do that to one of the bastards for years.

*

Hamish finished his meal, paid the waiter and walked off up the hill. He guessed that all roads ran towards a central point somewhere near the top of the village. He reached the village square a few minutes later just as the shops closed. The bells of Eglise de Saint Felix et Saint Blaise rang the hour on the far side and five minutes later they rang again. Hamish was intrigued. Surely the peels must have come from different churches.

The square was bedecked with long tables covered with white cloths. Women in yellow shirts and red neckerchiefs walked back and forth from the bar on Hamish's right with cutlery and glasses. A cart appeared and a small man with a stoop staggered to the nearest table with huge bunches of red gladiolis. On a stage at the back of the square, below the rear wall of the church, an African woman blew into her saxophone while a boy strummed harmonies on his guitar. Dogs and cats mooched around the tables. The shutters in the houses surrounding the square were ajar, their owners hoping to keep the light out of their bedrooms before they retired for their siestas but still wanting to hear the sounds of the square being prepared for the festivities.

Hamish walked over to the bar and sat on a bench under the window. He ordered another glass of wine, and asked the waitress, 'à quelle heure?' He nodded to the square.

'à cinq heures monsieur. Vouz avez une invitation?'

'Non. Je suis Anglais, Mademoiselle.' *It's amazing how often I've said that*, Hamish thought.

'Ah. Il faut que vous aviez une invitation pour la fête monsieur.'

Hamish looked at her blankly.

She smiled and shouted something into the dark interior of the bar. An unshaven man with red-rimmed eyes appeared, scratching his ample stomach through the dirty vest. He was about forty years old and had a scowl that would have done justice to a Parisian sewer worker.

'Vous êtes Anglais?'

'Oui,' replied Hamish squinting at the man under his open hand.

'You need an invitation for the fete.'

'I know. How do I get one?'

'You cannot.'

'I see. Can I sit here, then?'

'Non.'

'Why not? I will drink your wine.'

'All day?'

'Oui, all day.'

'D'accord monsieur,' said the barman in a 'you know you will regret it' manner. The barman took the wine list from the waitress and opened it.

'You choose a bottle,' he said without charm as he gave it to Hamish who was enjoying himself hugely.

'I'll have a bottle of the Bisconte please. I think I saw a sign for the vineyard when I arrived.'

'Oui monsieur, you did.' And then he disappeared muttering something about 'Les Anglais' under his breath.

Hamish sat back and took in his surroundings. A wall, about forty feet high protected the square from the north, behind which lay a row of orange-pink houses that rose towards to the top of the hill. To the west ran the wall of the church, windowless in its mystery. Another group of ancient houses formed a barrier to the south, but the east was open. Over the roof of the Marie below, with the words 'Liberté, Egalité, and Fraternité' engraved below its roofline, Hamish could see the sweep of the Vermillion bay as it passed across Argèles and Perpignan.

That afternoon, in the hours before he fell asleep on the bench Hamish experienced a high that nearly made his recent experiences worthwhile. He managed to understand from an old man sitting near him that the church did indeed ring out twice, on the hour and five minutes later so that anyone working the vineyards in the small valleys surrounding the hill would have twice the chance of hearing it.

He found that his French seemed to improve with the quantity of liquor that he drank. Words that he had not spoken since school at fourteen seemed to come to him out of nowhere.

In the far, darkest corner of the square, four men, dressed in red and yellow dragged a huge, black, metal dish on a wheeled frame to a position under the plane tree and lit a fire in the grate under the dish. A long table was placed nearby and the men worked feversishly on onions, garlic, peppers, tomatoes, spices, mussels and the biggest shrimps that Hamish had ever seen. The ingredients were poured into the hot oil and stirred with six-foot long paddles, not unlike the ones that he and Jim had used to row the river Severn. He watched the bowls of water passing, person to person, across the square from the bar to the dish, as if there was a fire that needed putting out. The water hissed and steamed as it was poured into the mixture.

*

Hamish awoke with a start. The band made its way up the slope to the square in front of where he sat, head leaning against the terracotta flowerpot on the windowsill. The glass was still in his hand but the red wine had spilt onto his white shirt and down the right leg of his corduroy trousers.

'Bugger,' he said out loud. Some of the people sitting around his table looked at him, then his clothes, then at the empty bottles of wine on the table, and they smiled sympathetically.

Hamish held his head in his hands and stood up too quickly. He tottered and had to spread his feet to stop himself from falling into the table. He held onto the wall as he made his way towards the entrance to the bar and ran across the empty room and found the toilet just in time to empty the contents of his stomach. He kneeled on the footings of the latrine until the retching stopped. Slowly he rose, washed his face and hands in the sink and re-entered the bar area using the wall as a prop as he went.

'You are not used to the alcohol, I think,' said the barman, drying a glass.

'I used to be, Monsieur,' replied Hamish.

'Here, have some Pernod and water. It is good for the breath.' He winked at Hamish as he passed him the drink.

'Thank you. I am sorry for messing your toilet.'

'It will be worse by tomorrow morning. This is our biggest night of the year. The fête de Paella. Very Catalan, very noisy, lots of passion.' He winked again. 'Catalan ladies are the most beautiful in the world, I think. You are English. This is good for you. Because you are not French, nor Spanish. And you are brave, as you fight the Hun.'

Both men looked at each other. The silence was painful. Hamish could sense the barman's confusion about his presence in the village. 'Monsieur, if you are a deserter then you are amongst friends here. This is a town of 'passeurs'. We have lived off the secret movement of people and merchandise for hundreds of years. The area is riddled with paths that only the local people know. The towers that you see at the top of hills were built to allow us to see when pirates were coming, so we are good at hiding people. The church here is a 'salle d'armes,' where the village people would go when the bells didn't stop. One small window to the south, monsieur, near the roof. You can't get in that way, even if you are a pirate. Hannibal used our people as guides when he took his elephants over the Col de Perthus more than two thousand years ago. For a small fee we can get you over the border to Spain. It is not a border that we recognise anyway. Ours is further south, below Barcelona.'

'What's your name?' asked Hamish.

'Luis. Luis de Soto.'

'And I am Hamish Rutherford. Yes, I am a deserter Luis, but I have to stay in the village for a while. A wealthy relative has let me use his house here. When the time comes, I will pay you well for your silence and for passage over the mountains.'

'Let's drink to that, monsieur.' Luis grabbed his brandy from the bar, and they clinked glasses. 'If I were you Hamish, I would take advantage of the hospitality.' He nodded to the party that was getting into full swing outside. 'Would you like to help me serve the drinks? I'll tell you what people want. You can deliver.'

*

He sat in the middle of the long table, below the high wall that ran along the side of the square between the bar and the church. He was sweating and exhilarated. Hamish had been on his feet for four hours and his clothes were a palette of splashes from the drinks he had served, and he had loved every minute of it. The other tables in front of him had been cleared and happy, drunken people danced to the Latin band music in the space vacated.

'Votre paella monsieur.' It was the waitress that Hamish had spoken to earlier. 'Gracieusement offert par Luis.'

Hamish looked along the long bench and saw his new friend leaning against the entrance to the bar. They raised their glasses to each other. Hamish looked at the food in front of him and breathed deeply on the vapours. 'Very Catalan,' he said as he realised that the colours of the dish mirrored the flags around him. He prized open the mussel with his knife and was about to scrape the contents into his mouth when a voice said, 'Not eat, monsieur, not eat.' A hand gently took the shellfish from Hamish's hand and put it on the table by the side of his plate.

Hamish looked up at her, his mouth open like a stunned fish. 'I am sorry, monsieur, but that moule is perhaps…how do you say…. poisoned.'

Hamish's mind raced. 'Who by?' he said, looking suspiciously around the party.

Rosa giggled, covering her mouth with her delicate fingers, her eyes reflecting the fire-torches that hung from the wall behind him.

'No one. You must eat these, the open ones. Not closed ones. They make sick.' Rosa mimed someone retching.

'How did you know I was English?'

'Everyone knows you are English. You serve us drinks but cannot speak French or Spanish. Also you have red hair. So we find out you are English.'

'I speak French. A little.'

'Oui, bien sûr, mon ami.'

'Now you are making fun of me.'

'Oui, bien sur, mon ami.' She giggled again.

Hamish crossed his arms and leant back against the wall. He was intrigued at the unaffected confidence of the girl. 'What is your name?'

'My name is Rosa Jouie, Hamish.'

'Your English is good.'

'I have an aunt who lives in London. I have stayed there sometimes.'

'Will you dance?' he asked.

'I will love to dance with you.' She held her hand out and they walked the length of the table, the other diners ducking under their arms as the couple went by. She untied the red bandana and shook out her hair, letting it cascade down her dress.

'Rosa. Elle danse avec l'Anglais,' a girl shouted from a first story balcony. Rosa blew her friend a kiss and guided Hamish to the dance floor. People turned to watch the couple find their way to the middle of the floor.

'Do you dance jazz?' asked Rosa.

'No. Irish.'

'D'accord Hamish. I dance jazz, you dance Irish.'

'No contest,' said Hamish in his best Dublin accent. He put his hands on his hips and stamped his heels on the cobbles, the nails in his boots sending sparks flying as he circled an impressed Rosa. He didn't care if it wasn't in time with the music. It was what he knew and it worked for him.

And the smile on Rosa's face said that it worked for her too.

*

Hamish lay in his bed, staring at the cicada preening itself on one of the slats in the shutter. He could clearly see its four front legs rubbing against one another and then occasionally one of them would go to its mouth, as if it were trying to feast on the remaining debris of last night's meal. Hamish couldn't work out if he was fascinated or revolted at this beast that was so much larger than the 'hoppers back home.

Rosa had been right. He would have a hangover, or 'gueule de bois' as she called them. He closed his eyes and put one of the pillows over his head, trying to silence the din from the garden.

He looked back on the previous day. After disgracing himself in the afternoon, the evening had been what he and Jim called a 'brigger', a made-up word that could mean being drunk, or getting into trouble, or getting off with a girl. Anything that was worth an hour's retelling and embellishment. Except that Hamish had no one to tell and no need to exaggerate.

The first dance with Rosa had been a typical cock-and-hen affair with Hamish throwing his legs and arms around in the way that many did at the Free 'n Easy, a drunken mixture of Irish and Gypsy. Rosa had countered with a quickening flamenco in the imaginary circle that Hamish had made for her while the other dancers backed away from the gyrations and flying kicks.

When the music stopped everyone clapped the band and started shouting 'Sardana, Sardana.' The band complied and as the first bars were played by the wind instruments the dancers got into groups, holding hands at head height in circles of different sizes. Even those who had appeared happy to watch now joined in. Children, old men even. A leader was appointed for each circle as if by telepathy and the groups rotated as one in time with the music. Each group except Hamish's. The sympathetic expressions of earlier had disappeared as his fellow dancers realised that they had a renegade in their mist and Hamish bowed out, embarrassed.

Rosa stayed in the circle and Hamish watched, entranced at the spectacle of a whole village dancing in harmony. Each circle seemed to have a mind of its own. He ran up the lane behind the bar and leaned over the parapet of the wall that bordered the square, watching the circles turn, always stopping and starting at the same moment, without ellipse or pause. They reminded Hamish of the wheels that turned the belts on the side of the new threshing machines that toured the farms in late summer, only far more beautiful.

He watched Rosa look for him when the Sardana finished

and he whistled and waved to her from the wall above. She ran up the lane to join him and hugged him as if to reassure him. Then she took him to the small tower at the top of the village that stood behind another labyrinth of streets and low arches. It was dark at the top and she held his hand, guiding him over the rough ground. He wondered how many men she had guided up here, until she said that she was surprised how different it was in the dark.

She found the bench at the front of the tower. The sun had gone down an hour before but Hamish could make out the silhouetted feet of the hills as they met the plain to the west. Above and below them lay blackness. The few lights in the valley mirrored the stars above and Rosa said that this was the only place she knew where you could feel like you were floating in the heavens. To close your eyes was to spoil it. Their eyes tracked the red mast lights moving across the bay miles away to the east.

And then they kissed, tentatively at first, but their passions were palpable to each other and they wanted to give more than their experience and respect would allow. They walked back to the party hand in hand and Rosa had introduced Hamish to her parents, who had been looking out for her.

'Vous êtes deserteur?' monsieur Jouie asked. Hamish looked at Rosa and then at his feet.

'Oui monsieur. Je suis deserteur. Mais il est difficile à expliquer…'

The father turned his back on him and led his family away.

But Hamish wasn't going to give up that easily. He could not tell anyone the real reason why he was here, why he felt anything but a deserter. He knew that this girl had fire in her soul. She was courage and passion in one body and she liked him without knowing anything about him.

So as he lay in his bed, he played with his beard and hatched a plan.

12

The man whose passport said his name was Jeremy Hayes walked sleepily to the full-length shutters and opened them to one of the most uplifting sights that he had ever seen. The winter afternoon sun sparkled off the calm green-blue water a hundred feet below him. He put his hand up to shield his eyes as they took in the mountains around the bay and the city in the far corner, about ten miles away. The air was mild and the sun's rays warmed the skin of his almost naked body.

He stretched and placed his palms against the frame of the doorway at shoulder height. Instinctively he pushed himself up so that his long legs hung six inches above the tiled floor. He stayed there, hardly moving for nearly a minute and then gradually lowered himself down before going inside and picking up the towel that sat neatly folded on the dressing table. He caught a glimpse of himself in the mirror and pushed the top back a little so that he could get a better view.

He was not a vain man but he considered that the punishment that his body had taken in the past three months justified the occasional compliment that he paid to it. This was one of those moments. Given that in August his mind and body were shattered, even the harshest critic would admit that he had made extraordinary progress. His hair was completely grey but otherwise he looked like the supremely fit twenty-one-year-old that he was. His head was supported by thick trapezius muscles that curved their way from the back of his skull to the top of his muscular shoulders, his chest was deep and well-defined and the contours of his upper and lower arms only hinted at the deadly power that lay within. The stomach was a mass of muscled knots that were framed by sheaths of smooth sinew which ran from the latissimus muscles at the top of his thighs. Even his jaw was more prominent.

But it was his inner-self that was most enhanced. The

nightmares had gone and so had the scars on his hands. He awoke each morning with a clear head and an eagerness to get into the day. He believed completely in the urgency of the work that he was being prepared to carry out and had been looking forward to this day for a long time.

The training now complete, this was the real thing.

He had been given the relevant documentation, cover story and details of the target and its defences. It would not be an easy job, but at least he did not have to make any pretence that the targets died a natural death. These were marked men, pursued and defended by many.

Jeremy Hayes, known to himself as Jim Downing, got dressed and went downstairs.

'Good evening Jim, did you sleep well?' asked Bernardo Verro.

'Excellently, sir.'

'Are you ready for the task ahead?'

'Yes, sir.'

'Good. I want to say that we are all pleased with the way things have turned out, Jim. From start to completion in three months is unprecedented.'

'I had a good teacher. I've also spent two years in a trench. We learnt a lot about killing.'

'I am sure.' Verro shook Jim's hand. 'Good luck. These are particularly evil people. Much blood on their hands, even women's and children's. There is a saying in Calabrian dialect: 'Nun saacia, nun vidi, nun ceru, e si cere durmiv.' It means, 'I know nothing. I didn't see anything. I wasn't there, and if I was there, I was asleep.' Give them a taste of their own medicine, Jim. They hate socialists like us. Look on it as a trial. If you succeed, we make the targets a little more interesting.' He grinned and watched Jim go out into the garden and down the steps to the sea. He suspected that the targets weren't quite the type that Jim had joined the organisation to kill. Still, it was a test and it removed a threat.

*

Jim tied the small rowing boat to the trawler that lay anchored about a hundred yards from the cliff face, checked the waterproof bag that hung from the belt at his stomach and slipped into the cool, dark water.

He swam slowly at first, making few splashes of white water. There was no moon and he grew more confident that his black clothes and cork-blackened face, hands and feet could not be seen from the cliff above. The current took him from right to left as he pushed on faster. The torches at the entrance to the cave reflected off the surface of the water as he got closer to the low, rock platform. He swam underwater for as long as he could, coming up for air for only a couple of seconds as he had trained to do.

He reached the rock at the far right hand side of the cliff face. He looked along the jetty, saw no one and pulled himself up. He untied the bag at his waist, withdrew the Browning .45 calibre semi-automatic pistol and twisted the sound suppressor onto the barrel. He waited until the water had stopped dripping from his body and moved on towards the entrance to the cave. The rock felt cool against his bare, blackened feet.

Reaching the entrance, he dropped to one knee and peered into the darkness. An overweight man sat on a chair just inside the cave, his chin resting on his chest. Jim slipped the gun into his belt, unclipped the buckle around the hilt of the stiletto knife tied to his left ankle and withdrew it from the sheath. He moved behind the sleeping man, put his hand over the man's mouth whilst pulling his head to the left. The knife entered the man's neck from the right to a depth of four inches. The body tensed as the blade severed his carotid artery and then relaxed. Jim laid the man against the wall of the cave and moved on up the steps, knife and gun in either hand.

As he got near the top of the steps he saw a shape silhouetted against the dim lights of the garden, facing away from him. Jim ran forward, put his outstretched arm over the shoulder of the man and smashed the inside of his forearm against the man's voice box, the other hand punching him hard in the small of his back. Jim caught the unconscious man and gently laid him on the ground, keeping his hand over his mouth and nose until he suffocated.

He moved out into the garden using the bushes and trees for cover. Three guards stood on the walls but they were looking for threats from outside the property, not inside. He reached the pillars that framed the entrance to the glass double doors. They were not locked, to allow free passage to those who defended the target. Once inside the dark house, Jim waited by the door to the cloakroom. His own breathing slowed and he could hear the low murmur of voices further inside the house. He followed the noises until he found himself in a small corridor leading from the galleried hall to the kitchen. Two voices. The training took over. Jim walked slowly away and went up the stairs to the bedrooms where he had been told the targets would be asleep. He found the first one easily, having mentally rehearsed this night using the hand-drawn map and sepia photograph that he had been given in Switzerland. He recognised the face of the man lying alone in his large bed. He didn't hesitate. He grabbed a pillow and pushed it onto the man's face, shooting twice into it as he did so. The body tensed, twitched and then lay still. Jim stayed still for twenty seconds listening to the sounds of the house. Nothing. The sound suppressor had done its job.

He returned to the hall. He closed his eyes to remember the plan of the house, took three steps to his right and slowly turned the door handle and pushed. He walked confidently into the room with the pistol out in front of him, saw the large shape on the bed, pulled at the sheet from the bottom and shot three times into the body. He stopped again and listened to the house. A creak in the corridor. In two strides Jim was at the opening side of the door with his pistol at face height. A man in pyjamas walked down the dark corridor away from him, and went to the bathroom. Jim waited. Ten minutes later the sound of running water alerted Jim to the man's return. He listened as the footsteps passed down the corridor, slowly opened the bedroom door and walked to the door at the end of the hallway. Light shone on his feet. Jim swore under his breath. He waited again. A minute later the light went off and Jim turned the handle and went in. The man in the bed sat up but Jim shot him between the eyes before he could utter a sound. He changed the magazine in the pistol, walked out of the room, down the stairs and out of the same doors through which he had entered. The guards on the walls were in the same position as before. One had lit a cigarette. Jim moved along the stone path and into the entrance to the cave. Keeping his gun and knife ahead of him he descended the damp steps, passing the two bodies as he went. He lowered himself into the water at the end of the platform and swam to the boat. Jim looked back at the cliff. There was no sign of activity.

He rowed out to sea for a while, changed into his dry clothes, and then rowed back to the small harbour below the hotel. The whole operation had taken less than two hours. He would be on a train to Naples at dawn, mingling with the thousands of people yet to read about the deaths in the Tomasi family.

But first he needed a cigarette.

*

Jessie Appleby put the brake of the pram to the 'on' position by the pump at the top of the high street and shook her hair, sending water in all directions. She had tried to hold the open umbrella whilst she pushed the pram with the other hand along the rutted road but it was impossible. The pram's hood and cover kept her child dry while she struggled the three miles into town for the essentials that the local village shop didn't stock. She was soaked to the skin.

The streets of Shrewsbury town centre were deserted. People huddled in doorways trying to keep dry and Jessie could see faces pushed to the windows of the shops. She pulled at the pump handle and filled the metal cup, downing the contents in thirsty gulps. She positioned the pram closer so that the chain attached to the cup reached Poppy from the pump.

'Excuse me,' said a voice behind her. She turned around. A boy, about ten years old stood in front of her, one hand behind his back.

'Yes?' she said.

'I 'bin told to give this to yah. It's 'cos your man was a coward.' He handed her a grey and white feather. It was small, no more than four inches long. Then he laughed and ran away.

Jessie stared at the feather. Spots of water rested on the barbs. She looked up at the miserable scene around her. It seemed as though the whole town was looking back at her, laughing at her from the dry. She flushed and moaned through gritted teeth. *'I will not cry,'* she said to herself. *'I will not cry!'*

She let the cup and the feather drop and pushed her pram back down the street, only realising the brake was still on after a few paces. The metal cup swung on its chain, clanging on the pump as she raced back down the hill.

*

It was Saturday evening and the bells for six o'clock mass rang through the streets of the village and into the valleys below. The silver haired man pulled on the hoops at the bottom of two ropes that dropped from the belfry into the small church, smiling to the people as they drifted in through the small opening in the thick wooden doors. A queue formed as they waited to dip right hands into the bowl of cool water. They genuflected in well-practiced, fluent movements like a conjurer making a card appear out of an empty hand and idly found their places in the pews, talking to friends as they went.

Rosa and her mother took their seats towards the front, kneeled and prayed.

Just as the door was being closed a clean-shaven Hamish stepped through, nodded to the black-suited old gentlemen standing at the back and found a place just behind where Rosa knelt.

It had taken Hamish a week of waiting in the shadows opposite the church entrance at six o'clock for Rosa to appear. He did not know where this girl lived, in fact he knew next-to-nothing about her and he didn't want to ask anyone in case it aroused suspicions. He knew from experience how small towns loved intrigue and he didn't want Rosa's father to look on him as a threat any more than he already did.

Now that he knew that Rosa attended Saturday mass, he had waited another week. He had shaved this afternoon, hoping that she would appear today as well. His experience of women told him that they were creatures of habit. That was about the only predictable thing about them. He hoped that his beard had become the signature of l'Anglais in the way that a kilt was only worn by a Scot. Without it he could be anonymous for a while, just long enough to give Rosa a message.

The pale pink plaster that covered the walls extended upwards and met in the centre of the ceiling. There were no beams, no paintings or murals. Even the walls were bare apart from small wooden crosses in line with the end of the pews. There were not even any windows and yet the church was bathed in light. Hamish looked behind him and right at the top of the rear wall, just where Luis said it was, a small window, no more that a foot square burnt with western light.

His moment came at the altar rail. Hamish positioned himself to Rosa's right, on the other side to her mother. Rosa closed her eyes while she prayed, only opening them to take the bread. He had been confirmed and had no idea if he was allowed to take communion in a Catholic church and frankly he didn't care; religion had never been a particularly important thing in the Rutherford household.
After he had eaten the bread Hamish swiftly withdrew from the rail and in the same movement placed the small folded piece of paper between Rosa's shoe and her heel. She didn't flinch.

Later, as the congregation filtered out of the church Hamish stood in the queue behind her.

'Look in your shoe,' he whispered. She turned around and gasped as she recognised the smooth-skinned man who had knelt next to her at the altar.

Hamish put a finger to her lips and moved past her through the door.

He grinned as he made his way to his favourite bar and tried to put away the thought that the next twenty-four hours could decide how happy the rest of his life would be.

*

Rosa went straight into the small vineyard as soon as she and her mother reached the Romengas' house. Guests milled around in the large hall but she made her excuses and went to the rear of the house. She had felt the note as she walked down the hill and as she talked idly to her mother she felt a rush of excitement and frustration. Who was this man? This mysterious Englishman who couldn't dance and seemed both hopelessly naive yet somehow…. knowing. It was in his eyes. There was so much that he wanted to tell her but couldn't. She could see that. She had heard horrible stories about the war in the north, of the terrible losses there and in the Alps. Hundreds of Italian deserters had passed through the village on their way to Spain. They were accompanied by a spatter of French and even some Germans. But this was the first Englishman. Indeed this was the first Englishman that she had met for many years, apart from her teacher, a thin, gaunt man who was drinking and smoking his way to an early grave.

She leant against the toilet wall and took off her shoe. She opened the note and read,

'Dear Rosa, I think that I have fallen in love with you, but is that possible in an hour? Will you meet me at the gate to the path that goes into the hills, opposite the church door, tomorrow evening at five? I respect your father's feelings about me but I am not what he thinks I am. Please do not ask me about this. Hamish Rutherford.'

She put the note back in her shoe and went back to the party hoping that her cheeks were not too red.

*

She walked past the church and saw Hamish waiting at the gate. She put her hands behind her back and sauntered lazily up the gravely road towards him, occasionally pretending to see something interesting on the ground in front of her.

'Good evening, mister Rutherford,' she said cheekily.

'Bon vesper senyorita Jouie,' he replied.

'Catalan! You spoke Catalan!'

'Un poc tros, senyorita.'

Rosa skipped with delight, and pulled him up the path into the woods.

'Come, we must go before we are seen.'

They climbed the steep path, sometimes clambering over rocks until they came to a man-made stream that formed a 'T' with the little canal that ran past where they had walked.

'This is how we water the fields and clean the streets,' said Rosa as she pointed to the sluice gate. 'We go right. Always go against the current for the hills, with the current for the villages and the sea.' Hamish smiled at her sympathetically. Rosa marched off embarrassed at saying something so obvious.

Ten minutes later, she stopped and held Hamish's hand. She pointed into the shadow of a bush that overhung the path. 'Dragonfly,' he said.

'Libel-lula. Libel-lula negre. They are tame. Watch.' Rosa walked forward slowly, holding her arm out in front of her. To Hamish's astonishment, one landed on Rosa's open hand, and then another.

He held his hand out and walked towards her. A dragonfly alighted on his fingertip. He brought his hand closer and studied the insect, now no more than six inches from his face.

'It's beautiful,' he said and the dragonfly flew away.

'We are lucky. These are rare. Tomorrow they will be gone.' Rosa blew the dragonflies off her fingers and walked on, followed by an enchanted Hamish. He turned as he walked, holding his hand up for the dragonflies to land on.

They reached the pools half an hour later. Water cascaded over the smooth grey rocks above and splashed into the pool in front of them. The couple looked at one another, hoping that the other was thinking the same. Rosa pulled the blue dress over her shoulders, kicked off her shoes and removed her white knickers. She walked over the pebbles and dived into the water.

Her face slowly appeared. Hamish could see her breasts and long legs through the clear brown water.

'Come in Hamish. It is English cold.'

Hamish removed his shoes and socks and undid his waistcoat and shirt.

Rosa looked at her Englishman removing his clothes and tried unsuccessfully not to smile. She had to put her mouth below the water to stop him hearing her giggles. She had no idea what this was leading to but it didn't scare her. Her life had recently come to an unexpected crossroads. She could either take the high road or the low road. This man would decide for her. She would not push him.

Hamish stood naked on the edge of the pool facing her, his hands on his hips. He had never shown his adult body to a woman before, not even to his mother. If someone had asked him three months ago whether he would rather attack a German trench single-handedly or strip in front of a woman that he hardly knew, he would have picked up a gun and jumped into no-man's-land.

This was not how he expected it to be. He smiled back at her, feeling that he was being tested and that he was doing well. He dived in and swore as the cold mountain water drenched his nerve endings.

'Bloody hell. It's fucking freezing,' he shouted before he could help himself, as his head cleared the surface.

Rosa laughed. 'Yes, it is cold, isn't it!'

They treaded water for a while, waiting for the other to say something. The reflections from the pond danced on their faces and on the leaves above their heads.

'What would you say if someone saw us?' asked Hamish.

'I would say that the priest told me to do this, to cleanse you of your sins.'

'What sins?'

'Passing notes at communion is not a sin in England?'

'I don't know. I've never tried it.'

Rosa laughed again. 'You are a funny man, Hamish.'

'Will you go out with me, Rosa?'

'We've only just got in,' she toyed.

'No, I mean as boyfriend and girlfriend.'

'My father does not approve of you.'

'He doesn't know me.'

'And you know me?'

'In England if you see someone naked, you know them.'

'I do not think that you know me, Hamish.'

'Yes. Yes I do, Rosa.'

'And who am I?'

He paused. This was the harvest weather question. Get it wrong and you were poor for a year. Get it right, and….

'The most b….' He paused again. She was more than that. 'I see me in you, Rosa, and the pieces that I wish I had. I see fun, defiance, sympathy, love. I see a need to understand the world, to experience things that most people don't know even exist. God knows, the stuff that I have seen this year has made me realise that there is so much more out there than you can possibly imagine. Some of it is frightening, Rosa. But we can change things for the better, so long as you have….beliefs. Fate is lazy, sometimes you have to kick him. I see this belief in you also.'

'I thought fate was a woman,' replied Rosa.

'A man, definitely a man.'

Rosa looked at Hamish and then sank below the surface. She dived to the bottom of the pool and put her fingers into some of the gaps between the rocks. She rose to the surface and put her cupped hands out towards Hamish so that he could see what they held. As the water and the sand fell through her fingers he saw them. Black dragonfly wings.

'I agree,' she said. 'Life is too short. I do not want to be a dragonfly. And I *will* be your girlfriend.'

*

Over the next few weeks Hamish and Rosa became inseparable, not even bothering to hide their relationship. They walked into the hills, ate together at the safe house and in cafes and once her father had resigned himself to the pointlessness of resisting young love, Hamish had even accompanied Rosa and her mother into Collioure.

One evening, on the way back from riding in the mountains, they made love for the first time. The snow was heavy as they came off the mountains and Rosa took Hamish to a shepherd's lodge. They tied the horses up in the stable and lit a fire with the flint that was lying to the side of the grate. Rosa showed Hamish how to uncork a bottle of wine with her thumb and index finger and they stripped off their wet clothes.

Hamish lowered Rosa onto the sheepskin in front of the fire, kissing her as he did so. His hand slid up her side and stroked her breast. She gasped as he turned her nipple between his fingers and her hand went between his legs. His cock hardened in her hand and she gently massaged him until she thought he would come. Grabbing his hand she guided him to the soft flesh above her wetness. She groaned into the gap between his chest and his arm, kissing him feverishly as she approached climax.

He leant over her, moved her legs further apart and pushed his manhood into her, gently at first and then thrusting hard and fast as she implored him to.

*

Lying on the rug once their breathing had become shallower, Hamish asked Rosa to marry him. She accepted on condition that her parents agreed. They rode back to the village in the morning, the happiest that either had ever been. Hamish took Rosa to her home but finding that her parents were not there, he took the horses back to the stables and walked home alone.

He turned the key in the lock, walked into the dark hall and closed the door.

A voice in the darkness said, 'Stop right there, Rutherford.'

Hamish did as he was told. A faceless man stood in the shadow cast by the shade of the standard lamp

'Please sit down. Thank you. I work for Cumming. Prepare yourself, Rutherford. I am afraid that I have some bad news for you. Your father is dead.'

'What?'

'He died two weeks ago.'

'How?'

'We think it was meant to look like a heart attack.'

'What do you mean 'meant to look like'?'

'We did an autopsy and found a tiny hole in his breastbone and heart.'

Hamish looked at the man, stunned.

'Neville Milton's father drowned two days later, so we had a Home Office pathologist look at your father and he found the hole under magnification.'

'Jesus. Does Neville know?'

'He will do by now.'

Hamish put his head in his hands. 'I have to get back.'

'I am ordered not to let you do that. You see, we believe that somehow this organisation of yours has found out that you and Mr. Milton may have escaped from the trenches. They did what they needed to do to get you to come out of hiding.'

'But I must go to the farm!' Hamish picked up the coffee table and threw it against the wall.

'No, you must not, Rutherford. Special Branch is protecting your family and Mr. Milton's family. They are safe. We do not think that the organisation will come for them. They have nothing to gain. We will be at the funerals should they turn up looking for you and Neville. But we need to take the fight to them'

'How?'

'Ken Downing was given a few names by someone he used to know when he was working undercover. So we put a tap on their phones.'

'A tap?'

He signed. 'It's a listening device. One of the names spoke to a Bernardo Verro in Sorrento, Italy, about preparations for next year. Vernon Kell didn't like the transcripts of those telephone calls, particularly when he was told by Ken that Jim and Verro met a couple of years ago. So we are going to pay him a visit. You leave on a boat from Collioure this afternoon.'

'This afternoon….? But why me?'

'Because you are a bloody good soldier, Rutherford, and Kell and Cumming thought you might like to talk to the chap who saved your friend. We link up with a Royal Navy frigate in three days time. You will be joined by a squad of Lovat Scouts who, by chance are on their way to Flanders from Salonika. Cumming thinks the Italian navy isn't up to the job, particularly in that region.'

'Lovat scouts!' exclaimed Hamish. 'Even Randle admired that lot.' Hamish stared at the floor, trying to collect his thoughts. 'Where's Neville?' he asked.

'Still in London, again protected. His work is too important to the war effort for him to help you, I am afraid. Quite a gentleman is your friend.'

'I know. I've seen him play cards. How will my family cope without Dad?' Hamish wiped the tears off his cheeks with the back of his hand.

'They'll have to fend for themselves I am afraid. All departments' budgets have been stripped bare by the war. We can't help them.'

Hamish suddenly stood up. 'Randle's mother! If they know that Neville and I escaped they will work out that Randle must have known. He reported back that we had been taken prisoner!'

'They may not know for definite that you escaped. Men literally vaporise if they receive a direct hit from a shell. And the Germans behind their lines might have shot you. They would know for sure if you attended the funerals.'

'Or if you were waiting for them.'

The man thought for a moment.

'I see your point. We will be discrete.'

'Christ, if you screw up, Randle's mum is dead. So is Randle,' said Hamish.

'There are a lot more than a few people at stake here, Hamish. If we are right about the seriousness of this conspiracy, the future of democracy in Europe is threatened. I have packed your bags. We leave now!'

'Now? But I have to say goodbye….'

'Don't be stupid, Rutherford. The more people who know you, the more you put in danger. Particularly the ones you care for. This is the way that this group appears to work. It's the same with the Orientals. Revenge is carried out on those you love, leaving you to grieve for the rest of your life. Nasty, but effective. Now move. I have a motorbike in the garage.'

*

Jim watched the lively party over the top of his coffee mug from the cafe on the other side of the road. He sat with another man whom he knew only as 'Red'. They had exchanged small talk for an hour over the meal of omelette and bread. Red's English was faulting but they had managed to get along fine, sharing their interest in books and politics. They never discussed the target; this had all been worked out in the hotel beforehand.

Prague's red-light district was starting to warm up. Scantily-clad women walked up and down the street outside, looking incongruous with their frozen breath and gloved hands. Shutters opened onto window displays that did their best to distract Jim from the task-in-hand.

Jim had noticed the two heavily-set men guarding the entrance to the restaurant opposite. He had no intention of challenging them. His training had taught him many things, the most striking being the importance of patience. If that meant waiting for hours or even days for a target to present itself, then so be it. Better to endure the discomforts before a hit when you were in control of your environment, than face the consequences of an operation gone wrong.

Jim pulled his coat collar up, sank into his chair and nodded to Red. It was understood. They would take it in turns to watch the party. Jim fell asleep almost immediately.

He felt the kick to his feet and opened his eyes. Red was getting ready to leave and Jim followed. As they stepped into the street, Jim saw the group of men leaving the restaurant, laughing and back-slapping as they walked along. Jim and Red followed for a few minutes and at the pre-arranged signal, Jim turned into a side street and jogged around the block. A minute later he was at a corner looking back on the group. He curled his right hand into a tight fist and squeezed the muscles in his forearm. The needle inside the brace dropped and with pressure from his left hand it clicked into place. He opened the small bottle in his coat pocket with his other hand and smeared the alcohol around his lips, enjoying the taste. Then he stepped into the street.

He remembered a teacher once telling him that to act drunk on the stage was one of the most difficult thespian challenges. Too obvious and it looked contrived; too little and the audience would think you couldn't act. So he walked slowly and stared into the distance, veering towards but not looking at the approaching group of men. The target was obvious. He was small and surrounded. The firecrackers went off when Jim was about ten feet away from the target. The group turned to see where the noises were coming from and Jim staggered into them, right forearm horizontal.

'Get out of my way!' he said in English. The target turned to face Jim as he brushed passed. They looked at each other. Jim carried on through the group and along the street, without looking back. No-one called out.

The group continued towards the square for another fifty metres, joking with each other about who had jumped the highest when the firecrackers had gone off. Only when he was a good distance away did Jim turn and watch. The men stopped in the middle of the square and debated which direction to take. Then the small man dropped to his knees and fell forward onto his face. His arms stayed by his side; he was dead before he hit the ground.

Jim turned the corner into the next street, took off his hat and pocketed it. As he came to the crossroads he nodded to Red and the two men walked towards the station. *This beats strawberries, any day,' thought Jim.*

13

The small converted trawler entered the Bay of Naples on a dull November dawn. The distinctive shape of Vesuvius rose to the north above the bustling city and the newly exposed ruins of Pompeii. The island of Capri rose to the south, its hills wrapped in cloud. Sorrento lay straight ahead.

Hamish stood in the cabin with the Captain Bob Healy. 'Captain' was probably too strong a word for the role that Healy played. With a crew of two including himself, the personal qualities that he was required to show in carrying out his job did not include an ability to lead legions of men into battle. A lean, mean, sailing machine as the Orsini undoubtedly was, it was rarely called upon to do anything other than transport individuals and special equipment around the Mediterranean on behalf of the British Secret Services. Its main route ran between Gibraltar, Malta and Cyprus. He and his crew just got on with the job and didn't ask questions.

'The most beautiful bay in the Med, and that's saying something,' said Healy in his Hampshire accent. 'And the most dangerous.'

Hamish looked at Healy. 'Because of the volcano?'

'Aye. And the earthquakes and the tidal waves. And the pirates.'

'Pirates?'

'Oh yes. They didn't all die out after Captain Long John Silver you know, and they don't raise the Jolly Roger and swing from the rigging flashing their sabres neither. In these parts they sneak up on you pretending to be something else and then slit your throat while they shake your hand. The straits that we came through yesterday between Corsica and Sardinia, 'Bonfacio' I think they call them, used to be impassable 'cos of pirates. You had to go around the islands either way and then the bastards would get you just when you thought you were safe. They don't touch us, though.'

'Why not?'

'Because they know who we work for. If there's one enemy that pirates do not want, it's the Royal Navy.' Healy glowed with pride. On the journey Healy had told Hamish many yarns about his time in 'The Profession' as he called it; how he had been discharged for nearly killing an officer who had caused the death of two of his friends in an ill-advised mine-clearing operation. Someone had saved his bacon and had him transferred to a new venture set up by the First Sea Lord, Mr. Winston Churchill himself and he had stayed ever since.

Hamish had left Collioure six days earlier. He didn't cry easily but the thought that he would never be able to introduce Rosa to his father had made him weep. They would have got on famously, Hamish was sure. His father would have flirted with her as he always did with pretty girls and Rosa would have loved his sense of humour and bluff manner.

As for Rosa, Hamish tried in vain to banish the image of her face as she came to the inevitable conclusion that he had 'done a bunk.' Her father's worst suspicions would be confirmed and eventually he was sure Rosa would move on, having consigned Hamish to the bin entitled 'No moral fibre.' And Hamish knew he was lacking anything but that. That was why he was here, risking his neck to save his friend and about to do it again for the British Secret Service. He tried to be philosophical about it. After all, if Cumming had not sent him to Laroque, he would not have met Rosa. The irony, not that Hamish was one to see the irony in things, was that his love for Rosa was what was preventing him from seeing her again.

Ingram Hobart, the man who had surprised him at the French villa, had come with them as far as Sardinia where he had another job to do. Hamish quipped that he hoped Hobart spoke Latin, remembering something that Neville had told him about the Sardinian shepherds and olive growers being the only people on Earth who spoke it as an every day language. Hobart was confident Verro would be where he should be because he only travelled by boat, which he was currently unable to do because the pump mysteriously kept breaking down. Hobart ordered Hamish to take Verro to Gibraltar where Cumming was attending a meeting of Allied Heads of Intelligence.

The boat made its way across the small harbour of Sorrento. Hamish could see a dog lying on the beach in front of a hotel and the small fires where families were cooking some of the day's catch. Large balconied houses clung to the cliff tops, a myriad of pastel colours that had faded over the years. Statues of the Madonna and child guarded the entrances to the narrow ravines where fishing boats bobbed on the calm sea. A man stooped over his boat and pulled a wriggling octopus up on a line. Gulls dived into the inky depths, returning moments later with silver fish flapping helplessly in their beaks. Hamish caught the smell of seaweed and was taken back to holidays on the Welsh coast.

It was getting lighter now and the lights of Naples across the bay started to disappear into the blue mountain. A mile east of Sorrento along the Amalfi peninsula the boat rounded a huge rock that had fallen into the sea. In front of them lay a warren of holes in the cliff, spotted with fire-torches that hung from the soft, volcanic rocks. The signs of devastating seismic activity could be seen along the rock walls, the layers undulating and twisting wildly. Ancient coral sat fifty feet above the sea, below the decaying battlements. Carved steps wove their way across the outside of the cliff, sometimes ending in thin air and more disappeared into the interior of the rock. It reminded Hamish of a snakes and ladders board.

Eight men in British Army uniform climbed up the steps from the boat's interior and silently took up positions around it. Four of them raised rifles with telescopic sights to cover the cliffs in front of them. Hamish watched spellbound as the rifles steadied on their targets despite the roll of the waves. He could make out the badge of the deer with antlers below the words, 'Je suis pret,' on the caps of the men.

As they approached the torches, silhouettes moved along the

jetty against a background of reflected water dancing on the walls behind them. The scouts fired and five bodies fell back into the cliff and lay on the jetty.

Healy put the engine into reverse and expertly manoeuvred the boat to the side of the jetty. The small crew fastened the boat as the soldiers covered the cliff top and entrance to the cave with their guns. Six men jumped ashore and ran into the cave while the remaining pair stayed on board scanning the cliffs for signs of movement. Hamish heard the sound of rifle and pistol fire and grenade explosions inside the passageway as he stood in the wheelhouse. He had been told by the scout sergeant that he didn't want Hamish involved. He would only dilute the effectiveness of the well-drilled manoeuvre.

Ten minutes later the shooting stopped and the soldiers returned with Verro. 'Yours, I believe. He's unarmed,' said the sergeant to Hamish in a Scottish accent. 'Three of ours wounded, nothing serious. Now get us out of here.'

*

Two hours later the boat was well out into the Mediterranean and the scouts had been transferred back to the frigate. Hamish sat opposite the handcuffed Verro in the small canteen.

'Any idea why you are here?' asked Hamish.

'No, but I am glad you are British and not Italian. They want to slice me up and feed me to the pigs!' he hissed.

'I am looking for Jim Downing. We believe that you know what has happened to him.' Hamish saw the flicker of surprise pass across Verro's face. 'I'll make this easy for you. We know about Small's link to Lord Sidney-Coke and his link to you. We have telephone call recordings, so we know that you were planning something in England. Jim knew Small and he knew you. He was also my best friend.'

Verro stared back at Hamish. His head lolled on the movement of the boat.

234

'You are too late.'

'What do you mean, "Too late"?'

'The world has changed. No-one can resist the storm that is coming.' Verro smiled a relaxed, almost resigned smile. 'It is the time of the people. As Engels said, with much foresight, "To stir up a general war for the sake of a few Herzegovinians which would cost a thousand more lives than there are in Herzegovina isn't my idea of proletarian politics." Jim believes this also.'

'Verro, I don't care much for politics but even Jesus had disciples. You can't let everybody run everything.'

'That is a very naïve thing to say,' replied Verro.

'Is it? People need to dream to have that big house, that interesting job. We are all individuals, Verro. You can't tell people what to believe in, what to hope for. You'll just replace one corrupt system with another.'

'There will be some pain,' said Verro. 'All great social change requires it. But sometimes the more pain there is, the stronger the recovery.'

Hamish knew at that moment that Verro was mad, and like all arguments with madmen, it was boring. Neither of them was going to change their minds.

'So where's Jim?' asked Hamish

'Doing excellent work for his comrades.'

'You don't really think that bumping a few people off will bring about a revolution.'

'I depends on who you 'bump off'. If the people are already unhappy with their lives and with their leaders and then something happens that makes them believe that the government is trying to take away their freedom of expression, then you have the conditions for a revolution.'

Hamish didn't understand what Verro was staying at first. Then he involuntarily took a sharp intake of breath. 'You wouldn't do that! Not to the people who believe what you believe.' Verro smiled back. Hamish was appalled. 'Please tell me you aren't expecting Jim to kill your own supporters!'

Before Verro could answer, Baker poked his head around the door.

'Captain wants you,' he said.

'We're being followed,' said Healy as Hamish came onto the bridge.

Hamish looked back along the white lines of the boat's wash for a while. 'I don't see anything. A few boats, but nothing coming this way.'

'Two boats zigzagging. Trust me, they're following us. They're waiting until we are out of Italian waters before they jump us.'

'Can we escape?'

'Not with this engine. Great for long-distance, but a sprinter she ain't. Pirates probably.'

Hamish peered into the morning mist, still not able to identify which boats Healy was concerned about.

'Of a type,' replied Hamish. 'If they are who I think they are, then we are in trouble. Can you telegraph for help?'

'Help? We have never needed help before and I don't intend to start now. We'll just wait for them to get closer and see what they are made of. Pass me that telescope.'

Hamish did as he was asked. After what Verro had told him, he had no intention of getting mixed up with this lot.

'Listen, I have a very important message to get to Gibraltar. We must do everything we can to get there safely.'

'Scared are we?' asked Healy.

'No, I am not bloody scared, Healy. I just suspect that I know the type of people that we are dealing with here. They will do anything to find out what I have just been told. And I mean anything.'

'In that case would you go with Mr. Baker here and unlock the gunroom. You should find some interesting stuff in there.'

The two men went below. Baker unlocked the padlock on

the steel door and slid it open. Hamish couldn't believe his eyes. Behind glass doors and strapped to frames around the room was an armoury. Webley semi-automatic pistols, rifles, one with telescopic sights, bayonets, grenades by the dozen and two Vickers-Maxim machine guns on their stands, with boxes of ammunition. There were even clubs, daggers, helmets and shields.

'No wonder we had shortages in the trenches,' exclaimed Hamish.

'You were on the Western Front?' asked an impressed Baker. 'It must have been terrible.'

Hamish said nothing. How do you describe something like that to someone who wasn't there? In any case, he understood that since he got out it had got a whole lot worse.

'Give me a hand with these,' said Hamish.

Hamish and Baker took the machine guns and ammunition to the bridge and set them up on the deck just inside each door, pointing to port and starboard. They then retrieved a box of grenades and the sniping rifle.

'This chap was in the trenches, Captain,' said Baker.

'Was he now? That'll be useful. We are now in international waters, by the way.' Hamish and Baker looked back at the chasing boats and saw that they were speeding towards their flanks, about half a mile out.

'I don't think these chaps are out fishing, gentlemen. Keep your heads down,' suggested Healy. No sooner than he had spoken when a bullet ricocheted off the steel skin of the bridge.

'Amateurs,' sighed Healy. 'Can you shoot straight, mate?'

'Just give me the opportunity. What is the sight zeroed to?'

'Two hundred yards. Try to take out those on the bridge of the boat to port. That's that side. I'll move in closer. Baker don't shoot that thing until I give the order,' replied Healy.

'I can't anyway. Not without someone feeding the bullet belt.'

'Prop the bullet belt over a stool. I've seen a very capable

237

Welsh machine gunner do it for real,' said Hamish.

'Blimey. We've got a real soldier here, Captain,' said Baker, looking up in admiration at Hamish. Hamish rested the barrel of the rifle on the lock in the frame of the open door. He peered through the sights and his heart beat faster as the adrenaline coursed through his veins. He tried not to smile. Another bullet pinged off the hull on the other side.

Hamish could clearly see the two men on the bridge. Moustachioed and dark skinned, they looked straight ahead, occasionally glancing at the boat turning towards them.

'Three hundred yards, two fifty, two hundred…' said Healy.

Hamish fired, the noise causing the other men to duck involuntarily. In one fluid movement Hamish lifted the bolt with the heel of his right hand, pulled it back and returned it to the starting position. It took a second. He fired again.

'Both down,' said Hamish.

Healy looked at Hamish disbelievingly, then at the boat, saw it skewing increasingly towards them and shouted at Baker. 'Fire Baker, fill the fucker.'

Baker gave it two five-second bursts, filling the bridge of the Orsini with a deafening noise and the smell of cordite. Hamish and Healy both put their hands to their ears as a hundred .303 bullets smashed into the boat opposite at two thousand feet per second.

Hamish had seen the effect of machine gun fire on trenches and human beings but never on a floating structure made of wood. The middle of the boat literally disintegrated, the bow and stern lifted slowly towards each other like a dead leaf in sunlight, and the boat slowed in the water.

'Now the other boat, men.' Hamish and Baker ran to the other door. This time Hamish belt-fed the machine gun while Baker aimed and pressed the trigger until the other boat exploded, spraying bits of wood and people in all directions.

Healy kept the Orsini going straight ahead. Hamish scanned the water for survivors of either boat through the sights, and saw none.

The first boat broke in two and disappeared beneath the waves.

'Bloody amateurs. Don't these chaps know who they are dealing with?' Healy said as he looked out through the windscreen. Hamish saw the tremble in Healy's hands as they sat on the wheel. Then he went below.

Verro's body was slumped forward on the canteen table. The glass in the small window where Hamish had sat earlier was shattered. Blood dripped onto the floor, forming a puddle two foot wide.

'Oh, bloody hell.' said Hamish.

*

Vladimir Ilich Ulyanov's breath froze as he spoke. The castle walls had lost their summer warmth after a month of snowfall and now even the fire could not break the stranglehold that the cold had on the temperature and the mood in the room.

'We still go on! We still go on! We must not be cowards. Comrade Verro's loss is a mere inconvenience in the battle to overthrow the bourgeoisie. It was probably local thugs anyway. They have tried often enough.'

Gabriel nodded in agreement. 'There are so many people relying on us, comrade Ulyanov.' The arrival of the Russian had galvanised everybody at the castle. The loss of Verro had been a shock, particularly the way in which he had been taken. Everybody on his property had been killed, as if whoever had taken him wanted to either send a message or to hide their identities. The Sorrento newspapers were full of details of the attack's aftermath, including the two boats belonging to local families that had followed the perpetrators and had not come back. But there was no doubting Ulyanov's genius. Where Verro had been a thinker, Ulyanov was all action, backed up by a great intellect. His reputation preceded him. This man was Jesus to Marx's John the Baptist.

'Gabriel, I shall be returning to Russia early in the year. The Germans have promised me safe passage.'

'That is great news, comrade. Great news.'

'But I need you to watch my back for me, Gabriel. Literally. My return will be monitored by every government and intelligence agency in Europe. They know my feelings about this war. It is not in the interests of Britain, France or Italy for me to succeed in Russia. If Russia is out of the war, the Allies will have to fight a Germany that can throw everything at them! It would be hugely beneficial to me if one of those countries was diverted by their own internal problems. Comrade Verro was planning something in England, I believe.'

'Yes, he was. The timing is perfect. The war is going very badly for the British. Many, many men have been killed and some cities are close to starving. There is much industrial unrest. Best of all, the newspapers are demanding a complete rethink about the war and are criticising the leadership about everything from the economy to military strategy.'

'Excellent. But what about the people's trust? If they lose trust in their leaders then change is inevitable!' Ulyanov thumped his gloved first on the table.

'Comrade, last month the British Secret Services were in court explaining how a new department called PMS2 persuaded a group of socialist students to try to poison the Prime Minister. There has been an outcry. The press is accusing the government of framing people who disagree with their policies. There are even comments that the public were manipulated to support the war in the same way. They have lost trust in their leaders, comrade.'

'This is all excellent news. I think you should carry on with comrade Verro's plans for England as soon as you are ready.'

'We are ready now, comrade. There is going to be a general strike next month organised by the Pacifist Union of Democratic Control and the Independent Labour Party. The strike will lead to violence in London where the army will be forced to return fire to defend themselves. There is also going to be the wedding of a war hero. He is much loved in England for his pacifist poetry, and his death will be seen as another example of the Establishment's attempt to silence people it is scared of. A communist agitator will also die in mysterious circumstances.'

'Very good. Sometimes you have to think the unthinkable in order to achieve the greater good. Now, please tell me about security. Give me confidence that your group's activities are still a secret,' asked Ulyanov.

Gabriel rubbed the bridge of his nose with his thumb and forefinger. 'We have a small situation in England, comrade. We have taken all the necessary precautions, like changing our channels of communication with our contacts there. We don't think there is anything to worry about.'

'Go on.'

'The Red Cross records show no sign of two British soldiers, supposedly captured during a raid on German trenches in August, at any of the POW camps or hospitals.'

'So what?' asked a frustrated Ulyanov.

'One of these men was meant to have been disposed of during a raid on a German trench, after he unfortunately discovered one of our resurrection operations. The agent thought it better to let the soldier carry out the execution and then see to him later.'

'I see. What has happened to the agent that failed to dispose of him.'

'He died on the raid.'

Ulyanov thought awhile. 'The soldier who discovered the resurrection, was he told the implications of telling anyone what he saw?'

'He was. And as a security measure we have killed both of the missing soldiers' next-of-kin, as we always do, comrade. If these men are alive we expect them to come to the funerals.'

'Where they will disappear?'

'Yes.'

Ulyanov looked at Gabriel. 'Aren't you forgetting something?'

Gabriel was taken aback. *How could he have forgotten anything to do with security? This was what he was meant to be good at.*

'Who said that they had been captured?'

'The British Army…' Gabriel stopped. Suddenly he saw the flaw in his own ruthless logic.

Ulyanov's face formed what could only be described as a pained smile.

'Perhaps comrade, you can make a few enquiries about the person who said that they had been captured. It is probably nothing, as you say. Red Cross records can be awfully out of date. But it is best to be sure, don't you think?'

'Absolutely, comrade.'

'Good. I bid you goodbye for now. I will call you when I need your services again. You did a good job in Moscow, by the way. You have avenged my brother's death. Happy Christmas.'

*

Gabriel waited by the phone, looking impatiently at his watch. *How could he have made such a mistake, such an oversight? And for comrade Ulyanov to find it! That was unforgivable.*

The phone rang. Gabriel picked it up immediately.

'Gabriel.'

'The gentleman you are looking for is on his way to Shrewsbury, for a funeral.'

Gabriel thought fast. 'This doesn't mean that the cat is out of the bag. He may know nothing. He may just be paying his respects to his missing friend's father.'

The only sound at the other end of the line was of shallow breathing.

'Can we get to his next-of-kin before he returns?'

'Why bother? We can get him at the funeral.'

'Yes, of course. But he may have told his kin something.'

'I doubt it. This is his first home leave since he joined up in August 1914. He would never have written anything to endanger his friends which could be picked up by the sensors. The British Army would then know that they had deserted and that would make our man culpable. Telephone contact with England has to be authorised and is monitored by the Army.'

'I see your point. However we must follow the policy that has kept us secret for so long. Please arrange it.'

'Very well. Who shall I send?'

'Is 'Black' ready?'

'Yes, but he has only just returned from Italy. And even in disguise, I think this is the wrong job for him. He knows those involved.'

'Who then?'

'Blue is available. He would do a good job.'

'Fine. Please let me know when it is done. Goodbye.'

Gabriel replaced the receiver on the cradle. He felt a lot better.

*

'Well, my boy. Haven't we been busy? We must do something about your spelling though. I think you have the same problem as my dear son had. Both of you are bright but you have problems showing that in the written word. Shame about Verro, too.'

Cumming closed the purple folder marked 'Most Secret,' and laid it in the desk in front of him. Vernon Kell sat in a leather chair in a corner, looking at his shoes.

Hamish sat opposite, embarrassed and irritated. He was tired from the journey across the Mediterranean. He hadn't slept well since he lay with Rosa for the last time. He had written his report in the small cabin and read it over and over again. It was not a good bedtime story.

When they had berthed, Hamish had refused to give

Cumming's adjutant his report, insisting that he gave it to him in person. He had waited all day to see the great man and now as he sat in the room under the Rock of Gibraltar, he hoped it had been worth the effort.

Cummings was wearing his Marylebone Cricket Club tie and a big smile. 'Have you ever seen the 'tube and envelope' trick, Hamish?' He leaned over to the far side of the desk and retrieved a metal tube, about three inches long and an inch in diameter. He opened a drawer, found an envelope, wrote some words on a piece of paper, folded it in half, put it in the envelope and sealed it.

'If you hold the envelope to the light and look through the tube you will be able to read what I have written, even though the paper inside is folded. Can you see?'

Hamish did as he was told and read the word on the paper. 'Crecy!' said Hamish. 'What's that?'

Cumming raised his eyes to the rock ceiling. 'Crecy, my boy, was a great battle where the English beat the French against all the odds. It was raining and the French crossbow archers couldn't wind their bowstrings back because the rain had tightened them. The English on the other hand, had kept their longbow strings under their hats where they kept greasy and free of damp. Hence the expression, 'keep it under your hat.' Don't they teach children anything in school these days?'

'It depends on what type of school you go to,' countered Hamish, irritably.

Cumming looked at Hamish with a glare that would have withered lesser souls. He saw no fear there. He smiled. 'Quite so, quite so. Your discussion with Verro was very illuminating, Hamish.' He tapped the folder, got up and started limping around the room. 'We can at least surmise that their seditious strategy is to undermine the country's faith in…in us, the people they trust to do a good job and remain faithful to the creed of the gentleman. We haven't done very well on either count. However, without Verro we can't do much, other that watch the known agitators and keep an eye on the families in Shropshire. We don't know who these people are or where they are, even. All we know is what they want and why they want it. We have no idea about timescales, either. Until we know the answers to at least some of these questions, we have to wait until they show their hand. Let's hope we win the war before they try anything.'

'I agree,' said Kell. 'Sir Sidney-Coke certainly won't tell us what's going on. His calls to Sorrento were useful in as much as we found a link between Jim, Small and Verro. But he didn't incriminate himself because we can't use the transcripts as evidence in court and vague language was deliberately used. And we can't exactly take him down to a Special Branch station, stick a bag over his head and get him to talk.'

'But you would if he weren't a Knight?' asked Hamish.

Kell didn't answer.

'You have forgotten why I came to you in the first place,' said Hamish.

Cumming stared at Hamish for a few moments. 'Ah, yes, your friend.' He walked around the room, looking at the designs on the rough carpet below. 'Jim, I am afraid, is lost. You have not uncovered evidence of his whereabouts nor did I expect you to. We cannot find him without unravelling the whole organisation. Which we cannot do for the reasons that I have just given you.'

Cumming looked down at the crestfallen Hamish.

'We will provide protection for your family and Neville Milton's for three months. That is all I can give you Hamish. Captain Kell's resources are stretched to breaking point trying to stop the unpatriotic bastards blowing up our munitions factories and bringing our mines and shipyards to a halt. For my part, I have been ordered to focus all of our attentions onto identifying Germany's plans for next year and doing what we can to prevent an implosion in Russia. Who knows, perhaps your friend will show his face, in time.'

Hamish was drained. He had come all this way for nothing. He felt used.

But Cumming and Kell were not the only ones in the room

who knew a trick or two.

'Alright, thank you for the protection,' said Hamish. 'Would you be able to send me back to my unit? We can say that I escaped from the P.O.W. camp.'

'Give me time to think about it, my boy.'

'I'll need a pass for the next fast boat back to Blighty and a leave pass for a month. I need to tie things up at home.'

'That can all be arranged. You know you are too late to get to the funeral.'

'Yes. I will leave that in the capable hands of Special Branch. I've seen them in action, defending the King against flying strawberries no less.'

Cumming raised an eyebrow. 'Thank you for your understanding of my position.'

'War is a nasty business,' said Hamish. He got up to go.

'Yes it is, and it requires taking some very difficult decisions if you are to be successful. Happy New Year,' replied Cumming, putting his arm around Hamish and walking him into the corridor.

Hamish stooped under the electricity cables in the cramped tunnel until he came to the entrance. He handed his pass to the guard and walked up the steps to find his hotel. He thought that he saw the man in the moon wink down at him.

He smiled to himself. A poor speller he may be but stupid he wasn't. If Cumming and Kell weren't going to find Jim, he would try to find him, himself. He needed some help. And he knew just where to find it.

He went to his hotel and placed a call to Shrewsbury, England. Ken's last words before he put the phone down were, 'Hamish, you know we could all hang for this.'

*

Neville Milton, senior cryptoanalyst in the anonymous

department that was Room 40, went through the motions of deciphering last night's intercepts, but he wasn't concentrating. At least, not on what was in front of him. Ever since the tense telephone conversation with Ken Downing the previous day he had not been doing his job in the thoroughly inspired manner that his colleagues had grown used to. He hadn't agreed to Ken's request, nor had he declined it. What he was asking for was easy to supply. A name and address for a telephone number that his department had tapped for Vernon Kell. There couldn't be too many Sir Sidney-Coke's around, let alone one that had been investigated by the Secret Services. Ken couldn't take the chance of talking to the wrong one, so he needed the address from Neville, but easy as the information was to find, if he were caught giving it to someone without authorisation, he would spend the rest of his life in jail. He wasn't prepared to take that risk, but neither could he do his job and that probably had even more serious consequences for the country, given the importance of the messages that he had already deciphered. The fact that the information might lead to the people who killed his father made the decision easier.

So at lunch he took a bus and walked a mile from Whitehall, made sure he wasn't followed, found a phone kiosk and called Ken. 'The address you are looking for is Lethersett Hall, Buxton, Staffordshire. The number is Buxton 5659. His name is Percy Sydney-Coke. Lost two sons at Loos, which may explain why he wants to see an end to the war at any cost. Spends a lot of time in the water mill that he is restoring. The telephone call transcripts also hint at him being very wealthy so he may have been bank-rolling this organisation of yours.'

'Thank you, Neville.'

'Ken, if you find Jim Downing, let me know. Otherwise I'll see you after the war.'

*

The families spilled out of the ancient Catalan church into

the cool, evening air and made their way home like a returning tide finding its way into familiar rock pools. Rosa and her parents walked slowly and silently past the windowless church and over the small irrigation canal that formed a border to their vineyard. All around them were dormant vines. Candle lights flickered in the cottages on the hill sides.

They passed the wooden sign that said simply 'Bisconte' and Rosa's father stopped and leaned on his cane. 'Rosa, we have to sell the vineyard', he said. 'Your Mama and Papa are too old to carry on this work. We have to stop'. He wasn't able to look Rosa in the eye and coughed as if to underline what he was saying to her.

Rosa was stunned. She had watched her parents slave between the vines in every season almost as long as she could remember. *The vineyard was more than their livelihood, it was their lives.* 'Papa, please don't sell it. I could run the vineyard. We could get help in. You and Mama can rest. Please, Papa'.

'We cannot afford to pay people, Rosa. The market for this wine is dying. The soldiers want cheap wine, from large estates in the north. We are already using up our savings just to stay in business. Soon we will have nothing.'

'No! I will not allow it, Papa. We have spent our whole lives here. I want…I want to die here,' she shouted.

'Rosa, you are not thinking clearly. Ever since that Englishman came here you have been thick-headed'.

'Papa, this has nothing to do with Hamish.' She started to cry. 'This is the wrong decision! I will not allow you to sell it. I will get help. You'll see. In the spring I will get help from the village, cheap help, and the vineyard will still be owned by a Jouie, even if it is me and not you! This war cannot last for ever. Then the vineyard will be healthy again.' She turned and walked away with her father calling after her.

When she got to the house she went straight to the hiding place that she had used since she was a child. She lit a candle and descended the circular, stone stairway to the cellars. There, she walked across the uneven floor to the far wall and rested against one of the barrels and as her breathing steadied, she reached up and took a glass from the wooden rack above her head, she went to the front of the barrel and turned the tap. Black wine poured into the glass and she put it to her lips. *'Too good for soldiers'*, she thought.

She looked around the cellar. The light from the candle turned the whitewashed walls near her to a warm gold and strips of light bounced off the cellar ceiling, reflections from the metal bands engirdling the barrels. *What* had *happened to Hamish? How could he just disappear the day after asking me to marry him, after making love for the first time?* The concept of cold feet was not one that Rosa thought Hamish was capable of understanding. *And yet why had he not left a note or a message for her?* She had gone to Hamish's house early the next morning. The house was locked up, the shutters closed. She had banged on the door again and again and then climbed over the garden wall that ran beside the path to the hills behind. Nothing.

She had sat in the garden and cried. *How could he do this? They loved each other so much. She was no expert in men but she had ample reason to trust her instincts. She had even helped him kill his lice for God's sake! They had both laughed when she called them 'Spaniards'. Something must have happened. Hamish would not walk away from her without good reason. And the reason had to be connected to the subject that she was not allowed to discuss with him. Why was he here in the first place? If he wasn't a deserter, then what was he?* She had asked the Notaire to tell her who owned the house but his enquiries ended when the deeds could not be found. No-one in the village seemed to know anything about the house.

So now she was stuck in an emotional no-man's-land, not able or wanting to move on. She thumped the top of the barrel and finished her glass of wine. *Her father was right. She wasn't thinking clearly. If only Hamish were here!*

14

The captain with the huge moustache stared dreamily out of the train window onto the snowy landscape, sucking on his pipe. This was not his favourite time of year. The countryside was inert, biding its time until the earth warmed under the lengthening days of late Winter. The solstice had just passed but it wouldn't make a lot of difference to the wildlife for another month or more. The hibernators stayed asleep and the birds stayed low, protecting themselves from the cold. He wished he could find a way of doing the same. The journey from London had taken six hours and his feet felt like blocks of ice.

He could not deny however, that the sight of Shropshire under a blanket of snow was a bewitching one. Blocks of red brick speckled the whiteness and slate roofs showed a foot or so around the warmed chimneys. Friesian cows huddled together for warmth and ivy boasted its evergreen leaves against black trunks and branches.

Before the war he would go out with his gun to bag a few partridge or pheasant, but it was too easy. To use a dog with a net was far more challenging. Snaring vermin using only a strip of wire in the right run at the right time in the cycle of the moon, that was what hunting was all about.

This and a lot more he had taught the soldiers, his students at the Sniping, Observing and Scouting School. He had been a revelation to those running and attending the school, particularly Hesketh-Pritchard, now back to his previous rank of Major. It was not every man who could teach others to shoot, to read and make maps, make camouflage, survive in the open and defend themselves without a weapon.

He had not for one minute let it go to his head. Randle was in his element, doing a job that could have been designed for him to do, making a big difference to the way the British Army fought the war. He was grateful for the way that fate had dealt him this wonderful hand.

But his first visit back to England in over a year was a sad one. He had been dismayed when he heard the news of Brendan Rutherford's death. The man had been a true gentleman. Randle had known many who would have taken a poacher straight to the police once they caught him on his land, notwithstanding his saving of the young horse. But he had made good friends with the farmer and his family, often mending machinery and fences and even treating the animals with his ancient remedies. Major Hesketh-Pritchard was sympathetic to Randle's request for leave, now that the trenches were ice-bound and quiet.

He wondered about Hamish. Would he be there? If he were, then Randle would have to answer some awkward questions about why he had said that he and Neville had been captured. Somehow he knew that Hamish wouldn't turn up. Whatever Hamish's love for his father, and Randle knew that they were devoted to each other, the risk to everybody of Hamish being found as a deserter would prevent him from attending. He was sure of it.

He smiled as he remembered the times that they had together. The go-carts, the pranks, the poaching. But most of all he remembered the trenches. The stupid games that they had played: alphabet diseases, rat sticking. The cruel furnace of war had welded their relationship and many others, for all time. They would never be the same again as individuals. Only the friendships got better.

The train slowed as it moved into Shrewsbury station. Randle stood up, brushed down his captain's uniform and collected his bag from the rack. He said goodbye to the other soldiers that he had met on the trip and stepped into the slush on the platform.

A horse-taxi was waiting when he got outside the station, and as he got in he shouted across to the masons making a memorial to the local men who had died in the war. 'That'll be the first of many, lads. You'll need new chisels by the New Year.'

He sat back in the carriage and regretted the cheap remark. But he had adopted the same black humour as his fellow soldiers, protection against the awfulness of the Western Front. He was grateful to be based a few miles behind the lines. On more than one occasion he had been caught in trenches preparing for a sniping job when the shells had come in. Nothing prepares you for the explosions, the eardrum shattering noise, the shock, the earth falling on top of you, the shell splinters, the screams, the dead.

The horse pulled the carriage up the hill past the castle where he had last seen his mother. He was looking forward to getting home. His mother's face would be a picture when she saw him in a captain's uniform. Vanity, he knew, but then he hadn't had much opportunity to show off in his life. Randle looked at the people of Shrewsbury shuffling past, securing their footing on the slippery pavements. He felt nothing for the men still to enlist, still to fight. He knew the horror that they would face one day. They didn't.

He asked the driver to wait outside the bank. Randle walked in and operations came to a standstill. The clerks behind the grill all turned as one as the enormous, uniformed shape moved to the back of the queue. One of the clerks darted in to a room and the manager came out, nodded to Randle and opened a door at the side.

'Welcome home, Mr. Pugh. May I say how distinguished you look?'

'You've put on weight, Paul.'

'Yes, well. Mrs. Walton looks after me very well.'

'Considering the shortages,' remarked Randle.

The bank manager looked up at Randle over his gold-rimmed spectacles, not sure whether to look affronted or respectful. He shut the door to his office and they both sat down at the polished table.

'Now then, Mr. Pugh, since your phone call yesterday I have made enquiries into your savings and the funds in your syndicated account.'

'Just tell me the amount in the syndicated account, would you Paul?'

'Certainly.' He opened the file and wrote a sequence of large numbers on a clean sheet of paper, one under the other. He added them up in the same way that he had earlier in the day.

'Six thousand, three hundred and ninety two pounds and eight shillings. You have invested very well, Mr. Pugh.'

'Thank you. We can all benefit from wars. You just have to use y'r 'ed. Every cloud 'as a silver lining as they say.'

'Indeed, indeed. And may I ask what you intend to do with the money now, Mr. Pugh?'

'I'd like you to keep a thousand pounds in the account, sell the gold investments, give me one hundred in cash now, and with the rest I want you to buy a country estate, 'bout a hundred acres. There'll soon be a lot for sale, mark my word. Wait until the prices come down and keep me informed of progress.'

'Certainly, certainly. We would be delighted to act as your agents.'

'Lastly, I intend to give Mrs. Rutherford access to this account. Can you arrange that?'

'Of course. Awful business. Poor man. He was always in such rude health.'

Five minutes later Randle left the bank and made his way in the taxi towards the hills. He had one more stop to make before he went home.

*

Jessie Appleby opened the door to the small cottage next to the village post office. In front of her stood the tallest man that she had ever seen. She stepped back into the porch before she saw his uniform.

'Miss Appleby?'

'Yes.'

'My name is Captain Randle Pugh. I served with Jim Downing.'

'Jim Down… but, but what has he to…how did you find out about me?'

'A mutual friend.'

'What do you want, Captain?'

Randle removed his cap and placed it in the crook of his arm. 'May I come in?'

Jessie said nothing but retreated into the living room having first glanced up and down the street. Randle stooped under the lintel. A child cried quietly at the back of the house and the room smelt of recently washed clothes.

'I'm sorry about the state of the house, Captain. But I am on my own, you see.'

'I know all about you Jessie. I even know who pays for this cottage.'

'You do? Who then?'

'Amongst others, Jim. He was a good card player and a few of us arranged for his winnings to come to you.'

Jessie was stunned. 'He must have been a bloody good player!' she said, looking around the room.

Randle laughed. 'Yes he was and he was a fine soldier too.'

'Funny that they shot him then.'

'Jessie, I am here to tell you that there has been an enquiry into Jim's court-martial. He should have been pardoned but they are worried about the effect this would have on the troops. Morale is very poor as I'm sure you can understand, given what they've been through. He disobeyed an order to try to save some injured men. He should never have been shot.'

Jessie's eyes welled up. 'A bit bloody late, wouldn't you say, Captain?'

Randle met Jessie's eyes for as long as he could and then had to look away. The pain of the news of his death was still in her eyes and he could see the link that she was making between him and the machinery that killed her lover, the father of her child.

'Look under the Christmas tree, Captain.'

Randle saw the two small presents.

'They are both to Poppy, my little girl. One is from me and one is from Jim, although obviously I bought both.' Her arms were folded tightly across her chest and tears found their way slowly to the corners of her mouth. 'She thinks she has a daddy in the war, you see. I think it makes her feel special. She smiles every time I talk about him, probably because I do too. By the time I tell her that he isn't coming home she will be old enough to understand but won't feel the grief of someone who has lost someone they actually knew.' She sobbed, holding her head in her hands. 'This bloody stupid war. How many more widows are they going to make?' She rested her head on Randle's huge chest and he gently put his arms around her.

Randle's insides were twisting. He wanted, needed to tell Jessie that he thought that Jim was still alive. But what good would it do? He didn't know for sure and he certainly didn't know where he was. That was for Hamish and Neville to find out, if they were still alive.

'I've brought a present too,' said Randle weakly. Jessie looked up, her cheeks red and damp.

Randle put his hand in his breast pocket and retrieved a brown leather cylinder. He gave it to Jessie. She opened it and pulled out the object inside.

'It's a kaleidoscope. Look into it.'

Jessie lifted it to her eye and squinted. Her face lit up. 'It's beautiful.'

'Now turn it.' Jessie turned the cylinder and for the first time she laughed. She took the tube through to her daughter. Poppy Appleby grabbed the object in her tiny hands and put it up to her eyes. Jessie turned the top and the child giggled with pleasure.

'Definitely her father's daughter,' said Randle looming over the pram. 'He was good with a telescope too.'

*

Randle paid the taxi driver at the gate outside his cottage and asked him to return at nine the next morning. He looked at the tiny two-roomed house. The light within glowed through the sheet curtains and smoke rose into the windless, darkening evening. A cloud of starlings pirouetted around the sky, its defined edges defying nature. He opened the gate quietly and stepped forward, his huge feet crunching the snow underfoot and he saw the shape of someone under the gas lantern as he moved slowly towards the front door. He smiled as he noticed the seaweed barometers that his mother insisted on bringing back from her seaside jaunts, hanging from nails in the wall. His knock on the stable doors was followed by silence. He knocked again, more urgently.

'Who is it?' asked a woman's voice.

'The big, bad wolf and if you don't let me in, I'll huff and I'll puff....'

The two parts of the door opened as one and Randle's mother and the dog, Josh ran out to greet him. He bent over so she could get her arms around his neck and he stroked the furiously barking dog.

'Randle, Randle, my boy, my son!' she shouted. 'You've come back. You've come back. Oh, what joy!' He gently lowered her to the ground and they stood there grinning at each other as the snow fell into their hair and onto their shoulders.

'My, look at you,' she said. 'All togged up like a groom with no bride.'

And then she hugged him again, this time around his waist. 'And look at that moustache.' She playfully tugged at its ends. She didn't know what to do with herself, she was so happy. They went into the tiny cottage and talked for an hour, mainly about the urine that had wasted in the bottle above the doorway and the Welsh witch that had laid low all the pigs on the nearby farm, before Randle said he was hungry. 'But I haven't got any food in, Randle,' she said.

'Do you want to go out for dinner?'

'Go out? Whatever for boy? We've got everything we need here. There's vermin aplenty since you men went off to war. Go and catch a couple of rabbits and we'll have a stew. I still go out and get pheasants where I shouldn't.'

Randle smiled and took his bag through to the bedroom that they had shared for the best part of ten years and put it on his bed. He took the rifle down from its hook above the fire and found the .22 bullet box where he had left them in August 1914.

'You'll have to be quick, my boy, it's getting dark.'

'The moon's up, Ma. It'll be like playing marbles in torchlight. Josh'll help me.'

*

Randle made his way through the bracken back towards the house with Josh. Two rabbits in half an hour in the near dark. He was a bit rusty but it wasn't a bad effort for someone shut up in a missen hut for most of the last six months.

He opened the door.

The pistol pointed straight at his head. Another one was held against his mother's temple, her mouth gagged by a thin white cord that Randle could see was cutting into the sides of her mouth. Her eyes were bulging, pleading as they stared at Randle. Her hands were behind her back, obviously tied.

Josh growled, showing his yellow teeth.

The gun spurted fire into the gloom and Josh whimpered and slumped to the floor..

'You bastard!' hissed Randle.

'Here, closer,' said the foreign voice. Randle did as he was told. 'Drop the gun and the rabbits.' Randle dropped the soft, lifeless animals to the floor next to the dog's body and placed the gun near them.

'Very slowly, remove your belt. That's it. Drop it. Now remove your shoes and socks. Good. Now turn slowly around and walk out of the door and follow the path to the left of the house. I want to have a good look at you. If you try anything then I blow your mother's brains out. If you even stumble, I kill both of you. Pat down your trousers. Good. Roll up your trousers to above the calves.

Put your hands on your head. Now move.'

Randle turned and walked out of the house followed by his mother and the man with the guns. Randle tried but failed to slow his breathing and thinking. He had never expected his mother to be involved in anything dangerous, let alone a situation that could only be resolved by him or a man holding a gun to her head. Nothing could have prepared him for this moment.

Randle understood that whoever this man was he knew exactly what he was doing. He hadn't touched Randle but he now knew that Randle was unarmed. He also had control over something that he knew that Randle would never risk.

They walked into the forest. The moon reflected off the snow as it balanced precariously on the branches and bracken tops. Their feet crunched and their breath froze in the cold air. Randle could see footprints pointing in the opposite direction. The man must have come this way earlier. But where were they going?

After a few minutes he told them to leave the path and walk through the bracken deeper into the wood. Randle saw the footprints again.

And then they came to it. An old ditch, probably carved out centuries before but now mostly grown over with moss and undergrowth. Here though, it had been freshly dug in places to make it deeper and wider. A spade lay by its side.

'That must have taken some digging,' said Randle turning towards the two guns.

'Not really...'

A roe deer jumped from the bracken. Randle reacted instantly. In one movement he picked up the spade at its nearest point and threw it towards the guns. The swirling instrument caught the man's right arm near the shoulder. He staggered back without a sound. Randle was on to him in a flash. He slammed his cupped hands onto the man's ears, bursting his eardrums. Still the man was silent. Randle passed his right arm over the man's chest and under his shoulder, his other arm passing underneath the man's knees. He lifted him, took a short pace forward and bent his right leg. With all the force he could muster he smashed the man's body onto his knee. The spine broke with a loud crack. Now the man screamed.

Randle picked up one of the two guns and aimed it at the man's heart.

'Look away, Mother,' shouted Randle. He fired twice and the screaming stopped. He lifted the man's trouser leg and found the knife that he expected to be there and ran over to where his mother was kneeling, sobbing by the side of the pit. He cut her gag and her bindings and hugged her. 'We're alright Ma, we are alright. He's dead. I'm going to look after you, Ma.' She rocked and sobbed until eventually she was still and silent.

He looked into her eyes and wiped away the last of her tears.

At last, she spoke. 'I suppose there is no chance of you telling me who that was, Randle?'

Randle laughed and hugged her again. 'You're a hero, Ma, a bloody hero.'

*

Neither of them slept that night. The adrenaline and fear in their veins took hours to seep away. Randle walked his mother to a friend in a nearby village. She would explain to her friend that she was feeling unwell after the shock of Randle coming home. It was weak he knew, but it was the best they could think up at the time. Either way he needed to know that she was safe so that he could think clearly.

Randle realized that someone must have made a connection between him and Hamish and Neville. This was the only explanation. The man that he had killed and buried last night was a professional and he didn't think that any of the gentry in these parts would order a hit on an ex-poacher.

His mind went back to when he last saw Hamish. They were in

the German dugout. Randle had suggested that Hamish and Neville speak to Jim's father. He had not heard of them since, neither dead nor alive, so he had to assume that Ken had helped them in some way. He decided to wait for Brendan Rutherford's funeral. Surely Ken would be there.

Randle walked through the fresh snow and followed the worshippers into the church. He was the last in and he took a place in one of the small pews at the back. The bells stopped ringing and Randle looked around the congregation as the service started.

He recognised the Rutherford family sitting at the front, arms around each other's backs, heads down. In front of them was the large coffin, a simple posy of wild flowers lying on its top. There were many others, acquaintances and workers of Farmer Rutherford. The wheelwright, the auctioneer, the shepherds, the railway worker, the banker, even the gamekeeper. Most had the ruddy complexions of outdoor people. Randle felt amongst friends here. He was 'legal' now, on the right side of the law. Fighting for your country in the Great War was about as credible an occupation as one could have and some of the congregation turned to look admiringly at the big uniformed man at the back. Even the gamekeeper nodded an acknowledgement. Randle felt no danger here and he thought he was well-placed to feel any that was about.

A few minutes later, one of the church doors quietly opened and Ken Downing walked in, followed by three tall men wearing grey mackintoshes. Ken saw Randle and shook his hand. The other men sat in pews where they could. Some of the ladies looked up, disapproving of their tardiness, not knowing the real reason for their being there.

When the service was finished the crowd watched the coffin being taken out of the church by the six pallbearers and followed as it wove its way through the churchyard to the freshly dug hole. It had stopped snowing but the day was still dull and cold. Brendan Rutherford's widow and daughter supported each other in their grief as the cortège reached the grave.

'We need to talk,' whispered Ken into Randle's ear as they walked.

'We certainly do,' replied Randle. 'If those friends of yours are here to protect us, then thank you. However I think the people you are trying to protect us from were looking for me.'

'I agree Randle, but even you may not be strong enough to deal with this lot.'

'A dead body lying below my woods says otherwise, Ken. Let's meet in the King's Head after we have buried Brendan. Poor man. I can only 'ope that the man I killed was the same as got Brendan.' Randle wiped a tear from his eye and walked on.

Ken stood rooted to the spot, mouth open.

*

Ken brought the two pints of Bass back to the table in a quiet corner of the bar.

'Cheers, Randle. Happy New Year. Did you know that Shakespeare was caught poaching? To absent friends.'

'Aye, to absent friends. Wherever they may be.'

Ken's eyes narrowed, searching Randles' for any sign that he knew more than he was letting on and decided that he would never be able to know, not with this man. 'Well, I can help you there, Randle. Neville is in London and Hamish is on his way back from Gibraltar. Should be in London sometime tomorrow.'

'Aren't we both full of surprises today?' He supped at his beer, and wiped away the froth from his moustache. 'You go first, Ken.'

'You came close to breaking the Official Secrets Act when you told Hamish about me.'

'I told him nothing, Ken, just that you were more than a publican and that you may be able to help find your own son.' Randle was not in the mood for games.

Ken held up his hand. 'I know Randle, and I am grateful. Just be aware that the Act is there for a reason. Neither you nor I fully understand the importance of the Intelligence Community to the safety and success of this country. Those that do understand it are ruthlessly efficient at keeping the Secret Services secret. We have to assume that their ends justify their means. There is too much at stake. Particularly now.' Ken cast his expert eye around the pub. Nothing of concern there.

'Anyway,' Ken continued, 'the boys did visit me and nearly got their heads blown off for their trouble. We met up with Cumming and Kell.'

'Mansfield-Cumming?' asked Randle. 'You kicked high, Ken.'

'I thought he would be interested and he most certainly was. He even invited us down to Hampshire. He had done his research before we got there. Neville's languages and other skills have got him sent to a special unit in London. Hamish was sent to France to await instructions. These came through three weeks ago. He went to see someone in Italy, who told him that Jim is part of a communist plot to destabilise this and other countries by playing one side off against another.'

'How do you know this Ken? Are you still in contact with Cumming?'

'No. Hamish called me from Gibraltar last week to update me with what was going on. Hamish gave Cumming his report on the meeting in Italy and Cumming thanked him but said he couldn't do anything for Jim because of a lack of anything to go on, and other priorities.'

'That's what he gets paid for,' suggested Randle. 'To make difficult decisions. Tough on Hamish but I can see what Cumming may be thinkin'.'

'But Randle, if this organisation succeeds we won't have any other priorities because we'll have lost the war and a whole lot else besides.'

Randle nodded, realising that Ken was much closer to the

big picture than he was.

Ken continued. 'Hamish said that the Service would provide Special Branch cover for the Milton and Rutherford family. That was Special Branch with me at the church.'

'Not very covert, Ken.'

'They weren't meant to be. They were there to scare off anyone who shouldn't have been in the church. Listen, Randle, I need your help. I know who is running this end of the coup.'

'What? How the hell do you know that? Have you told Kell or Cumming?'

'No. I came by the information only yesterday and definitely by illegal means. The Secret Services can't touch him because they haven't got evidence that would stand up in court and his being a Knight of the Realm, they think their more....exotic methods of extracting information may blow up in their faces.'

'So you want me to do it instead?'

'Randle, if we can get this bastard to talk we may save a lot more people than my son.'

Randle leant the back of his head against the cold window pane. 'What if he isn't there?' he asked.

'He will be. I called him this morning pretending to be from the Waterways. I told him we needed to divert the supply of water to his mill. He was most concerned.'

'When do you meet him?'

'This afternoon. Come on. I'll drive.' Ken downed his pint and walked out of the bar with Randle following. Randle thought of asking Ken how he came by such detailed information, but knew with complete certainty that Ken would never tell him.

*

The young man slowly stepped down onto the platform from the rear door of the rear carriage of the 9.52 a.m. boat train from Portsmouth. It had been a few minutes since the train had reached its destination. He wore a flat cap and carried a battered leather box in his left hand. He put the case down, removed a silver case from his jacket pocket and put one of the two hand-rolled cigarettes to his lips, lighting it with a match from the box in the other pocket. He squinted through the blue smoke towards the barrier at the end of the platform. Those from second and third classes waited their turn to have their tickets checked and the young man noticed the high proportion of women in the crowd.

Immediately in front of him was a line of shining black carriages harnessed to equally shining black horses, sometimes one, sometimes two abreast. Their livery was immaculate as was the clothing of the footmen that stood on the footplates holding the reins. Long jacketed and mustachioed porters went about their business of locating trunks and cases before loading them onto the waiting vehicles. A policeman sauntered through the chaos. Headwear defined the classes; black visored hats for employees of Great Western, boaters for the aspirational, bowlers and tops for City and Country types, and trilbies and panamas for the deliberately indefinable. And then there were the ladies. More soberly-dressed than the young man remembered from previous visits to London but still sporting the only gay colours in the scene before him. Reunited families and friends hugged and slapped one another's backs.

He stood there, waiting, watching for a while. His eyes rose to the station roof, pockmarked with spots of dark cloud beyond the strips of rusting steel and his mind went back to January 1915 when he was last here on week-end leave.

When he had observed all that he needed, he picked up the case and walked towards the back of the diminishing queue, feeling for the revolver in his breast pocket. He was twenty-one years old but looked older. He suddenly felt very exposed. The time spent as a trained killer who made his home in no-mans-land and working for one of the world's most secret organisations had not fully prepared him for the enormity of what he was about to do. He was back in his home country, about to commit an act that would get him killed if he were caught and killed if he failed. But Gabriel had insisted that he was the best man for the job, this task that was part of the final reckoning with the bourgeois classes that had taken Europe to the brink of disaster and beyond.

He remembered the poem by Henry van Dyke which he had seen in a Parisian bar:

'Oh, London is a man's town, there's power in the air,

And Paris is a woman's town, with flowers in her hair.'

This week, Jim Downing definitely needed to be a man.

He gave his ticket to the collector at the platform gate, found the sign for the new underground railway and made his way to Cambridge.

*

The platform attendant doffed his hat as Marjorie Singleton walked by. She found a position on the crowded platform in line with the advertisement on the far wall of the underground. It was Kitchener's We Need You poster. The finger pointed directly at her as it did to anybody bothered enough to look. *'How ironic,'* she thought. *'He's been killed by a German mine. You need me to stop this war, not join it!'*

The noise of the approaching train drew louder and as one, hands went up to hats to hold them in place.

The fearless anti-war campaigner turned to face the train as it rattled noisily through the station. She glanced at the man in the black uniform who was shoving his way through the crowd nearby, felt the push on her shoulder and fell helplessly into the path of the train. A lady screamed as she saw Marjorie Singleton's terrified face disappear beneath the wheels.

The platform attendant walked quickly along the ten yards of platform before climbing the steps, passing the travellers as they ran to see what was causing the screaming.

15

Ken knocked on the door of the mill. The sound of metal striking against metal stopped and a minute later the door opened. A corpulent man of about fifty with wisps of silver hair above his ears stood in the shade. He said, 'Can I help you?'

'Sir Sidney-Coke, I am Mr. Harper and this is Mr. Green. We're from the Waterways. We spoke on the telephone this morning.'

The man rubbed his dirty hands on a rag and shook with Ken and Randle. 'Ah, yes, do come in, gentlemen. I am afraid that I must ask you to leave that pipe out here. Flour dust is very explosive. I do hope that you are not going to go through with your threat. I am very well connected you know and I know my rights.'

Ken looked around the ground floor of the mill and listened. No sign of anyone else in the building. Just the sound of water falling and the rumble of heavy machinery turning slowly. An enormous metal waterwheel rotated at the back of the room.

'I'm sure you do, sir. We are just here to explore a few ideas.' Ken looked up at the beams supporting the floor above. 'I've never been to a mill before, sir. This really is impressive.'

'Restored most of it myself, with the help of my two boys. Unfortunately, they didn't live to see it working.'

'The war?' asked Randle.

Sir Sidney-Coke nodded. 'Still, life goes on, eh? Did you know that the saying 'on tenterhooks' is a milling expression? Look up there. The tentering gear can be altered by a fraction of an inch, so that the millstones, the water and the amount of grain work in a way that produces flour, but not so much heat that we all blow up!' He laughed.

'Sir, is there anywhere we can talk privately?' asked Ken.

'This is private. There is no-one else here.' He looked quizzical and then worried.

This was all the information Randle needed. He launched himself at the miller, gripped his collar and threw him to the ground. Randle sat on him and pulled the man's arms behind his back and pushed. Sir Sidney-Coke shouted, 'Please, God, stop! Who are you? There is no money here!'

Ken squatted in front of the man's face. 'We aren't after money, Sir Sidney-Coke. We are after some information. Who was Bernardo Verro working for?'

The man was silent. Randle pushed again. 'I don't know who you are talking about. I swear!' he screamed.

'Sir Sidney-Coke, the game is up for you and whatever you are planning. We do not want to hurt you even more, but we will if we have to. This is too important for niceties.' Ken knew that he was talking to himself as much as Sir Sidney-Coke.

The panting man stayed silent. Randle pushed harder until there was the sound of a bone cracking in one of the man's arms. He screamed again. 'Please, I don't know what you are talking about!' he cried. Ken started to worry. He had been witness to many interrogations. Broken bones were usually the point at which they talked. Had Neville given him the wrong information? What if he had been set up? He gave it one last try.

'We know that you are planning to shoot innocent people in order to discredit us. We know that Jim Downing is one of your assassins. We know that you are the key operator in this country. What did you stand to get out of it, sir? Did you think that these communists were going to put you in charge?

'Comm....?

'Ah! The penny drops. You didn't know they were communists, did you? You just wanted the war to end. Well, so do I and so does the captain here, and so do millions of people, everywhere. But please, not the communists. I would rather die than lose hope. How can you hope for anything when everything is the same? Have you ever met a happy communist? Who, what, when? Now!'

Sir Sidney-Coke was sweating profusely and his breaths were

short and sharp. He closed his eyes.

Randle stood up and pulled the man through the mill by his collar. Ken followed. They took him round to the back of the mill to where the wheel lifted and dropped the water from the pond. 'Give me a hand. We'll keel-haul him.' Randle got hold of the screaming man's legs and pulled him along the grass towards the rotating wheel.

'What are you doing? No! Not that!' Sir Sidney-Coke tried to grasp the fence post with his good arm but he was too slow. Ken and Randle lifted the fifteen stone man towards the wheel. He wriggled and screamed but they weren't listening. They pushed his legs between two of the trays on the ascending side of the wheel and squeezed his torso, arms and head in just before it descended into the water. Twenty seconds later, he came up and shouted, 'Please! Get me out. I don't...... ,' between wheezes before he went in again. Randle and Ken said nothing. 'Don't leave me here, please!' he screamed as he came up. They let him go round twice more.

'Information. We want dates, times, places,' shouted Ken over the noise of the water.

'Alright! Alright! I'll tell you, just get me....'

'Information, first!'

'Tomorrow, Sidney Sussex, Cambridge, wedding, four o'clock.'

'Who's been sent there?'

'I don't know. Honestly. He's English. That's all I know.'

'What else?'

'There's one more. Get me out! I'll tell you!'

Ken nodded to Randle and they pulled on his collar but he was stuck fast. 'Get me out of here...' he shouted as he went under again. This time he took longer to come up.

'He'll drown, Randle!' They pulled as hard as they could, and the wheel slowed further. As he descended into the water he shouted, 'The tenterhooks! The wheel is too.....'

Ken and Randle watched the wheel stop with the man still

underwater. They ran to the front of the mill and dived into the machine room and located the gearing system that Sidney-Coke had pointed at. Ken turned a small metal handle and the water wheel turned again, faster than before. They ran back to the wheel and pulled again at the stuck man. But there was no sound.

'He's dead, poor blighter,' said Ken.

'That's what I call grinding to a halt,' joked Randle.

Ken winced. 'We've got to leave.' They walked back towards the car. As they passed the door they could smell burning.

'The flour dust!' shouted Ken. They ran to the car, got in and Ken started the engine.

'Hold on!' shouted Randle. He opened the car door and ran back over the bridge to the mill, grabbed the pipe from the windowsill and ran back. The car fired mud in all directions as Ken spun it around the yard. The mill exploded in a fireball of bricks, metal and wood just as the car rounded the corner of the farm building.

*

The telephone on Ken's study desk rang and his hand was on it immediately. 'Downing,' he said.

'Ken, it's Hamish. I've just got to London. I'm calling from Euston. About to get the train to Birmingham, then onto Shrewsbury. Bloody hell, it's cold here.'

'Hamish, listen very carefully to what I am going to say. Do not come here. You must go to Sidney Sussex College in Cambridge for a wedding at four this afternoon. I think Jim is going to be there. You need to stop him.'

Hamish looked at his watch. 'Four o'clock! But that's only three hours from now! Haven't you called the local Special Branch?'

'Hamish, listen to me. Neither Special Branch nor the Secret Services, nor the police can go anywhere near there. Have you heard the news?'

'No. What's happened?'

'Marjorie Singleton was pushed under a train yesterday. The press are speculating that the government ordered it. If we go to Cambridge and anything goes wrong, they will have all the proof they need that we are being subversive, with all the consequences that that entails.'

Hamish was silent.

'Hamish, I think Jim has been sent to Cambridge to do something similar to the groom. I've looked through the announcements in my newspapers. The groom is Captain Huw Nightingale, a highly decorated hero of Le Cateau. Lost his arm at Ypres. One of the few Old Contemptibles left alive. Also a writer of brilliant anti-war poetry.'

Hamish still said nothing. 'Hamish, whoever has been sent to do this will not be expecting you. Try to stay close to the groom without arousing suspicion. It is vitally important Hamish, that you get some information from the assassin that could seal the fate of this country. There is going to be another attack. We need to know where and when. Use whatever methods you deem necessary to get this information. Good luck, my boy.'

Hamish replaced the receiver, looked at his watch, ran out of the station and hailed a taxi. He suddenly realised that he wasn't armed.

*

Jim Downing sat in the sunshine outside the Bull & Bear public house in Green Street, Cambridge and looked up the street to the west. The sun was setting between the tall chimneys of a large Tudor house at the end and long shadows moved slowly towards his bench. He could hear a broken pipe spewing water onto the cobbles somewhere in the darkened passage on the other side of the street. A small stream filled the gutter in front of him, sparkling in the dying sun.

He opened the silver cigarette case with the initials J.J.G.

engraved on the underside which he had found in no-mans-land during one of his sorties as a sniper. He had kept it ever since, as much a reminder of how his life had improved, as something in which to put his beloved cigarettes. The last hand-rolled cigarette presented itself behind the piece of shoe lace in the lid. Jim took it out and put it to his mouth, retrieved the box of Swan Vestas from his waistcoat pocket and lit one behind his cupped hands. He squinted, moving the cigarette closer to the flame. He sucked twice in rapid succession and tasting the warm smoke fill his mouth, he took a deep, satisfying chestful. He leaned back and spread his arms over the bench and looked to the left.

Sidney Sussex College.

The sandstone walls were topped by spiked railings, woven by centuries-old Wisteria whose branches wound their way round some of the points as if they were embarrassed by a violent image so close to a seat of learning. Bicycles leaned against the wall. On top of the roof above the college building at the back of the court stood a large black bell and a clock with gold hands.

He nervously felt the revolver through the fabric of his trousers, finished his coffee, had a discrete look around to see if he were being watched and walked towards the huge oak gates in the college wall at the end of the street. Students, some in gowns, others in tweeds, cycled across his path and moved on towards Christ's college. He took a last drag of the cigarette, dropped it, rotated his foot over the butt and stepped across the road.

He strode casually through the open gates, his hands in the pockets of his black waiter's uniform, passing the Porter's lodge to the right. He glanced at the gargoyles and Countess of Sussex's coat of arms above the door. Turning again to skirt the court lawn he looked ahead to see the Gothic arch over the college hall entrance, just where his map said it would be. The lights from the street reflected off the windowpanes. He hoped that anyone looking up from their studies would see only their own reflection and not the details of his face.

His shoes crunched on the gravel until he came to the two stone steps under the archway. He moved confidently up into the small hallway, leaping up the steps that had been deeply worn by centuries of feet. The warmth from the heat of a dozen fires found their way to the open door and the sound of laughter and excited conversation drifted through the double doors to the left. Kitchen staff busied themselves beyond the hatch in the opposite wall. A vicar appeared from nowhere, passing Jim with a 'Good night'.

'Night', replied Jim, noticing the irony. He continued to the end of the corridor, turned the small key in the lock and opened the door. He stepped into the darkness and closed and locked the door behind him, leaving the key in the lock. No voices behind him, only the happy sounds from the wedding reception beyond the stairs in front of him and his own shallow breathing. Everything was going as planned.

*

'Vicarage,' answered the plump lady holding the duster.

'Hello. Please can I speak to Nigel?' said the voice on the other end.

'Certainly, who's speaking?'

It's a private matter, I'm afraid'.

'Oh, right. Certainly.' She called up the stairs. 'Sir, it's for you. It's private'.

'Righteo. I'll take it up here, Mrs. Davies.' He closed the door to the bedroom and picked up the receiver. 'Hello, this is Nigel Hall.'

'Afternoon, Nigel, this is Paul at the bank.'

'Paul, what a surprise. How can I help?'

'Well, Nigel. I have an offer to pass onto you from an important client of ours. A confidential client.'

'Oh, yes?' replied the vicar, trying to keep the excitement out of his voice. 'Mrs. Davies, put the receiver down would you?'

Mrs. Davies replaced the receiver on the cradles and dusted the table furiously.

'My client wants you to christen Jessie Appleby's daughter. Apparently you have already refused her request.'

'Jessie Appleby? Oh, yes, the woman with the child. Boyfriend was shot for cowardice.'

'Disobeying orders, actually Nigel, but that's unimportant. My client is willing to offer ten pounds towards the maintenance of your church, should you carry out the christening.'

The vicar thought for a while. 'I'm sorry, Paul. But that's really not on. I can't accept money for compromising my values.'

'Which values are we talking about?'

'The ones that decide who is fit and proper enough to receive God's blessing.'

The line was silent for a while. 'Hello? Paul, are you still there?'

'Yes, I am still here, Nigel. My client has authorised me to give you a final offer of fifty pounds.'

'Fifty! This must be a very important client, Paul.'

'It is, Nigel, and it would please the bank if you could find it within yourself to rethink your stance on this.'

'I see. How do I get the money?'

'Pop in next time you are in town and I'll give it to you in cash. Unless of course you'd like a cheque made out to the church fund?'

'No, no, cash is fine. I'll collect it in the morning. Goodbye, Paul.'

The line went dead. The banker put the receiver down and said to Randle, 'This one's on me, Mr. Pugh. I have a feeling the cash will come back to the bank anyway, once I make a note of the serial numbers. I can imagine the bishop's reaction when I tell him that one of his employees has spent church funds on his mistress. Values indeed!'

*

Jim took the pistol out of his breast pocket, opened the chamber and checked by touch that all the bullets were in the magazine. He felt for the phial of poison that was in his jacket pocket. All he needed to do was find the target and put a drop of the poison into his food or drink.

He waited.

The sound of a heavy chair moving back across a wooden floor filtered across the mezzanine and down the stairwell to where Jim stood in the darkness.

He heard the light tapping of a spoon against crystal.

Complete silence.

'The bride's father.'

Everyone cheered, thumped the tables and stamped their feet.

Jim opened the door behind him and went out into the hallway. He followed a waiter into the large room where the banquet was being held and stood at the back of the room, watching the proceedings unfold.

'My friends,' started the bride's father, 'I am delighted to be here today...'

The audience cheered. More banging on tables with cutlery and the stamping of feet.

'...to support the wonderful institution of marriage.'

'Here, here,' shouted someone. More banging. A child shouted something.

'Shit,' whispered Jim. He hadn't reckoned on children. It just hadn't occurred to him.

'My wife and I understand the secrets of a happy marriage. We go out twice a week. I go out on Tuesdays and she goes out on Thursdays.'

The room erupted. Someone threw a scrunched-up napkin at the father.

'Every marriage needs rows. The quickest way to end an

argument is to lose it. When a row is over I always make sure that I give my wife something expensive that she doesn't need. Last week I bought her a ticket to watch the Arsenal.'

More laughter. Jim took in the top table and its guests and those sitting at the tables below. Everyone was facing the speaker, a large, ruddy-faced man wearing a black and red striped blazer. His thin hair stretched across the bald head from one side and he puffed at a cigar between jokes, winking at the elegantly dressed woman to his left who grinned lovingly up at her husband.

Behind the top table was an enormous painting of Queen Elizabeth I. Close by was the portrait of Oliver Cromwell that the landlord of the Bull & Bear had told Jim was covered with a black cloth when the monarch of the day visited the college. The bride and groom sat at the centre of the table facing the audience.

The father finished his speech. His wife supported his arm as he sunk slowly into his chair, cigar firmly between his teeth. Jim watched the smoke rise as the room filled with rapturous applause and more cheering. He leaned his head on the cool stone wall and looked around the room. Ladies' bobbing hats, tables laden with half-empty glasses and plates. Saucers bearing candles and holly sat at regular intervals down the lengths of the tables. Children wriggled on laps, drunken men gesticulated across the white tablecloths and waiters placed fully charged champagne glasses on tables from silver trays. The smell of cigarette and cigar smoke mingled with perfume and rich food. It was a happy scene, warm, welcoming and very English.

This was not going to be easy.

The MC rose again. The guests fell into a respectful hush. 'The groom'.

Jim didn't move a muscle as the groom stood and looked around the room. He wore a dining suit over a white shirt with high collars. A red cravat hung at his throat, set off by a gold stud. He looked about thirty years old but there was something about the quick movement of his features that hinted that he was much younger. He awkwardly took out a sheet of paper from the inside pocket of his jacket. Jim automatically looked at his other arm that had not risen to hold the jacket open. The sleeve was empty.

'Ladies and Gentlemen. I am a very lucky man. I have just married a most beautiful and wonderful woman and I have also married into a marvellous family.'

'Quite so', muttered his new father-in-law.

Laughter rippled across the hall. The dignified, respectful air seemed to lift and the guests relaxed into their seats.

'This is a very, very happy day for me.' He swallowed hard, and for a moment the lights reflected off moisture in his eyes. He paused, and looked up at the ceiling as if looking for some kind of inspiration.

'When I was writing this speech I wanted to achieve two things. First, to honour my wife. Second to recall the family and friends who cannot be here today. Well, to be honest, words have failed me when I try to describe my feelings for Winnie. I hope that you have all seen how completely devoted I am to her. How I radiate when we are together. How I move faster on returning to her than on the leaving. Winnie, I love you. You are my world and my home.' He blushed in unison with his new wife.

'If there is anything else that I should have said, then I am sure that Phil will fill in the gaps because he has fancied her for years. And now I want to say a few words about those who could not be here today.' He paused again and looked around the room of sad faces. Some were staring at the floor.

'We are lucky. Every one of us in this room today is charmed. We are alive. Many, many people that we knew in 1914 are not here today but should be. John, David, Charlie, Pete, William, Graham, Alf, all of them. War makes a man hard, but I still grieve for them, the poor buggers and I know that you do too.

'You all know of my feelings about this war, but you will be glad to hear that I will save further ranting and raving for another time. Today is a celebration.

'However, I have heard some say that they feel guilty about being here instead of others. Don't be. They wouldn't want that. They would want us to really enjoy days like today and may there be many more of them. Live lives that are noble and full. Live the lives that they would have wanted to live and that they fought and died for. They died so that we could have days like this today.'

Jim flinched. Something had turned over. He felt it in his brain but he wasn't sure it wasn't elsewhere in his body. The back of his neck started to warm and itch. Feelings that he thought he no longer felt, emotions that he thought he wanted to leave behind, welled up inside him. He could not understand why this man had to die. Who could possibly want that? He needed to know more. This man was not going to die at his hand until he had an answer. If that meant his own downfall then so be it.

The groom continued,

'Remember me when I am gone away,
Gone far into the silent land;
When you can no more hold me by the hand,
Nor I half turn to go, yet holding stay.
Remember me when no more, day by day.
You tell me of our future that you planned:
Only remember me; you understand
It will be late to council then or pray.
Yet if you should forget me for a while
And afterwards remember, do not grieve:
For if the darkness and corruption leave
A vestige of the thoughts that once I had,
Better by far you should forget and smile
Than that you should remember and be sad.'

He looked down at the folded piece of paper that he hadn't opened, reached for his full glass of champagne and raised it.

'Ladies and gentlemen. To the Fallen'.

Jim Downing had already turned to leave once during the speech but had stopped himself before he had taken two steps. He took another as the groom finished but the power of his training held him in check. That, and the irresistible logic that he had not got this close to striking a blow against the continuation of the war only to walk away from it. Perhaps this man was a fake, an imposter in the employ of the institutions that gained from the war or which just didn't care about the slaughter. Gabriel had explained to him again and again that the apparent randomness of the targets was one of the reasons for the organisation's success. There had to be a good reason for this man to be killed. Jim watched the guests rise, lift their glasses and say as one, 'The Fallen.'

He walked to the kitchen, got in the line of waiters and took a tray of filled champagne glasses from one of the white-suited chefs.

'Keep those turning round, boys. Pissed punters pay plenty, remember,' said a waiter quietly.

Jim balanced the tray on his upturned fingers above his head and made his way into the banquet hall, excusing himself past the guests. He put his other hand into his pocket and gently pushed the two halves of the phial apart until the cool liquid spilled into the pocket lining. Jim started to sweat freely as his blood pressure rose. He wanted this over quickly. Indecision is fatal, Gabriel had repeated. Jim focused on his target about twenty feet away, ten, five. He lowered the tray and slid it onto the top table. 'A recharge, sir. Complements of the college,' he said to the groom. Captain Huw Nightingale looked up at the waiter and said 'Thank you.' Jim dipped his finger into the glass on the left, before placing the four flutes closer to their intended owners with the other, clean hand. 'A fly, sir'. He showed the captain the black dot on his fingertip and turned to go.

'Just a minute! Don't I know you?'

Jim stooped in his tracks. 'No, I don't think you do, sir'. His heart was racing now and his shirt stuck to his back.

The captain's eyes bored into Jim's. Jim could see he was trying to place him. 'In the papers, a year or so......damn it. It's gone. It was you, I'm sure of it'.

'No, sir. I'm sorry'. Jim shook his head and walked away a little too swiftly. He had to get out. He went straight to the kitchen, ran some water and washed his hands and the tap. He undid his cravat as he walked into the sunshine.

Hamish was walking towards him on the other side of the lawn. Instinctively Jim reached for the revolver and levelled it at Hamish's chest with both hands. Hamish stopped in his tracks. 'Jim....Jim,' he said. He opened his hands at his sides.

Jim said nothing. He was too shocked. His heart was fighting with his training. Was this a saviour or a threat?

'Jim, you've got a daughter. With Jessie...'

'What...?'

'   A daughter, Poppy. Jessie thinks you're dead, Jim. I broke out of the trenches to find you. That's why I'm here. Am I too late? What have you done in there, Jim?'

'Nothing, Hamish.'

'You're a liar! I know you. Jim, what have you done?'

A woman screamed by the porter's lodge. Someone exited the hall, swore and ran back in, shouting.

'Jim, give me the gun. We know all about the people you work for. Neville and Randle helped us find then. Your father too.'

'Dad? What..?'

'He knows people in the Government, Jim. You were tricked. Verro wanted you to kill your own people to make it look like...like we did it.'

Jim's mouth went dry. He looked behind him. Guests poured through the doorway, forced out by those behind wanting to see what the excitement was.

'Hamish. Help me!' Jim fired into the air and ran at the group of guests, shouting 'Get out! Get out!' People screamed and dived out of his way. Hamish followed behind him.

279

Inside, Jim fired again, filling the entrance with a cloud of centuries-old masonry dust. 'Get out of my way!' he shouted as he leaped over the falling bodies. He ran into the hall. The few guests that were left in there shrank from sight under the oak tables. Jim stopped and looked at the top table. Only the captain was there, his hand resting on the rich cloth.

'Have you touched the champagne I brought you?' asked Jim as he approached the table. Hamish stood a few feet away.

'I have, as a matter of fact. Never been able to resist free alcohol, particularly when it's champagne. Will it kill me?'

'Yes.'

'Well then, young man, will you please tell me what you were doing in the newspapers?'

'I won the Aldershot medal in 1915.'

'Seems we are fated. I won it the previous year.'

The captain and the assassin looked at each other, their expressions identical. Both were doomed. One physically, one morally.

'Is there nothing you can do?' asked Hamish.

Jim shook his head. His jaw was set and his eyes were closed.

'Jim, I've got to get you out of here. Given what we have done for our fucking country, there is no way that I am going to let you die, not now. You're an idiot, Jim, for those stupid politics of yours. But you were pissed on by Bartlett and taken advantage of by whoever you are working for.'

'*Were* working for,' replied Jim.

'I did expect it, you know,' said the captain. His face was turning grey. His lips darkened. 'You can't run a successful war with people like me undermining you in your own back yard. SIS? Did Vernon Kell send you?'

'No, sir…' Jim seemed distracted, almost removed from the scene. "Though this be madness, yet there is method in 't." he recited.

The war hero smiled painfully. "Men at some time are masters of their fates: The fault, dear Brutus, is not in our stars, but in ourselves, that we are underlings." We have all been deceived, I fear, Jim.'

Hamish pushed Jim towards the ancient gothic door at the rear of the hall. He turned the handle and the door opened onto a cloister. Hamish pulled Jim through as he glanced at the dying captain. They started running. Jim took off his waiter's jacket and Hamish copied him. When they got to the first right-angle Jim sprinted to a large modern building on the other side of an orchard. He looked in three windows until he found what he was looking for. Spreading his jacket over the pane with his hands he kicked the jacket and the bottom of the glass gave way with a dull thud. He put his hand through the hole and retrieved a cap and black gown, gave the cap to Hamish and put the gown around his shoulders.

'Hamish, there's an anti-war march in London, in three days' time. It's meant to be peaceful. It won't be. Various groups are trying to turn the people against the army. The organization will be there to provide the spark.'

'Were you meant to be there?'

'No. Gabriel, my teacher...' said Jim, 'Gabriel is the one who...'

'Alright, Jim, it's alright. Will you help us stop him?'

Jim suddenly looked fearful. 'Yes. But alone. They have to think that I am working alone. If I work with anyone else, these people will go after their next of kin. Goodbye, brother.' Jim held Hamish's shoulders. 'Find a bike. Cycle to Ely. Take a train from there to London via Bishops Stortford.'

'What about you?'

'Goodbye Hamish. See you after the war!' Jim turned and walked away.

*

Jessie awoke as Poppy stretched and yawned next to her, just as she had many times over the past twenty months. People brushed past and she remembered where she was. On a train, a stationary train, next to a platform. Jessie gathered up her belongings from the rack above the seats, took Poppy's hand and joined the shouting and singing throng. A drum beat up ahead somewhere. The scene reminded her of the men going to watch 'The Town' play football at Gay Meadow before the war, before this bloody, futile war.

That was why she had travelled to London today, for the anti-war march. She had heard about it by word-of-mouth only in the last week. It had been whispered about in shops and pubs in the town and she presumed up and down the country. The train was packed when she caught the connection in Birmingham but more than one person had offered her a seat because she had a young child. She sat opposite three soldiers in uniform, two of whom were blind. They were all going on the march. Jessie felt part of history-in-the-making and she wanted Poppy to be part of it too.

*

Randle and Hamish stood behind the retreating company of soldiers, rifles at the ready. One company wasn't enough, not by a long way. The crowd of protestors was much bigger than the authorities expected. They should have listened to Ken. He had tried to get hold of Kell and Cumming and even Commander Hall from Naval Intelligence but they were all at sea, returning from Gibraltar and the telegraph hadn't been able to make contact. Their second-in-commands had listened to what he had to say if only because of Ken's reputation but none of them knew anything about the investigation. Kell and Cumming had kept it very low key, waiting for information that they could use. The idea that a bunch of assassins was trying to bring down the government seemed ridiculous to those left behind in London. Even the confused events in Cambridge hadn't persuaded them. The head of London Special Branch agreed to let the two lads from Shropshire join the hundred soldiers guarding the entrance to Whitehall but he had refused to issue the two sharp-shooters with telescopic sights on the grounds that this would probably make matters a lot worse if the crowd saw them.

As soon as the thousands of marchers and marshalling police entered Trafalgar Square those at the front saw that their way to Downing Street and Parliament was blocked by the soldiers. The mood of the crowd changed. They chanted 'scabs, scabs, scabs!' and 'peace murderers,' and 'end the war now!' They threw blocks of paving slabs and placards at the soldiers and then they rushed them and fights broke out. The soldiers had no choice but to retreat into Whitehall. Someone ran a message to Downing Street to prepare for evacuation via Horse Guards parade.

But Randle and Hamish weren't looking at the crowds. They were looking higher, at the windows and roofs overlooking the wide street. They had no protection from anyone up there. They were all sitting ducks.

Hamish instinctively understood the import of the moment. His search for Jim meant nothing compared to what was happening here. Even the war was subordinate to it. Today's events would determine the future of the nation, and by implication, the future of the world.

Two army trucks suddenly appeared from behind them, screeched to a halt at the end of Horse Guards Avenue, reversed and turned so that their backs were facing the advancing mob. The soldiers inside unbolted the tailgates that fell with two loud thuds. Inside each lorry there was a crew around a Vickers machine gun, ammunition belts dangling into their boxes. The gunners pulled back the arming pins at the sides of the guns, making a sound like the groans of a straining rack.

It had the desired affect. The mob gradually grew quiet and stopped. The soldiers on the ground turned to see the contents of the lorries and slowly backed away from the crowd towards the safety of the machine guns. Hamish and Randle didn't budge.

A tall officer came to the side of one of the lorries and lifted a tin loudspeaker. 'This is as far as you get. We cannot let you go any further. This is the seat of government. Go back to your homes.'

'We don't want a government! We want peace!' someone shouted.

'Then go home!' shouted the officer.

'We want our men home!' A brick landed harmlessly in front of the officer. He didn't flinch.

Another brick landed at his feet. The mob started to walk forward.

'Please, do not make me do this,' he called. 'There are children here, think of them!'

Hamish looked at each of the machine gunners. Hard men, without a trace of emotion in their faces. Then he looked up at the windows. God, he wished he had a telescopic sight.

A gun-shot rang out from the direction of the crowd and the officer went down holding his shoulder. Immediately, the machine gun nearest Randle started firing into the crowd at point-blank range. The two friends instinctively ducked. Bullets tore into the people sending blood and shreds of flesh and clothing in all directions. The other gun crew joined in, the screams drowned out by the explosions of the cartridges, sending thirty red hot bullets into the civilians every second.

'No!' Someone from the edge of the crowd nearest Randle raced at the nearest machine gun, firing a revolver as he did so. He vaulted into the back of the lorry and into the path of the bullets. His momentum carried him onto the gun and it collapsed through its stand.

Hamish fired at the block of the other machine gun and sent it crashing against the far side of the lorry. Screams of pain and panic pierced the air, echoing down the wide avenue. Randle and Hamish rounded the back of the lorries and aimed their guns at the men in there, the expressions on their faces leaving the gunners under no illusion about what would happen if any of them moved towards the guns. One of the soldiers raised his hands and kicked the machine gun towards the back of the lorry and over the edge onto the cobbles below.

'You bastards!' shouted Hamish. 'You fucking bastards!' He turned to the appalling scene behind him. From one payment to the other and for fifty feet back, men, women and children lay on the ground. Beyond them stood the crowd, still holding their placards, silent in their shock.

The lines of soldiers and protestors faced the other across the sea of dead and dying for a full minute, neither side knowing how the other would react. Slowly, almost imperceptibly, the people started withdrawing, as if they were a single body directed by a common force. Those at the back heard the firing, felt the shock waves through the crowd in front of them and understood the meaning of the minute's silence. So they turned away and walked back whence they came. The ones who had witnessed the slaughter at the front followed them, dropping their banners and posters as they went.

Only then did the soldiers attend to the wounded. Randle and Hamish ran to the lorry that the protestor had attacked. They didn't need to turn him over to see that Jim was dead. Half-a-dozen bullets had ripped through his body leaving scorch marks in the clothes in the middle of his back.

'Gabriel!' said Hamish, 'The shot came from the crowd. He must still be here!' They jumped from the lorry and joined the soldiers attending the wounded. Hamish scanned the bodies around them. He stepped over one, then another. There was blood everywhere. He bent over and rested his hands on his knees. Randle put his hand on his back.

Snow started to fall and the bells of approaching ambulances filled the air. The two men moved quickly, running their hands over the jackets and trousers, occasionally wiping blood onto their own. Then Randle found it. A Colt .45 lying under the body of a man with short, dark hair. He had been shot in the chest. 'May his soul burn in Hell! How could he do this?' Randle put his hand up to his mouth and surveyed the scene of devastation around him. Then he heard a child's voice that he recognised. 'Hamish….Hamish, look!' Randle pointed at the woman and child lying amongst the bodies furthest away from where the machine-guns had opened up. He ran to them shouting 'Jessie, no! Please, no!'

Randle bent down and lifted Jessie's head. Poppy sniffed and cried 'Mummy!' as she hung on to Jessie's neck. He held them both to his huge chest and Jessie's head fell back, mouth open.

Hamish looked down on the little group, not knowing what to do. The catastrophe had just turned into a something much worse. Fate was playing with them.

Then he noticed something. He pulled at the child and placed her on the road. 'Randle, there's no mark on her!'

Randle carefully turned Jessie over on the ground and found no wound. 'Randle, remember what you used to do to bring the lambs back….?'

The captain looked up at Hamish and then at Jessie's body. He crouched over her and pushed at her chest, then again. 'Sometimes it works, sometimes it…..it might have been too long since she stopped breathing,' said Randle.

Hamish crawled over to Poppy and held her in his arms. They looked on as Randle pumped Jessie's chest and breathed into her lungs. White and red ambulances screeched to a halt next to the lorries and white-coated men and women rushed to help the wounded.

Jessie groaned and coughed. 'She's alive! She's bloody alive!' shouted Randle. 'Look Hamish, Poppy. She's alive. Mummy's alive!' Poppy ran to her mother. Jessie's glassy eyes looked up at Randle and then around her. It seemed to take an age before she understood. 'Jim?' she whispered.

Hamish shook his head and Jessie buried her face in her daughter's hair.

Hamish and Randle just stared at each other as they knelt. 'Well done, big man. Well done,' sighed Hamish.

16

The two horses made their way slowly up the road that snaked from the river basin to the monument at the top of Breiddon Hill, known locally as Rodney's Pillar. The enormous edifice that overlooks the Welsh hills and Offa's Dyke had been erected a hundred years before by the forestry people of Montgomeryshire to celebrate their contribution to the defeat of the French navy by the great oak ships of Admiral Rodney.

This was ancient border territory. Caractacus, a prime candidate for the original King Arthur, made his last stand against the Romans in these hills in the year that the Empire came to Britain. The path wound through woodland that lay between three extinct volcanoes, the peaks no more than a mile apart. Millennia of erosion had formed a shallow valley lying a thousand feet above the plains below. Jim and Hamish had named it 'The Lost World' in their childhoods, after Conan Doyle's novel about the table mountain where dinosaurs roamed. In the summer, the haze from the circling Severn made the colossus appear as if it were floating in the sky, but today the hills slumbered under a counter-pain of bluebells.

The woman with the grey hair coaxed her horse to the edge of the woods, lifted the panting dog off her lap and dismounted. 'I think Jim would have been proud of his little girl.'

Jessie smiled. 'That he would,' she said, holding Poppy tightly. Ma Pugh untied the net that was strapped to the saddle and walked into the wood followed by the dog.

A pair of crows rose into the sky and screeched at a circling bird of prey.

When she got to a rise in the path she knelt down and put her hand on the back of the greyhound-sheepdog. She whispered in his ear. 'See those pheasants? They don't know we're here 'cos they're facing into the wind, keeping their feathers down, see? But I suppose you already know that, seein' who your dad was.' The dog looked at

Ma Pugh, then the birds. His long tongue dangled from the side of his mouth and his tail wagged furiously. 'Randle'll be back on leave soon, and we can't have him being hungry, can we, Scout?'

*

The warm breeze drifted up from the Vermillion Bay and into the villages and valleys of the Pyrenean foothills, covering everything with the clean smell of pine. Old ladies swept their doorsteps and talked with the neighbours whilst their husbands sat in the bars and on benches under the trees.

Hamish pulled at the bottom of his British Army uniform as he walked up the hill to the bar. He hadn't tried to contact Rosa since his enforced absence months earlier. It wasn't the right way. If he were to find out that he was too late, he would rather hear it as he looked at her beautiful face and not read the cold words of a goodbye letter. At least this way he could explain to her the reasons for his leaving. A telephone call to Luis had given Hamish Rosa's whereabouts. He asked Luis not to tell him anything else about her and not to tell her that he had called.

Hamish had to hand it to the British Government or whoever it was that managed the aftermath of Whitehall. He was convinced that there would be civil war when the photographs appeared on the front pages of the newspapers under headlines that put the blame squarely on the shoulders of the Establishment. In the days that followed, there were anti-war demonstrations in every city, followed by ransacking of official buildings, particularly enlisting centres. Strikes paralysed the docks, the mines, the steel and ammunition industries.

But an amazing story started to unfold. Pieces of information leaked to the press told of a communist plot involving an escape from a firing squad; a soldier who risked everything to find the friend who eventually gave his life to save innocent strangers; and the vital role played by British Intelligence in uncovering the coup attempt. How the plotters had killed Marjorie Singleton, Huw Nightingale and Sir Sidney-Coke and had shot at the soldiers guarding Downing Street. A gun was discovered and Scotland Yard matched it to the bullet found in the officer's shoulder. The fingerprints on the gun were from those of a still unidentified body found in Whitehall. The mood in the country changed from one of anarchic belligerence to anti-communism, anti-socialism, anti-anything in fact that could be seen as undermining the traditional British values of courage and tolerance. The public were told that the names would be released once the full extent of the conspiracy was uncovered. But it never was. Vernon Kell had weaved his magic once more.

Jim's funeral had been a quiet affair. Special Branch insisted that only those who were 'aware' could attend. There was no sobbing. Jessie whispered, 'To the genuine article' as she threw the sod of earth onto the coffin and walked back to a puzzled Poppy who was holding one of Randle's giant hands. Jessie looked over to the stony-faced Ken, who returned her gaze. They both understood the other's feelings. The real sorrow had hit them several months before, when Jim's execution was announced. Jessie hadn't had time to hope it was all a bad dream until it was too late. Ken, on the other hand, had got used to the numbness that he felt when he thought of Jim's possible return to him. If Jim wasn't in a box, then Ken's country, as he knew it, would have expired.

For his part, Hamish had seen so much death that the sight of Jim's coffin being lowered into the grave made him sad only for the thousands of men left to rot without anyone to mourn them. He had done his duty, to himself and to Jim. But his mind kept going back to Neville's story of Doctor Faustus, told while they were making their way back to England from the trenches. Faustus had sold his soul to the devil in exchange for knowledge and power. Neville thought Jim may have accepted a similar offer. Hamish now knew differently. Jim had no choice, and Hamish wasn't convinced that the people who manipulated Jim were wholly evil, either.

Hamish sat at a table outside the bar and waited. And waited. As he was about to stand up and look for service a dark-haired girl wandered out, leant over the table and cleaned it without looking up.

'Bona tarda, mademoiselle,' he said.

The girl turned her head to Hamish, her hair falling over her face. She looked at him for what seemed like an age, her face set but her eyes ablaze. Hamish thought that she was going to walk away.

'Hamish,' she said, 'do not try to speak Catalan. It was because you were not Catalan that I loved you.' She resumed her cleaning of the tables.

'Loved?'

'You cannot love a ghost, soldier Hamish.' She looked into his eyes, waiting for his response.

'You'll wear a hole in that table,' he said.

Rosa laughed so loudly she had to put a hand across her mouth. Then she moved between the seats and the table, held Hamish's face in her hands and kissed him. 'Can you still dance Irish, Hamish?' she asked.

'You never forget,' he replied.

Rosa took Hamish's hand and walked the few yards to the centre of the square. She lifted one side of her skirt and danced around him. The old men and women of the square looked up from their game of boulle in the shadows of the palm trees and started to cheer and clap. Someone shouted, 'Rosa dance avec l'Anglais,' from a balcony.

Luis arrived at Hamish's table carrying three glasses, a bottle of Bisconte and an enormous plate of moules. 'For you, Hamish. There are no closed ones. Rosa checked.'

'You told her! You untrustworthy toad,' Hamish shouted back.

'I had to. So many boyfriends….' Luis winked at Rosa and went back into the bar.

Epilogue

On 3rd April, 1917, Vladimir Ilich Ulyanov, later to be known universally as Lenin, returned to Russia to direct the disintegration of Tsarist Russia and its rebirth as a communist state. His transport was arranged by German Intelligence in order that he would spread his ideology 'like a virus,' to quote Winston Churchill. The Russian armies gave up their fight against the Germans four months after Lenin's return. For most of the rest of the twentieth century, half of Germany and all of Eastern Europe reeled under the yoke of the same virulent ideology.

Some historians are convinced that Lenin was a German spy. If true, it would probably qualify as the worst intelligence blunder of all time.

BIBLIOGRAPHY

I Walked By Night	Anonymous
Sniping In France	Major H E Hesketh-Pritchard
Secret Service	Christopher Andrew
The Puppet Masters	John Hughes-Wilson
The KSLI 1881-1968	Peter Duckers
The 6th Battalion KSLI 1914-19	A. J. Burgoyne
The War The Infantry Knew	Captain J.C. Dunn
With A Machine Gun To Cambrai	George Coppard
Kitchener's Army 1914-16	Peter Simkins
Rural Britain, Then And Now	Roger Hunt
Britain, Then And Now	Edmund Swinglehurst
The Penguin Book of War	John Keegan
The Working Countryside 1862-1945	Robin Hill and Paul Stamper
World War One, Day By Day	Ian Westwell
The Romanov Conspiracies	Michael Occleshaw
British Tommy	Martin Pegler and Mike Chappell
Around Shrewsbury	Dorothy Nicolle
Terrorists and Terrorism	David J. Whittaker
Essential Militaria	Nicholas Hobbes
The Sceptred Isle: The Dynasties	Christopher Lee
The Victorian Public House	Richard Tames
The Hunting Of Man	Andy Dougan
A Glimpse of Old Shrewsbury	David Trumper
Sun Tzu	Translated by Samuel B. Griffith
Shropshire, Photographic Memories	Dorothy Nicolle
The River Severn, A Pictorial History	Josephine Jeremiah
The Sixteen	John Urwin
The Cosa Nostra	John Dickie
Democracy Needs Aristocracy	Peregrine Worsthorne
Remember Me	Christina Rossetti

With special thanks to Acton Scott Historic Working Farm in Shropshire, Blists Hill Victorian Village, Ironbridge Gorge Museum, Shropshire Regimental Museum, Shrewsbury Records Office, Letheringsett Mill, Norfolk and The Imperial War Museum, London.